Cowslip

a novel

by

Kirk Sigurdson

Terminus Books

cutting-edge literary genre fiction
terminusbooks.com

Published in the United States by Terminus Books, 1090 Farraday Road, Durango, Colorado, 81303.

www.terminusbooks.com

This book is a work of fiction. All the characters and events portrayed in this book are fictitious, and any resemblance to real people or events is purely coincidental.

Library of Congress Catalog Control Number: 2002093481
ISBN: 0-9722893-0-5

Printed in the United States of America

Book design Kurt Lancaster
Text set in Minion

Cover design Kurt Lancaster
Cover photograph by John Dowland © PhotoAlto

Every angel is terrifying.
And yet, still, I summon you,
almost deadly birds of the soul.
For I know you.
—Rilke

Foreword

What you are about to read is not a novel. It is a long and painfully honest journal with a newspaper article tacked on the end. Presenting the whole thing as a work of fiction was the publisher's idea.

As you will soon find out, this journal began as a project in Julia Fleischer's writing class at Portland Community College. Although it spans some five months, only the first thirty-four pages were handed in for credit. The remaining pages are, as Julia says, a record of "life experiences." They chronicle her beginnings as a cowgirl in Mt. Angel, Oregon, and the steps leading up to her explosive rise into the professional rock scene.

Two years have passed since her death, two long years, but there isn't a day goes by when I don't feel her presence. When she died, Julia had it all: a talented band, a million-dollar recording contract, dozens of friends who would have done anything for her that was humanly possible.

She also had Creutzfeldt-Jakob Disease, and eventually, it caught up with her. Yet she got further than me or anyone else in her position could have gotten. I should know. As Julia's best friend, I saw her change from a jubilant young woman into something else entirely: A wide-eyed mystic with tales of angels and demons—accounts gathered from sojourns in a murky realm that divides our world from the next.

Julia's brushes with the supernatural were neither welcome nor appreciated. But rather than shrinking back in fear, she utilized each new experience to create a working model of God and the universe.

By this I don't mean to suggest that Julia Fleischer was some kind of spiritual seer or prophet. That's not for me to say. Everything she felt, everything she experienced in the last few months before her death has been recorded here. Along with the songs on her album, those memories are all she had left to give, her legacy.

Bringing this manuscript to an agent was the hardest decision I've ever had to make, but ultimately I think it was the right one. Now Julia's message can reach the world—and by extension, you, the reader. That's who she had in mind when she wrote down her most personal secrets.

So if you begin to feel a bit like a voyeur, don't worry, it's part of the experience. To Julia, artistic integrity meant full disclosure. She wouldn't have had it any other way.

—Ruth Cohaine
New York City

Journal of Life Experiences

Julia Fleischer
Writing 121
Professor Oden

ENTRY ONE

Jeff called to ask if he should buy me a ticket for Dee-Dee Ramone's show at the Satyricon. "We can watch the punks slam themselves into oblivion," he said. "It might be the last chance we'll ever get to pogo dance along to the Blitzkrieg Bop."

After hearing that, I couldn't possibly go. It would spoil the memory of the time I saw the *real* Ramones when Joey was up there on stage—all six and a half feet of him jumping up and down with his long black hair flying and his big nose sticking out in the most adorable way.

I tried to explain, but Jeff took it personally. He got all defensive and choked up, like he does when he feels not in control. The last thing he said before he hung up was, "Alright, fine. I'm going with or without you. And either way, I'm getting ripped. For Joey."

Excuse me, but is that any way to talk to your girlfriend of sixteen months? I think Jeff's starting to get the impression I'm stuck up because I've lost so much weight and other guys are looking at me for the first time in my life. If he keeps it up, maybe I *will* go out with some pretty boy just to piss him off.

ENTRY TWO

I'm supposed to be keeping this journal for my English teacher. His name is Mr. Oden and I'm in his Writing 121 class at Portland Community College. He said we could either write daily reactions to things that happen in Oregon and the rest of the world or just keep a personal journal of our lives.

We also have three essays and a pass/fail final exam that's an in-class essay. On top of that, he's got daily assignments and readings in our textbooks. Can you believe it? God, does my life suck. I won't even have time to pick my nose this term.

Yesterday when I got home from school, I almost went ahead and started the boring current events journal because I thought Mr. Oden might be a perv or something, you know, like he might want to spy on my personal life in a voyeuristic kind of way. Most English teachers are either pervs or homos. That's what my friend Ruth says. But I don't think Oden is either one. He didn't mean "personal" like that. He just meant a diary of the significant things that happen to us as our lives unfold and how we relate to the world.

I've had some time to mull over the whole thing, and I've come to the conclusion that if I'm really going to do this assignment right, then I should pretend that I'm only writing for myself. I can edit out the private parts later.

ENTRY THREE

I like Mr. Oden's class, I guess. It's not always boring. But he tries a little *too* hard during the lecture. Especially if he's drinking coffee that day. His jokes are really weak but sometimes I can't help laughing. He makes all these puns and I've never heard a really good pun from anyone ever.

According to Ruth, puns aren't *kosher*. She's also in my class and she's Jewish. Her parents are transplants from New York (pronounced "N'Yawk"). She uses a lot of slang that she calls Yiddish. When I asked her about "kosher," she said it means that you can eat something without feeling religious guilt if you're Jewish. I guess it must have broader applications because you can't eat a pun.

Ruth has very long blonde hair that's too frizzy and jet-black at the roots. I told her to let it go straight and natural, but I don't think she listened to me. I tried to convince her that guys notice if your hair is *long* and *silky*, the color doesn't matter as much. But she says blondes have more fun—at least according to Marilyn Monroe.

Ruth also plays dumb whenever a guy talks to her but I refuse to do that. She's way smarter than me, and I need to utilize whatever brain cells God gave me to the fullest.

Mr. Oden plays drums. He's in a band called Mammy Jammer. I think he must have thought up the name himself because it sounds suspiciously like a pun. Word around campus is Mammy Jammer's an alright band, at least by Portland standards. They've got a young lead singer who's a dead ringer for Ally McBeal. Also, they're the only act in Portland with three keyboardists.

In this week's *Mercury*, it said they're playing Dante's on Saturday night: The warm-up band for Saving Ophelia, this local band that sounds exactly like Dido. Maybe I can get Ruth to go. That would be too weird seeing our English teacher rock out. Two Friday nights ago, the line outside Dante's stretched practically all the way to the Burnside Bridge.

And Saturday night's even more popular than Friday. So I guess Mammy Jammer's front girl can do more than strut around on stage looking like the most annoying bulimic star on television.

ENTRY FOUR
Time for a little background info. This is probably the one and only chance I'll ever get to write my own personal liner notes:

Julia Annika Fleischer
   ø   Born: June 14, 1979
   ø   Height: 5'10"
   ø   Weight: 153 lbs
   ø   Hair color: "Dirty" blonde
   ø   Eye color: Blue
   ø   Born: Mt. Angel, Oregon
   ø   Favorite bands: Hooverphonic; Björk; PJ Harvey; Esthero; Mazzy Star
   ø   Favorite book: *Animal Dreams* by Barbara Kingsolver
   ø   Favorite movie: *Jesus' Son.* "We're wrecking like trains"
   ø   Favorite night of the year: Halloween, or sometimes New Year's

I moved to Portland on my eighteenth birthday. For the first couple of years, I displayed my wares at the Saturday Market and shops in Old Town—handcrafted candles mainly. When I wasn't at work, I spent a lot of time hanging out with people on the street.

But I was different from most of my friends at that time and what separated me was a love affair with books. On my twentieth birthday, I calculated that I'd read approximately one thousand of them. And we're not talking about light reading, either. Just because I was out of school didn't mean I lacked ambition.

In some ways, I think I learned more in those two beautiful free years than all my hours in the classroom put together. I was like a girl possessed. Whenever I walked into the library, all the big names jumped out at me—Plato, Kafka, Einstein, Dante, Shakespeare—and I devoured them whole, picking my teeth with their spines.

Eventually, though, I wised up and decided to go to college. Even if I swallowed the entire canon of English literature, it wouldn't get me hired without a degree.

I still don't know what I want to do in terms of a career, but I've been taking classes at PCC for the past three semesters. It's not like high school. The teachers don't even talk to you (unless you ask them a question). Some things are more formal and some things are less. Half my teachers introduce themselves by their first names to the class. I'm sorry, but that's just plain weird.

I want to go to Portland State University after I get my associates degree at PCC. Or maybe Reed College on Woodstock Blvd; it's supposed to be pretty wild, a throw-back from the sixties. And it's famous. Even Ruth's uncle in New York City has heard of "those crazy Reedies."

Most of the classes I've taken here have been in the sciences, but I'm starting to get interested in English. Fall term, I took Drama As Lit, and then I decided to go back and start taking writing classes because my instructor said I definitely had some talent there.

At first I wanted to take Creative Writing, but my drama instructor said I'd be better off taking WR 121 first—so I did, and that's what I'm doing now.

I met my best friend Ruth in Human Biology. She wants to be a doctor of some sort. She doesn't know what kind, but I'll bet she becomes a plastic surgeon or something totally useless to society. Don't get me wrong: she's got a big heart and all. She's just a little hung up on things that don't matter. Like looks. I think she should try to become a writer but I've never told her that.

I saw one short story that she wrote, totally amazing. It was about a girl who lived in a Kibbutz in Israel and had a housemate who discovered that datura, this hallucinogenic drug, was growing all over the countryside. He brewed up a big pot of the stuff and they all had a datura party. He was into Carlos Castañeda's books and so he knew how to prepare it using a little of the flowers and a little of the stems and a little of the roots, to get the balance just right.

Everyone got totally lit except for the narrator of the story. She just kind of kicked back and watched the freakshow. One girl took a bus to Tel Aviv and got lost and came back several hours later wearing only her bra (but it was a sports bra so it didn't look that unusual). The rest of the people had some pretty weird experiences.

Weirdest of all was the guy who made the datura soup. He disappeared and went out in the desert for the longest time. When he came back, he looked different. *Changed.* A little while later, everyone around the fire looked over at him in the shadows because he was laughing this really freaky laugh; it almost sounded in stereo, like there were *two* voices laughing together.

Of course, it was only him standing there, but he had has his arm hanging out in the air, like there was someone standing next to him. The way he was leaning, his weight seemed more on the invisible friend than on his own two feet and that just totally wigged out everyone else because they noticed this. They overheard part of the conversation he was having with this invisible friend and they realized it was another language. But when they listened closer, it didn't sound like a language any of them had ever heard before.

The next morning, they asked the guy what he'd been speaking and he couldn't remember. He said he only knew how to speak English and Hebrew. Over the next few weeks, he started experimenting on all kinds of concoctions made from datura. Nobody else wanted anything to do with the stuff because they'd gotten such a splitting headache from the party, but this guy was hooked. He kept going and going until one day they found him out in the desert half dead. So they sent him to a clinic and kicked him off the Kibbutz.

I'm not really describing the story very well, but you get the idea. It was a cool plot and it had the added bonus of being 100% true. When I asked her about it, Ruth said she'd read a few of the Casteñeda books the housemate had left around. Don Juan, the narrator, explained how datura has a reputation for putting people in touch with the other side. And what better place for that sort of thing than out in the deserts of Israel where it's absolutely crawling with demons and angels?

I didn't want to seem *too* impressed with Ruth's story because she was kind of aloof about it, but I did ask for a copy. She seemed really flattered. I think I might submit the copy Ruth gave me to the school newspaper. I'll bet you anything they offer to publish it. Ruth will be so psyched if they do. Then she'd officially be a "Woman of Letters."

ENTRY FIVE

I've been a vegetarian since the seventh grade when I saw the butcher truck come out to the ranch and slaughter two of our best cows. Dad told me not to name any of the cattle or sheep, but I did anyway. All of them. It wasn't fair because the bulls and rams always end up with names, but I guess that's because they don't get slaughtered; they live like kings, the spoiled brats.

So Janet and Chrissie took a spike for us that day. Right through the head. The weapon looked like that thing in *The X-Files* they use to kill aliens with—the ones who can't be killed with a normal gun. This spike shoots out faster than the eye can see. It shot right through Janet's and Chrissie's foreheads and knocked them out so their throats could be bled with a minimum of fuss. One second they were scared and mooing—and the next, *wam, bam, thank you mam!* Goodbye Janet Jackson, soft chocolaty brown fur, big eyes and the prettiest moo you ever heard. Goodbye Chrissie Hinde, you sexy thing. No more shaking that tail to drive the bulls wild. No more pro lapses for me to sew up, no more nothin'.

My brother, Hans, thought I named Janet and Chrissie from the characters in *Three's Company*. He even tried to mess with my head and called the butcher "Mr. Roper." I hate *Three's Company*. All those stupid seventies'd-out shows. But I kind of liked the fact that Hans didn't know the real connection. I should never have told him their names in the first place.

That night, my mom served steak, of all things. I couldn't touch the food on my plate. Not after seeing Janet and Chrissie get the spike. Gravy is just cooked blood and it was soaking everything in death. I had to run to the bathroom. After hanging onto the toilet for dear life, puking my guts out, I went straight to bed.

And when I woke up the next morning, I just knew: Meat is murder, especially the red stuff. I'd never be able to touch it again.

ENTRY SIX

A lot of religions have this thing about cows. Mohammed wrote a whole chapter in the *Koran* about them. A kind of extended proverb. The Hindus think cows are sacred. In my opinion, that's going a little overboard, but they must be higher up on the cosmic pecking order than, say, chickens or turkeys.

There's a turkey farm on the way from Mount Angel to the rodeo grounds in St. Paul and it's the stinkiest most disgusting place on earth. One time, late at night, some activists from the Environmental Liberation Front cut the fence to set all the turkeys free. But instead of running away, most of the birds just cowered inside. A few intrepid ones got away and they ended up getting hit by cars on the road.

When the farmer who owned the place discovered what had happened, he rang the dinner bell and they all came waddling to the food troughs. While they were gorging themselves, he and his neighbors tended to the fence. As a joke, he even left up the "calling card" ELF had spray-painted on the side of his barn:

Deaf to the language of the birds? We hear!
—ELF

Ah, well. Better luck next time, guys. I read all about it in the local newspaper. A grainy B&W photograph of the turkey rancher standing triumphantly in front of ELF's slogan; it made the front page—not once, not twice, but three times. For months that's all anyone in Mt. Angel would talk about. "Those environmentalist wackos."

Yackety, yack yack. Day and night. Night and day. Enough to make you scream. And not one of them ever breathed a word of regret for those poor turkeys that died in the name of liberty.

If I'd been born a sorry bird in that feedlot, I would have run out of there so fast that no one could have caught me. So what if I got squashed in the middle of the highway? It would sure beat the heck out of a visit to the butcher so a family of humans could eat me, celebrating a holiday that's supposed to embrace freedom but really just reinforces the same dull round.

Beast of burden, beast of prey: *One law for the lion & ox is oppression.*

I remember in Sunday School hearing this Bible story of a king who had a dream: Seven fat cows and seven skinny ones rose up out of a river and the thin cows devoured the fat ones. The king called in all his magicians and wizards and Nostradamus-like servants, but no one could help him, except Joseph, this Jewish kid who knew all about what the king's dream really meant because God told him. God said it foretold a famine that would eventually starve all these Egyptians to death if they didn't get their butts in gear and store enough grain to last them seven years.

Anyway, the point is, I had a terrible dream that night. The Bible is supposed to be comforting, but it can really scare the crap out of you when you're little and impressionable. What a nightmare! Don't let anyone tell you that people don't dream in color. That dream was more vivid than the biggest movie screen you've ever seen in your life.

Time has faded the images, thank God. All I can remember now is that I had to relieve myself (in the dream) so I got up out of bed and went into the bathroom. While I was sitting on the pot, I happened to look down at my stomach. It was clenched tight because I couldn't go pee-pee—even though my bladder was totally full—and I noticed in this horrible realization that my ribs were skin and bones, like those pictures of starving African children, all covered in flies—only my skin had a fine dusting of hair. And between my legs I'd grown a tail.

The next morning, I told my folks about the whole thing and they laughed it off. Dad said that being skinny was the least of my worries. If I ate my Wheaties, he promised I'd never turn into a cow. Maybe a pig, but not a cow.

ENTRY SEVEN
Before dad passed on at Portland Health Sciences University, he'd been having some absolutely God-awful dreams. The doctors said it was just a

side effect from the Alzheimer's, but I know they were lying. It was a side effect from all the drugs they were pumping him full of. Even when he was awake, he would scream at the things he imagined were creeping up the blanket.

Every time I visited him, I tried to pick off every particle of lint or dust, anything that could pass for creepy-crawlies, but he still saw the things come alive and crawl up the sheets that he'd tucked so tightly around his neck.

That was near the very end after he couldn't really talk anymore.

When he could still put whole sentences together, and he was still himself, he would never have dignified a nightmare or bad daydream by speaking of them. Instead, he always wanted to hear about me and my life. Something to take his mind off his troubles. As I sat looking out the window of his room in the hospital, I tried to pick out only the good things: finding these really cool new outfits at thrift stores, going to see my favorite rock bands in concert, playing my guitar, getting the job at Rose City music.

Happy details, the little things that reminded dad of the outside world, cheered him up the most. Near the end of my visit, he would smile so warmly and blink the way he did when he wanted to show his love for you. Then he'd close his eyes and whisper how I'd made him proud. So slim and trim, so pretty. "Yes, m'dear, all the cowboys are gonna be fightin' over you. A few more years and you'll have your own ranch and a whole house full of little snot-nosed devils runnin' around!"

ENTRY EIGHT

It's Sunday afternoon and the weather is nice for once. Summer's definitely on the way. I'm writing this journal entry at a table in front of Café Lena. I like it here because it's one of the few places around that actually pays homage to writers. They've got pictures of all the great Beats on the walls. My favorite is this picture of Jack Kerouac and Neil Cassady. I've read *On the Road* three times and it just keeps getting better.

Last night at Dante's was awesome! Everyone was there: Ruth; her friend, Ginny; Joan Compton, who I've known since I first moved to Portland; and all these other students from Writing 121.

I've driven by Dante's a million times, but I've never actually gone inside because the cover at the door is always very steep. But Ginny told us that if we got there before eight o'clock it would be free. We all met at Hung Far Low's, a Chinese restaurant in the oldest part of downtown Portland. I ordered this plate of chow mien that ended up being totally disgusting, but the drinks were cheap and really strong so it made up for it.

We ended up getting to Dante's around nine o'clock. The bouncer—this really cool black guy with dreads—let us in without paying cover. I bet if we'd brought dates he wouldn't have been so willing to make an exception.

It was totally deserted inside. The décor was nice, though. Everything painted in red and this burning pot of coals by the window that flamed up like hellfire. I guess it's supposed to look the way Satan might choose to decorate his palace if he were entertaining, but I'm sure most people don't make the connection. How many clubbers in Portland know the difference between *The Inferno* and *The Towering Inferno?*

I put a few quarters in the pool table and played Joan a game of 8-ball. Then people started showing up and before we knew it, some guys had bought us these really expensive drinks, the kind with little umbrellas in them.

Usually, I don't accept drinks from people I don't know because of Roofies, etc., but I talked to these guys for a while and we played another game of pool with them as doubles and I could tell after that that they weren't the types to drug up girls. Judging by the way they were dressed in matching G-style suits you would have thought they were gay for sure. But they definitely made a point to check us out. One of them kept looking down my blouse every time I'd get down low to shoot the ball. I think he liked the black bra I was wearing. After they won the game, they went in the bathroom and came out with red watery eyes.

Joan, who's really brazen, asked them for a hit of whatever it was they had, but they acted all surprised, so she let up. It was obvious they'd done some lines, though, because after a few minutes they got more drinks and started talking non-stop about themselves: fast cars, model girlfriends, vacations to Belize and Costa Rica . . . bla, bla, bla.

Finally, Joan gave them the brush off. It didn't take much because of their big egos. By then there were other girls at the bar for them to impress.

Mr. Oden was the first "Mammy Jammer" to get there. He brought a really nice Gretsch drum kit and it took him forever to carry all the pieces inside and set them up on stage. Some guys from Writing 121 offered to help, but he politely declined. I guess he figured it could be construed as a bribe.

Once Mr. Oden got his drums in place, he didn't bang on them and show off like most drummers. A few light taps here and there, and he was good to go. After that, he sat at the bar and drank by himself.

I took the opportunity to walk over and say something. He didn't recognize me, but when I mentioned 121, he perked right up. He looked quite a bit different outside of class: a more stylish pair of glasses, a tank top that showed off his arms. He must work out, because he's got fairly wide shoulders despite a spare tire around the middle. Not bad for a guy in his 30's. I could tell that he didn't want to talk about his day job, so I asked him about Mammy Jammer: How long had they been together, stuff like that. He seemed preoccupied. Stage fright, probably. Then the singer got there and he had to go consult with her. She wasn't dressed up or anything. Just a T-shirt and jeans. How lame. I mean, if I were playing Dante's, I would have put a little more effort into my outfit. That's the one time looks are important; as a rock star, it's part of the job description.

Mammy Jammer went on late, about eleven. Usually the warm-up band goes on earlier. I have to admit, they were pretty good. A hell of a lot better than Saving Ophelia ending up being later on. Mammy Jammer had lots of cool synth samples. I was wrong about them having three keyboardists—they only have two. The other guy plays guitar with a million effects pedals, which is practically the same thing, at least if you're listening and not watching.

Mr. Oden played with a lot of feeling, especially in the slow parts. It was cool how he rocked along with a drum machine most of the time. A lot of drummers are afraid to use click tracks and machines because it gives away their bad time. Not so with Oden; he nailed down those beats and hit plenty of loud cymbal crashes.

The singer didn't talk between songs. Ruth thought she was stuck up, but I think she's just shy. Her voice was a little on the weak side. It was obvious she'd never had any formal training; she had to work twice as hard to get the notes out, but they were always right on key, with a fairly strong accent—Danish maybe, or Dutch.

That picture in the *Mercury* didn't really do her justice: she's much more striking in person. Very petite and delicate. I don't think she looks like Calista Flockheart at all. In a few of the songs, her voice reminded me of a cross between Portishead and the Cocteau Twins. I think maybe she doesn't speak English too well and that's why she didn't acknowledge the audience. Plus she seemed kind of depressed.

ENTRY NINE
OK, here's the deal with Jeff: I love him, but he's got a few issues that I'd rather not deal with at the present time. We've been dating since my first term at PCC. At first, I was attracted to his personality; his looks grew on me later. That's a polite way of saying he's not the most handsome man on the planet.

But he's not ugly, either. He's probably a good fifty pounds overweight, but it doesn't really show since he's over six feet tall. Like the saying goes: "he carries it well." He's also very sweet when he wants to be, and he's got amazingly clear skin with blushing cheeks and the cutest little boy dimples that make you want to reach out and pinch them when he grins.

Jeff comes from a small town on the coast (Coos Bay) where he played football in high school. He also lost a parent (his mom) recently. So we've been a great comfort and a support to each other in that regard. It formed this amazing bond that made us both stronger.

I guess the biggest gripe I have about Jeff is his lack of ambition. He doesn't know yet what he wants from life. And that's kind of a turn-off because it means he's got an excuse to bomb out. Take school, for instance: He could get straight A's but he's never gotten anything higher than a B in any of his classes. Mostly he gets C's.

And he doesn't try very hard in his jobs, either. I think he must have had around four or five in the year-and-a-half we've been dating. Usually, he ends up getting fired because of personality conflicts with his boss.

Right now, Jeff's working as a fry cook at McMenamins under The Crystal in downtown Portland. I call it "McMinimals" even though it's technically named Ringlers. That really pisses Jeffrey off because he says he's finally found an organization that cares about its employees. Yeah, right. As if. He just likes to work there because they give him free beers after work.

Jeff called me up yesterday and we went out for brunch. I was kind of surprised because I thought he'd have a raging hangover from the night before. It turned out he did go to see Dee-Dee Ramone at the Satyricon. And *yes,* it had been the best show of his whole life.

I didn't know whether or not to believe him because he would have said that even if it sucked just to make me wish I'd gone. After he went on and on about it, though, I could tell it really was an exceptional show, not just a ruse to make me feel bad. I sat there almost wishing I'd broken down and gone, even after Jeff had dissed me so bad on the phone. I could have showed up with Ruth and ignored him for a while until he got drunk and apologized.

He said the crowd was just like the old days when the Ramones ruled. I didn't contradict him, but I couldn't help smirking inwardly because how the hell would he know? Dee-Dee Ramone is old enough to be his father! Jeff wasn't even born yet when the Ramones cut their first album (back when everyone bought vinyl—not CD's or cassettes).

I let Jeffrey go on and on about the show, how there were all these fights, how he broke one of them up right on the dance floor and how Dee-Dee was spitting on the crowd and they were spitting back, how it was kind of surprising that Dee-Dee didn't say a word about Joey, but that was probably because everything that could be said had already been said; you can't mourn forever, especially if you're the last Ramone on earth who can still rock the house.

After brunch, we rode bikes over to Jeff's new pad. It's kind of a weird set-up down on Water Street by the Ross Island Bridge, freeway on-ramps and off-ramps all around it, hundreds of feet up in the air, dwarfing what might otherwise be a rather agreeable three-story house. From the kitchen, it almost feels like you're a troll living under a bridge in your own little troll cottage waiting for some unsuspecting person to come along that you can catch and boil in a pot for dinner.

The landlord is fairly cool, as far as landlords go. He owns everything on the block and he calls Jeff's house the "pumpkin" house because it's painted a pumpkin shade of orange. Despite the fact that he's a yuppie from the tip of his nose down to his Birkenstock-clad toes, he responds quickly if something breaks and generally acts polite and respectful. He's also got the house fixed up pretty nice considering.

The backyard opens onto a deep grassy ravine, and there's an old May pole down there from the hippies who used to live on the block way back in the 70's when all the houses were falling-down shacks. Jeff told me they used to have Moonlight Madness parties where they'd get drunk on dandelion wine and dance naked around the May pole. He vowed to carry on the tradition, but May is already half over and I know he won't get around to throwing a party for another couple of months.

Since none of Jeff's other roommates were there, we had the place to ourselves. After we talked for a while and drank coffee on the deck overlooking the ravine, we went up into Jeff's new room and made love. It was OK. We went through all the right motions (and positions) but the old tenderness just wasn't there. Part way through, I started wondering if maybe Jeff has been cheating on me. He tried a kinky move that I seriously doubt he could have thought up on his own.

Maybe I'm just paranoid now that he's working at a popular bar. Especially with all the free beers and late night barflies drifting down from Crystal Ballroom on the weekends.

Afterwards, instead of taking his customary bong hit, Jeff went over to the big chair by the window. He stared, grinning his boyish grin. "Hey, Jules: why don't you stand in front of the mirror and pose for me?"

When I did, he said I looked the best he's ever seen me. How much weight had I lost? I told him I didn't have a scale. He said he'd buy me one. In the meantime, I'd better watch out. Another five pounds and I would be too skinny; most of the weight so far had come off my boobs and ass. Pretty soon there'd be nothing left to grab.

We had a pillow fight over that one.

Later, I started thinking about what Jeff had said. Me too skinny? It didn't seem possible. I'd lost a few pounds, so what? Plenty of girls on campus were skinnier than me. *Way.* And they probably starve themselves. You'd never catch me throwing up in the bathroom. "Ewe, like, *ohmygod*! Gag me with a spoon!" Not this chick. I'm still a corn-fed dame at heart. So what if I woke up one morning to discover that I'd become a clotheshorse? These things happen when you lose your baby fat.

Which reminds me, I've got to call Ruth. She promised to go shopping this week and help me pick out some new outfits. We'll hit all the best thrift stores in Southeast, then we'll have dinner at the Old Wive's Tale. I hear they've got a new salad bar that's to die for.

ENTRY TEN

After class today, I asked Mr. Oden about Ruth's short story. He said the school paper wasn't the right periodical to send it to. PCC has a special journal that's published twice a year called *The Alchemy*. But it probably wouldn't be such a good idea to submit another writer's story without her permission, even if she was your best friend.

Somehow the conversation got switched to Oden's rock band. How were things going? He said that Helena (the singer) had to fly back to Belgium for a family emergency. The band was dead in the water until she got back.

Jokingly, I mentioned that I sing and play guitar, I could fill in for her in the meantime. Mr. Oden didn't laugh. Instead, he asked if I had a demo tape. Can you believe it! *Holymama*! I almost died.

Mr. Oden walked me out to my car where I had a few extra tapes in the glove box. I was so nervous that my legs were shaking the whole way.

ENTRY ELEVEN

After I gave Mr. Oden the tape, I popped another copy into my car stereo. *Damn*! I'd forgotten how old the songs were! Really ancient stuff, back when I was still into Portishead.

Sometimes I can be so daft. I should have brought a copy of my latest demo, the one I recorded a couple of months ago in my friend Kyle's basement (he's got an eight track, but you can split each one twice and get sixteen). Those songs are so much better. Kyle even brought in a friend to play real drums on a few of them.

On my first demo, there's just a drum machine and me on a four track. I'm playing guitar and singing. In retrospect, I suppose it's fair to say my style didn't change that much from the first demo to the second. The vocal tracks turned out better on the first one, even if the production value is garbage.

Now that I think about it, I guess I'm glad that I gave Mr. Oden my first demo instead. I should think about recording another one soon. Jeff knows a sound guy at Crystal Ballroom who said he'd let me use their board to record myself live on a Monday or Tuesday night when the place is closed. I've got at least seven brand new songs, and one of them is probably the best I've ever written. It's called "Cowslip," about how my Dad's always called me that since I was little because I was always picking the wild flowers Opa had brought back with him from Europe, the bright yellow ones that took over the ranch and started growing like weeds. I don't actually mention Daddy dying, just all the big-hearted things he did for me in his life. I'm pretty sure it could be a hit if I got the right band behind me.

I should probably stop this entry right now because I'm starting to fantasize about "making it" and that could go on for pages and pages. I've always wanted to play in a band, but it hasn't materialized. Not yet, anyway. If Mr. Oden likes my demo, he'll tell me. If not, he probably won't say much. Either way, I'm cool with it.

ENTRY TWELVE

Ruth and I went shopping today. It wasn't as fun as I thought it would be. Ruth said she's worried about how much weight I've been losing. She said, yeah, I looked fabulous, but was I taking diet pills or anything? I told her no, but I don't think she believed me. She probably also thinks I'm making myself throw up, which is totally bogus. The thought of doing that is so repulsive, I can't even tell you.

After Ruth gave me the third degree, I didn't feel like driving all the way over to the Old Wive's Tale, so we went to a Thai restaurant just up the street. It had the most succulent tofu pad Thai. I think Ruth felt better when she saw me clean my plate. I'd made a special point to go to the bathroom *before* the food came, just in case, so she wouldn't think I was going in there to ralph up my lunch.

Things were pretty much cool after that. I could see her begin to relax. We drove down Hawthorne as far as Uncommon Grounds and had a cup of coffee. Then we walked up Hawthorne a little farther and browsed in the shops before we headed into Powell's Books, where we can hibernate for hours and hours, no problem.

ENTRY THIRTEEN

On Friday night, Jeff called in sick and we went to one of the newer music venues in Northeast called "Beulahland."

The name reminded me of a place mentioned in William Blake's prophecies, but I bet it's just a coincidence. I like Blake a lot, and I've read a couple of books on him. It's cool how spacey he could get without taking drugs. In *The Marriage of Heaven and Hell*, he writes that if the doors of perception were cleansed, everything would appear as it is: infinite. The words of a true prophet. When he was a child, he saw angels dancing in a tree outside his window.

In Blake's poetry the word Beulah is usually associated with a heavenly consciousness. That was fitting in a poetic sense the other night because I really wanted to have a good time with Jeff. We drank a few beers and then the first band came on. Their lead singer was a dead ringer for Richard Ashcroft of The Verve, but his nose hadn't been broken like Ashcroft's. He played a giant old beat-up synth from the 70s that surged through the PA. You couldn't really hear his vocals.

The music was so loud Jeff called it a "bombast." That really cracked me up. Once in a while, he comes up with these great $10 words.

I spent the night at Jeff's house. When we got there he gave me a present, all wrapped up and everything. I knew without opening it, that it was a scale. For some reason, I just started to cry. Jeff looked puzzled because here he thought he'd done a nice thing, showing concern for my welfare. But I couldn't help it. I cried and cried and he held me. It felt good to let the tears go. I haven't cried so hard in a long time.

We fell asleep in each other's arms. When I woke up, it was still night. The moon was full outside and the window was open. Cars whooshing across the overpass. Skyscrapers glaring defiantly up at the cosmos.

The air was warm, but I couldn't help shivering. I didn't have goosies, though. My skin was curiously warm to the touch. Inside, underneath, was what seemed cold: an icy dampness in my bones.

For a second, I thought maybe I was dead. I jumped out of bed and ran to the window, trying to see if the world looked the same.

It didn't exactly. In the moonlight and city-wash, everything seemed morbid, drained of color. The ravine was stretched bare and the grass looked like dust on the surface of the moon. Even the maypole was strangely diminished.

I pinched myself. *Ouch!* It stung, but I've had dreams where I did that, so I went back to bed and pinched Jeffrey, just to be sure. He flinched and rubbed his arm in his sleep. That made me feel better. I lay back next to him and stared at the ceiling: Shadows dancing across like angels.

Or *demons* pretending to be angels. The shivering got worse and I thought I could hear a band of people whispering, calling out my name, just outside the window. Their voices piggy-backed on the whoosh of passing cars: "*Julia, Julia . . . .*"

Suddenly, I felt more hungry for sex than probably at any other point in my life. Desperate for the close reassurances of the flesh. I leaned over, rolled back the sheet, and took Mr. Happy in my mouth. He got really big before Jeff woke up. We made love then. It felt delicious when he slid between my legs: warm, so warm, the rush of him within me, beating in time with my heart, and the final outpouring: A thousand seeds for a thousand microscopic souls lying in wait.

Too bad for them, I'm on the pill.

ENTRY FOURTEEN
School is really starting to get me down. I think I took too many credits this term. Sixteen is a lot when you're working almost full time. I would so love to quit my job at Rose City Music.

Stephen (my boss) put me on commission, but I'm still not making diddle. At least I can do my homework without him yelling at me now. He's got another sucker to do all the menial jobs when there aren't any customers in the store. According to Steve, right now is the slowest time of the year. Yeah, right. *Wax on, wax off.* He's so full of crap, it's coming out his ears. Even though I wasn't working at Rose City last summer, I know for a fact that May is nothing compared to July or August when most everyone goes on vacation.

I should get a second job to pick up the slack. I could start making candles again for the Saturday Market. Maybe set up a table at college during the week. If I play my cards right and get the wax cheap this time, I could easily make an extra grand by the end of summer.

ENTRY FIFTEEN

Well, it's final: I've officially been dropped from my morning yoga class at PCC. The instructor said she thought I should go see a doctor. I don't know what her problem is. Just because I shake a little during the stretches, she thinks I'm a tweaker?

That's total bullshit. She never actually came out and said it, but the whole class knew what she was getting at. She gave me this pamphlet on drug abuse in front of them, and even had the nerve to write down the name of a guidance counselor! I'm definitely going to the Dean of Students about this one. At the very least, I should be able to get my money back.

ENTRY SIXTEEN

Got to quit drinking coffee. It's making me so jittery, I can barely bring the cup to my lips without spilling. Then afterwards, I feel a little nauseous with these yucky gaggy coughs.

Can you imagine life without coffee? That does seem a bit drastic. In Portland, there's espresso machines on every street corner! Maybe I should just lay off for a week or two and see what happens.

I can't help thinking about my dad when he first got Alzheimer's. His doctor nixed coffee right away. And lots of other foods, including chocolate. Anything with caffeine. Dad was forty-three when he started to get sick. That's kind of young for Alzheimer's.

Too bad I don't have any health insurance. I'm due for a physical. How long has it been? Two, three years? That bitch in my yoga class has me spooked. It's probably nothing. I've got a very active imagination.

But can your imagination make you shake for real? I guess they call it "psychosomatic" when you make yourself sick just by thinking about something. Fearing it. I've got to keep control and think happy thoughts.

OK, Jules, from now on, when you think about dad, remember only the good things: his smile, the way he used to tip his hat and call you the prettiest cowgirl on God's green earth. No more freaking yourself out with paranoid theories. Take a deep breath, relax. Chill.

ENTRY SEVENTEEN

My roommate, Deeksha, is driving me nuts. She's convinced that I'm insane because I jump if she comes up behind me when I'm not expecting it. And let me tell you, this woman rushes *everywhere*. She can't just walk into a room. Everything about her is on fast-forward.

Except when she's meditating. Then it's the opposite. Then she moves like she's underwater and you want to smack her, especially if she's standing in the middle of a doorway and you need to get past.

Deeksha's the only person I know who can meditate anywhere, anytime: Standing up in the living room, in the backyard, on the basement stairs with the light off. I've even caught her meditating on the toilet, "ohming" with her arms out.

Good thing our house has two bathrooms.

I really don't think I'm unusual in my response (to the fast-forward Deeksha). I mean, damn it, anyone would be surprised if their housemate snuck up behind them and yelled a strange Indian word they didn't know, like *dahl!* or *Nataraj!* It's more than a little disconcerting.

This morning, Deeksha did this to me yet again for the hundredth time. I was fixing myself some breakfast in the kitchen. One second, I'm looking down peacefully at my bowl of cereal, and the next, there's a big loud voice yelling, "*Namaste!*" in my ear.

So I panicked and dropped the sugar bowl, and it broke into a million pieces. I guess Deeksha was very attached to that bowl, a family heirloom or something. Anyway, she yelled really loud and called me crazy.

Yeah, right. Good one. This coming from a person who worships idols. She's got these little shrines of Bhagwan Shree Rajneesh set up everywhere in the house, including the bathroom.

Deeksha is probably the only follower left in Oregon who goes by her Rajneesh name. Even Bhagwan changed his name to "Osho" before he died. But Deeksha will always be Deeksha. That name will ride her to the grave. And her relatives had better put it on the headstone, or she'll come back to haunt them, spike all their sugar bowls with salmonella.

I think Deeksha's real name is Catherine because one time this guy called up and asked if Cathy still lived here, and I told him the same person has owned this house for the past ten years but her name is Deeksha. He goes, oh yeah, right, is Deeksha there? I called her to the phone, and, sure enough, she knew him. He must have called her Deeksha because she didn't frown or correct him or anything. She's very touchy about her "spiritual" name and anything else that has to do with her religious beliefs.

Actually, she's very touchy, period. I'd move out in a heartbeat, but I only pay two hundred a month here and that's super cheap for Southeast Portland, especially so close to Ladd's Addition. I've got this huge bedroom that overlooks the most incredible garden in the backyard. Deeksha keeps it immaculate all by herself; she won't let me pull a single weed. On some days, she'll spend the whole afternoon out there. I'm not sure, but I think it has a religious significance: Her dedication to Bhagwan's principles of living in harmony with nature, etc.

The garden has flowers that bloom in weird colors and shapes most people have never seen. Totally exotic. And all these plants and miniature trees from India. It must have cost a fortune, but I know Deeksha could afford twenty gardens just like it. This much, I've figured out. She never talks about money, but she always buys exactly what she wants exactly when she wants it. To me, that's a sign of being rich.

Don't ask me why the fancy trees and shrubs don't freeze in the winter, but they don't. Maybe it's because Bhagwan keeps watch over them. Yeah, that's right, you guessed it: Deeksha's got a giant picture of him out there in the garden, hanging from a tree.

By now, it should be obvious what I'm up against. If I pander to my housemate's eccentricities, she's usually very cool. Only today, she was a total bitch and there was nothing I could do about it. I offered to buy a new sugar bowl to replace the one I broke, but she just crossed her arms and said, was I also going to buy back all the memories that went along with the old one?

That did it. I told her to pick up the longest, sharpest piece of the broken bowl, and shove it where the sun don't shine! All the way to India!

Well . . . not really. I *wanted* to tell her off. In real life, I just stood there and took my medicine like a good girl.

ENTRY EIGHTEEN
Took a copy of my journal to class today and showed it to Mr. Oden
during our independent conference. He said he was very impressed, but
that I shouldn't let it detract from the time I was devoting to my essays.
Especially the second one, it could have used a rewrite.

Oh, please. I'm so sure. Last week, Oden gave me a B+ on it. And
when he was handing it back, he'd even confessed that he usually rounds
up if the grades, especially if my other essays were in the A range.

Now why would any student in their right mind bother to do a
rewrite if the instructor tells them that? Besides, the journal is worth
more than that first two papers and I got an A on the first one. I've
already written Essay Three, but I didn't bring it with me to class. When
I told Mr. Oden that, he shut up about the other one. Now he's probably
pegged me as the most anal student in his class.

Essay Three is due next class for a "peer review" session. We're
supposed to team up with another student and let them look for
mistakes and offer suggestions. It sounds good in theory, but in practice
I think it's a total waste of time. Still, it's better than sitting through
another boring lecture.

Well, I shouldn't say that. In most classes the lectures are boring, but
Oden's aren't so bad. After a brief introduction and a little bio on the
author of whatever essay we were supposed to have read, he turns it over
to the class and asks us what we thought. Then we break up into groups
and do the discussion questions. I liked my old group better than the
new one because Ruth was in it and she always does the readings. I'd say
over half the students in WR 121 haven't even cracked open their
textbook yet. They cheat on the quizzes to make up for it, and Mr. Oden
doesn't seem to notice. The whole system is really pathetic. That's
community college for you: Slackers, jokers, and 'tards.

But the real reason I wanted to mention Mr. Oden's class is because
during the independent conference today, he told me that he'd had a
chance to listen to my tape and was very impressed. He also let drop that
Helena isn't planning on coming back to the States any time soon.
When I asked him why, he seemed kind of pissed. He said she was
homesick. "Missed her Mammy." And now that she was officially out of
the band, Mammy Jammer was looking for a new singer. They'd be

holding auditions all day Saturday at their rehearsal space—a little warehouse across the street from Pub At The End Of The Universe.

I almost died. That's only ten blocks from my house! I could ride my bike there in, like, two minutes! Mr. Oden put me down for five o'clock in the afternoon. Mammy Jammer has a full PA and everything. I don't even need to bring an amp, just me and my axe.

Mr. Oden gave me a CD of their latest material and said if I wanted to learn the first two songs that would be great. He gave me a sheet with the lyrics, typed front and back. Extremely professional. I can't wait for Saturday. It's only five days away, so that doesn't give me much time to learn the songs. Already I know that if I want to make a good impression, I should memorize the lyrics for the first song.

On my way home from class, I sang along and almost had an accident on the Terwilliger Curves so I put the sheet down and didn't look. I wish I had a CD player in my car instead of this cheap cassette player.

When I got home and put on the CD, everything fell into place. I'll be able to learn the first two songs by heart with no problem. My voice isn't quite the same as Helena's: she's very professional, and the production values definitely made up for the fact that it's a little on the weak side. It has this cool ethereal quality, sort of haunting. Maybe that's only because I know how beautiful she is; sometimes you can tell a woman is beautiful just by her voice.

I'm thinking now of those gothic babes who court death in the Edgar Alan Poe stories like "Morella" and "Ligeia." I had a teacher in high school named Mr. Grabenhorst who was majorly hooked on Poe, and he made us read all these tales, most of them dealing with *femmes fatales*. Kind of a repeating theme you might say, and he used them to teach us words like "symbolism" and "irony."

Mr. Grabenhorst was one of those English teachers who definitely fits into Ruth's little theory. One time he ate a jelly doughnut in class while everyone was reading, and when Margery Clemmens happened to look up, he sucked out the red jelly in a way that was just totally sick and wrong. She told us after class in the hall. We didn't believe her at first because she was a little gossip hound. But then as the term dragged on, we did, because there was something about Grabenhorst that instinctively made you cringe. The way he looked at you with those watery green eyes pickled in their own juices. Yeah, I'll bet he would have made a pass at Helena for sure, if she'd been in his class. She belongs in a Poe story, I can tell you that right now.

Yet, despite Helena's "haunting" presence on the CD, I'm pretty sure I could do a better job in person. For instance, that night at Dante's, I could have kicked her scrawny Belgian ass right off the stage. I definitely have stronger pipes. I just have to watch out that I don't go sharp. Sometimes, when I get nervous, I have a tendency to overshoot the high notes a little, and that can be murder.

When I relax, it's no problem. Like my voice coach in choir always said, "You have to open up your diaphragm to let the little birds out. If you don't, they can't see the sky and they won't sing."

Kind of gay, right? Well, I guess it is, but it works. Next Saturday, I've got to remember to let my little birds see the sky. Then everything will be cool.

ENTRY NINETEEN

I want to do something nice for Jeff. After giving it some serious thought, I've come to the conclusion that I should go a little more easy on him. The only reason I feel like bailing on our relationship sometimes is because I try to picture us in ten years together and I can't. Not the way we are now. Time has a way of changing people, especially men. I know that *I* can't change him, and if I try it will only push him away. I also know that if I'm walking down the street with him and there's a cute baby in a stroller, it makes him uncomfortable if I lean over and talk to it.

I guess Jeff thinks that when I do that, I'm subconsciously sending a signal to him that I want one for myself, and he might actually be right. A baby is the last thing we need right now. It would make everything difficult and ugly. We wouldn't really want it, and that's got to be the worst possible way to bring new life into the world.

These days, in the new millennium, I think it takes guys longer to mature. Part of it has to do with the way they're raised, and part has to do with the fact that people are living longer in rich countries like America and that means you have longer to party and just be a kid.

Still, I have to wonder when I see twenty-five year-old skate punks on the street. Do they know how silly they look in those baggie shorts and candy-striped Vans with a glow-stick around their neck? Do they know they're imitating teenagers? They think they're leaders, but in the larger scheme of things they're followers. Sure, they might be top dog in their own little pack, but meanwhile their former high school classmates (at least the brainiacs) are making six figures a year and living in their own houses instead of squatting under the Burnside bridge or couch-hopping from basement to basement.

Jeff is different from those skinhead losers, but he could end up like them if he's not careful. My latest pet peeve is the pot plants in his closet. He must have at least five or six now. Even though he doesn't deal (he "gives away" buds) people treat him differently, always doing him little favors. That's pretty much the same thing in my book. You don't have to be a genius to see it could lead to worse habits, not in terms of drug use, but in terms of job-sloughing. Especially when Jeff only has to pay half the rent as the other guys. If there was ever a raid, they'd all be accessories. And so would I, if I happened to be there when the cops broke down the front door.

But that's not going to happen. I'm more concerned about what it's doing to Jeff's mental outlook. Being a successful grower keeps him from trying his hardest at work or looking for a real job with a future. I have to admit he has a green thumb. And his expertise with all the high-tech equipment is also impressive. That's what tells me he could succeed in chemistry or biology if he really applied himself. When it comes to his CO_2 levels or measuring the precise amount of phosphorus in the soil, *bang!*, he's an expert. But if he's confronted with the task of memorizing the periodic table of elements, he just totally spaces out.

For what it's worth, I need to come to grips with the fact that I've fallen in love with the guy. I miss him so much at night that sometimes I cry when his cell is turned off and he's unreachable—especially when I want him next to me, to feel the heat from his body under the sheets, warming me, keeping me safe, even in my dreams.

In the interest of being the best girlfriend ever, I've decided that I'm going to buy Jeff that new Sony PS-2 Playstation he's been wanting so bad for his birthday. I saw in the paper that Fry's Electronics is having a Memorial Day sale. They've got one advertised for only $199. That's the lowest price I've ever seen anywhere. I was going to buy myself some new clothes with the money, but what the hell, I know how to sew. A nip here, a tuck there and *presto-change-o*, I've got a new wardrobe!

Jeff's birthday is the day after Memorial Day. If I get him the Playstation this afternoon I'll have to keep my mouth shut for six whole days! He's getting off work early this Friday night, so we can go have a drink somewhere. I can't wait to see the look on his cute face!

ENTRY TWENTY
I'm writing this entry instead of hooking up with Jeff. It's ten o'clock Friday night. He called at the last minute and said he couldn't make it, they were working him until closing. It's a good chance for him to schmooze his way into a bartending gig. Pouring drinks is where the real money is, especially at a crowded place like Ringlers where the tips fall like manna from heaven.

Last time Jeffrey closed, they let him bartend from eleven to closing. He already knows how to pour beer out of a tap and mix drinks, but it gave him a chance to prove himself. He said the manager's going to be there, so that means he might end up snagging a few regular nights behind the bar instead of the kitchen if he does well. I know he will. When it comes to pouring drinks, there's nobody better than Jeff. He can spot a drunk a mile away and knows how to cut them off without getting them riled. He's also got a nice "barside manner." That's because he's such a good listener and knows when to keep his mouth shut (if he's getting paid for it).

By the way, I did end up getting him that Playstation last Wednesday. He'll be so surprised! All I have to get now is some wrapping paper to do it up right. He said he'll make up for tonight by taking me out tomorrow. I hope the audition for Mammy Jammer doesn't go too late. That might mean I can't hang out with Jeff and he'd probably take it personally. I'll call him tomorrow and tell him just in case. He's always been very supportive of my musical aspirations, so he'll understand. How long can practice possibly go? If I get there at five o'clock, the latest we'd probably jam is, like, nine or ten. And if that happens, I know I'm in for sure.

God, I'm shaking. Just writing about it is making me nervous. It's probably good I'm not going out tonight because I need to get some quality Zs.

ENTRY TWENTY-ONE

Well, it's settled. I'm in the band! They didn't even have to take a vote. No contest. The other singers might as well have stayed home. I got there early, around 4:30. All the guys were just hanging out waiting for me. And guess what: they had my demo playing!

After I warmed up and sang the first two songs on their demo, they turned around and played the first song on my demo! I couldn't believe they'd actually taken the time to learn all the changes. Then again, they're such good musicians, they probably could have picked it up that afternoon while they were waiting.

Niles, one of the keyboardists, said he thought I could sing even better than Helena. Everyone else was super complimentary about my voice, too. Part of it was the fact that they have such an amazing PA. It would've made anyone sound good. Their sound board is bigger than the one at Dante's.

Mr. Oden had the delay and everything already set up for the first song on their demo, so when I started to sing, my voice sounded almost exactly like Helena's. I guess a lot of that waifish mystery was digitally "enhanced" you might say. But I didn't have her accent, that's for sure.

The accent was a nice touch. Ever since Björk made it big, everyone and their mother has been faking her Icelandic drawl, at least in techno bands. Even quality acts like Esthero sneak it into the mix, and there's just no excuse for an Icelandic accent when you were born and raised in Canada.

I really like the practice space. It's quite large, at least a thousand square feet. There's this little office where they've got a 24-track set up, isolated and everything, and then there's the main floor. It's obviously an old warehouse, but they've got it fixed up so nice you can barely tell: Carpets on the floors, three or four couches and futons, cool artsy foam things hanging from the ceiling to break up the echoes, tapestries on the walls. A serious party pad. There's a big yard in back with a patio and a pretty good-sized lawn. I was surprised to see they even keep the grass mowed. I think one of them must live there, because I also saw a microwave by the sink in the bathroom and the medicine cabinet was fully stocked.

I hope they don't ask me to pitch in for rent, especially if someone's living there. I'm so broke now that I bought the Playstation, I'm scrounging just for beer money. Jeff better appreciate it!

Oh, that reminds me: after practice, the guys wanted to hang out and get to know me better, so we walked over to Pub At The End Of The Universe. I called my homeboy's cell from there. Jeff picked up on the first ring and said he'd be right over.

Later, when I was introducing him to the band, I stopped at Mr. Oden because, strange as it may seem, I still didn't know his first name. I introduced him as "Mr. Oden" and everyone cracked up, even Jeff. It was pretty funny. Mr. Oden said to call him Lars from now on.

Pub At The End is my kind of place. I hadn't been there for quite a while, and I'd forgotten how many good European beers they have. They also have a big poster behind the bar from one of Mammy Jammer's shows. I guess that some of the bartenders must be friends with the band. I ordered a Newcastle because I like the sweet flavor. Northwest beers can get old after a while. Skunky and hoppy. My favorite beer in the whole wide world is called John Courage. It's from England and the only place I can get it is at this little Korean deli on Milwaukie Avenue.

Lars said he likes to drink at Pub At The End Of The Universe because it reminds him of his college days. He said a lot of Reedies drink there. I looked around and realized he must be right. Most of them looked really granolaed-out, with dreads, hemp clothes, etc. So that means I'll get the chance to pick some of their brains about Reed College since this will obviously be one of my new hang-outs, it being right across the street from the practice space. Mike, who plays guitar in the band, refers to our space as the "Compound." I think he's the one who lives there.

After we finished our first pint, Lars bought three big pitchers and we all settled into some serious, contemplative drinking. Mike said that he'd find out if Mammy Jammer still had the gig at Crystal Ballroom.

I could see Jeff's ears prick up when Mike said that; he went on to explain how originally they'd been booked to warm up for Red Angel Rising, but when the management heard that Helena had gone back to Brussels, they pulled Mammy Jammer from the line-up. Mike also said he'd recently heard through the grapevine that Red Angel was having a tough time of it finding a local band in Portland that they liked. So there was a window of opportunity, albeit a small one, before they went looking to another city like Seattle for a warm-up band. We should hurry up and record a few songs with me on vocals, just to let Red Angel's manager know that I could sing as well as Helena. The only problem was, they were playing The Crystal on June 7th. That only gave me about two weeks to learn one set's worth of material *and* record the new demo.

I must have looked a little dazed by all this information, because Jeff put his arm around me and gave me a little love squeeze to let me know that he was supporting me. I really appreciated that a lot. Then Lars said the new demo wasn't going to be as difficult as it sounded: They had a studio master tape in the Compound with all the original tracks.

I didn't quite follow, so he explained that all they had to do was record the new vocal parts and mix them into a digital copy of the master. If we did, say, three songs, it should only take a couple of days. And if we were pressed for time, we could just leave in Helena's backup vocals and blend them with my lead. That actually might be a good idea anyway, since we were doing the whole thing to prove we sounded pretty much the same with no drastic differences.

Well, I said that sounded fine with me. Especially if it could mean getting a gig at Crystal Ballroom. Lars held up his glass for a toast and we all drank to the band. It felt really good sitting there with my fellow musicians. Part of me couldn't quite believe it: *Pinch yourself, girl! You're the lead singer in a band that's one step away from playing the best venue in town!* My head was spinning, it had happened so fast.

At this point, the waitress brings over a bottle of champagne and Mike does the honors, but when he gets to my glass, he stops. I look up. Everyone has these sheepish grins on their faces. Mike puts his thumb over the bottle. He shakes it and sprays champagne all over me. Then he sprays everyone at the table. I was so surprised I didn't know what to do, so I screamed.

Champagne dripping off my hair, into my eyes. More on my head than in my glass. It was beautiful, really beautiful, like something a rock star would describe on MTV during an interview: *The initiation.* I felt so overwhelmed that I started to cry. Nobody noticed except Jeff. He kissed me real soft on the lobe of my ear, and whispered, "You've finally done it." Then he licked some champagne off my cheek.

Everyone howled in appreciation, even the bartenders. The whole place was watching. A crowd had gathered, and I could hear people whispering, telling their friends who we were—that I must be the new singer to replace Helena.

God, just thinking about it right now, I'm getting goosies. It was, hands down, the absolute coolest moment of my life.

ENTRY TWENTY-TWO
This morning, Hans (my brother) happened to call and I told him the good news right away. I don't think he quite grasped the magnitude of getting in a band as big as Mammy Jammer, but he certainly did his best to congratulate me.

After the usual pleasantries, he started asking some really personal questions about my social life and I felt my face start to burn. God, tell me this wasn't happening, not again. Mom up to her old tricks, listening on the other phone. She'd probably even written out the questions for him to ask.

I told Hans that I loved him, but next time he called, please do it *alone*. Then I hung up before he could stammer out a lie. It would have been too much, especially considering that none of it was really his fault. Mom was using him like she'd used me when I lived under her roof.

And that's just the point: I don't live with her anymore, so if she wants to know who I'm screwing and if I'm taking the pill, then let her call me herself.

Of course, she'd never do that. It would give me the opportunity to unload twenty-one years of frustration: "Mom, mom, mom. Let's not kid ourselves. I stopped being your daughter years ago."

In a way, I can't really blame her. She associates me with the ranch, how it slipped through her and dad's fingers . . . *the accident*. I know she still blames me for that. Dad blamed me for a long time, but eventually he forgave me. If only he'd taught me about engines, I would have known what to do. I could have stopped the whole thing from happening. But I was a girl to him, and girls didn't belong on tractors. They belonged in the kitchen next to their mothers, cooking jam and preserves, tossing the salad, blanching the green beans, baking the pies. Cleaning house, scrubbing and waxing the floors, folding the clothes, hanging them out to dry in the summertime when the fields were gold and the skies were blue and the air smelled of clover and mint.

Well, shit. I might as well get this over with, telling about the accident. Sooner or later, I'll end up making some vague reference to it. If I wait too long, I'll just try to cover my tracks.

It happened the summer before my freshman year in high school. Hans, my brother, was working on the big hay tractor. He called me over and asked me to fire up the ignition. I was excited. It was my first time behind the wheel.

The engine started right up, I kept it going with my foot on the gas. But something happened. I lost my concentration, started fiddling around with the controls. Hans must have known, because he shouted at me to knock it off. I did. I just leaned back and stopped fiddling. No problem. Except my foot bumped against the gearshift and the tractor lurched forward with Hans underneath.

Once it started moving, real slow, I tried to shut it off, but the key wouldn't turn and the gearshift was stuck. I could hear the emergency break whining, straining against the powerful engine. It was a big tractor, strong enough to pull a plow, a hay bailer, anything.

My father ran out of the house and caught up with me. He hit this little switch—the kill switch—and the engine died immediately. That was one of the few times I ever heard him curse. "What the hell's the goddamned big idea, taking off like that?"

I told him it wasn't my fault. Hans had told me to do it. He was working on the engine. Dad's face turned white when he heard that.

He raced to the barn, I followed.

We heard Hans before we saw him—moaning off to one side, in the hay. He was leaned up against the wall. Somehow, he'd propped himself up in that position. He was fiddling with the buttons of his jeans, trying to pull them off. As soon as he caught sight of his legs, the blood and torn muscles, he started screaming, each scream higher in pitch, until it was the cry of a little boy. Dad told me to run in the house and call 911.

After two unsuccessful operations, Hans found out he was never going to be able to walk again. He didn't believe it, though. You could see it in his eyes that he was determined to get his legs working again, even without knees. How could the star quarterback of John F. Kennedy High be a cripple? It took him a long time to concede the fact . . . weeks, months, years.

But my father gave up instantly, as soon as he heard what the doctors had to say. He accepted the verdict and its consequences: now there would be no one to help at the ranch, no one to carry on the family name: The legacy that had been passed down from his father who had immigrated to America from Germany.

I'll never forget what he said then. He turned to me in the hospital waiting room and said very calmly, very quietly, "Well, are you proud of yourself, little lady? Because of your horseplay, Hans will be an armchair quarterback for the rest of his life."

Things changed after that. Everyone told me that I was forgiven—only an accident, these things happen. Dad even apologized for what he'd said in the hospital. And Hans, well Hans was the most amazing of all: he never even acknowledged that I'd done anything wrong.

When he told the story to friends, he made it seem like the whole thing had been his fault. This kind of surprised me because for most of my life, he'd treated me with borderline contempt. The pesky little sister. Now, all of a sudden I was cool. He let me take him places, lots of places, around the ranch on Misty, my pony. His favorite was the old swimming hole down by the brook. After the wounds on his legs closed for good, he started swimming again. He'd splash out into the icy cold water, right out in the middle, and just float there, belly-up in the sun.

The thought of Hans swimming terrified my mother, I could tell, but she never asked him not to. His arms were as strong as ever, and there wasn't much current. He wanted to go and I took him, leading Misty by the reins with him on her back. She ended up being his pony more than mine because she was low to the ground and easy for him to mount. Which was fine with me because I'd always enjoyed riding Duke, his prize thoroughbred stallion.

Even without his legs, Hans was a much better swimmer. He liked to tease me about it. "Hey, you wanna race to the rope swing? No? Whatsa matter? Afraid the gimp'll beat ya?"

Finally one day, in a fit of anger, mom called me the black sheep of the family. Running Hans over with the tractor wasn't enough. I was determined to see him drowned!

Well, that was too much. I barricaded myself in my room and wouldn't come out for days. Mom apologized, but I never really forgave her.

One of the ways I nursed my resentment of my parents' darkening moods, the heaviness that hung around the house, was calling them by their first names, Loretta and Buck. This went on for over a year. I think they must have understood why I did it. In my mind, they had ceased to be my parents. I was their slave, and they dragged me along with them everywhere: 4-H livestock competitions; square dancing jamborees on Saturday night; church on Sunday; even to the Biergarten where dad sang and played the banjo in a local band called "The Reapers."

God, how I grew to loathe blue grass music but country was even worse. At least the blue grass players knew their way around a scale, but country music stars were just a bunch of dumb hicks with guitars, as far as I was concerned. I traded in all my old CDs for new ones by artists like PJ Harvey and Liz Phair that I read about in *RollingStone* and *Spin*. The fiddle my dad had given me on my tenth birthday never came out of the closet. I took up playing guitar, and when I'd saved the money, I bought an old Fender Mustang and a beat up Vox amp. Music was one of the ways I could escape from my parents, the ranch, Mt. Angel, everything.

Another way was through books. I started reading anything I could get my hands on. Barbara Kingsolver was my favorite. I loved the way she wrote about small towns without glorifying or disparaging them. She told it like it was. The flow of her words soothed my chafed nerves, helping me feel like I belonged in the world, like I wasn't a stranger, a temporary resident, a drifter. When she came to Portland and read from *The Poisonwood Bible,* I was sitting in the front row.

Mom took all the changes in my life as a direct insult. Purposefully "unladylike." She went in my room without asking and took back the fiddle my dad had given me. And she tried her best to ground me every chance she got, which only heightened my sense of isolation from the outside world. I started to smoke pot and rebel. Mom never found my stash, but she knew what I was up to. Small towns like Mt. Angel have more eyes than a nest full of spiders. Word got around that the Fleischer girl was trouble. I cropped my hair really short and wore grungy clothes to school just to piss off my parents. It worked. They stopped taking me places with them and even let me quit going to church without so much as a word.

Life on the ranch got pretty bleak around this time. Without Hans to help with the chores, dad had to hire part-time help and that totally sapped our budget. I dropped out of band at school and doubled up my chores, helping out where I could, taking on the things Hans used to do, like feeding the livestock, irrigating the pastures, etc.

In the winter things got really bad. Three of our sheep died from scrapies, this weird kind of brain-wasting disease. First they went blind from staring at the sun and then they wouldn't eat. You also had to be careful if you went near them; the sound of a human voice could send them into hysterics. Dad found this out the hard way.

One time he started talking to them, like he usually did in his soothing voice, and a few of them reacted strangely, bunny hopping straight up in the air. Then the smallest one, not much bigger than a lamb, fell on the ground and had a seizure.

An inspector from Animal and Plant Health Inspection Service (APHIS) came out to the ranch and took a look at the rest of the flock. He said many of the sheep were exhibiting the early signs of scrapies; we'd better keep them separated from our other livestock—quarantined—especially from the other flock in the upper pasture by the highway.

A week later, the man came back with a big semi truck and a crew of workers dressed up in orange suits with masks and hoods. They rounded up all the sick sheep and took them away. I was surprised they didn't just kill them right there, but dad said their spilt blood could infect the ranch since scrapies wasn't like a normal disease. It could hibernate in the soil for years, so better safe than sorry. APHIS would kill the sheep in a special warehouse and incinerate their remains. They didn't charge for the service, but we were out the sheep. I asked him if people could catch the disease and he said no, absolutely not. The inspector had assured him it only affected sheep. I didn't say anything, but I couldn't help wondering why those men were wearing special protective suits, if it wasn't contagious. Maybe they didn't want to infect other sheep elsewhere. I'd heard that could happen with hoof and mouth disease; it wasn't much of a health problem for ranchers, themselves, but they could inadvertently track it onto a ranch on the soles of their shoes, on their clothes, even in their lungs.

Dad was hesitant to buy more sheep after that. He even wanted to sell the flock in the upper pasture, but no one would buy them. Instead, he bought more cows to make up for the lost sheep. His insurance policy covered everything. He even was able to buy our very own milk cow with the extra money he saved on the transaction because he bought from Mr. Taggert, who owned the nearest ranch (in Mt. Angel, "next door" can often mean over a mile away).

There was a spell of good luck after that. Beef prices went up, and for once in our lives, we could relax. The hired help was doing a fine job keeping things running smoothly and Hans was feeling much better. So dad made the announcement that we were going on vacation that summer. Right after the Fourth of July. A driving vacation down to Mexico, where the ocean was as warm as bathwater. We'd drive all the way down to the Yucatan peninsula and check out the Aztec ruins.

But then, just as the clouds were clearing and we'd caught a glimpse of blue sky, a new storm front moved into our lives. As I was doing my chores, feeding the sheep in the upper pasture, I noticed several of the older ones were itching themselves in a funny way on the fence posts. Barnie was the worst. He scratched his butt as usual, but then he pressed his head against the post for a long time.

At first I laughed. "Barnie, you silly boy!" Then I realized he wasn't normal. If he'd been a person, I would have thought he was drunk by the way he was standing, weak at the knees, swaying slightly with his head balanced on the side of the post.

I fed the rest of the flock, keeping an eye on Barnie. He didn't come for his food. He seemed caught in a mental fog. Then I looked into the eyes of all the sheep around me and they started to frighten me. There was a presence there, a foreign presence, like the herd of pigs in the Bible that Jesus filled full of demons when he took them out of Legion, a man possessed. They'd run down to the river and drowned themselves. Right as I was trying to shake off the dark thought, little Shamus came up and nipped me on the leg.

Well, that did it: I took off running. I know it's absurd, being afraid of a flock of sheep, but they weren't normal. If rabies turned even the most harmless animals into killing machines then maybe this was no different.

From the other side of the fence, I watched them. Barnie was just the farthest along. The rest of the flock was definitely sick, too. Some of them were nipping at their knees and gnashing their teeth at each other, smacking their lips like they'd gotten into a jar of peanut butter. I prayed to God it wasn't scrapies.

The man from APHIS came out again. He joked with my father that it was starting to become a tradition. When he examined the sheep, he got very serious. No, it wasn't a false alarm after all. They were quite a bit farther along than the last flock had been. He was very sorry, but they had to go. Right away. He would also need to do a thorough search of the premises. "For what?" dad asked angrily. The man wouldn't say, but when he got to the barn, he seemed very interested in three old bags of feed he found there. He wrote down all this information on the labels, then he left.

We found out later that the feed was technically contraband, banned from sale in the US because the ingredients could be traced to England. It wasn't our fault, we couldn't have known, but we had technically broken the law by feeding the ingredients to our sheep.

Dad got really nervous. He wanted to know if it mattered that he'd fed it to our cattle. The man said no, it would only affect the sheep. Cows didn't get scrapies, so they would be immune. Because of the man's report, our insurance company wouldn't cover the rest of the sheep. They were very sorry, but since we had technically broken the law, they couldn't cover the loss. Dad was devastated when he heard that. He'd lost a whole flock and they wouldn't cover anything?

That's when he started losing it, I think. The weight of the news was more than he could bear. He tried to put our ranch up for sale, but no one would buy. Word got out the place was riddled with scrapies. Our neighbors stopped visiting. They wouldn't even drive their trucks past the main gate. It was horrible. All my friends at school started treating me like a leper.

And then, to make matters even worse, dad went on a marathon bender. At first, he spent most of his time in town at the taverns. When the money got tight, he did most of his drinking at home. He never got raging drunk, but it made us uneasy because we knew he might explode at any moment. He was going through a bottle of Jim Beam almost every day.

At dinner, he'd tell stories we'd never heard before, personal stories about high school and all the girls he'd dated, stuff like that. From the way he talked, you would have thought his life was behind him, that he was an old man. Hunting and fishing stories, all the stuff he would have told his buddies in the bar.

We had the added displeasure of watching him make a fool of himself: Two-stepping with an imaginary partner outside on the porch in the rain; throwing pennies in the bottle and drinking them down with the whisky; balancing a shot glass on his nose. He couldn't sit still, even for a second. If he did, his hands would shake furiously. Playing the banjo was out of the question. He made several half-hearted attempts before putting it away in the closet for good.

Gone were the days when you could ask dad a question and expect a straight answer. He would laugh when nothing was funny. Stare into space for hours, and then burst out in a fit of laughter. The air, the rain, the sky. Our faces. Everything was funny. It was as if this terrible demon had moved into the house, kidnapped our father's soul, and now it was determined to ruin what was left.

Sometimes dad's head would ache so bad he couldn't even see straight. When the pain finally let up, instead of tending the ranch, he'd stay inside and play chess and checkers all day with Hans. To make matters worse, he started giving us all these really annoying nicknames. One day we were Huey, Luey, Duey, and the next, Curly, Mo, Larry.

He would spout off about how all the cattle were sick now, too. Those jackasses from APHIS didn't know a goddamned thing about it. Cows could get scrapies, pigs could get scrapies—hell even people could get it! Good thing we hadn't eaten that feed from Jolly Olde England, or else we'd be biting our knees, goose-stepping like Nazis and smacking our lips at the sun.

Mom was beside herself. She thought we should take the vacation early, just go. Let the hired hands run things while we were gone. There was still savings in the bank.

Dad thought it was a grand idea: "Mexico or bust!" He would pack his suitcase every night, and then in the morning when he was almost sober, he'd shake his head and unpack it.

This went on for the better part of a week before my mom gave up and put her things away in the dresser. She knew dad couldn't leave the ranch. He was like the captain in *Dracula* who lashed himself to the wheel. So what if the ship had a devil on board? He wouldn't desert his post. Nothing could pry his hands off the wheel so long as he was alive with blood flowing through his veins.

I tried to talk to Hans about what we should do, but he wouldn't listen. I could tell he was just as worried as me, but he felt like saying anything negative would somehow be disloyal. He stayed in his room most of the time and watched television. One of his friends brought over an old SEGA and he played that thing into the ground until it finally gave out. He was miserable. If it hadn't been for the painkillers, I don't know what he would have done. When he wasn't watching TV, he was sleeping or so doped up you couldn't reach him.

My whole world had changed. Walking around the house, I felt like a stranger in a strange land. Around that time, my friend Gretchen took me in, and her parents let me stay with them. But then her older brother, Frank, sort of took advantage of me one night, so I had to move back home.

When my graduation rolled around, nobody said anything—not even my mom. I went over to Gretchen's to get ready. We smoked bowl after bowl from her bong. Good ole Gretch. She made sure that I was properly stoned. It was a form of self-medication and we both knew it.

Walking across the stage without my family in the audience would have been surreal—even without the pot buzz. There was this hole in the crowd, up near the top of the bleachers, where dad, mom and Hans would have sat. I stared up there during the long, boring Valedictorian speech and imagined a giant hand had reached down out of the sky with a giant pair of scissors and snipped them out of the picture.

After the ceremony was over nobody said a word about my situation. There was an implicit understanding. Teachers and friends made a special point to congratulate me, polite little hugs all around. It was obvious they knew my family was cracking up. I tried to smile a cosmetic "everything's OK" smile, but I felt like a leper. Contagious.

Maybe it was just the pot making me paranoid. I didn't care. By then, my mind was on one thing and one thing only: getting myself thoroughly shit-faced.

That summer after graduation, I got fed up. If my parents were flaking on the ranch, that was fine with me. I was ready to move out, anyway.

So I did. Gretchen and I found an apartment in downtown Portland. It wasn't very big, but it was cheap and we had enough money to make first and last month's rent, which was all the landlord required.

The day I left, mom took me aside, begged me to stay. She wouldn't explain why, just that I had to stay. *Please.* If I left now, I was leaving forever, deserting the family. I thought she was being dramatic, that it was part of the weaning process. So I turned a deaf ear. I packed up my belongings, put them in my old beat-up Volkswagen bug, and braced myself for the final goodbye on the porch.

Everyone came out of the house except dad. We all cried. It was very emotional. I got in my car and started to pull away.

But something made me stop. I glanced in the rearview. Sure enough, there was dad, jogging to catch up. He motioned for me to roll down the window and when I did, he leaned inside, panting.

As I type these words, I can picture the moment so clearly: Dad's pale blue eyes moving back and forth in his head. He's all worked up, without any way to express himself, like an engine revving up dangerously high in neutral.

"Why?" he says. "Why didn't you kiss me goodbye . . . *Tipper*?"

There's something very wrong. Tipper is our sheep dog. Even in his condition, dad wouldn't make that kind of joke. It's too much. I peer into his eyes, hoping for a sign.

By now, he's laughing because he knows that he's made a mistake, but the reaction seems automatic, a defense mechanism.

"Dad, what's my name?"

A little gasp of surprise. No one has spoken directly to him like this in over a month.

"My name, dad. What's my name?"

His face drops, an obvious admission of guilt. He slides down on the ground next to my car. I get out of the car and shut the door.

"I'm your daughter, remember? Don't you know my name?"

He looks up. "I, I . . . can't . . ."

So it's true. My hunch was correct. He's been forgetting our names, lots of things, for the past month, trying to cover up with his lame jokes. And now he has absolutely no idea who this girl is that's hunched down next to him.

"Are you OK?" I ask. "Can I get you something?"

He falls into me, trembling, and presses his forehead against my shoulder. I can sense the frustration welling up inside of him. He tries to explain, but it comes out wrong, childish nonsense:

"Toot mere light, tote mere light. Toot-toot, tote! Oh, ha, ha. . . ."

I want so badly to put my arms around him, to comfort him. But I can't. All of a sudden, there's a sense of danger. Dad's gone. In his place there's a big strong man who could get out of control. He goes on spouting gibberish.

"Tooty . . ."

It's like another person—a zombie—has attached itself to me.

"*Tote.*"

"STOP IT! LET—GO!" I pry off his fingers and jump into my car, pulling away slowly so as not to injure the zombie who used to be my father.

In the rearview, I can see him sitting alone and bewildered in the middle of the driveway, clutching his knees, rocking back and forth. Mom steps off the front porch. She's walking towards him, but there's nothing she can do. He's fallen and he can't get up.

ø

Christoph "Buck" Fleischer died three months later at Portland Health Sciences University. I visited him regularly, once a week. Every time I walked into his room, a stranger looked up at me from the hospital bed. Yet, I wasn't afraid. Not any more. I was visiting a *patient*—not a zombie—the victim of Alzheimer's, a disease with a very respectable name. President Reagan had made sure of that.

If my father had died without being able to say one last goodbye, it would have been a lot harder for me. I would have carried around a lot of guilt and sorrow for years to come.

But I was lucky. Out of everyone in the family, he chose me. I was the last person to speak with him before his spirit passed on, leaving behind a wrecked body that confused Hans and mom because they thought dad was still inside, lashed to the wheel, hanging on.

Our last meeting: It was a sunny afternoon in July. I'd been sitting at a table in the middle of the skybridge that links PHSU to Graubacher Children's Hospital, drinking coffee and half-heartedly skimming through a novel by Albert Camus.

Some nurse crossed over the bridge and walked right up to me. I braced myself, certain she was here to deliver the news of my father's death.

"Julia? Julia Fleischer?"

"Yes."

"Your father has asked to speak with you."

"What?"

"He called you 'Jules'. Is that your nickname?"

"Oh my God. He said that?"

"You'd better hurry. I've never seen anything like it. A patient in his condition. It's a miracle."

When I walked into his room, the first thing my father did was hand me a sealed envelope with my name written on it. Then he pulled out a letter (he'd probably composed it months earlier and, by some miracle, kept it hidden from mom) written in flawless script, a second or third draft, obviously designed to help him remember not only what he wanted to say to me, but how to say it, how to act with this young woman standing before him, his daughter.

He read the letter as if it were a script at first. The flow of words became more natural as he went along. He said that he wasn't himself anymore, but he loved me very *very* much and wanted me to know. He pointed at the envelope in my hands and told me it would be our little secret. I was to take all the money, one thousand dollars, and buy myself a new guitar, one to replace the violin that mom had taken away. He said he was very sorry she had done that, it had been *his* to give not hers, and she'd had no right. He was happy that I'd started playing music again, learning songs, even if it was rock n' roll. Maybe one day I'd write one for him. But please, after this visit, I was never to come here again. This would be our last time together.

As he said these words, there was a quiver of regret in his voice and it surprised me because it meant he was actually *there*, connected to the moment.

He looked up with eyes clear and bright. "Goodbye Julia. My little cowslip."

I gasped. It was like a ghost had just spoken. The ghost of my dad speaking through those ruined lips, that ruined face. Even without looking, I was sure that he hadn't written the word "cowslip" anywhere in the letter.

Daddy! He was back! He put down the letter and smiled his old confident smile. The proud face of a cowboy. I leaned over, hugged him, fell on his neck, kissed him.

For the first time in ages, he hugged me back. A real hug. It felt so good, so pure. And then a shudder ran through his body like a cold wind. Those big strong arms began to sway out of control.

"Go!" he said, pulling away. "Hurry!"

I ran back across the skybridge, out of the hospital, down the steps to the parking lot—ran, just ran—as fast as I could, the tears flying off my face. And I never went back there, not even when my mom begged me to come one last time because my father was dying. *No shit he was dying.* But it was only a body. Why should we torture ourselves by sitting and holding the hand of that *thing* in the hospital?

I wanted to explain what I knew, that dad would have wanted us to stay away, instead remembering him as he was: proud and strong. I even hinted about our last meeting without giving away the secret completely.

Mom wouldn't listen. She was the opposite of dad, who'd tried desperately to listen despite the fact he couldn't hear. With her, there was just no getting through. She'd purposefully sealed herself off from the world. I was no longer Julia, her baby, flesh of her flesh, blood of her blood. Now, I was the deserter. AWOL. A bad girl who played rock music and cropped her hair short like a boy's.

Farewell green fields and happy groves where lambs have nibbled. Julia's turned black and she'll never turn back.

ENTRY TWENTY-THREE

Holy shit! I can't believe how long my journal has gotten! It's due in class tomorrow and I'm sure it will be the longest in the history of Portland Community College.

Mr. Oden—I mean Lars—says that I don't even have to proof it for errors. He's probably not going to make me write the fifth essay, either. He hinted at that when we met at the Compound yesterday to get ready to record the new demo. At first, we were going to do it all there, and then at the last minute Mike came through with some free time at this real recording studio in Northwest. I forget what it's called. So all we have to do is take the master over and I'll lay down the tracks there.

The timing of all this couldn't be worse. I've got a biology final coming up this Friday and if I mess that up, I could lose my financial aid. The contract states that my GPA can't drop below 3.7. If I keep it up, the college pays for everything (tuition plus books) and even gives me a small quarterly stipend. I guess that I can't really complain, but if I lose it, I'll be up Shit Creek without a paddle.

Last night was Jeff's birthday. We agreed to meet at Dots Café, right across from the Clinton Street Theater. If I hadn't had the Sony Playstation waiting for him back at my house, I would have felt like a total gad because I kept him waiting for almost an hour. By the time I got there, he was already on his third pint of ale. He didn't complain, though. He knew without asking that it wasn't thoughtlessness; I'd been over at the Compound working like a dog.

Originally, the game plan had been for Jeff and me to have drinks at Dots then go someplace fancier. But we decided to eat dinner there. Jeff said he really liked the way they grill the barbecue chicken and I liked their middle eastern "caravan" platter.

After dinner, I took him over to my house and gave him his present. You should have seen the look on that boy's face! He nearly passed out from shock. Last year I gave him this lame-o sweater and I'm sure he was expecting something else like that. He hugged me so tight. Then he said, "Alright, we're outa here!"

The dirt bag. He was so psyched about his present that he wanted to stop by the video store before it closed so he could rent a few games.

We made it just in time, but all they had was the old version of Resident Evil. Jeff almost didn't rent it because he knows how much I hate games with zombies and stuff, but I said it was OK, get whatever floats your boat, so he did.

We went back to his place to try out the system. It looked amazing on his 27" Sony Trinitron. I forced down a few hard ciders and watched him battle all the evil-in-residence.

God, I swear, that game is the worst. Beyond freaky. I actually played a few rounds, but had to stop because it was giving me the shakes. The way all those monsters creep up and try to kill you in the dark. I know it's just a game, but it seems real when you get into it. You forget all about reality and your life temporarily revolves around keeping yourself alive.

For some reason, after playing Resident Evil, I felt super horny. At first I wanted to cuddle, then I was reaching for Mr. Happy.

He was definitely one step ahead of me there! I let Jeff do anything he wanted because it was his birthday. Naturally, he went straight for one place that's usually off limits. But strangely enough, it didn't feel so bad. Not like the last time. He was very gentle. I couldn't help wondering again where he'd learned his new moves. Was there a silent partner? One minute he's reaching for the K-Y, and the next, he's already inside and it's not even hurting. I think I might even have liked it. Just a little. I'll never tell Jeff, though, because he'd push his luck, the ass clown.

Usually, I like to make love, not "fuck," and you just can't be very loving when you're on the verge of pain. It's animalistic. My pussy is a life-giving place—womb, safe haven—but there? That's where all the poison comes out, it's death.

Awoke in the middle of the night with a terrible thirst from drinking so much alcohol, so I got up and went into the kitchen for some cold water from the pitcher Jeff keeps in the fridge. As I was standing there, pouring the water into a glass, I thought I saw something outside, moving down in the ravine: A shadow, flitting across my peripheral vision.

When I looked directly at the spot, I couldn't see anything. But when I looked away, sure enough, there it was again. Right in the corner of my eye. Probably some bum coming up from the river.

Back in bed, I couldn't fall asleep. Resident Evil messing with my head. I started imagining the *way* the shadow outside had moved: sort of creeping low to the ground, hopping along on all fours, yet with the awkwardness of human-being forcing itself to walk like an animal. I got majorly freaked out visualizing it, even with Jeff in bed next to me. Despite the fact he was right there, mentally it seemed like we were a thousand miles apart.

Some things you can't fend off with guns and knives. For instance, you can't shoot a bullet through the face of "evil." But it can get into your head and twist your thoughts, change you. Like a disease or a virus, it contaminates the purity of your soul and the only way to get rid of it is to be good.

And if the evil is too clever, too strong to resist, the only way to get rid of it is to pray to God for help. How many times had I prayed as a kid in church? A hundred, a thousand?

My present situation was no different. I got out of bed and knelt down with my hands pressed together, eyes closed tight:

"Dear Lord, I know it's been a while since I've talked to you, but I'm really scared and I need your help. There's a creepy man crawling around outside. At least I think it's a man. Lord, I'm asking you—no I'm *begging* you—please keep him from getting inside the house . . . ."

The prayer got worse and worse until it totally went sour and I felt like this naked fool on my knees, blabbing to a dark, empty room. It had been so long since I'd gone to church. Besides, if there really was a God in heaven, who could say whether or not he'd even want to help a black sheep like me? He'd probably side with mom. She was the one who went to church every Sunday. I couldn't even remember one of the Ten Commandments—except maybe, "thou shalt not kill."

Sixteen years of Sunday school and that's the only thing that came to mind. Totally useless. The harder I tried to concentrate, the more it felt like there was this dark energy messing with my head . . . whispering voices I couldn't quite make out, trying to distract me, laughing at my desperate attempt to reach heaven.

Or maybe it was the Lord God Jehovah, himself, laughing at me. Maybe he'd sent the demon to torment me for all the things I'd done wrong in my life: *Forgive us our trespasses as we forgive those who trespass against us.* What did it matter to him, anyway, the plight of one more stupid soul?

When I finally got back to sleep, I had the worst dream of my whole entire life. So real. It started like the scariest ones always start: from the exact moment when I shut my eyes.

Outside the bedroom window, comes a faint scratching: Afraid to move, afraid to breathe, I lay in bed imagining all the things that could make such a sound: tree limbs swaying in the wind, stray cats climbing on the roof, owls nesting in the eaves. But none of these seemed likely. There was a raw intelligence behind the scratching: Zombie Morse code. Whoever or *whatever* it was very much wanted to be in here with me.

Eventually, the scratching stopped. I waited and waited, hoping the scratcher had gone away. Pure agony. After a while longer my curiosity got the best of me (just like in horror movies) and I got up to have a look.

When I pulled up the blind, I came face to face with the last thing in the world I expected to see: my father sitting there, perched on the windowsill, as if it were the most natural thing in the world.

He wasn't zombied-out or anything; he just looked normal, like he had before he'd gotten sick. As soon as he saw me, he started tapping on the glass frantically.

"Please," he begged. "Open up!"

He had something very important to tell me and he couldn't say it from outside. I quizzed him over and over: "What's my name?" But he kept evading the question, pretending not to understand.

Something in the back of my mind warned me that if I opened that window, the real danger wouldn't come from my father, but the thing I let into the room. Whatever it was *pretending* to be him.

But what if it really was daddy? What if he had something important to tell me? A matter of life and death?

Against my better judgment, I gave in and unhitched the latch before jumping back into bed and pulling the covers up over my head. After a great deal of fear and trembling, I worked up the courage to peep out.

Nobody there. Damn. Where had he gone to? I crept back over, hesitating within an arm's reach of the open window.

In time, I grew more confident. If he were close by, he would have reappeared. And if it wasn't him, the ghostly imposter would have tried to grab me by now. Or maybe he was down below on the grass. If I didn't hurry up, I'd never know what he'd been trying to tell me. I stuck my head out for a quick look.

The air was cold and damp. A wash of moonlight shone down the steep slope of the ravine. All of the usual sounds in the distance were absent: traffic on the overpasses, trains, planes. Also, I noticed the skyscrapers downtown were dark, lifeless. There was only the moonlight and the rustling of wind through the trees.

I felt thirsty again, so I went back down to the kitchen to refill my glass. The sliding glass door was locked. Nothing out of the ordinary. I walked to the window, peered out.

Before I knew what I was doing, I'd already stepped out onto the deck.

A gust of wind caught my nightshirt, blowing it up over my knees. I tucked the thin fabric between my legs, pressing them together while I crossed my arms. *F-f-freezing.* I could see my own breath in the air. And now that my eyes were getting accustomed to the dark, I also noticed something else: the ravine was filled with sheep. They were grazing peacefully, as if it was the most normal thing in the world to be in Jeff's backyard. I tried to count them all: at least two flock's worth.

And that's when I caught sight of a familiar shadow, the same one that I'd seen from inside the kitchen. I squinted. Yes, there it was. Down near the bottom of the ravine, fighting its way through the brambles.

"Hey!" I shouted.

Whatever it was stopped and turned. I could feel its eyes resting on me, despite the distance between us. *"Es tut mir leid,"* said a voice, weak but unmistakable.

"Dad? Is that you? *Daddy!*"

I cried out again and again, but there was no answer. The figure had gone: Slipped into the brambles, leaving me standing alone in the cold, shivering and dazed.

I awoke with a start to find Jeff had rolled himself up in the blanket, leaving me nothing. *A dream, thank God it was only a dream.* I was shivering so badly, my legs had begun to cramp, so I got up, went to the closet for an extra comforter.

Jesus, it was cold. Wait a second . . . the window, it was wide open! I shook Jeff awake, asked him if he'd opened it.

No, he hadn't. Shut it and come back to bed!

I felt this sickening compulsion to go downstairs and check to see if the sliding glass door was locked. But I was too scared. Jeff parted reluctantly with some of the covers, flopping a lifeless arm over my waist.

Gradually, the heat from his body warmed me, and I was able to relax a little. But I still couldn't fall asleep.

Outside, the full moon: Plenty of light. I was relieved to hear the familiar whoosh of traffic coming in through the window. Headlights and taillights flickering back and forth on the Hawthorne bridge. And in the distance, the buildings of downtown Portland looming tall and bright.

The only thing left from the night before was a killer headache, worse than any hang-over. But still, the pain was somehow comforting because it was real, part of this world.

ENTRY TWENTY-FOUR
This is the first entry that I won't be turning in with my journal assignment. I was going to stop writing, but I just couldn't bring myself to abandon the project. Not now. In a way, it's only just begun. I think I'm addicted.

Lars told me that I was excused from doing any more work in his class. The journal was so impressive, he was giving me an A+. That is such a relief, truly a load off my mind, but I guess part of me feels like he's only doing it so I can spend more time recording the new demo for his band. And if that's true, it's kind of a hollow victory.

I've been going in the recording studio all week and our demo is almost finished. I had to take Thursday night off to study for my biology final, but other than that, I've been practically living in the studio. It's called "The Cell" and it's located in this old warehouse just off Burnside, in the heart of the Pearl District. They've got a huge board with a zillion tracks. More than we'll ever need. Cynthia, the producer who's helping out, says my voice is even better than Helena's, fuller and stronger. And since I know how to sing from my diaphragm, she won't have to "massage" it nearly as much on tape.

I was very flattered to hear that, but I usually take those kinds of comments with a grain of salt. In the record business, confidence is everything and I know that.

Cynthia wants me to feel at home. Still, she seems like she has a lot of integrity and since she's not getting paid, I don't see what she'd have to gain by buttering me up. Except she did hint that if we get a major deal, she would love to work on the project. Mike and Cynthia are dating, I guess. I know they're sleeping together, I picked up that much.

Mike knows practically everyone in town, at least if you believe all his big talk. Last week, he claimed that he had drinks with the Dandy Warhols when they came through Oregon, just back from their Australian tour. He said he even knows Art Alexakis from Everclear. According to him, all the rumors are true: Art's a total egomaniac.

One time, last year, I saw Art coming out of a gallery on Broadway, and I wanted so badly to stop and tell him how much I admire him, but I chickened out. I know that Everclear's sound is kind of poppy and cliché, but I really do like the way their songs aren't just sappy love songs like most of what you hear on the radio. Art gets some real life things in there about his childhood in a broken home and that takes guts. I heard him say in an interview on a local station that he likes to juxtapose these really sad lyrics with happy melodies. The way he said it, you would have thought it was all his idea. *Duh!* Ever hear of a guy named Brian Wilson?

But even if Art's sound isn't the most original, his lyrical content makes up for it. Most of the band members are from Portland. There's never been a band from anywhere in the state that made it as big as Everclear.

ENTRY TWENTY-FIVE

Spring term is going, going, GONE! I dusted my Spanish final, it was so easy, and I'm pretty sure I got an A in Calc. There was just one problem I couldn't solve before class was over. Usually, I'm the first one finished, but not this time. I think my instructor was a little surprised.

When I turned in my test, she smiled and said thank you, but I could tell she'd noticed how I was agonizing over the last problem. Sometimes in math, either you get it or you don't. That last question threw me, but I should clear ninety percent, even if I got the answer wrong. Mrs. Davidson is a pretty cool instructor, so she might even give me partial credit if I was on the right track with most of the problem, until near the end when I had to bring in those equations we learned last week in class when I was so busy.

I guess I could go ahead and mention that the demo is finished and Red Angel's management has it, but right now I don't really care. This other thing happened and I have to get it off my chest.

It involves Jeff. My suspicions were right; he *has* been cheating on me. I should listen to my gut when it comes to these things. It was so obvious, I've been dating the guy for almost two years, I ought to know when something's wrong.

Thank god for Ruth. She's the one who found out and told me right away. From her friend, Marty, this really nice (gay) guy who also works at Ringlers.

Here's what went down: Ruth was at this party in Northeast and she got to talking to Marty and my name came up because of Mammy Jammer. Marty was all bummed out that they'd "broken up" and Ruth told him we were still together, I was singing lead now.

Marty put the pieces together: Me and Jeff. A couple. He hadn't known. Jeff's probably been all hush-hush because of this affair he's been having with one of the new waitresses. So, of course, when Marty realized that I was Jeff's girlfriend, he spilled the beans.

Ruth called me as soon as she got home, bless her heart. I think she even left the party early, she was so upset.

The bitch's name is Nadja. I guess she's from one of those Eastern European countries. She's married, but it's just an arranged marriage, totally fake, to this dweeb from Gresham so she can live here. Man, I am so ready to sink my claws into her face. She'll wish she never set foot on American soil. Ruth says all I have to do is call up the INS and faster than she can say goodbye in her mother tongue, BOOM! She's back on a plane to Romania or wherever she came from.

But that would be too easy. Marty told Ruth he promises not to breathe a word of this to anyone. He says Jeff and Nadja started requesting the same shift and leaving at night together. And since they also come in together, Marty even thinks she might be living at Jeff's.

When I heard that, I could barely contain myself. Some cunt named Nadja sleeping in the same bed where Jeff and I . . . oh, man, that's too much to even think about.

Even if she's not sleeping all night in the same bed with him, she's still "sleeping" with him, if you know what I mean. One of the cool things about Jeff's new pad is this little attic room with a skylight on the top floor, just down the hall from his room. He could have holed the bitch up in there; his other roommates would barely even notice.

Holy Mama, if she's actually been *living* there, creeping around, hiding in that room every time I came over . . . I'll throw a complete shit fit. It's going to rain, sleet, and hail shit! A typhoon, a hurricane! Mount St. Helens will erupt and bury Jeff's house under pyroclastic shit-flows so deep, he'll be sleeping with Harry Truman. And then I'll take that Sony Playstation and break it over his head!

ENTRY TWENTY-SIX

Well, it's official: I've got chlamydia. And guess what that means? Marty was definitely right. Jeff *has* been cheating on me. You don't get chlamydia from toilet seats, that's for sure.

I figured it was just a mild bladder infection, until I looked in the toilet and my pee looked more greenish instead of yellow, like pea soup. Yuck! *Blaaah*! I screamed, "Me, VD? I've never even had a cold sore!"

But I already stopped by the free clinic today and guess what: Oh yeah. You know it, baby. I've joined the ranks of proud Romanian hookers everywhere who smoke cigars, piss green and wipe ass-backwards!

When I told the nurse how horrified I was and how bad it hurt to pee, she only laughed and gave me a little cup. Would I mind doing her the honor? After she'd had my sample analyzed, she told me to go to the pharmacy and buy these special pills; it would go away. I kept waiting for the catch, but it never came. You mean, that's it? Yes, honey, she said, giving me a little hug. It's not like you got AIDS or anything. Chlamydia's a microscopic parasite, easily killed by antibiotics. But if you don't take your medicine, it could get serious. You might develop urethritis, or worse. And while you're taking the pills, you shouldn't drink alcohol or take other medication. I thanked the nurse, reached out my hand to shake. That's when she looked down and noticed I was trembling.

She asked was I on meds? What's going on? By the grave expression on her face, you would have thought she expected me to say junk or something. I told her no, I wasn't on "meds." She gave me another critical look. Why was I squinting like that? I told her I had a raging headache. She nodded to herself—as if she'd made her mind up—told me to shut the door and come back inside.

After that, I was a different kind of patient. The nurse put on another pair of latex gloves, took my temperature and a bunch of other things. Then she told me to sit tight, the doctor would be along shortly. I asked her what this was all about. She just smiled and said probably nothing. But I wasn't convinced. Her voice was hard, not like the first time when she laughed that easy laugh that sisters do when they're relaxed and just hanging out chilling together.

I must have waited for almost an hour. The room was air-conditioned and I felt so naked sitting there in my paper smock on the paper sheet they put over the examining table. I put my clothes back on, and waited.

There were all these pamphlets in the rack by the door. Since I had nothing else to do, I started to thumb through them. Big mistake. All those gnarly pictures of STDs just got me totally freaked and my paranoid self took over. What if I had something else? What if Jeff had caught something really serious from Nadja?

The longer I waited, the more nervous I got. And the more nervous I got, the more I started to shake. Finally, the doctor came. He was this young uptight white boy, Joe Wonder Bread compared to the nurse.

While I was getting back into my paper gown, he scrubbed his hands and snapped on a pair of gloves. There was no small talk, not even a forced smile. His bedside manner made the nurse seem like Florence Nightingale.

Next thing I knew, he'd lubed up his finger and was feeling around inside my vagina. He put in one of those metal stretcher thingies and went to town with his flashlight. I thought the whole thing would never end.

Dr. White seemed pleased by the results of his little snipe hunt, but I didn't know if that was a good thing or a bad thing. He changed his gloves, washed his hands, put on another pair of gloves. He took my temperature again, checked my tongue, my eyes. Because he was so serious, I couldn't really tell what he was thinking. Judging by the scowl on his face, I could have had the black plague or just a common cold.

Next, Dr. White tested my reflexes. He took a rubber mallet and whacked my legs a few times to check my reflexes. Then he gave me a little rubber ball and told me to hold it in front of me, give a little squeeze.

My whole arm began to shake. It was really scary. I almost dropped the ball. He told me to do the same thing with my other hand, and when I did the same thing happened. I told him I was just a little out of sorts. Too many cups of coffee, my doctor says it makes me nervous. He didn't laugh.

We went through a bunch more tests, then he told me I could get dressed. While I was putting on my clothes, he checked things off this checklist. Had I ever taken methamphetamine or recreational drugs of any kind? I confessed to the occasional bong hit of pot. That and good ole fashioned rocket fuel. Nothing else.

Dr. White nodded, making a note in my file. Then he asked me the question that I'd been dreading to hear: did I know of any hereditary diseases that might run in my family? I told him no, but he must have picked up on my hesitation. He asked if any of my immediate family had a serious illness. I told him no, but that my father had died recently. Complications due to Alzheimer's. He asked how old my father had been when he died, and I said forty-four.

That did it; the doctor raised an eyebrow. Uh-oh. He turned over a fresh sheet in his clipboard, started asking all these questions about my dad: his full name; where he'd been treated; his social security number (which I didn't know). Then he left the room and the nurse came back a few minutes later.

She wasn't smiling. I could see that a big line had formed out in the waiting room. This made me feel bad for getting impatient because it was obvious the doctor had taken extra time for me, despite all the patients piling up. And it also made the nurse's job twice as hard. She hustled me out of examination room, gave me a prescription for the pills, and asked if I needed to apply for financial assistance. I noticed the line for the free meds and said no thanks, I'd just take the prescription and pay for my own pills. She told me which drug store chain was the cheapest to buy from. Then she reached into her pocket and pulled out a business card.

When I saw PHSU printed at the top of the card, along with some neurologist's name, my heart nearly stopped. I asked the nurse what this was all about, did it have anything to do with the chlamydia? No, no, she said. Just call the number on the card in two days and the receptionist in neurology at PHSU would take care of everything, it was all pre-arranged.

As soon as the nurse had moved on to the next patient and wasn't looking, I chucked that card in the trash and rushed out the front door. Why hadn't the doctor told me himself? Why had he given the card to the nurse? What the hell was going on?

I took off running down the sidewalk—*Go! Hurry!*—an instant replay of two years earlier when I'd rushed out of the hospital room, daddy's voice echoing in my head, the last words of a dying soul.

Running felt good. I lost track of myself, letting my body take over—the necessity of gulping down oxygen to feed the blood as it rushed madly through my veins. When everything else fails, the limitations of mortality can have a strangely calming effect. You can only run so fast, so far. And then you've got to stop and catch your breath.

I found myself standing in the middle of a little park that I'd never seen before. It was very beautiful with big alder trees, ash trees, all kinds of trees. They looked very old because the trunks were so big around and covered with big woody carbuncles. Heavy green benches, circular in shape, were wrapped around the trees, almost as if they'd been designed to keep the trunks from getting any wider. I sat down and let the tears plunk down onto the pavement. It felt good, shifting my attention away from my arms and legs; when I stopped thinking about them, about the shaking, it stopped magically, like I'd tripped an off-switch in my brain.

The sun was filtering down through the leaves. I noticed this bum watching me from where he stood across the street panhandling. When I looked at him and made eye contact, he crossed the street.

I knew what he was going to say before he even said it: "What's a cute young girl like you cryin' for? You should be smilin'!" I told him to get lost. Why should I be smiling? Just because I'm young and female and pretty? Was it my job to smile for people, to make them feel better? Who did he think I was, Julia Fucking Roberts?

The bum listened really well, nodding in all the right places. I was kind of surprised he didn't get agro.

Instead, he just said, yeah, well, OK, I hear you. But check this out: smiling doesn't just make other people feel good. It makes *you* feel better, too. What goes around comes around, you know? It's like that old Beatles song says, "The love you take is equal to the love you make."

What could I say to a pearl of wisdom like that? I gave the guy a dollar. He was starting to impress me. I mean, here he was, totally down on his luck, probably sleeping under a bridge somewhere, and he was absolutely beaming with positive energy. I also liked the way he didn't just bail on me when I gave him the money, when he could tell I wasn't going to cough up any more no matter how many pearls he let drop.

We sat there together watching the squirrels bury their nuts, trying to be as sneaky as possible, turning their tails at each other. The guy laughed and pointed. He knew most of them by name. The squirrels reminded him of this story about a girl he'd known, a pretty blonde student like me, 'cept she was going to Portland State. She used to come here and play with her pet rat. He even remembered its name: Ginger.

"Lemme tell you, that little critter was the smartest animal you'd ever see. Way smarter than dogs or cats. Used to climb way up high in the trees and look down. Very curious about everything. But when the girl hollered 'Ginger!' it would come scampering down, jump up onto the bench, and perch on her shoulder, how do you do?, just as slick as a parrot."

I asked the guy if he'd seen Ginger lately. He smiled and said that was another story. The girl had gotten a second rat to keep Ginger company, and when she was gone from the house, this other rat, which turned out to be a juvenile delinquent, had taught Ginger all these naughty habits like chewing through power cords, how to open up cupboards in the kitchen—really destructive things. So the girl had been forced to get rid of both rats.

Despite Ginger being abandoned, the story cheered me up and helped take my mind off my own troubles. I gave the homeless guy another dollar. He picked up his garbage bag full of cans and went off on his rounds.

My headache was almost gone, but my bladder was starting to hurt again. I could feel the pain welling up between my legs. And I knew that when I urinated, it would be that awful green color. What they say is true: A healthy body is practically invisible. It's only when you're sick, that you start to notice it. I caught myself thinking back fondly on the good ole days before I'd gotten sick, when my pee had been pure and clean: Golden.

Golden showers, that's what they call it when you pee on somebody else. But who in their right mind would want a *green* shower?

Hang on . . . oh, now that's wicked, really wicked. No, no, girlfriend, don't go there. A green shower? *Could I? Should I?* Jeff gave it to me . . . why not literally give him back a "taste" of his own medicine?

I could play innocent, tell him I heard about this thing, a golden shower. Did he know anything about it? Yeah? Well, how about trying it? Would he mind if I pissed on him in the shower?

Poor baby. He wouldn't know what to say to that. Especially considering I'd let him do what he wanted to me the other day. A little pissing would only be fair. Lately, he'd complained that I wasn't "assertive" enough in bed. What could be more assertive than that?

ENTRY TWENTY-SEVEN
3:45 in the morning and I'm sitting in front of my iMac typing. The screen is a uniform grey, illuminated from behind like the clouds of an Oregon sky. Deeksha's snoring in her room across the hall. It's really intolerable. A high, raspy chainsaw. I want to go and stuff something in her mouth to shut her up.

Today, she asked for the rent with the snidest expression on her face. To her, it's an amusement. She keeps me here as a boarder just to amuse herself.

Sometimes I feel so weary. I need to go on vacation and get away from the Pacific Northwest, take a bus down to Mexico, crash on the beach. Live in one of those little huts for $3 a day. My friend, Simon, did that one winter. He packed up some food and clothes and drove all the way down, three thousand miles, deep into the heart of Central America and ended up on some nameless beach somewhere with his van and his surfboard and his girlfriend.

Man, that sounds so good. All I need is a van and a girlfriend. Right now, the thought of another woman's body doesn't repulse me. After the men I've been with, it would be a refreshing change.

Even in the animal kingdom, females are invariably cleaner than males. Take cats, for instance. The females spend much more time preening themselves and they don't go around trying to mark their territory. Instead, they greet you with an air of indifference. Perhaps a bit more aloof than the males, but they don't want as much in return. They don't demand obeisance. Instead, if they trust you, they'll roll over on their backs and offer their tummies to be pet.

Everyone in Portland can be so passive-aggressive, especially the men. They never tell you how they feel. Jeff is a perfect example. Instead of asking for a favor, he tries to weasel it out of you with small, calculated acts of manipulation. Instead of saying, "The sight of your body intoxicates me. Come, let's make love," he'll offer some weak compliment about my hair or my clothes, trying to flatter me, thereby drawing me closer.

Lately, it's been my weight, how good I look. "Skinny." There's something forced about the way he says it, like he's thinking the exact opposite. I wonder about this Nadja of his, how she looks. Is she a waif, a tall thin scarecrow? Or a big-boned Slavic babushka—a tit-flapping, bear-hug of a mommy?

I'd wager the latter. Jeff said he was attracted to the "gravity of my presence" when we first met. I never quite knew what he meant. But he's a chubby chaser, alright. I know that now. He wants a big, fat ass to pound, to absorb the shock of his desire: A *big* girl.

Well, I've got news for him: I'm not super-sized anymore. I'm me. And if that's not good enough then he doesn't deserve what I have to offer.

There's more to sex than reproduction. I'll never have a child, I know that now. It's not my destiny. I can touch more lives with my music, my art. This leaves more time for exploration, change. Discovery.

I'm thinking of Ruth: the warm voluptuousness of her skin, so smooth; the gentle curve of her breasts, her hips, her calves. If she were here now, I would try to seduce her. I would come to her and take her in my arms, envelope her in my newfound passion, the transience of life, of our time here on earth. My lips would hold the first cry of a babe and the final gasp of a dying breath. Alpha & Omega. I would promise her everything and nothing. My gift would be moments, and you can never measure those—for a single moment can last a millisecond or a century, depending on what is being experienced, how it's interpreted.

Ruth comes from the oldest surviving civilization on earth: The Israelites. Her ancestors were building great cities and worshiping their God when mine were living like savages in forests of hemlock, sleeping on pine bows and washing themselves in mud-choked ponds and bogs, rinsing their faces in the same waters that claimed the flesh of their children, where they drowned them as sacrifices to death-hungry gods.

Ruth, you are like a warm breath from the East, instead of this cold blight that Jeff has embraced, this adulterous whore of Babylon. Your sex holds the secret to my salvation. So wise, so giving. Even if I never tell you that I find you attractive, it is enough for me to write these words tonight. I love you, Ruth. You are the greatest friend I've ever had. We've only known each other for a short time, just under a year, but I feel a kinship with your soul as a fellow writer, a blasphemer, a priestess at the altar of life. You are the antithesis of everything I hate in the male ego—this green death in my loins burning and eating me from the inside out, a testament to my hatred, each stabbing pain giving me strength.

Whatever doesn't kill me only makes me stronger. I know that. But I also know that I can't hold out forever. Loneliness is a contest no man or woman can ever hope to win, holding out against the immensity of the universe.

Like the lapping waters of the Tigress, I will go back for more . . . letting the bastards enter me again, hoping for a new release that will never come. And so will you, my love. So will you. It is our fate as women. The compulsion we can't ignore, no matter how much it tears into our flesh and binds us with cords of violence. I wish you were here with me now, lying in my bed, just being here, not even touching. I want a friend more than anything else in the world. I just want to be loved as much as I can love.

Where are you tonight, Ruth Cohaine? Are you sleeping, dreaming of a man, a bird, the sky? Are you happy in your dreams? I hope so. Because if you can be happy then there's still hope left for me.

ENTRY TWENTY-EIGHT

Just got home from the hospital this morning. It was crazy. I feel better now. A little shaken up, but as well as can be expected. Jeff called an ambulance last night from his house, but I didn't really need one. I was just tired, that's all. Too weak to protest.

The ambulance took me to Providence St. Francis, pretty much against my will, and then, later, after a doctor had looked me over and given the green light, the receptionist tried to make me pay for it. Can you believe it? That's America for you. The richest nation on earth, but if you get sick and don't have health insurance you're done for. I told that receptionist I'm not paying a red cent. She acted like I was mental or something, so I had to calm down and tell her very quietly that I didn't have any insurance and was a college student on financial aid.

There was this black guy waiting in the lobby who overheard the whole conversation. After I went over into the waiting area to catch my breath, he told me not to worry. I didn't have to pay, just blow it off. The hospital would harass me for a couple of months, send these threatening letters from a collection agency, but that was just a front. He'd done it more times than he could remember. And so far, they hadn't gotten anything out of him.

That's not what I want to write about, though—the accident. Not yet. First things first.

Lars called yesterday morning. We got the gig at Crystal Ballroom! Red Angel's manager called him to say that the new demo sounds every bit as good as the last! I'm not sure if that's a compliment or not, but I suspect that Cynthia had something to do with it. She probably mixed out the low end. I have more range than Helena, so there's no way that I would have sounded much like her without some fancy footwork behind the control board. Oh well. I don't really care. That's typical. A strong voice can be threatening, especially if it's a woman's.

These days, the big record companies are hung up on a cult of youth. They want female vocalists to be charmingly rebellious teenagers like Britney Spears and Christina Aguilera. "Flash us your most spiteful bedroom eyes." The whole thing is a ruse for male domination. It's more fun to conquer a woman with spirit—the crazy, bucking mare that needs to be broken.

If I have any say in the matter, I'm going to change that. Even though I hate Madonna's music, I really admire the way she was able to go from this bubble gum chewing hairy-pit poster girl to the single most powerful entertainer in the record industry, with her own label and everything.

When Mammy Jammer plays The Crystal, I'm going to let the audience have it: my voice, my body, my vision. And if they don't like it, they can just "F" off. Even though I haven't played any major venues yet, I still know a thing or two about performing.

Crowds are different than fat cat record producers. They thrive on power, whether it's feminine or masculine. A crowd is like a flock of sheep: they always follow the shepherd. Well, I'm their shepherd, not Helena. That means the band is going to learn a few of *my* songs. And if the gig goes well, I'm going to sit them all down and we're going to have a talk. If they want to keep me as their front woman, they're going to have to make some changes.

Like the name: *Mammy Jammer*. That's gotta go. A cheap euphemism for "Mother Fucker" as it turns out. A cheap shot, period.

But enough about Julia's BIG PLANS. I've got to keep my sights on what's in front of my feet, as well as on the horizon.

School's out for summer! I was going to take a few classes, but I've decided that I need a break from studying; it won't affect my financial aid if I nix the summer term. Besides, who knows? Maybe the band will get a record deal. Then I'll put off school for a while. I definitely want to get my degree, but I won't be young and beautiful forever. So if the opportunity presents itself, I've got to grab it while I can and follow my dream.

Now, here's the skinny on what went down at Jeff's. I called him up yesterday and asked if he wanted to get together. He hesitated at first, but I said that I really wanted to see him. I had a big surprise. That got his attention.

We met at Tiger Bar and socked down a few drinks, then we went for Chinese at this place Jeff likes that's just down from the Magic Garden. I didn't touch anything on my plate. Jeff noticed this and asked what was wrong. I told him I was excited. He asked why and I said he had to wait until later, I'd tell him back at his place. He wanted to go drinking at a few more bars, but I asked to go straight over to his place.

He looked at his watch. The gears were turning in that predictable little brain of his. I knew instinctively that he was stalling. Must have something to do with Nadja. Was she over there right now? The thought of seeing her, confronting her face to face, beating the shit out of her . . . Oh, man, it pumped through my veins like fire. I told Jeff that I'd pick up a sixer of whatever he wanted, my treat. He laughed and said I didn't have to do that, his birthday was over and it was the best one he'd ever had.

We stopped at the store and I bought a six-pack of Black Butte Porter even though I hate dark beer. Jeff laps it up like milk and that was fine with me. Let him get drunk. He'd turn into a big teddy bear. I could get him into the shower without even trying. So what if the pills had already started to work and my pee wasn't green anymore. I'd make him leave his clothes on so he could smell my disgust after I left.

He'd have to wash my scent off him, off his clothes. My disdain would linger on him, give him something to ponder. And while he was soaping himself down, I'd stop off in his bedroom and pee all over his bed just to wash off Nadja's stink.

Back at Jeff's place, I let him drink a few more beers. He was all smiles. I tried my best to be happy and carefree, but I had my eye on the stairs the whole time, waiting to see if Nadja would come down.

She didn't. After an hour or so, I told Jeff that I was getting thirsty. Did he have any Hornsby's hard cider left? He laughed and said I'd drunk the last bottle on his birthday. I pulled out a ten-dollar bill and asked him if he would be a darling and ride his bike over to the 7-11 for another six pack. He groaned, fumbling for an excuse. He was too drunk . . . a cop might see him swerving and, uh, pull him over. I said, what, did they give RWI's now? "Riding While Intoxicated?"

Jeff couldn't think of a comeback. The teddy bear phase was setting in. As soon as he left, I ran up to the spare room, knocked. There was no answer, so I opened the door.

Instantly, I knew that everything Ruth had told me was true. The room was filled with stuff, totally lived in. On a crate beside the bed that was doubling for a night stand, I spotted a thick book with a foreign title embossed in gold letters on the cover that obviously spelled The Holy Bible. I ripped open the top drawer of the dresser: Bras, panties, post cards and a passport, a Polish passport, belonging to one Nadja Renata Sobieski.

So she wasn't Romanian, after all. She was a Pollack! Goddamn Jeff, shacking up with a Polish whore! I held my nose. Her clothes were saturated with cheap perfume, the reek of it, marking the room. I ripped open the other drawers, throwing out clothes, belongings, until I came across the bundle of pictures.

Nadja, Nadja, Nadja. There she was. In the flesh. Blonde like me, a natural blonde, with brown eyes. A little older and a little taller, judging by her height compared with the other people in the group shots. Most of them were conspicuous, doofy-looking foreigners with bad teeth, pale waxy complexions, dark circles around their eyes from too much liquor, cigarettes, late night parties in *Amerika*, all wearing these really tacky sweats and tennis shoes. And just as I'd suspected, Nadja was indeed a tad on the plump side. "Big boned" like I used to be. When I got to the last picture in the bundle, I felt a bitter smile creep across my lips.

There they were, the happy couple: Jeff and Nadja caught in the kitchen at Ringlers—he with his arm around her, and she leaning back into his chest, holding up her hand at the camera—*no, stop, please!*—giggling.

That was all the proof I needed. I turned off the light, shut the door and went back downstairs to wait.

Jeff took a long time getting back. I couldn't help wondering if he'd gone off looking for his new love. It was over a half-hour later when he came stumbling in, clutching my six pack to his chest as if it were a rare jewel that he'd brought back with him from some distant foreign land, a knight in shining armor with his "booty."

I noticed one of the bottles were missing and then I saw Jeff's elbow, it was bleeding. Oh, the poor thing, he'd taken a spill. What a shame. He put the five-pack in the fridge, handed me a bottle. Warm. He said the 7-11 was out of Hornsby's, they only had the kind of cider I hated, so he'd ridden his bike all the way up the hill to the store that had all the brands. I think he was a little surprised that I didn't comment on his elbow. He washed it off in the sink, picking out a few chunks of gravel. He'd wiped out coming down the hill, trying to balance the six-pack on his handle bars. One of the bottles had broken, he hadn't drank it.

I just sat there. No comment. I could see that he was nervous because he started blinking his eyes. After almost two years together, I could read him like an open comic book.

All at once, I knew that I wasn't going to go through with my little revenge scenario. There was no way I could pull it off, giving him the shower of his life. I was too angry, and it wasn't like me anyway. I'd never wanted to hurt Jeff. Not really. But I knew for sure that I didn't love him any more.

So what was the big surprise, he asked. I told him I'd gotten the gig at Crystal Ballroom. We were playing Thursday after next. Warming up for Red Angel Rising.

He jumped in the air. "I knew it! All your hard work has finally paid off!" I could tell that he was going to bound over and give me a hug, so I put up my hand to stop him. Then I pulled the picture out of my pocket, laid it down calmly on the table, without even looking.

But Jeffrey looked. Oh yeah. He drank in the sight of it, everything it implied, and then he coughed. A dry little cough of defeat. He opened his mouth to say something. I told him to can it. No excuses, that would make me hate him and I didn't want to hate him. Not anymore. I felt nothing now. An empty hole in my heart where his love had been.

But, but, he stammered. He wanted to know all the details, how I'd found out. It wasn't really how it appeared. Nadja was only staying here until she saved up first and last month's rent.

I could tell he was lying. Right through the gap in his front teeth.

I got up from the table, stepped over to the sliding glass door.

There it was: the ravine from whence my father had come, warning me in the dream. I felt a tear glide down my cheek, quickly wiped it away.

No, stop. Don't cry. Jeff will think it's for him. My hands were shaking uncontrollably and there was a warm buzzing in my ears. The room began to fade. I felt Jeff's strong hands catch me, but he couldn't catch my soul—even as I was lying on the ground and he was crying, "Please don't faint. Fuck! Should I call 911? Jules, wake up!"

Sinking down through the floor, into the basement, deeper and deeper, past the concrete foundation, nothing to stop me from falling inside the earth where the ground is cold and damp.

I try to call out, but my mouth won't open. Everything is strangely alive down here. Crackling, whirring. Shapes and colors whizzing past at incredible speeds. Other wills, other souls reaching out, wanting to touch me, to be near. I hold up my hands in front of my face: They're steady, peaceful. No shaking. And a faint luminescence radiates from them. My entire body seems to be giving off a signal like a radio transmitter and this attracts the shadowy forms, hungry little wingéd vermin buzzing in my ear.

And then I hear a familiar voice, high above, steady and true, calling down: "*Coooooowslip!* Come back! You can do it! Concentrate!"

My head clears and I can make out the sounds of a police radio, the sensation of my body being lifted into an ambulance, flashing red lights bleeding through my eyelids. Jeff's voice, strong and clear, talking to a policeman, telling him that I'd only had a few drinks. No medication, no drugs. I was his girlfriend, yes that's right.

When I heard Jeff say that, I tried to object. The attendant noticed and told me to lie still. *Shhhhhhhhhhhhhh. Juuuuuuuuuuuuust relaaaaaaaaaaaaax.* He was holding my hand. I wanted to tell him that

Jeff wasn't my boyfriend, not anymore, but it was like my mouth had been filled with sand. The granules slid down my throat, into my lungs and I couldn't breathe. One of the attendants pushed something down my throat that made my windpipe open up so air could get through. The other guy jumped behind the wheel and off we went!

I was their cargo, en route to a destination of their choosing. They were taking over the reins, doing their jobs. After we traveled through the night, they would drop me off at a hospital with a room like the one where daddy died and that would be it, the end of the road.

But I knew, even as I lay there in the ambulance with the siren wailing over my head, that it wasn't really the end. It was the *beginning* of the end.

ENTRY TWENTY-NINE

That black guy in the lobby at St. Francis had been right: I've already gotten four calls from the hospital trying to strong-arm me into paying. They want almost five hundred dollars! Ninety-nine for the ambulance and four hundred eighty-seven for the emergency room.

Can you believe it? Those bloodsuckers can take my paperwork and choke on it. I barely have enough money to buy Advil. The headaches keep getting worse and worse—constant pounding, knocking, "Hello? Anybody home?" Tiny imps beating on the hot coils of my brain.

Deeksha heard me on the phone all morning. After the last call, she finally broke down and asked what was going on. I thought she was uptight about me not paying the rent, but she said she didn't give a flying fuck. It was *me* she cared about.

Frankly, I was more than a little surprised to hear her talk like that. She never curses. Part of her *sannyassin* training, her duty as a follower of Osho. She said she used to have a really bad "potty mouth," cleaning it up had been one of the sacrifices she'd made to join the inner circle at Rajneeshpuram.

As I filled Deeksha in on all the gory details, what happened at Jeff's, the hospital, she sat there across the kitchen table and gave me her undivided attention. For once in her life, she really listened. When I got to the part about my fainting spell and the way I've had problems shaking lately, she came over and put her arms around me. She told me not to worry, she'd take care of the ambulance bill. I couldn't believe my ears. I said no way, she didn't have to do that. But she said it would ruin my credit rating. That could come back to haunt me later. I said I didn't care about my credit rating, buying an expensive car or a house was the last thing on my mind.

Deeksha said alright enough negativity, let's go outside. We can sit together in the "sacred spot" next to the koi pond.

It was a warm day, very beautiful and peaceful in the garden. She told me to sit cross-legged and close my eyes. We meditated like we used to do when I'd first moved in. It felt really good. Then we did some stretching and yoga.

For some reason, it didn't bother me this time when Deeksha started preaching from Osho's lessons. She told this story that was a little corny but kind of interesting. I think it came right from one of the books she's always reading. She said we must strive to be fearless because fearless thought is like the powerful roaring of a lion. When other animals hear this sound, it strikes terror into their hearts. Even the biggest elephant runs off, forgetting his dignity. But if you have a really good heart, unfettered by guilt and self-doubt, you can become like the old dragon who hears a roar and welcomes it with calm delight.

I wasn't sure exactly what that meant, but I knew I wasn't supposed to say anything, no questions, so I just sat there with my eyes closed. Deeksha kept talking. She explained how she thought of men as lions. Women, on the other hand, were calm disciples, accepting the roar as a part of nature.

That's when I had to speak up: Did she know that female lions did all the hunting? Males just lay around, eating, sleeping, and humping up a storm.

Deeksha laughed very hard. She came over, kissed me on the forehead and said that's why she loved me so much, because I was a thinker. The way she'd kissed me kind of surprised me. It seemed a little more passionate than the way Bhagwan might kiss one of his followers. But I knew she was "ecstatic," carried away on the moment. She started preaching again: Only women possess the key to the universe. It's in our safe keeping, locked up in the strongbox of our wombs. But if we chose to open our hearts to each other, we could share this life-force, this *chi*, and the floodgates of consciousness shall open up to embrace our love, reinforcing it with all the glories of Zen.

When I opened my eyes Deeksha was sitting naked in front of me. I'd seen her body before many times, but never like this.

She was opening herself to me, and I knew I had three choices right at that moment: 1) to reject her, which would mean moving out, 2) to postpone rejecting her so that I would have more time before I had to move, or 3) to make love to her.

I looked at her body: ample breasts, the long graceful contours of her neck, a warm inviting smile, and the place between her legs, already moist and glistening in anticipation of my response. Part of me wanted to surrender myself, turn the key and unlock her corner of the universe, but I knew I couldn't. Not now, not ever. The attraction wasn't there. Deeksha was far too old, a mother hen. Having sex with her would have been like having sex with my mom, and that has to be the single most disgusting thought I could ever conceive of.

All of these thoughts kind of short-circuited my brain, but I still managed to fudge my way out of the predicament, somewhere between the second and third choice, reassuring Deeksha that I wasn't upset, but that now wasn't a good time. To reinforce my open-mindedness, I even slipped off my shirt and closed my eyes, meditating topless for a while.

I knew then that Deeksha would be more than happy to take care of me if I wanted her to, that she would bend over backwards to be my "sugar mama," but this was inconceivable. If I let her pay all my bills, I'd be no different from Nadja.

A whore is a whore is a whore . . . .

If the seduction had happened at any other point in my life I would have been angry. Livid. A fire-breathing dragoness!

Deeksha hadn't even given me a chance to catch my breath from what happened the night before. I was just getting over the chlamydia and was sick with God only knows what else. Also, I was an emotional wreck from Jeff's betrayal.

So no matter how much Deeksha tried to prove her motivation to help me was genuine, her bad timing only reinforced my impression of a pampered and basically selfish person who had never done an honest day's work in her life because she came from a filthy-rich family.

Still, I need as many friends as I can get right now. Deeksha is on my side and that feels good to know. Even if she does want to jump my bones.

ENTRY THIRTY

There's no use pretending anymore. Just because I fooled that doctor in the emergency room at St. Francis, telling him I'd mixed antibiotics with alcohol, lack of sleep, that I'd been distressed, beside myself about a personal matter involving my ex-boyfriend, it doesn't mean I have a clean bill of health. It only means I can trick those who want to help me, or at least those who show a pretence for trying to help.

Yesterday, I was sitting at Café Lena, working on these poems that I'm secretly writing for Ruth, and I felt the awful slipping feeling come over me, stronger than ever before. People's voices at nearby tables kind of slowed down, or sped up, and I could see these shapes moving all around me, out of the corner of my eye. I thought of ghosts, but that would be silly, like the movie *Ghost Busters*.

The grey shapes, shadows—whatever you want to call them—didn't really seem to be aware of the other people. But they were *painfully* aware of me. That I know. The more attention I paid to them, the faster they came—rushing over like insects, huge grey shadowy insects drawn to the heat of my presence until they were pressing in around my table.

As soon as I got my "tofurkey" burger and started to chow down, I was fine. My conscious mind shooed them away. Eating must have had something to do with it. Maybe they were literally the manifestation of hunger. My body trying to communicate on a subconscious level. There's no way to tell for sure, but the whole experience was beyond freaky.

OK, time to change the subject.

Remember that story I mentioned, the one Ruth wrote about that Kibbutz in Israel? *The Alchemy* at PCC accepted it! They're going to publish it in the fall! Bless her heart, Ruth was so excited! The Chair of Creative Writing sent her a personal letter of acceptance!

That's another reason Ruth should come with me to the poetry reading tomorrow night. We've got to celebrate! Ruth is such a sweetheart. I feel embarrassed about what I wrote about her last week, all those sensual things.

The next morning, I read through the entry and blushed. It didn't even sound like me talking. It sounded more like Deeksha. I came very close to deleting the whole entry; can you imagine how embarrassing it would be if Ruth ever read it?

I wonder what she'd do if I told her that I'm attracted to women as well as men. Would it get in the way of our relationship? Despite how "progressive" Ruth likes to think she is, with parents from Manhattan, she's never really discussed her sexuality with me. It's just sort of taken for granted that we're both straight. We talk about other guys— appraising their faces, legs, asses—but that's only for laughs. I wonder what Ruth would say if I told her I thought another *girl* had a nice ass?

Life is so mixed up right now. I don't want to jeopardize our friendship. Ruth is my rock, my fortress. Even though she doesn't know it, she's helping to keep me from cracking up.

Sometimes I get this impulse when I'm walking down a busy street to take a few steps sideways in front of a bus or a big truck. I could end it all, so simple. No more changes, no more dark energy, nothing. God, how I wish things could be the way they used to be. I just want to be happy again.

These days, it's really weird at home with Deeksha. I think she's been kind of embarrassed about that time she came on to me in the garden. We haven't discussed it. But she doesn't walk around naked anymore. Instead, she wears this slinky Japanese kimono made of silk. I almost feel like doing her just to get it over with. But that would be so wrong.

Even when I go into my room and shut the door and put on my headphones, it doesn't feel private. I imagine Deeksha listening from the next room, wondering if we'll ever get together. Touching herself, thinking of me.

That's part of the reason I could never tell Ruth how I feel. If I somehow put her in the same position, I'd rather curl up and die. But there's one good thing about my predicament with Deeksha: I don't feel guilty about the rent anymore. All that tension in the house, it's such a drain that I'm earning the rest of this month's rent just putting up with it.

And Jeff. He's been calling me at the house. Deeksha has a nose for his timing. She always picks up the telephone first. Then she gets this really sarcastic tone in her voice and says, "Oh, Julia . . . it's for *you.*" Jeff hasn't mentioned anything about getting back together, he claims he just wants to check up with me now and again to make sure I'm hanging in there. According to him, Nadja moved out, he never sees her outside of work. Not that it really matters. I guess she found some other teddy bear to squeeze.

The other night still has Jeff rattled. I know he feels guilty, like it was all his fault, my passing out and stuff. And he's partly right. Every time I start to stress, the shaking gets worse. Fainting isn't out of the question, especially if I've missed a meal. I haven't told Jeffrey about the illness, though. He doesn't have to know. It's really one else's business but mine. Jeff thinks I've got an iron deficiency because I'm a vegetarian. He's been pushing for me to start eating fish, to become a "vegaquarian" like Ruth. Whatever. I wish he'd just give it a rest and quit calling.

Next time he does, I'm going to say so. Enough is enough. He can see me at the show. That's the soonest I'd want to see his big dumb baby face. He can stand out in the audience and watch all the other guys get hard-ons and remember "once upon a time, she was all mine."

God, I'm totally rambling. It's getting late, past my bedtime. When I'm tired, it's hard to concentrate. These last few entries have taken me a lot longer to write than usual. I should write in the morning first thing when I get up, but I usually have to rush to get to work on time.

Maybe if I go to bed earlier, I can get up earlier and do the writing then. A glass of orange juice, one piece of rye toast, along with a Morningstar Farms breakfast patty, and I'll be set. No more coffee, though. No more caffeine, period. That's taboo. If I drink anything with caffeine these days, I'm a basket case. I get the shakes so bad it's all I can do just to keep my teeth from rattling in my head like a maraca.

I'm going to call Ruth now. Three rings and then I hang up if no answer. But she's probably still up. Girlfriend's a night owl like me.

ENTRY THIRTY-ONE
Forget writing in the morning. I've been sitting here for ten minutes just staring at a blank screen. That whole early morning thing was just bogus. You can't deny your nature. Plus, there's the Deeksha factor to contend with. In the morning, she's in full gear, puttering around, banging pots in the kitchen, vacuuming in the hall outside my door—all in an effort to get my attention.

Why put off the inevitable? I've got to move out. Like, immediately. Things have gone from bad to worse. Deeksha's been making these elaborate dinners, expecting me to drop everything at the last minute, wanting to "talk" about my life, which basically ends with her dishing out a liberal helping of Osho vomit every chance she gets, cramming it down my throat.

I was going to write about what happened at Café Lena, when I read my love poems about Ruth with her there and everything, but it's going to have to wait until after work. Screw this. I can't even type, my hands are shaking so bad.

ENTRY THIRTY-TWO
Ahhh. Much better. I'm spending the night over at Ruth's, so I'll have to transfer this file back to my computer on disk.

Gotta stay out of Deeksha's lair. She thinks she's helping me, but she's only making everything worse, much worse. I almost told Ruth about her coming on to me, but then I thought better of it. So I just said that she was on the rag, PMSing, and that I had to get away, which is probably not far from the truth.

One of the bogus things about living in Deeksha's house is the way she and I synchronize our periods. I don't know how it happens or why, but I'd rather not "share" my cycle with her.

Now Ruth, she's different. There's almost something endearing about her cycles, the way she groans and leans on my shoulder as we walk to class: "Oh, Jules, I'm not going to make it. Can't you just carry me?"

We both get cramps really bad. If we were synchronized, we could sit around and moan together.

The other night at Café Lena was probably one of the best nights of my life. I was kind of burnt from work and band practice, so Ruth invited me over to her place and we took a nap together.

Oh, heaven! It was absolutely *amazing* lying next to her! We kept our clothes on but I was tingling all over! We must have slept for at least two hours because the alarm clock never went off and we were late getting to the reading.

I'd already brought my poems, so we drove straight there. Ruth had a few of her own, which sort of caught me by surprise. I didn't even know she wrote poetry; she's never mentioned it before. I think every writer worth her salt should write poems. As far as I'm concerned, they're the purest form of literature.

We got to Café Lena about twenty minutes late and I was really bummed out because I figured we'd be around twentieth on the list, but guess what, Tina Blanchard, a friend of mine who knew I was coming, put my name under hers, which was third! That meant I was going on fourth. Perfect! Just long enough for people to settle into their drinks.

But then I remembered Ruth, so next to my name I wrote "& *Friend*." Tina thought that was really clever. She had a table in the corner by the window, our favorite place to sit. I think she must have gotten there really early because it's usually taken.

The first poet who read was totally boring, rambling on with a fake Irish brogue about wine, women, and song, trying to sound like this latter-day Odysseus from Ireland. He fell flat on his face, but everyone clapped loudly because that's one of those things, at least at Café Lena. People are understanding, since most of them are nonprofessional writers. It's a kind of embarrassment insurance: that way, if you end up sucking the big one, at least you'll get some applause. There's nothing worse than a room that's totally quiet after you've just poured your heart out.

The next poet was this slam type, yelling in the microphone about titties and beer, a real turn-off. I discreetly took out my poems and started to arrange them, figuring out which one to read first.

When Tina's turn came around, I put everything away and gave her my undivided attention. She's so adorable, this really petite girl, and they always have to lower the microphone for her. But she has a great presence despite her height and her squeaky voice.

Tina's poems were about places and natural things, very little about people. That's cool. Most poets at open mics tend to go off about poppy Americana like game shows and Elvis, so it's always refreshing to hear some well-crafted poems about nature.

Since the crowd really loved Tina's first two poems, she took out a third one—this really long one that was totally different, about her brother and how she'd felt after he committed suicide. I hadn't even known she'd had a brother.

The poem was so touching that I saw a few people get misty-eyed. I probably would have too if I wasn't nervous about reading next. When Tina finished, there was this awkward silence. People didn't know if they should clap, but then Roger (this tall, skinny flamer who only writes sonnets and heckles the bad poets) stood up and clapped.

Everyone took his lead, standing up. The emcee came over and said a few words of encouragement to Tina as she was sitting down at our table. She was crying, so the whole thing must have been true. Man, that took guts. Ruth and I patted Tina's little hand, told her she'd done great. Then it was our turn, we were up.

I decided to let Ruth go first. She'd always been more confident than me in class, raising her hand a lot, so I figured she wouldn't mind and she didn't. She read this one poem about a trip she'd taken back to her grandmother's house in Brooklyn. It was very polished, like something you'd read in the *New Yorker* and people were obviously impressed. But it lacked emotional conviction, especially after Tina's reading.

Still, Ruth's voice was strong and clear and she came across well, much better than most people who read.

The audience clapped and I was up.

All eyes shifted on me, and that's when I realized how bad my hands were shaking. I couldn't even read the words on the page. Ruth gave me this worried look that said, *OK, go ahead, you can do it!* I felt like I was going to cry. The people in the audience seemed a little caught by surprise, too, because I'd been reading at the open mics for over a year and this had never happened before.

Ruth put her arm around me and gently took the pages, holding them for me to read. My whole body was shaking. I could tell because Ruth's arm felt so calm and steady. I felt the dark energy flow out of me into Ruth and it anchored me down. Once I started reading, the poem found a voice. I just relaxed and let the words spill out of my mouth:

Summer
I wait for the coming of summer
Like a sparrow saving up her twigs.

I wait for the chance to brush
Against the cross-currents of your hair,
Trailing in the wind.

You are the season of my release,
Bending your arms like the boughs that hold me.

Your essence clings to the roof of my mouth,
Lofty as the arches of a cathedral set against the clouds.

You have a soul as generous as the sun,
Yet dangerous as a storm cresting over the fields.

The voice of the wind calls your name to me as it rushes
Through the branches of proud oaks, waving at the sky.

After I finished, Ruth rubbed my back, turned the page. Everyone was clapping really loud, but I almost didn't like it because I knew part of the reason was because at least some of them were my friends worried about me. Also, it felt so weird standing there with Ruth's arm braced around me, reading the poems I'd written for her, *labored* over, agonized for her sake.

And then I smiled because I realized that it was beautiful. She would never know, I'd never tell her, it was just one of those things. Now, I was getting the old rhythm back. I felt my "sea legs" as I launched into the second poem:

Dreaming Open Days
Where do the winds go on days that move like beetles
Across a heap of dry driftwood?

Where does the rain go in summertime
When the firs smell of pitch
And dreams leave me open to chance?

I reach out to the sun and your voice spreads
Its rays into the pores of my skin.

Take me in your arms, and I will sigh the sigh
Of open days

That rise up like steam from milk-washed lips
Toward the window of hours yet to come—
Hours spent together
In the bosom of a blue-streaked sky.

The crowd clapped even louder as Ruth turned the last page, but I didn't need to look at the words. This one, I knew by heart. I'd been reciting it earlier that afternoon, committing it to memory as I lay next to my love, watching her sleep, cherishing the rush of her breath, the rise and fall of her breasts:

Your Body
I drink in the sight of it
With reverence
Like a sip from the Holy Grail,
Nakedness spilling down my throat,
Hips smooth as the bank of a slow-flowing river
That has caressed a favorite bend of sandstone
Lovingly
For a millennium.

Ruth put down the sheets and hugged me right there in front of everyone. She took my hand, led me back to the table. Tina scooted her chair over next to mine, asked if she could get me anything. Everybody was looking.

All of a sudden, I didn't feel so well again. I thanked her and said yeah I'd really like a Tofurkey burger. Tina looked nervously over at the waitress who said she was terribly sorry but the kitchen was closed.

That's OK, I said. Maybe a glass of soymilk. Then I got up and went to the bathroom to compose myself in front of a mirror.

Edgar Alan Poe would have fallen in love if he could have seen me: Chest white as snow, fine blonde hair starting to get long, already going light from the summer sun, from sitting outside cross-legged meditating in the garden.

Funny how life works, strange. Without meaning to, I'd finally done it. I looked like a rock star, an actress, a model. The weight had slipped off my body, leaving behind a different person. There was a wildness about the eyes—larger, wider. A look that said: "Tomorrow I may die, but you shall remember me forever."

I'd never thought of myself that way before: beautifully doomed, with a sad, haunting transience. But my face, my body, everything about me accentuated this fact, and now it was undeniable.

A knock at the door, Ruth's sweet voice: "Jules, honey. You alright in there?" I burst out, throwing open my arms to give her a tremendous hug.

I could tell she was chafing at the bit, dying to ask what was wrong. Slyly, I took her hand, dragging her back to the table. Not another word. We had to support the other poets, that was our solemn duty. We had to clap for them as loud as they'd clapped for us!

A big glass of soy milk was waiting for me. Tina winked. I leaned over, gave her a peck on the lips. Her eyes went wide and she giggled nervously.

That's right, baby, get used to it! The new Jules can do anything she wants! People were looking again, whispering about the change that had come over me, a fresh new glow in my cheeks. They probably thought I'd shot up in the bathroom. Well, fuck 'em. They could think what they wanted.

I signaled to the waitress, ordered a glass of wine. Tonight was a celebration! After the poetry reading, I'd invite Tina to join us next door at Chez Grill for a bottle of champagne. Life was a celebration, especially with Ruth at my side: *O, for a draught of vintage that hath been cooled a long age in the deep-delvéd earth!* Wipe away your tears! Come, run with me through alien corn!

And when night is over and the time has come to resign ourselves to the morning minions' mercies, then and only then will you count me among the darkling drawn . . . not lost, but passed, like the bridge of a song.

ENTRY THIRTY-THREE

Went back to the free clinic today, not for a prescription, but to ask the doctor for that card again, the one from PHSU. He wasn't there, so my visit turned out to be pointless. The nurse was there, though, she remembered me.

When I asked her about the card, she couldn't recall. It had been a very busy day, she'd had people coming in who looked quite a bit sicker than me. But she was kind and told me that I could schedule an appointment with the doctor for next week. He was at a conference, out of the state, but he'd be back the following Monday. I thanked her and made an appointment for eleven-thirty, Monday.

Now I've got five days to stress out about it. Oh well. Them's the breaks.

After going to the clinic, I was exhausted and hungry. The weather sucked, a light misting of rain—more the rule than the exception in Portland—except for July, August and September, the sunny months when it actually warms up.

Today was cold, dark clouds drooling, not the kind of day to sit outside in a park looking for my friend, the can scrounger, for a pick-me-up story. I thought about calling in sick to work. I was due to come in at one o'clock, and it was only eleven-thirty.

I hadn't really eaten breakfast yet, so the changes were starting to kick in. Just barely. I'd been fighting them on and off, ever since that night when I had passed out at Jeff's, but a morbid streak in me was curious to find out what would happen if I didn't eat. I wasn't particularly hungry, though. My stomach had already started to shrink.

I drifted west, up toward the Pearl District where I knew there were lots of interesting cafes. At Ninth, I turned left and followed Burnside up to the biggest, most famous branch of Powell's Books, which has always been a safe haven for me, the perfect place to experiment. What psychologists would call a "controlled setting."

Powell's Books was fairly deserted inside, it being the middle of the day and all. I went straight to the literature section and started browsing.

I just love the way Powell's is laid out, not like most bookstores: One whole city block with three big floors (four if you count the rare book archive upstairs). It reminds me of an ancient library from Borges' *Fictiones*: Seven rooms, each a different color. I went straight to the Blue Room where all the literature is kept. The clerks put their favorite books with the covers facing outward to attract your attention with all these little tags that say which employee recommended them. And they usually have good taste. That's how I've come across many of my favorite books—by going for the yellow and blue tags.

As I strolled down the isle, I could feel a low, resonant whir start up in my bones, like a big generator straining way down in the basement. But I knew there wasn't any such generator—not really. It was a telltale sign the changes were already upon me.

Thumbing through a novel, I began to hear voices whispering behind the stack. This time, I could understand what they were saying. Instead of calling my name or jabbering amongst themselves, they were mocking me through a new and ingenious method: *reading aloud!*

If I hadn't known better, I would have thought the books *themselves* were talking—the souls of long-dead authors leaking out into the cold, stale air.

It took every ounce of restraint not to dash outside, into the broad daylight, where the Shadow People wouldn't be able to track me so easily. But a part of me knew instinctively that I had to find out more about them in order to beat them at their own game. And Powell's was the perfect place.

I rushed over to the "K" section. *Animal Dreams* wasn't on the shelf, so I picked up a nice, big hardcopy edition of *The Poisonwood Bible*. I squinted down at the first page in Kingsolver's latest book. To my relief, I could make out the words, despite a few backwards letters here and there. Reading aloud, I hoped the sound of my voice would steady me.

I froze, mid-sentence. What was that? It came from down in the Rose Room: A long, plaintive howl. The man standing just down the aisle from me hadn't even flinched, but I could hear the Shadow People jabbering. No more fun and games. Now it was everyone for themselves!

Another howl and another—more animal than human. This time it was much closer, over by the stairs.

I listened for the Shadows' reaction: Nothing. They'd bailed, leaving me alone to confront whatever it was coming up the stairs. *Fuck that!* I bumped into some lady, knocking a book out of her hands. She backed away, as if I were some kind of lunatic.

When I got to the Coffee Room, I scoured the shelves for anything of substance, but there were only starchy foods—bagels, muffins, scones. The girl behind the counter asked if she could help. "Yes!" I said. "Do you have any protein?"

She blinked at me stupidly. I began to get desperate: "You know! Soy, meat, anything!" The girl shook her head. This was a *cof-fee shop,* not a restaurant. But there was a pizza place right across the street.

"OK, fine" I said, trying to calm myself. "Is there a back way out of here?" The girl forced a smile, "Uh, no. Not really. Your nearest exit would be that way." I followed the tip of her finger down the stairs to where she was pointing, even though I knew exactly where the front entrance was.

No sooner had I glanced down there, than my eyes tracked the movement of something that didn't belong. At first, it seemed like the shadow of a large dog on the wall, elongated by the lights down in the Rose Room. And yet, I knew this was no mere shadow. Not this time. Shadows didn't have bristles . . . the bristles of a coat, *hair.*

The realization took a second to register. In the flicker of that instant, the creature froze and turned its head. I looked away, but not before I caught sight of the monstrous black lips and fangs. There was something about them that lingered in my brain like the flash of a light bulb. What was it? A smile, horribly animalistic, yet conscious of itself like no animal could be. I'd seen that look on the faces of sportsmen in photographs displaying their wares, gloating over the carcass of some poor sad being that had fallen victim to their deadly game.

"Please," I begged the girl, reaching into my purse and whipping out a twenty-dollar bill. "Don't you have *anything?*"

The girl glanced down at the money. "Hang on," she said. I scrunched behind the trashcan as she went into the back room. She came out with a sack lunch. "There's a sandwich in there," she said. "It has meat."

"What kind? *What kind, damn it!*"

"R-roast beef! I, uh . . . made it fresh this morning. It's my lunch, but for twenty bucks you can have it."

"M'RO USHÁLYIN!" The creature looked right at me, getting ready to pounce up the stairs—its eyes hypnotic, burning yellow. I grabbed the lunch sack and dropped behind a shelf of magazines.

Crouching down, I ripped the sack open. *Red meat.* Of all things, it had to be red meat, cow. I stripped off the bread, wolfing down huge bites that made my eyes water as the cold flesh slid down my throat.

As soon as it reached my stomach, I could feel my body start to come back online. The roaring in my ears stopped. Just to be double sure, I ate the potato chips and the orange. Then I pulled my knees up to my chest and waited.

Several minutes passed. No sign of the demon. Not even so much as a growl. By this time, I knew I was safe. The headache told me so. It pounded mercilessly on the coils of my brain, bringing tears to my eyes.

When the security guard came to escort me out of the store, I didn't have any objections. He was this really nice Hispanic man in a green T-shirt who didn't say much of anything.

Outside, on the sidewalk, I apologized. The security guard smiled, no harm done. Just don't come back for a while, OK? I asked him how long that would be, and he said one month, maybe two. I could tell he thought I was on drugs by the way he was looking at me, studying my eyes, making a mental note of my hair color, height, weight, etc., obviously for a report of some kind.

ø

Oh, man, I'm exhausted. All this talk about shadows and demons has drained my brain. I can barely type another word. Such heaviness, heavy thoughts. Instead of focusing on dark energy, next time the changes come, I'm going to keep a lookout for angels. Surely, they must be there, waiting, just out of reach, wanting to help.

ENTRY THIRTY-FOUR

Speaking of angels, my father's spirit seems to have some connection with light. I'm remembering that time at Jeff's when my soul left my body and the voice shouted "Cowslip!" to keep me from sinking too far.

Or maybe it wasn't my father, maybe it was an angel who didn't want to frighten me.

Whatever it was, I have the feeling it would help me again. Whenever I feel myself start to sink, I'm going to listen for it. A few words of encouragement from above. There's so much blight and ugliness. I just want to be good.

Even if this whole thing is just one massive hallucination—a soul that's packing up and getting ready to leave behind a spare body—I can deal with that. At least I'm trying to make some sense of it: The possibility that I'm searching for pearls of wisdom in a lump of crap.

Putting everything down here in this journal makes me feel better. It's like a breath of pure oxygen, helping to give my life a purpose. Yet another outlet for my soul, along with my music.

So much to think about: Fame, fortune . . . *fate*. Will I die rich and famous, a victim of some rare degenerative brain disease? Locked away in a special wing of some hospital. Or worse, in a lunatic asylum.

I can't help speculating about the obvious parallels between the way our sheep acted on the ranch after they'd contracted scrapies and the way my father acted once his so-called "Alzheimer's" took over, filling his brain with paranoid visions until the very lint on his blanket roared loud enough to make him cower in fear.

And now I'm the same way, hearing voices in bookstores, running from my own shadow. Reality is starting to break down. I can't tell what's real and what's illusion. If my suspicions prove correct, then both my father and I must have caught some kind of human form of scrapies. I know it seems unlikely. The man from APHIS told us that could never happen, but it doesn't take a genius to see that allaying our concerns was in his best interest, not ours. He certainly didn't care one peck about my father's well being. He knew the implications of his report, how it would bankrupt the ranch, and yet he walked away as if it was nothing.

Thinking back on it, I'm sure that doctor at the Free Clinic must have made some kind of tentative diagnosis if he gave me that neurologist's card at PHSU. And I threw away the card he gave me. Why? That was stupid, childish. From now on, no more rash decisions. I've got to keep on top of this thing if I want to get anywhere at all.

ENTRY THIRTY-FIVE

Ruth had me over last night. She's sick of her housemate, too. We're thinking about looking for a place of our own, just the two of us. Thank God her housemate's on vacation. Bill Green. He's this older guy, a retired construction contractor, who owns the house. Mostly, he stays upstairs. Ruth says he watches TV nonstop and drinks whisky, even in the morning. He looks a lot like Charles Bukowski but he's uglier, if you can imagine.

One time, last fall, Mr. Green came on to me when Ruth and I made the mistake of drinking with him. That was right after she'd moved in, when she still was trying to make a good impression. He brought down his blender from upstairs and made the most delicious frozen margaritas. In a strange way, he seemed almost charming. Watching him grind that ice with such expertise, flexing the muscles in his forearm (still rock-hard from a life spent swinging a hammer) I imagined how he must have looked as a young man: Tall, strong, virile . . . and still ugly as sin.

Before he'd gone back upstairs with his blender tucked under one arm, Mr. Green had whispered that he felt a special "connection" with me because I possessed a "timeless beauty." This followed by a tender kiss on the cheek.

You know, I'd never admit it to anyone, but I felt strangely connected to him right at that moment. If there's such a thing as a "grandfather figure," he certainly fit the bill. Now is that messed up, or what?

Ruth did most of the cooking for dinner. She's got this dynamite recipe for tofu pad Thai and it was *soooooo* delicious! When she was boiling the noodles I told her that I ate a roast beef sandwich the other day and she dropped the spoon on the floor she was so surprised. I didn't tell her about the rest, though. I just said I'd been feeling faint; I'd need some protein really fast.

When I said that, I could see the wheels start to turn in her head. She twisted the corner of her mouth like she does when she wants to say something but thinks better of it. That didn't last long, though. Over dinner, she broached the subject very delicately. She said that she'd noticed I'd started drinking a lot. I could tell by the way she said it that she thought I was becoming an alcoholic. That kind of ticked me off, so I decided to go ahead and tell her about the scrapie/mad cow thing.

Ruth listened really patiently to my whole spiel. I told her about the sheep on the ranch, how my father had gotten sick. His symptoms. I also told her about the Free Clinic and everything.

We were done eating by then, so we went into the living room and sat on the couch. Ruth listened really attentively to all my theories on the disease without passing judgment. When I was finished, she gave me a hug. Then she jumped up and said she had a surprise. She opened the freezer and *voila!* A pint of my favorite: Haagen Daaz Vanilla Swiss

Almond! That was so sweet of her, always thinking of me.

She took the ice cream back to the couch with two spoons and we ate right out of the carton. I was impressed she didn't seem worried about catching anything, but that also made me realize that she probably thought I was imagining the whole scrapies thing. She told me that if I went back to the Free Clinic and got the name of that neurologist at PHSU, she'd go with me. The way she said it, I felt like she wanted to go *to make sure* I went.

After eating all that food we were both so drowsy that we decided to call it a night and turn in. This time, I took off my clothes and only left on my T-shirt and undies. Ruth went into the bathroom to get ready and came back in a cute little nightie. I put on this dreamy CD by Hooverphonic that I'd given her for her birthday and she turned off the light and got in bed next to me.

We started talking girl talk. I told her that I really liked the way she was growing her hair out. Eventually, it would look so killer: Long, black and sleek. Another two or three months and that blonde raccoon stripe along her bangs would be history.

Ruth said thanks and switched the conversation, wanting to know how much weight I'd lost over the past couple of months. I said beats the hell out of me, I'd thrown away the scale Jeff bought. She said she thought I looked good with the weight off. But some of the girls at school had been gossiping, saying I must be anorexic or something. She said she could never make herself throw up, could I? I said no way, that was totally wrong. In the silence of the room, I sensed her listening carefully to my answer, gauging it to see if I was telling the truth.

For the second time in one evening, I felt a twinge of irritation but I knew Ruth was only worried about me, it was friendly concern, so I let it slide again without calling her on it. She put her arms around me and gave me a nice hug: "I'm so glad that we're best buds."

I asked her about Chuck, this guy she'd been seeing lately. She said, oh Chucky, that loser, she was going to break up with him next week. He was *way* too immature, never listened to a word she was saying. All he cared about was sex, and even that wasn't so hot. She asked if I'd ever get back together with Jeff, and I turned to face her. No need to even dignify that with a response. As I propped myself up on one elbow, my night shirt slipped down and my left tit kind of popped out.

I looked down, back up at Ruth. She giggled. There was enough light in the room coming in through the window to see the look on her face. I knew right then that she was attracted to me, but maybe she wasn't quite aware of this fact. It was more of an impulse. All I had to do was lean over and kiss her. But I couldn't do it. Not tonight.

Instead, I just lay there next to my love, her long brown legs rubbing against mine under the sheets, and I felt my skin prickle in that familiar way up and down the inside of my thighs right before my little girl starts to get wet.

In the middle of the night, I woke up plagued with a terrible thirst. *Water, water everywhere and not a drop to drink!* I got up, stumbled into the kitchen. As I was standing there at the sink, I could have sworn I heard a creaking upstairs in Bill's room. The floor boards. Then I heard a sound that was too soft to really hear, but I recognized it anyway, kind of a whisper.

A big shadow was there in the room with me. I could see it out of the corner of my eye. Just one. Better to pretend it wasn't there. Sometimes when I did that, they went away. Acknowledging their presence seemed to encourage them.

I didn't feel hungry, but I looked in the fridge anyway. There was the tofu pad Thai, wrapped neatly in Saran Wrap. No, that wouldn't do. I needed something more substantial. Protein, a quick fix. I poked around. Ruth was a vegaquarian but alas alack, no fish. Then I noticed the shelves in the door. Sure enough, there was this jar with a picture of a fish and the word "Gefelte" written on the label. I couldn't find an expiration date, but when I unscrewed the lid, this vile smell came out. *Yuck!*

Right as I was putting the jar back in the door, I caught a glimpse of something moving closer to me, out in the dining room. Looking directly at the spot, I could see the carpet was shaded different like there was a huge invisible form standing there casting a shadow.

Whatever it was moved toward me again and I screamed. The jar fell out of my hands, shattering on the floor. Shadows popped up everywhere, and I saw something else, something horrible that I'd never seen before: It was like this little vortex had opened up right in front of my eyes and all these squirming beings were moving around inside.

I fell down to my knees without taking my eyes off the vortex and started feeling around blindly on the floor for a piece of that rotten fish. My fingers wrapped around a soft, fleshy chunk. As soon as I got it down and swallowed, the whispering in my ears began to fade away, and the vortex closed up like it had never been there. I looked down, grabbed another piece of fish, stuffed it in my mouth, chewing mechanically.

Now that I was a little more relaxed, I noticed how awful the Gefelte tasted. *Bleh! Gross!* And then it came bubbling up out of me, not the fish, but these giggles of relief. So what if my knees were bleeding with shards of glass in them? I sat back against the fridge to catch my breath.

And that's when I heard the new sound: it came from the living room—a sniffing gurgle. Every muscle and tendon in my body went tight again. The first thing that came to mind was the sound that demon had made in Powell's. If the Shadow People could follow me here then why not the demon?

I looked over at the knife drawer on the other side of the kitchen. Two, maybe three steps. They would take me into plain view of the living room, but if the demon hadn't come in the kitchen yet, then maybe it didn't know I was in here. I remembered the way it had followed my scent in Powell's, sniffing around the place where I'd been standing when I'd read from *The Poisonwood Bible.* My scent had been weak then because I was still alive with a soul insulated tight inside my body. But if I'd fainted in the cafe and my soul had slipped out, like what might happen now . . . .

OK, this is it, baby. Don't give a fuck. One fast, fluid motion and the knife will be in your hand.

I rose up slowly, cautiously, bracing myself against the bar like a sprinter getting ready to explode off the starting block. And that's when I recognized another sound, this little gasp, the familiar tone of a throat being cleared.

I peeped over the bar. There was Ruth. Her eyes were all red and her face looked strange—puffy and distorted. I wondered if maybe one of the Shadow People had done something to her, hurt her in some way, because if they had . . . and then I realized she was only crying.

"Oh, Jules," she said in a shaky voice. "Please. Don't." I looked down. My hand was clenching the handle of a big steak knife.

ENTRY THIRTY-SIX
I've been thinking a lot about light. Where it comes from: both here and beyond. When that vortex opened up in Ruth's kitchen it glowed pinkish-red like the inside of a womb, flickering or pulsing to the beat of some colossal heart.

Who knows? Maybe I was so scared at the time that I immediately assumed the worst. Maybe the squirming beings were really angels!

Yeah, right. Guess again. Even as I typed those words, I knew that I was only kidding myself. There's no way those grody ucky things were angels. They seemed more like human maggots, unhatched embryos—souls that hadn't ripened yet into fetuses made of real flesh and blood.

I think maybe what I saw was a cosmic rip. Instead of seeing forward into the future, I was seeing backwards. When the changes happen, it's like that: I slip out of time. My soul's no longer held in check; it starts to drift, a boat cut loose from its moorings. The Shadow People are attracted to me because I have the light of being alive, my soul gives off some kind of energy they lack. They want something from me, but I'm not sure what.

OK, enough! Change the subject: Christmas, the Easter Bunny, shiny happy people holding hands. No more demonology. Your heart's pounding like a drum inside that bony chest of yours, girlfriend.

Today, I started packing up my things when Deeksha wasn't home. I'm not sure if Ruth still wants to room with me after what happened the other night at her house, but I can't live here anymore. Deeksha is driving me insane. Partly, it's my fault. If I'd been honest with her that time in the garden and just said I wasn't attracted to her, maybe she would have left me alone. Yeah, and maybe she would have made me pay the rest of the rent money that I don't have. Business has been really slow at Rose City. I haven't sold a guitar in weeks. This commission thing is starting to backfire. I'm not positive, but I think it's illegal in the state of Oregon to pay commission without a base salary. I'm going to call up the Better Business Bureau to ask.

It didn't take long for me to get tired of packing my stuff this afternoon, so I poured myself a cold glass of water and went outside to sit in the garden. I'm going to miss that beautiful place, a little corner of paradise on earth.

After I finished meditating and doing some Yoga, I just lay back and soaked up the warmth. Oregon has the most beautiful skies when the weather is good. A deep robin's egg blue. The sun was shining from behind a tree and I could see its corona peeking through the leaves. It was so warm, nourishing. I had to fight off the urge to look at it.

When I was little, one time my mom had told me never to look directly at the sun. I asked her why and she said it could make me blind. The warning scared me quite a bit, but, I'd had to fight the urge to look at it.

Later that night, I'd looked at a light bulb in my room—really stared at it. After a while it made this black splotch on my irises that followed me everywhere. I screamed and ran into to my parent's room, confessing what I'd done. Mom chuckled and said it would go away, don't worry. A light bulb isn't as powerful as the sun. But if I'd kept on staring, who knows, it could do permanent damage. Never stare at anything that's really bright.

I think I'm attracted to the sun these days because it symbolizes divine illumination. Here on earth, it's the closest thing we have to heaven. *No one shall look on my face and live.* That's what God said to Moses. My Sunday school teacher showed us that passage one time and it immediately reminded me of the sun, how my mom had told me never to look directly at it.

I wish I were an angel, so I could fly into the sun, live in its warmth, a heavenly womb. I wish God would talk to me like one of the prophets. Because if there's really such a thing as heaven, I want to go there more than anything else now. I want to see the true light that comes directly from God.

Part of me feels like I've been there before, in heaven. It's sort of like how you feel when you're far away from home and you think about it and your heart grows fond, longing to return. *Deja-vu* of the soul.

ENTRY THIRTY-SEVEN

Ruth finally called tonight. When I picked up the phone she didn't recognize my voice at first. She said I was mumbling like an old woman. Really? I said. I wasn't aware of that. OK, she goes. Now you're talking normal. She asked how I was feeling and I said fine, I guess. No more "episodes," if that's what she meant. I'd been making sure to eat a little protein before bed, preferably meat.

Ruth launched into how she'd been thinking nonstop about what had happened. She wanted me to know right off that she didn't hold any of it against me. I thanked her and said I'd been worried that she might ditch me as a friend. What are you talking about, she laughed. Me ditch you? No way, girl! You're gonna be famous!

We both laughed. I was feeling better already. Ruth has a way of putting you at ease. She asked, had I gone back to the Free Clinic? I said yeah, I'd even called that number and made an appointment for the last Wednesday of the month to meet with the specialist at PHSU. Ruth wanted to know if I had health insurance and I said no, but the receptionist on the phone hadn't said anything about money. Besides, if the doctor at the Free Clinic had given me that card, it stood to reason there'd be no money involved.

Ruth got quiet when I said that. There was a long pause, then she asked if she could still come with me, and I said, yeah, sure, of course, I'd love the support. She said her uncle was a general practitioner in New York and she remembered him talking to her father one time about "test subjects" and how some doctors who were less than scrupulous would get kick-backs from the big drug companies if they tested new experimental drugs on some of their patients. So be careful, Ruth warned. This might be some kind of experimental study. But don't worry, because if it is, they're supposed to get your signature on a release form.

I was so glad Ruth was coming when she said that. She's much smarter than me about these kinds of things. She asked how band practice was going, and I said no worries. Mammy Jammer's good to go: Six of their songs, one of mine. It was hard to believe our gig at The Crystal was only a few days away. Ruth asked if I was nervous and I said not even—I had more serious things to worry about.

I tried to feel Ruth out then, to get a sense of how much she'd seen the other night when I freaked out in her kitchen. After I let go of the knife, she'd come over and given me this long, sad hug. I'd burst into tears and it made her cry, too.

Afterwards, she'd sent me to bed with a glass of water and cleaned up everything herself. I woke up the next morning all by my lonesome.

She'd taken the couch. So I guess that means I won't be getting laid any time soon.

Ha! Just kidding (sort of). Not that I really care about that, I just want to keep Ruth as a friend. Sleeping with her would be a bad idea, anyway. I wouldn't know what to do. I've never so much as touched another woman. Ruth and I would be totally new in the sack.

I told her that I'd be sure to put her on the list at the door Thursday night, and did she want to come back stage before the show and maybe hang out? She said, hell yes! She'd even bring a pair of her old high school pom-poms and be my own private cheer leader. I told her to just bring herself, that was more than enough.

And then I let it slip out, right as I was hanging up the phone. She said bye and I said bye and then I said "Ruth, I love you."

I'm not really sure if she heard me say that last part because I said it right as she was hanging up, but I'm pretty sure she did. Still, I don't see the big deal. It's just girl talk. Except I wasn't just saying it like that. I really meant it, and Ruth knows me well enough to be able to tell the difference.

ENTRY THIRTY-EIGHT
It's already Thursday and I'm writing this entry at 3:00 pm, exactly six hours before I go on stage at The Crystal. I can't believe it! I'm so excited.

Last night I spent the night with Ruth and some friends at the Compound. We had the most awesome time! Gretchen and Tina and Lilly and Mae-Ling and a half dozen others. There was only one rule for anyone who came: NO BOYFRIENDS!

I made the rule—not because I'm turning into a bull-dyke, but more because I wanted to keep things mellow and young guys tend to jack it up and get wasted. They'd probably end up screwing their girlfriends in places like the control booth and that would be totally annoying. Mike also kind of hinted that there was a lot of expensive equipment laying around when I asked him if I could have a sleep-over. That automatically ruled out the skate punks that half of the girls were dating. So I put the kybosh on *boys*, period, and it worked like a charm.

Everyone said they were just totally blown away after we played a couple of songs. I could see the girls were impressed. They sat there, sipping their drinks. No gossiping, no whispering—*nada*. Judging from the solemn expressions on their faces, you would have thought they were sitting in church.

Mike rigged up a blue spotlight on me and he also had this kick-ass strobe that he could trigger with his foot, which he thankfully didn't overdo, just enough to add a little variety here and there.

I swear, Mike is such a horn dog. Later on, after Cynthia took off, he glommed onto Mae-Ling like a fly on flypaper. I think Mae was flattered, but her parents don't want her dating white guys, so she ended up giving him the brush off. It was truly a beautiful sight to behold.

Instead of taking it hard, though, like I expected, Mike sucked up his ego and moved on to the next girl. Almost like a used car salesman. With guys like him, dating is a numbers game. I think he might have gone home with this one cute girl that I didn't know who'd came with Lilly.

The evening was fairly warm for June in Portland, so everyone gradually moved outside to the patio where Lars had the barbecue going. He was grilling all kinds of cool stuff like these big giant prawns and swordfish steaks that Ruth and the girls had brought. He also put on some hotdogs and burgers. I asked him to please grill my fish first; the thought of it brushing up against raw beef made me want to vomit. He laughed and called me a "Cow Lovin' Vegan." Yeah, yeah, whatever.

I kept him company, taking the opportunity to impart some wisdom I'd gathered over the years, growing up on a cattle ranch, etc. Lars nodded in all the right places, but he seemed fairly uninterested, like he was just being polite.

After he'd taken off the chef's hat and was sitting down to eat, I couldn't help noticing he went for a couple of seafood/veggie shish-kabobs, avoiding the red meat altogether. I think most people would think twice if they knew all the gory details. They'd rather visualize hamburger as cellophane packages that grow on trees.

Lars had to leave early. His snob of a fiancée, Margaret, was too good for our party. She put the guilt trip on him to come home. Three calls to his cell in the space of an hour. It was obvious who wore the pants in their relationship.

On his way out the door, Lars took my plastic glass full of wine and dropped it in the trash. "No more! Save a few brain cells for the show!"

I couldn't believe he'd do a thing like that in front of my friends. "Gee, dad," I said. "Thanks for looking out for me. Got any more advice?"

"Yeah, get some sleep."

"Anything else?"

"Nope."

"Alright, then." I grabbed Ruth's beer, chugged it down, handed him the empty bottle. "TAKE THIS LONGNECK AND GO FUCK YOURSELF! YOU GODDAMNED SONOFABITCH, NEVER TELL ME WHAT TO DO AGAIN!"

A collective gasp ran through the room. Lars tried to make a joke by sticking out his tongue and crossing his eyes, but I could tell he was shocked. I'd never said anything like that before.

Ruth escorted me into the backyard. She got me a glass of water, made sure I drank it all. People were gawking through the sliding glass door: "What's gotten into Jules? Is she alright?"

Just looking at them, you'd think they were a bunch of kids. I'd lost my temper, big deal. Shit happens. I threw open the door and pushed my way to the kitchen for another hit of red.

But somehow, it didn't taste the same. Not with everyone staring at the back of my head: carnivorous whispers, the gleam of the occasional eye tooth. I poured out the wine, refilled my glass with soda.

So much for having a good time. Without alcohol to steady my nerves, I'd start to shake, out of control. People would assume I was tweaking. Either way, it was a lose-lose proposition.

Niles, the guitarist, hung out until the "wee hours" as he put it (did I mention he's from Glasgow, Scotland?). It was kind of a drag, but he pretty much kept to himself over by the turn tables, our own private DJ.

Niles has really good taste so nobody complained. Mostly, he spun ambient techno like Kruder & Dorfmeister, perfect for the late-night vibe. Poor baby. I'm sure he was hoping to get lucky, but his face got in the way, especially when he smiled. All those gangly teeth. Not one of the girls went over to keep him company.

Cheer up, doll-face! You'll have your revenge! After we play The Crystal tomorrow night, you'll be fighting 'em off!

Most of us were getting tired by then, so we arranged our sleeping bags in a circle like at Camp Cascade. Gretchen and I thought of it because we both went there two summers in a row when we were kids. It was great hanging out with girlfriend, catching up on new developments in her life, giggling about the old days. She's not in school this term, so I barely ever see her anymore. We promised to call each other more often. She said she's already got tickets to our gig at The Crystal. I told her to come back stage and say hi, but I know she won't. Not with the ole ball and chain around her ankle. She's got this nerdy geek of a boyfriend named Alex and she lives with him out in Beaverton, near Intel's main complex where he works like a slave with a Pentium Processor for a brain. I feel bad for her because Alex is a total workaholic and she pretty much stays in the apartment by herself nights. She told me that Alex wants to get married. They went to the Shane Company and looked at rings the other day. It seems weird that he hasn't even proposed. Whatever. I guess I'm a hopeless romantic. If some guy just assumed I was going to marry him without even *asking*, I'd tell him to take his ring and stick it where the sun don't shine!

Before I fell asleep, Ruth gave me a bite of Swordfish steak that she'd put in the fridge. I asked her to come over and sleep next to me, but she said she was all set up on the other side of the room with Mae-Ling. I guess Mae was nervous because Niles hadn't left yet, and she didn't want to fall asleep with a strange (white) man in the room.

ENTRY THIRTY-NINE

We came, we played, we kicked ass! Damn. I've never had such a rush in all my life. If performing is a drug, then I'm hooked! From the moment we stepped out on stage, we were on, baby, ON! To be perfectly honest, I don't recall every detail even though it happened only last night. It's all this tremendous blur of lights and electricity.

Lars and the guys, bless their hearts, they did all the work moving our gear. I got to the Compound just after 5 pm and they'd already loaded everything up into the van. At first, I thought I must have gotten the time to meet wrong, but no, Lars smiled and asked how I was feeling. I said perfect and he laughed a relieved laugh. Then he told me to kick back at the Compound for a while. Just make sure I was at Crystal Ballroom by 7 pm for the sound check.

It was totally quiet in the Compound, empty and hollow. Most of the gear was on its way over to Crystal Ballroom. I'd started over to the stereo for a little tuneage, when I noticed a big gift basket on the table. There was fresh kiwi, blood oranges, grapes. A loaf of French bread. Three kinds of imported cheese. And fish. Lots of fish, smoked and pickled in these cute little tins. Nestled underneath was a bottle of expensive pinot. God, what a sweetheart! The card was the best:

> Dear Julia:
> Sorry about what I said last night. You were absolutely right. See you at at seven for the sound check. I've never told you this before, but I think you've got the best singing voice that I've ever heard. No need to stress out biting your nails. Just relax and everything will fall into place. Like my old drum teacher used to say, "Don't make it happen, *let* it happen!"
>
> Break a leg and both your arms,
> Lars

I skipped into the kitchen for a corkscrew. First, I opened the wine to let it air out, then I went out to my car to get my wardrobe. Once I got to The Crystal, I'd do my eyes and put the finishing touches on my face. Ruth would be there after the sound check, so she could help with that. She's really good at putting on makeup. I'd never put on stage makeup before, but I knew you had to exaggerate every line with plenty of blush and mascara. Otherwise, the audience wouldn't see it from a distance.

OK, now brace yourself: I know it sounds hypocritical since I don't eat beef and all, but I absolutely *adore* leather. Especially black leather. That's why I'd picked out this special outfit with leather pants, spike-heeled boots, and this tight red silk tank top. For the outside layer, I got a billowy white blouse from Buffalo Exchange. Oh, and I forgot to mention what I'd be wearing under the tank top: a black leather bra. Since I'd lost all the weight, my breasts had shrunk a whole cup size. I'd gone from a C to a generous B. So I could really use the extra "volume" the leather gave me. Also, I had a second outfit ready to go, but Lars said there probably wouldn't be time for a wardrobe change; it was sort of frowned on for the warm up band to take the time for that. But just in case, I'd bought this skintight black fishnet shirt and a red bra to go underneath.

Everything was totally over the top, I know, but that's show biz. I was going to give the crowd exactly what they wanted. Up on stage, I would be everything from that old Berlin song and more: a bitch, a blue movie, a little girl, . . . and we'll make love together. Tonight, everyone in the audience would be my lover. I'd open myself up to all of them, ride their hearts and their minds with my music, squeezing a little piece of myself into every verse, every chorus, every last snarl and groan.

At the club, things started to get complicated. The sound guy was this total asshole who barely even gave me a chance to say 'boo' into the microphone. Mike said he got paid by Red Angel, so all he cared about was them. I asked why didn't we have our own sound guy and Mike said we did, except "he" was a "she." Cynthia, that is. But evidently, according to this joker on the board, there was some kind of problem with the union. Cynthia wasn't a card carrying member. As far as Mike was concerned, the whole thing was just a scam just to keep us from upstaging Red Angel. Unions had never affected anything like this before. At Dante's, Cynthia had gotten behind the board, no problem.

I started to get stressed out when I heard that. Lars must have noticed because he came over and said something to Mike and Mike disappeared. Lars put his arm around me, all smiles. I hugged him, thanked him for the basket. And you know what? He actually looked bashful! Lars! I think he has a crush on me! All the usual signs were there: blushing cheeks, a sudden interest in his shoes.

I was so flattered that I planted this big wet kiss right on his mouth. So what if he was engaged? Tonight, I was dangerous with a capital D.

After that, Lars said he had to meet his fiancée downstairs in the bar and I was welcome to join him. I thought about it. Naw. A crowd was the last thing I wanted to deal with right then, so I hung out by myself in the powder room, putting on the finishing touches.

I was almost done when there was a knock on the door and Ruth ducked her head in. "Hello? Anybody home?" I screamed, ran over to hug her. She giggled, nervously fingering the backstage pass that was hanging around her neck.

I took the opportunity to model my new leather pants. Ruth had been there at the store when I'd tried them on, but she couldn't believe I'd gone back and bought them. She asked how I'd gotten the money and I said that was my little secret. (Actually, it had come out of the rent for July that I'd already decided I was going to blow off.) Ruth noticed the black leather bra on the chair and held it up: "Don't tell me you're actually going to wear this?"

"Hell yes," I said. In my spike-heeled boots, I was almost a whole foot taller than Ruth. I slipped out of my shirt, waiting for her to pass me the leather bra. I winked, hamming it up. There was this tantalizing instant when she looked down and noticed how hard my nipples were. The bra had a strap that tied in back, so I asked Ruth if she'd mind doing the honors. As she tied the straps, our eyes locked in the mirror.

"Hey," she said, "what do you say we go snag ourselves one of those free drinks you were telling me about?"

I pushed my breasts together, gave her my nastiest bad girl pout. We both totally lost it then, laughing like a pair of wild hyenas in heat. I strutted over and put on the red silk tank top and the white blouse. Ruth took one last look at me before we went out the door. She said I looked the best she'd ever seen me. Like a supermodel. I took her by the chin, gave her a quick peck on the lips. "Hey!" she gasped. "Watch it! You'll muss your lipstick!"

I lugged my gift basket with me to the Green Room. After Ruth and I had ordered our drinks, she took one look in the basket and shook her head. What I needed was pure protein, not that candy-coated stuff. It was far too rich, and besides, since everything was sealed up it wouldn't go to waste. No, what we both needed was a plate full of Japanese magic—*open sashimi!*

Despite Ruth's enthusiasm, I wasn't convinced. The idea of raw meat just didn't sound appetizing. She said no problem, she could order some smoked salmon, along with sake, teka maki, and some other cool things she liked. Oh, and they had this seaweed salad to die for! Did I want some of that? I said, sure, whatever. Just hurry the hell up! I'm starving!

We were the only people in the green room, but we didn't care. We just sat there and drank our free gin & tonics and laughed. The food came faster than I expected. It turned out that Kurumazushi, the restaurant, was just around the block. Ruth gave me a bite of the smoked salmon first. It was by far the best piece of fish I'd ever tasted. So fresh! I wanted to eat the other four pieces, but Ruth held me back. She was mixing soy sauce with this green stuff in a little bowl. She took a piece of light colored fish, dipped it in the soy mixture, gave it to me. The texture wasn't much different than the smoked salmon, just a little more chewy. But way more tasty.

After that, I was a believer. Raw fish? Who cares! I tore through that sashimi like a madwoman. And the best part was, I didn't even get full. The protein went straight into my system and for the first time in months, I felt totally normal. No shakes, nothing.

When everyone else in the band caught up with me in the green room, I was pretty lit. Lars gave me this nervous puppy dog look that said it all. I ordered a glass of H$_2$O. We were due onstage in about thirty minutes. All the guys looked kind of jittery and nervous but I was untouchable after my sushi and sake and gin. Fortified! A samurai without fear!

There was some kind of confusion with Red Angel's manager, so we ended up taking the stage a half hour late, which was fine with me. Let the crowd wait. That would only heighten their anticipation.

The rest of the band went out first, settling into their instruments. They looked back at me, but I waved for them to go ahead and start the first song. Lars clicked off the tempo with his sticks and Mike tore into the opening chord with a swing of his arm.

There was this orgasmic wall of sound. Right next to the stacks where I was standing, I could feel the song reverberating inside me, teasing my heart, my lungs, my womb. Right before the first verse, I charged out and ripped my microphone off the stand. By the time we reached the chorus, I was belting out the words, letting them rise up from my diaphragm in waves of release.

Behind me, all the guys in the band were staring in disbelief. I laughed, spun back around to face the crowd head-on. Some kid in the front row lifted up his shirt to show me his pierced nipples, so I lifted up my shirt and showed him my leather bra. The crowd liked that. A lot. I teased them a little more and a little more, until two songs later, I ripped off my tank top and pressed my breasts together like I'd done jokingly in the mirror to Ruth.

Well, that was it: they went wild and I knew this was going to be a show to remember. No one was yelling for Red Angel anymore. I glanced up at the hot stage lights, feeling their electricity warming my flesh, heating my blood. The next song was "Cowslip." Mike started feeding reverb into his amp and Niles melted into a dreamy synth part to set the mood.

Ruth was standing in the wings, holding out my guitar. I said into the microphone, "Whatcha got there, baby? Is that for me?" The crowd started calling out dirty things and I chided them playfully. "Hey! I'm talkin' about my guitar!" They laughed. I met Ruth halfway across the stage and when she turned around bashfully to leave, I slapped her on the ass.

The rest of the band kept ad-libbing on the same three chords. It started to get annoying. I cut them off and they kind of freaked, but since they were consummate professionals, they all stopped playing at the same time.

I started talking to the crowd, asked how they were doing, etc. Then I said, "not to put a damper on things, but my dad died two years ago right here in Portland. Up on the hill, PHSU. He was a cowboy from Mt. Angel, about thirty miles southeast of here. Anyone from Mt. Angel? No? I didn't think so. Folks there don't get out much. But anyways, when the banks foreclosed on our ranch and took it away . . . well, that just about broke daddy's heart, as well as his spirit.

"Right before he died, he gave me an envelope, and inside was money, lots of money that he'd managed to hide from the bankers. He told me to go ahead, take it! Buy yourself a guitar. A real nice one. And maybe, just maybe, if you ever feel like it, you can write your old man a song.

"Well, dad, I bought the guitar, here it is! And I wrote you this song. Hope you like it, cause it's the only one you get."

I drew out the first chord with my slide and then hit my effects petal to get some reverb going. The crowd hushed down when I started to sing. And it wasn't long before I could feel the tears streaming down my cheeks, cold against my skin that had been scorched by the lights.

I was singing about my daddy, how much I loved him, despite our differences. Telling everyone about his name for me: *Cowslip*. How I would always be his little flower, no matter what. I could see him walking back to the barn with a saddle slung over his shoulder in the evening sun with the dust kicking up, and even if I would never sing country music like him, that didn't matter because he was my cowboy, and our love was pure, the love of a good man for his daughter, and it could bridge the gap between worlds, between rock and country, and in this one song, I was a cowgirl with a fuzzbox and Marshall stack. He said, yes ma'am, he reckoned that was just about right, and it suited him fine.

When I finished the song, there was total silence. I thought maybe I'd lost the crowd, they hadn't liked the song. But then they started clapping and I knew they'd held back their applause out of respect. I walked over to the side of the stage, and strapped on my Fender Mustang, blasting them with a Hendrix-style riff:

"Alright! Let's rock n' roll!"

The band launched into our last song, arguably our best. Definitely our LOUDEST! After we finished, I was really surprised when this guy came out on stage and gave me a kiss on the cheek.

The crowd must have known him, because they went ballistic. He waved, blew them a kiss and then he was gone. Just like that. I leaned into the mic, kind of confused, and said, "OK, right. Thank y'all for coming! I love you! Also, I'd like to thank Red Angel for inviting us to play. This is the first time I've ever had the chance to see 'em, and I can't wait! I'll be right over there behind the curtain with a Perrier in one hand, and a bottle of Sapphire in the other. Best goddamned seat in the house!"

Getting off stage was this rush of roadies and people swarming around backstage. Ruth was nowhere to be seen. Everyone in the band had vanished.

No, wait! There was the back of Lars' head bobbing up and down on its way out a side door. I ran after him.

Once I got through the door, I didn't see him anywhere. It took me a second to get my bearings. Oh shit, I was standing out in the auditorium! All these girls and boys ran over and started asking for my autograph. They got behind me, cutting off my escape route. I didn't know what to do. My hand started to shake so bad that I could barely sign my name. It was totally illegible, nothing more than a scribble, but no one seemed to care.

My ears started to hum and I felt a hot flash run through my system. All the faces started to change; they looked hungry, licking their lips, baring their teeth. Instead of wanting my autograph, now they were pawing me, ripping my shirt. Animalistic snarls, a pack of wolves circling the kill. One hand reached between my legs from behind.

A few more seconds of this, and I'd be down for the count. Thank God a bouncer noticed. Right as I was starting to fade out, he grabbed my shoulder and asked if I was alright. I shook my head—*no, please, help!* He called over these other two bouncers, and they pushed through the crowd, whisking me backstage.

As soon as I was behind the curtain, I burst into tears. The same guy who'd come out on stage at the end of our set happened to be there. He noticed and came over. There was something about him. He thanked the bouncers kind of authoritatively—no worries, he'd take it from here. He put his arm around me, rubbed my back, shouted for a glass of water. Someone brought him another folding chair and he sat down next to me. I was feeling better already. I drank a little water out of a plastic bottle.

The humming in my ears let up, so I could hear again. Time had started to flow normally. I took a deep breath. How long had I been here with this guy? One minute, ten? It couldn't have been longer than that. He'd been soothing me, saying these nice things to take my mind off the crowd, calling them assholes who didn't understand it was just a show, show biz . . . *shhhh*, it's OK, that's right, get it out, everything's going to be fine.

Mike walked up then and goes, "Hey! Jack Thorne! What's up?"

When he said that, part of me was flattered. But part of me was embarrassed that I hadn't recognized the lead singer of one of the biggest bands in the world.

Jack stood up to shake hands with Mike, and Mike (being Mike) says, oh, I see you've already met Julia. I leaned over, gave Jack a friendly hug, whispered *thanks* in his ear. He kissed me fondly on the cheek and Mike said, "*Whoa!* You guys should get a room!"

I couldn't help laughing. What a dick. Always having to get his two cents in. As soon as Jack heard me laugh, he busted up. And then everything was cool, dead-on.

True to my word, I sat on the side of the stage for Red Angel Rising. They were *very* impressive. It was obvious they'd been doing the live performance thing for a long time. All the kinks had been smoothed out years ago and each of them knew what the other was thinking intuitively, so they could ad lib, stick a part in here, a solo there, cut a song short, whatever, with very little to no effort.

Yet, despite how good the supporting musicians were, it was obvious this was Jack Thorne's baby. He strummed rhythm guitar on all the songs and even switched over to lead a couple of times while he was singing. I'd never really cared for Red Angel before, I mean they were internationally famous—along with the really well established bands like REM and U2 and Sting—so I'd heard them on the radio all the time, but they were a little too mainstream for my taste. At least for me to actually go out and buy one of their CDs.

Still, despite my initial reservations, I could tell Red Angel's latest album was different from the rest: More ambient with some techno loops thrown in. And for the tour, Jack had added a keyboardist who triggered some tasty samples and loops, even scratching vinyl on a few songs.

Ruth joined me part way through the show. I felt much better now that I'd been nibbling at the gift basket. It was great to have her there with me. Lars and his fiancée were sitting off to one side in their own little romantic world. Call me crazy, but I could have sworn that Margaret (his fiancée) shot me a few dirty looks. Maybe someone had told her about the kiss I gave Lars. Or maybe she sensed with her subconscious feminine radar that he was paying a little too much attention to me.

Ruth came over with a couple of drinks. She said that when she'd told the bartender to make it strong, that it was for Jules Fleischer, he'd gone straight for the good stuff, pouring Bombay Sapphire.

"Cheers!" Ruth said, clinking her glass against mine. "You're famous!"

After Red Angel finished playing their second encore, I drifted back into the green room. It was packed. Mike had his nose to the wind, trying to figure out who could get us a recording contract the fastest.

While he was foaming at the mouth, Cynthia took the opportunity to come over and tell me how much she'd enjoyed the show. I said thanks. (It was probably the five-hundredth time I'd said it. My new mantra.)

Cynthia asked, had she gotten the levels right in my monitor? I must have done a double take because she said, "Oh, you didn't hear? Mike finally kicked that LA piece of shit off the board. I swear, he was so fat and greasy, I had to wipe his stink off the knobs!"

We both had a good laugh and I realized that's why the show had gone so well: Cynthia had been our soundwoman after all.

Ruth was busy chatting with a couple of friends from PCC that I didn't really know. Strangers everywhere, it was more crowded back there than out in the auditorium, but I felt safe. No sign of Gretchen. She probably hadn't even come.

Mr. Ball and Chain had kept her locked in a closet out in Beaverton.

Through all of this, I kept my eye on Jack. Like a true rock star, he had this aura around him. I could see it glowing like a nightlight in a hotel room after dark. And his eyes were so bright, especially whenever he glanced over at me. The last time he looked, his girlfriend followed his gaze until she noticed me standing there in the middle of the PCC rat pack.

I went back to the conversation with Ruth because I figured Jack's girlfriend might be jealous of the attention he'd been giving me. But instead of getting pissy, she came right over and introduced herself.

"I'm Tawny," she said with a heavy British accent. "Pleased to meet you. I caught your last two songs. That one about your father was touching—very touching, indeed."

Despite a rather large nose, Tawny was striking: A tall, pale brunette with these sparkling emeralds for eyes that made you dizzy if you looked into them for too long. She said that Jack and she were leaving soon. A party in the West Hills. Would I like to come? I looked over at Ruth. She was giggling with her friends. Yeah, sure, I said. Love to. Tawny smiled warmly and said to meet them at the stage door in fifteen minutes. She took my hand again, gave a friendly squeeze, then went back to Jack. He held up his glass, winking conspiratorially.

Ruth and I waited in back of the club with her friends for half an hour. Gradually, the friends lost interest and went off in search of excitement—clubs, bars, whatever. The night was young. Ruth and I were just getting ready to walk back to our cars when a bright red Porsche came screeching around the corner. It skidded to a halt in front of us. The passenger door swung open, and there was Jack Thorne with a big shit-eating grin on his face. He stepped out, motioned for me to get in. I held up the gift basket and he took it for me, helping me into the backseat. But when Ruth tried to follow, he shut the door. Some old guy was slouched behind the wheel and Tawny was reclining next to me. I tried to get out, but she put her arm around me, gently pulling me back down into the seat. "Wait!" I cried. "What about my friend?"

Jack mumbled something to the driver and the guy scribbled out an address on a piece of paper. He scrunched it up into a ball, chucked it at Ruth.

Before I could say another word, the car had taken off, leaving poor Ruth standing there in a cloud of exhaust. My heart sunk: *Oh, honey! Forgive me!*

Tawny must have noticed because she opened up her purse and took out a little compact. It looked like something for blush or foundation, but when she opened it, I saw this plastic compartment with white powder inside and a little spoon. She took the spoon and scooped up a dash of powder, held it up to her nose. *Sniff*! In one elegant gesture, it was gone. Then she scooped a generous amount onto the spoon, held it out for me. Cocaine? I asked. She nodded. *Just* cocaine, is it pure? Well, she said, you can't get *pure* anything. They always cut it with something. But it won't hurt you. There's more additives in a can of Coca-Cola. What about meth? I asked. Speed? Do they add any of those things? She laughed, touched my cheek. My dear, you needn't worry. Meth is the drug of choice for poor white trash, not us. Mr. Thorne may have been born in a trailer house park, but you'd never know it by his taste in drugs. Or women, for that matter.

Satisfied, I took a sniff and lay back. A gust of wind blew over the top of the windshield. I'd never rode in a convertible before, it was crazy. So much noise: the growl of the engine, my hair whipping in my eyes. Jack motioned for the spoon.

By the time we reached the top of the hill, it had gone around the car three or four more times. Cocaine was definitely *not* my drug of choice. I felt the changes swirling all around me: "JULIA! OPEN UP! LET US IN!"

The wind, only the wind. Don't listen! Holding my ears, I prayed that Ruth wouldn't get offended by Jack's rude behavior and bail. I needed her tonight. Up on stage, I'd been in control, but now . . . I didn't know the first thing about how to act around these kinds of people with their fancy drugs, fancy cars, mansions in the West Hills. Way out of my league.

In the guesthouse, down below, overlooking the lights of Portland with a glass of wine in my hand. The gift basket lies sprawled on the floor, half-eaten pieces of fruit next to it. I can feel my heart beating faster and faster. It's wonderful and terrible. Jack put me here after I made a scene up at the house. I can't really remember. He said that I'd screamed at the guy who drove us here, calling him a goddamned pervert.

Jack said he'd laughed pretty hard when I said that. They'd all laughed. This was the goddamned pervert's house. The goddamned pervert's name was Raleigh Davenport, the famous British film director, had I heard of him? I said that I was very sorry, the cocaine wasn't agreeing with me. No shit, Jack said. You were right, though: Raleigh *is* a goddamned pervert. And by the way, Tawny's his daughter.

At the guesthouse, time has sped up and slowed down: Auto reverse/ fast forward. I'm looking out the window at the pool. The water: a deep sapphire blue.

Black sky above, brimming with stars. There's another larger pool back up at the main house. I didn't even know there were places like this in Portland, mansions. This one seems fairly old, like it's been here forever.

Jack said he'd be right back. I'm waiting. The pool looks warm, steam rising into the air, vanishing over the Portland skyline. Twinkling arcs over the river, symmetrical rows of lights on giant boxes that look like cardboard models . . . . Up here, from on high, Portland could be the backdrop for a late-night talk show.

My shirt's ripped from where the fans got me. I'm taking it off. And my pants. It's hot in here, the heat must be on. Leather makes you sweat a lot more than I expected.

Screw it, I'm going for a swim. Forget all those people up at the house. They're laughing really loudly, the sordid cackles of drunks. Leaches, sinners, fakes. I'm here with them, so that must make me one, too. Can they see the pool from up there? It's on the other side of the guesthouse, but they're up higher. Maybe they can see over the roof?

Ah, fuck. Fuck-a-duck. Who cares? Not me, I've got nothing to be ashamed of. Perfect body. More beautiful than a Playboy centerfold, and just as real. The Devil's airbrush in all the right places. A walking corpse . . . nothing's more beautiful than that.

Most of the people up there at the party have heard of me by now, my whacked-out performance. They're gossiping. Tonight, Julia Fleischer is the main dish. Along with champagne and hors d'oeuvres. *Whore d'oeuvres.* Just a pinch between the cheek and gums.

Jack & Tawny, the perfect couple. They're sitting alongside the pool watching me tread water. Tawny's holding out her arm and Jack's patting it . . . oh, God. They're shooting up.

Now Tawny's doing Jack. Now Jack's waving me over, but I'm swimming the other way. Their laughter skims over the water and it sounds right next to me, even though they're way at the other end. I can see their teeth glittering in the lights.

Jack holds up a little blue bottle. Even from here, I know what it is: my favorite. "Come n' get it!" he yells. "Candy for the baby!"

Both he and Tawny are timeless, immortal, like vampires— hopelessly rich, undead forever.

Back in the guesthouse, things start happening. Too many drinks from the pretty blue bottle. Time slows down into seconds—speeds up into decades, a century, the new millennia.

Space is floating in my veins now, pumping sapphires through my heart, into my brain. We're all together on the bed: one body, our hearts pulsing into each other's veins: Jack's inside my mouth and I'm in Tawny's.

A roaring in the distance, far away . . . big waterfall through the trees. Jack's on top sliding his cock between my legs while Tawny gets ready to stick the needle in my arm. They're both more or less raping me.

I'm not resisting—couldn't, even if I wanted to. But they don't know. I haven't told them how sick I am. They probably wouldn't believe me, anyhow.

"Black and white nights," Tawny whispers, the heroin flowing heavy and thick in our veins, each and every nerve kissed, fondled. We're melting into each other, losing our bodies. *Ohmygod.* It feels soooooooooo good. Like, like . . .

"*Un petite mort,*" Tawny says. "The little death."

Awoke the next morning with a hiccup and a shudder. For a second, I totally spaced on where I was. And then I remembered: the guesthouse.

Ruth was sleeping next to me with all her clothes on: Beautiful, sweet Ruth. She looked so wholesome, her face scrubbed clean of makeup.

When I sat up, my stomach heaved. I ran to the bathroom. *Ewe!* Dried puke all over the toilet seat. That did it. I dropped to my knees and cut loose, coughing, gagging. But there was nothing to throw up. All that puke must have been mine from the night before.

In front of the mirror, I nearly screamed: A skeleton peered back at me with huge black holes for eyes, a red smear for a mouth. I rinsed off the makeup and scrubbed my face with a towel. There, that was better. Through the open door, I could hear the swish of Ruth stirring under the covers.

My right arm felt funny. Stiff. That's when I noticed the welt: Dark purple like a spider bite. I touched it. *Eh?* Still sore where the needle had gone in.

So this was what happened when you shot junk. Well, screw that. Never again. I looked around for some kind of disinfectant.

Under the sink, a bottle of hydrogen peroxide; it fizzed like crazy when I poured a little on my arm, but I could tell the bump was nothing to worry about. It just felt like the stiffness you get when you give blood. No infection—not yet, at least.

"God, what a night." Ruth was standing in the doorway. She gasped when I looked up at her. "Christ, Jules. You look how I feel."

"Thanks."

Ruth stumbled past me, wadded up a handful of toilet paper, wiped off the toilet seat, lifted up her dress. I watched her ease that beautiful ass down onto the cold porcelain.

"Hey!" she laughed. "Do you mind?"

Back to scrubbing my arm. Disembodied moments from the night before flashed through my mind, but I couldn't quite put everything together. "So, uh . . . when'd you get here last night?"

Ruth sighed. "You mean you don't remember?"

"Well . . . no."

"God, you must have drunk even more than me! That champagne was so good. Usually, I don't like champagne, but holy mama . . . ."

I giggled, starting to get my confidence back. Maybe she hadn't seen me with Jack and Tawny. She wiped herself, flushed. "You were asleep when I came in. Tawny's dad said you were resting down here in the guest house."

I blinked at myself, realizing for the first time that I was completely naked. Ruth said my clothes were on the floor by the bed. She'd brought them in from outside by the pool. I went over and put my tank top and underwear on. The leathers were folded neatly. When I picked them up, they were so heavy, I dropped them and jumped back in bed.

"What's that on your arm?" Ruth asked casually, getting under the covers. I looked down and said that I must have gotten a spider bite. There had been a big brush spider up there in the corner when I'd gone to sleep.

"You sure put on a show last night," Ruth said, yawning.

"At The Crystal?"

"No, silly! Here!"

"Here?"

"You don't remember *that* either? Skinny dipping in the pool! Everyone was watching! Don't tell me you couldn't hear them whistling from the deck."

"Oh, right."

"You didn't know they could see, did you?"

"Uh-uh."

"I knew it! You didn't even look up once."

"How much do you think they could see?"

"I don't know. Not much. At least not the part under water. Except for Jack's friends. They had a pair of binoculars."

"Get out!" I tried to recall what had happened right after my swim. Jack and Tawny shooting up. But they'd been under the patio roof, so obviously no one from up at the house had been able to see them.

Ruth lay back on the pillow. "*Oyvay*," she groaned, holding her head. "I think I must have killed about a million brain cells." After she said it, I could see her wince inwardly, kicking herself. But I pretended not to make the connection. It didn't take any alcohol to kill *my* brains cells; they were doing the job quite well on their own.

Instead of getting up and limping home like a couple of zombies from *Dawn of the Dead*, Ruth and I crashed for another couple of hours. It was fairly quiet in the guest house. No one came down the hill or bothered us, except for the snarl of a lawn mower up at the big house.

Later, Ruth took me to my car that was parked a few blocks from Crystal Ballroom, and I drove home. Since Deeksha's out of town for the weekend on some kind of retreat, Ruth said she might come over later and bring a video to watch, something mellow.

Considering what I've gone through in the past twenty-four hours, I feel amazingly good. No shakes, no fever, nothing. I ate a whole can of tuna before I started writing today and that probably helped.

Damn. I wish I had my guitar. The guys took it back to the Compound last night. If I weren't so hung-over, I'd go over there to get it. I feel like working on this idea I had yesterday for a new song. Ah, the life of a rock star: *Sex, drugs, rock n' roll.*

Jules, Jules, Jules. Your life is starting to feel like one of the characters from a Bogosian play.

ENTRY FORTY

Jack called today. He wants us to open for Red Angel Rising in Los Angeles this weekend. I should be thrilled, but the thought of getting up on stage again so soon makes me want to puke. Literally. Jack sounded really warm on the phone. Like a friend. Not even a hint of guilt or remorse. It kind of caught me by surprise and made me second guess myself: Had our night together been more "consensual" than I'd like to think?

Jack just assumed I could speak for the band. He needed to know if we could play the gig immediately because his manager was riding his ass.

I knew what that meant: He was doing me a favor. If I said yeah we'd do it, then he was prepared to bump whoever had been scheduled to warm up, or maybe add an extra band to the bill. He mentioned that a lot of important people would be there from "the industry" and there was going to be a party afterwards at some hotel. If I went to that, he guaranteed I'd have to fight off the A&R guys like those rabid fans that attacked me after our last show.

God, this was all happening so fast. No time to think. Jack sounded surprised I even had to consider it. He kept pushing: So what's it gonna be, girl? What's it gonna be?

After I hung up, I lay back on my bed and closed my eyes. The gravity of the situation was finally sinking in: Jack Thorne—the man, the legend— had literally *begged* me to play another show with him. Somehow, it didn't seem possible. I opened one eye, squinted at the telephone.

Who'd be next? Sting? Bono? Steven Tyler? "Hey, Jules, baby! Great to hear your voice! Listen, the band's coming through Portland on our way to Seattle and I was just wondering...."

ENTRY FORTY-ONE

Well, it's settled. We're in: LA or bust. I called Lars yesterday and he called Mike and they decided together it was a "green light." Neither of them quite grasped what went down between Jack and me on the phone. I tried to explain that Red Angel's manager had already booked us to play, signing the contract was only a formality. But they still acted like the final decision had been theirs.

When I got to the Compound for practice, Mike was polite but distant: The typical passive-aggressive male with a bone to pick. After we played for a couple of hours, working like dogs on three of our weakest songs, he finally got down to business and laid into me for forgetting lyrics at the show. I kind of fluffed up my feathers at the suggestion. Who was he to get all over my case? He'd missed two of the breaks on one of my songs. Besides, I couldn't remember any problems with the lyrics at all. I even said so and Mike laughed and goes, "that's because you were making them up as you went along!" He got totally agro and Lars finally had to tell him to cool it, what I'd sung had actually been an improvement, at least in a few places.

Mike flipped when Lars stepped in and tried to smooth things out. I've never seen him so upset. Lars told us to take five while the two of them went for a walk. That left me, Niles and Ernesto sitting there with nothing to do. I went into the kitchen for a beer and stood drinking it in the dark by the fridge.

Niles came over and said not to worry, Mike was a control freak, that's all. He was bent out of shape because Sylvia hadn't called him first about the show. I asked who Sylvia was and he goes, *duh!* Red Angel's manager! She was the one who decided to book us as a third band at the last minute.

Oh, right, I said, taking a pull off my beer. This was going to be a long afternoon. Niles put his arm around me and said: Don't worry. You're in a band now. One big happy family—or a giant cluster fuck, depending on how you look at it. Gross! I said, please stop, God. That's just the most horrible image. Niles laughed and said he knew, but, really, that's how it was.

Mike and Lars got back over an hour later. I asked them where the hell they'd been. Had they gone over to Pub At The End Of The Universe? Because if they had . . . Mike said, *whoa,* attitude. I said fuck yeah, we've been sitting around forever with our thumbs up our asses waiting. Mike said, oh, well if he'd been here, there would have been some real work getting done instead of giving each other rim shots. I asked what he meant by that and he said never mind.

Lars went over to the file drawer and pulled out some fresh lyrics sheets. He told me to go over them again and be sure I had them down by LA. Then Niles, bless his heart, cut in and said that he thought Lars had said my lyrics were even better than Mike's. Why not let me go ahead with the parts I'd free associated on?

There was a moment of silence as everyone processed the repercussions of what had just been said. Then Mike asked really snidely how he proposed we do that. Niles started to open his mouth, and Mike said, oh no. No way!

"Alright," I said. "Does somebody here want to tell me what's going on?"

Lars admitted they had the whole show on tape, Cynthia had taped it right off the board. I couldn't believe my ears! We'd just been practicing for two hours and no one had even mentioned it! We could have been analyzing each song, figuring out the weak points.

"Cough it up," I said, holding out my hand.

Mike started tuning his guitar. "We'll go over it later," he said. "Right now we need to work on our parts."

I said, "Enough with the top-secret bullshit. Me, Niles and Ernesto could have been listening to the tape while you and Lars were sitting over at the pub drinking a beer instead of 'going over parts.'"

Mike's face got so red, he looked like he was about to explode. "Look-it," he said, "I've had the past two days to go over the tape and I know *exactly* what needs to be fixed."

"Bull-fucking-shit!" I yelled. "And who are *you* to decide?"

"One of the two original members."

"So what does that make the rest of us? Your bitches?" Calmly, coolly, I strolled over to the fridge. Behind my back, really quietly, Mike said, "And no more drinking before shows. It's all there on tape. Especially the first two songs. You sound like shit."

Everyone went back to their instruments. I sat working on the rest of my beer, waiting for someone to say *something*. But no. They started an epic jam instead. Mike broke into this long, pointless solo that went on forever.

After about five minutes of the same boring chord progression, I walked up to Mike's amp and pulled the plug. There was this horrible crackling/popping sound. He came running over and pushed me—*pushed me*, like I was a guy he could fight.

I fell over backwards and Lars jumped up from behind his drumset. Mike was standing over me screaming. Lars pulled him off, then Mike pushed Lars and it looked like there was going to be a fight.

Before either of them could throw a punch, Mike got nervous and farted. Well, that did it. The spell was broken. Lars put down his fists and cracked up. Then I started laughing, and so did Niles and Ernesto.

Mike went over to his coat, took out a tape, gave it to me. He said to take it home and write down whatever I'd sung. And if I wanted to sing it again in LA, fine, but I had to get it *exact*. No more ad libbing on stage. Some night it would backfire and the whole show would fall apart. I had to learn the lyrics and stick with them. This wasn't some open mic at Café Lena.

God, he couldn't have pissed me off more. Especially with that surly expression on his mug. I took my empty bottle, threw it down, shattering at his feet. Then I stormed out the door.

He had no right to say that. Making light of my poems, ripping on Lena. Maybe if he tried writing a few poems, his lyrics would do more than suck wind. He could play guitar—no one was arguing with him there—but when it came to wordsmithing, Mike McKay was a clueless hack.

ENTRY FORTY-TWO
In the car driving down to LA: Hot and miserable, no A/C. The wind blowing through the window feels like a blast furnace. I hate being poor. It would have been so much better to travel by plane. I've only flown twice in my life and I was petrified both times, but only during take-offs and landings. Once you're up in the air, it's just like a big, oversized bus.

And speaking of which, trusty Niles is our driver at the moment. We're in his car, a giant boat of an Impala. It gets about eleven miles to the gallon, so by the time we get to LA, we'll have probably spent the equivalent of a plane ticket each.

Ernesto Santos, our backup keyboardist/auxiliary percussionist/ sampler-extraordinaire is sleeping next to me. He's a very nice person, I had no idea. Niles said he's only eighteen but he's got a fake ID that says he's twenty-two. He never puts himself first, always the other person. He and Niles get along great, no arguments.

After yesterday's fight at the Compound, it's a welcome change. I don't think I can take Mike's shit much longer. If he keeps it up, he can find himself a new lead singer. He and Lars drove the van with all our instruments and equipment (except Martin, my guitar; he's right here next to me). Mike says we should get reimbursed for gas money after the show. And maybe even food money. That would be so great because I'm getting extremely low on funds. Last week, I sold a brand new Mesa Boogie amp, along with a used Tama drumset and the usual miscellaneous crap, but I think I'm going to have to find a new job; it's just not making ends meet.

We left Portland this morning at 5:00 am. I don't think I've gotten up that early since I moved off the ranch. Ernesto took the first shift out of Portland, and then I drove from Grants Pass to just outside San Francisco, but when we hit traffic, I let Niles take over. This car does *not* handle well in traffic. This car doesn't handle well, period. It's a boat, a tuna barge. The suspension is so loose, you feel like it's going to roll over on sharp corners. Niles says that's impossible because the "differential" is so broad (whatever that means). I asked him what he'd be driving right now if money was no option and he said a Land Rover because they also have this amazing wheelbase. Then he started talking some technical mumbo-jumbo and lost me. I told him I'd drive a Jag or maybe one of the new Audis, the ones that look kind of like a Porsche only better. Considering how expensive Porsches are, I said, they haven't really come up with any cool new body designs. Niles agreed whole-heartedly; they've been resting on their laurels for the past thirty years.

Ernesto says according to the AAA map, we've only got about two more hours of driving and we'll be there. I don't know what city we're going through now. It seems like ever since we hit SF it's all been this one big, nasty urban sprawl. In another hundred years (if America is still around) I predict that SF and LA will merge together like one giant unibrow on the face of California . . .

Don't ask me why I just wrote that last observation. I guess I'm getting loopy. I wish Ruth was here. I'm never this way around her. I call her R.C. Mix-a-lot, because she's always talking trash, homegirl. That is, if you call Yiddish "trash." She couldn't come on the trip because of her job. I almost cried when she told me. I said we could have *sooooooooooooo* much fun partying in LA. I think she almost considered quitting her job when I said that, but then she came to her senses.

Last month, before school was out, Ruth landed a sweet summer internship at Spree, this athletic shoe company. Paid and everything. I think her father got it for her, but she won't admit it. She's the assistant to some big shot PR guy who gets to fly around the country meeting with all their endorsees, like Tiger Woods. Don't ask me how this job is supposed to relate to medicine. To be perfectly honest, I don't think Ruth knows what she wants to do with her life yet, and I can't blame her. She's only 22 years old. If I hadn't gotten lucky by meeting Lars, I wouldn't either. And of course my illness, well, that changes things considerably.

Ruth was very cool to loan me her laptop for the trip. She said she won't be needing it this summer, she's too busy to write much of anything. I know that's a lie. She loves this computer. It can even plug into the internet, but I don't know how. Maybe I'll ask Niles at the hotel—I mean, *motel*.

We're staying at this buttly dump in the worst part of Hollywood—at least that's what Ernesto says. He's got family down here, so he's pretty knowledgeable about the neighborhoods.

Mike always has to do everything *his* way, so instead of consulting with Ernesto, he called ahead himself to make the reservations—yet another dipshit move. Someday, we'll have a manager to handle these kinds of decisions. But for now, we've got to lump it. Oh well. That's showbiz!

I brought all these little cans of tuna with pop top lids. Every couple of hours, I chow one of them down. Tuna really stinks up the car. Good thing the windows are all open. Every time we stop for a potty break, I throw the opened cans away. Otherwise, it would be unbearable.

Niles says I eat like a pig; he can't understand why I'm so skinny. I told him I weighed 192 when they made me weigh myself in circuit training class last year. He said bollocks, so I took out my driver's license and showed him my chubby-wubby face in the photograph. When he saw it, he just about wrecked the car. He wanted to know how much I weigh now and I said beats me. Probably somewhere around 115, give or take. He asked how tall I was and I said five-ten and a half. He said that's way too skinny for my height, and I said look who's talking, Bony Macaroni! Niles laughed. I guess he's always been a beanpole.

Everyone in Mammy Jammer is "fashionably thin," except Lars. He's a burler. Six-foot-four and built like a grizzly. That's OK because he can hide it behind his drumset. I like the way he's so big. It's reassuring. If anyone jumps on stage at the show, he'll scare them off. Considering how rabid our fans were in P-town, I hate to think what they're going to be like down here.

ENTRY FORTY-THREE
2:00 am and we're all checked into our rooms at the Camino Reál. I've already heard gunshots. Niles and I were standing by this Coke machine in the lobby when two very distinct shots rang out. I've shot plenty of guns in my day, so I knew instantly what they were, and I ducked down in the corner. Niles made fun of me. Then another shot rang out. He screamed "oh shit!" and ducked down, spilling Coke all over himself. It was hilarious. I laughed so hard I cried.

Now, back in my room, I've got a serious case of insomnia. How can you get any sleep with gang-bangers killing each other outside your window?

The Del Rey Theatre is practically in our backyard, but still, it's not worth the convenience. Mike says we should leave the motel at least two hours early for the sound check tomorrow night because this is LA and it has the worst traffic in America. Three miles as the crow flies can turn into three hours in the car if we time it wrong.

I could tell that Mike wanted to grill me about whether I'd been memorizing lyrics on the way down, but he checked himself. Lars and he obviously had a long chat about *moi*. I was right the first time when I figured Lars as the leader of this band. He is, but his style is very hands off. He likes everyone to feel important. But there are limits. Mike is one of these people who's always pushing things, trying to get the upper hand. Everything has to be done his way, or the highway. Funny thing is, he's totally expendable, whether he realizes it or not.

Maybe he does and that's why he amps it up, because deep down he's insecure. I mean, think about it: his lyrical input is minimal, especially now with me in the band. True, he's written a lot of the music, but Niles and Ernesto take his ideas and make them work. He strums out the chords on his guitar or sings the lines and they convert his gobbledy-gook into a concrete sound. They make it happen. Without their help, Mike would be just another guitarist and let me tell you, Portland has a ton of guitarists with even better chops who could play him into the ground.

Riding down here in the car with so much time on my hands got me to thinking: What if Jack wasn't bullshitting and we really *do* get offered a recording contract? According to him, I'm the main attraction: my voice, my stage presence, my persona.

If I get approached by some A&R guy, that would give me some serious bargaining power with the band. The first thing I'd do is ask for a vote on a new name. Mammy Jammer would be out. History. And Mike's "grandfather clause" would suddenly expire: *Adieu! Parting is such sweet sorrow!*

By the way, I paged Tawny's voicemail as soon as I got in my room and locked the door. I was just getting ready to take a shower when she called me back and said, "Oh *dahling*, we absolutely must brunch together, first thing tomorrow. How does one o'clock sound?" It was my first taste of "Californication." Down here, they turn everything into verbs. That's what motion pictures will do to you if they become your God.

Hearing Tawny's sexy British accent cheered me up. She asked where I was staying and when I told her she got all serious and goes, "*No!* You mean that flea bag on Wilcox?" I said yeah and she said that I was a lot braver than her. I asked what she meant and she said not to worry. I had lots of big strong men around to protect me. Yeah, right. As if. We both laughed. Then she sighed: "Ah, well. If only you'd called yesterday. Sylvia could have wired you the money for a plane ticket and I could have picked you up at the airport. You'd be over here right now with me, sipping frozen margaritas poolside . . ."

After I hung up the phone, I couldn't help wondering about that last part of the conversation. Nice on the surface, but the underlying premise hadn't gone unnoticed: Tawny wanted me to understand that she was the one behind the controls—not Sylvia, not Jack.

You'd think after that night in Portland she'd want to cool it. What about her relationship with Jack? Didn't she feel even the slightest bit threatened?

Or maybe I've got it all wrong, maybe it's *me* she wants. For all I know, she's a double agent: bisexuality is merely a ruse to lure hot young puss into her bed.

When it comes to reading these jet-setter birds, I'm hopeless. Everyday words and phrases take on dubious shades and sometimes different meanings altogether, the *faux amis* of another, secret language.

Hollyweird: Already, it's playing with my head, making me feel like a stranger in a strange land.

ENTRY FORTY-FOUR

Holy mama, this is the life! A second show under my belt and I feel even stronger than before! Technically, it wasn't as good as the first one, but in terms of the crowd and my "theatrics" it was way better.

As soon as we got off stage, Mike walks up and goes, "nice job on those lyrics." I almost said thanks, and then I noticed the smirk on his face. What a complete dick.

So I forgot a couple of lines, big deal? The crowd loved us, and that's saying a lot considering we weren't even in the newspapers. Just Red Angel Rising and the band that came after us called Solaris. I watched from backstage: Six guys dressed in white lab coats. They played old fashioned analog synths and a seventh guy out in the audience put together this really amazing audio-visual show on a screen behind them using three film projectors and tape loops. The effect was brilliant, kind of like what Godspeed You Black Emperor does in their live performances.

Red Angel was terrific as usual. No surprises, there. Jack Thorne in all his glory doing what he does best: playing vicious guitar and tearing his lungs out. He's a born entertainer with enough charisma to charm even the most jaded of audiences. And that's exactly who he was playing for, so it was a good thing!

ø

I'm on a plane flying back to Portland as I write the rest of this entry, so I'll have plenty of time to let you in on all the juicy details. And believe me, there *are* some seriously juicy ones.

Where to start? I guess at the beginning, when I got up the next day in that flea-bag motel, the Camino Reál. I went into the bathroom and saw my first cockroach. I screamed. The thing was watching me, I couldn't help myself.

There was a knock on the door—Niles, my knight in shining armor. He asked if I was OK, and I just pointed at the thing where it was crawling along the floor and he laughed and got rid of it for me.

While I took a shower, he sat on the bed thumbing through a magazine. I think he was surprised when I came out to get my clothes. Now that I'm so thin, sometimes I totally space on being naked, or maybe it's the other way around. Kind of like a girl with a boob job who wants to flaunt it. Or maybe I'm losing my marbles and just forgot.

Poor Niles, I don't know if he was looking; if he was, he got an eyeful. He said all the guys were planning on meeting at 1:30 for lunch, but I said, oh, sorry, I already have lunch plans—Tawny Davenport, Jack's girlfriend.

"Ah," Niles said. "A *power* lunch."

"Actually, she called it brunch."

He laughed. "Brunch in the afternoon, *um hmmm* . . . only in LA." I think he was reading my mind.

Outside, on Wilcox, I didn't have any problem catching a cab. The driver knew the restaurant on Rodeo Drive, but you'll never guess how long it took to get there. A whole hour! We only drove maybe five miles. But the traffic, Jesus God, it was horrendous! Mike wasn't kidding!

Luckily the driver had a cell phone. He let me use it to call Tawny and warn her that I wasn't going to make it on time. She asked where I was. The driver told me the cross streets and Tawny calculated about how long it should take. And you know what? She ended up being amazingly accurate—within, like, five minutes.

So we ended up having brunch at two o'clock instead of one. The food was excellent. They have all kinds of seafood down here, not like in Portland. The menu was filled with so many options, I couldn't decide. Tawny laughed and said I didn't have to. The waiter was standing right there with his pad and pen poised in the air, so she went ahead and ordered four meals. Then she ordered these hurkin' Sapphire G&Ts that had something else in them, an extra ingredient; whatever it was made them even better.

We had this little round table, so when the food came, it filled up every square inch. Not enough room for extra plates, so we just reached over the table and helped ourselves to whatever. We were kind of tipsy by then, I guess, because Tawny started feeding me and I started feeding her and we kept reaching over each other and cracking up.

Tawny. I think I really like her. My first impression was wrong. She's so fun and casual. You never feel uptight around her. And she's more beautiful than I remembered. She had on this really classy sundress to show off her tan and that sweet little bod of hers. *Meow!*

After brunch, Tawny took me shopping. We must have hit at least a dozen boutiques and she kept charging stuff on her card left and right. She said she'd get reimbursed for all my outfits, but I wasn't so sure. I think she was just saying that so I wouldn't feel like a mooch. She's way richer than I thought. I asked about her dad's film directing and she went *pfff*, that's only a hobby to keep him out of trouble. Her family was from Newcastle, did I know where that was? I said, sure, Sting lives there and they've got a brewery that makes the best beer on the planet! She giggled. Yeah, but did I know in which part of England it was located? I said, what?, is this a geography lesson, and she goes, yeah, she liked messing with Americans' heads because we had no idea where anything was in the world. Her favorite pastime is to write "Australia" and "Austria" on a napkin and ask people if they know the difference. According to her, one out of four had absolutely no idea. I said that Hitler was from Austria and INXS was from Australia. As for Newcastle, I wasn't sure, but I guessed it was on the east side of England, sort of down from Edinburgh. She said not bad. A little more north and I'd have nailed it. What a snob, right? As if that's not bad enough, she then proceeds to tell me her family's been in the ship building business for two hundred years, "back when you Yanks were still wearing diapers." I guess that means the Davenports are super rich. I'm thinking, like, billionaires. She said her grandfather's company even helped build the *Titanic*.

I was starting to get nervous about making the sound check. Tawny said no worries, Jack never went to his. It was all just whistles and bells. The roadies could do it with their eyes closed. I said yeah, but we didn't have roadies yet, and besides, I liked my monitors just so. She shrugged, suit yourself.

A few blocks up the street, Tawny opened the door and stepped out of the car right in the middle of traffic. She kissed me on the lips and told the driver which way to go. I asked if she wanted to come with. She said that was sweet, but she'd catch up with me after the show. "Not to worry, I won't miss anything this time!" Right now she had some kind of dinner date. With Jack? I asked. No, some other "bloke." Jack's no fun before a performance. You've got to catch him afterwards, once he starts to loosen up.

That really surprised me. Jack Thorne, nervous? Who would have thought. Maybe he's got a few more chinks in his armor than I realized.

Despite the driver's expert maneuvering through traffic, he still got me to sound check about twenty minutes late. Everyone in the band was there, along with the same jerk of a sound guy from Red Angel who snubbed us at Crystal Ballroom. He smiled his sweetest smile. "Nice of you to show up." I smiled right back and said, "Yeah, nicer than Jack, right?" No one else except him got the joke, but he didn't laugh. He tried to give me some crap about the sound check being over. Bullshit, I said, get your ass behind that board and turn on my mic and monitors. He cocked his head to one side as he tried to think up a comeback, but I just kept walking and when I got up on stage my mic was on.

This time, the guy did a pretty good job getting the levels right. Even though he's a fat piece of white trash and I normally wouldn't give guys like him the time of day, I knew pretty much what I had to do: Smile really big and pretend he's my new best friend. On the other hand, I couldn't take his attitude, either. That would be a sign of weakness and weaklings get no respect from guys like him. Despite the fact that he was a biker and not a cowboy, the rules of the game were nearly identical, at least in terms of the psychology involved.

Afterwards, I walked up and shook the dude's hand because he could make or break our band that night and he knew it. I was still carrying all my shopping bags from that afternoon, so I reached inside and pulled out this totally kick-ass silver Harley Davidson belt buckle that Tawny had picked out for me. With this big lump in my throat, I held it out, remembering that dude had been wearing a Harley T-shirt at The Crystal.

When he saw the belt buckle, his pig eyes went all squinty. "What's this?" he said. I told him it was a peace offering. Cheers. But if he took it, then he damn well better get those levels right tonight.

Well, that did it: He busted into this big, cackling smoker's laugh and said, OK, deal! Mike and Lars were standing right there and I could tell they were impressed. Yeah, yeah. BFD. *Girl's gotta do what a girl's gotta do.* If getting a great sound tonight meant parting with my favorite belt buckle, so be it; this would probably be our first and last shot at the big time. We were playing with one of the biggest "cult" bands around, and we were doing it in Rock Label Heaven, the backyard of all the biggest companies.

Besides, I knew the score when it came to business: If you hear a squeaky wheel, grease it up. Friendly favors make the rock n' world go round.

Mammy Jammer was supposed to go on stage at nine sharp, but the stage manager said the show hadn't sold out yet, so could we maybe go on around ten instead? Lars told him sure, no problem. That would work in our favor anyway. More people to see us and we all knew what he meant by that: more of a chance that some A&R guy would be in the audience. I didn't mention that Jack had promised he'd be sure to give his label a tip-off and to send a guy. What was the point in getting everyone's hopes up? Besides, knowing Jack, he was probably just blowing smoke.

Waiting around for the show was like torture. Mike wouldn't stop pacing back and forth in the green room. I was getting hungry and my hands had begun to shake. I got up and looked through the phone book, but I didn't have any idea what Japanese restaurants were good and how close they were to the club. I ended up calling half a dozen before I finally got one that would deliver, but since I didn't know the street address of where I was, I just told them the Del Rey Theatre and hoped that would suffice.

Also, I really wanted a drink but the bars inside the club weren't open yet. I tried to get Lars to go outside with me for a drink at one of the old man bars, but he wouldn't budge. Relax, he said, the front bar would open in another half hour. He noticed I was shaking, so he came over and put his arm around me. Right then, I came so close to telling him about my illness, but no. The timing was off. That would just make the rest of the band nervous. And besides, they'd probably think I was imagining the whole thing. If Ruth had had her doubts, they'd chalk it up to paranoia for sure, a mental hang-up, and I was already cultivating a reputation for more than my share of those.

To take my mind off the shaking, I got up and started wandering around the club. It was a big place, much bigger than it had seemed at first. Especially the basement, which had labyrinthine passages all over the place: huge rooms filled with cobwebs and dust, broken furniture. I found an old wet bar in one of them, but no luck. Only empties. Then I remembered the Japanese restaurant. Shoot. I could have ordered beer and sake from the guy on the telephone! Too late to change the order now.

Upstairs, I waited and waited for my food to be delivered. People were starting to trickle in. I was kind of nervous going out in the crowd until I realized they hadn't seen me on stage yet. They had no idea who I was. I stood around waiting for the bar to open. Thankfully, the bartender took mercy on us and opened early. I ordered a double Sapphire with a beer back. To my surprise, they had Newcastle in big Imperial pint-sized bottles.

After I'd downed those, my food still hadn't come, so I went up into the front of the theater and asked if anyone had seen a delivery guy from a Japanese restaurant called "Golden Pavilion." The bouncer said that sounded more like a Chinese restaurant, but he hadn't seen anyone come in; ask the stage manager, over in the office. I walked through the door and there was my food, just sitting out on the table. Great. Room temperature sushi. Thanks a lot, guys.

The yellow tail was inedible and so was the tuna, but every piece of salmon was passably fresh. As soon as the protein hit my veins, I could feel this satisfied hum in my system and the shakes cranked down a notch.

What I needed now was a cell phone to call Ruth. Check in, see how she was doing. Nobody had one up front, so I went back into the main auditorium. The bartender had one. Was it a local call? I said no, to Portland, but I slapped down a ten and he said cool.

To get some privacy, I went downstairs into the basement and found this moldy couch. Despite all the dust, it was actually pretty comfortable. I dialed up Ruth's number. Come on, baby.

She picked up on the fourth ring. One more and it would have gone to voice mail. No sooner had I said hello, than Ruth starting chewing me out. She was really worried. How come I hadn't called earlier? I told her about everything and she wanted to know right away if I'd been eating right. I said yeah, as a matter of fact, I'd just put down some sush—mainly salmon, the other fish hadn't been fresh enough. She sounded vaguely concerned. "How long had it been sitting around?" I said I didn't know. "But it smelled OK?" Well, no, not exactly. The yellow tail smelled like ass. But the salmon hadn't been too bad. I'd eaten it a half hour ago. Ruth sounded relieved and told me not to worry. If food poisoning was a possibility, I would have felt something icky in my stomach by now, at least a few stabbing pains.

Ruth quizzed me on what I was wearing and I said, *Oooooo*, wouldn't you like to know! She laughed and said not now, stupid, later. What was I going to wear on stage? I told her my same black leathers and this other shirt that Tawny had helped pick out, along with this really wild clear plastic bra with sparkles. That got Ruth's attention. "PLASTIC? Won't that be sticky? Especially under the lights?"

I couldn't help it, I was letting my fingers do the walking. Ruth's sexy voice was turning me on. I wondered if she could tell what I was doing, so I kept talking but I really just wanted to lie back and listen. I asked her to tell me about her day, how was the new job at Spree? Meet any famous athletes?

She said no, it had all been deskwork, filing, boring stuff like that. The people in the office were awesome, though. Totally kick back. The guys had this long-standing joke that if you came to work wearing a tie on your first day, someone would sneak up with a pair of scissors and cut it off. Wasn't that just the coolest thing? I asked if she'd worn a tie and she just laughed and kept going on and on about her job. It was all I could do to mutter in the affirmative.

Finally, she goes, "Jules? Are you there?" I said yeah, still here. She wanted to know what was going on. Was someone else in the room?

"What do you mean?" I said, stalling, and she goes, "Oh, I thought . . . never mind." After that she didn't even pause for me to say the usual, "uh-uh" or "oh, really?" I think either she knew what I was doing, or else she thought I must be suffering from some other kind of delusion—the changes, etc.

Second guessing Ruth was giving me cold fingers. Low down, dirty. Coming was out of the question: Definitely *not* kosher. As it was, my fingers absolutely reeked of sex. Not only would I have to wash them, I'd also have to wipe off the bartender's cell.

There was this awkward pause on the line. "Jules? Are you still there?" I said yeah, still here. "Alright, listen: no matter what happens tonight, I really admire how talented you are, and you *know* that I'll always support you. So go out there and kick some major booty! You hear?"

I almost cried when she said that last part, because it sounded an awful lot like what Jeff would say.

Actually, I think I did start crying a little because Ruth changed the subject real fast to get my mind off of it. She said the Chair of Creative Writing at PCC had written her a letter asking if she knew any writers who might want to submit a few pieces to *The Alchemy*. Ruth had mentioned my name, and the chair had seemed intrigued. How cool would that be if we both got published in the same issue?

I told her that I'd have to think about it. Right now, I just didn't have much material. Ruth asked how many pages I'd typed in my journal and

I said that I wasn't really sure. Seventy, maybe eighty? Single or double-spaced, Ruth asked. Single. She laughed. Don't you know that's twice as many in print? You've written around a hundred and fifty pages! Yeah, I said, but not anything I'd feel comfortable getting published. At least not yet. It's *way* too personal.

Oy, Ruth says, not giving up. What about those poems you read at Café Lena? They were incredible! *The Alchemy* would publish all three in a heartbeat.

The moment was so ripe, I was just dying to tell her about my inspiration: they were for her and I didn't want to give them to anyone else. I didn't even care if they got me published. They were my gift to her, an offering of love.

Naturally, I wimped out. The story of my life. I must have sounded kind of down because Ruth goes, "Honey, what's wrong?" I apologized for being such a dud and told her it was right before my period, I was PMSing.

"Oh, poor baby," she cooed, and then proceeded to give me a pep talk to get me revved up for the show—exactly what I needed to hear.

When she was done, I asked her what time it was and she said about eight-thirty, just long enough to get dressed and put on your makeup. I told her I was already dressed from the waist down. She asked was I going to wear the same spike-heeled boots and I said yeah. She thought that was a good idea. With the extra height, I towered like an Amazon on stage, well over six feet tall. And they made my legs look even longer.

Then it was time to go. I didn't want to say goodbye, so Ruth did it for me. A little kiss and then dead air. She can be so firm. Take-charge. I love the way she bosses me around. Only her, though. Only my Rooty.

We ended up going on stage a little after ten o'clock. By then, I'd had more than my share of G&Ts (heavy on the "G"). I could tell Lars and Mike were nervous about it, but they didn't want to get me angry. Not right before the show. I glared at Mike as I took sip after sip. He wouldn't make eye contact, he was so pissed. Good thing Tawny didn't show up "with a little help from her friends." I probably would have snorted just about anything at that point, I was so nervous.

Even halfway drunk, I could feel my arms and legs shaking. I must have looked quite a sight. Mike and Lars kept mumbling to each other, appraising my condition. They probably thought I was tweaking.

But once I stepped out on stage under those brilliant lights, everything clicked. The shakes evaporated, my head cleared.

Our first song went alright. It could have been worse. Trailer trash kept my monitors cranked. The belt buckle was paying off. I started working the crowd, singing right at them, in their faces, like Gwen Stefano, dancing around, stealing a couple of her moves that she'd stolen from rappers.

In the back of my mind, I was remembering the night at the guesthouse: Vampires ravaging each other, *un petite mort*. It was like this force was filling my body, turning me into someone else—*something* else. God, it felt good. If one of those fans had stepped up on stage with a shotgun, I would have ripped off my shirt and bared my chest. I would have taken a silver bullet for the crowd.

Thinking back on it now, the rest of the show was pretty much like before at Crystal Ballroom: a blur of lights, a wall of sound. When the band got to "Cowslip," I almost turned around and told them to snuff it. But then I looked over and saw my guitar sparkling under the lights. It shone like a beacon, drawing me closer, pulling me toward the song I'd written for daddy, our last few moments together.

Instead of telling the story, I just sang. Mike filled in some textures with his Strat and the synth boys kept a low, almost indefinable creepy drone that really worked well for the acoustics of the space. No drums, though. Lars stuck to the tambourine, tapping it lightly to help keep the beat on the chorus.

We were in the home stretch now. Two of our most powerful songs left to go, and then we were done. Trailer Trash lowered my levels so I could scream into my mic without overloading the PA.

By now, I was covered in sweat; but instead of hiding it, I peeled off the layers until I found myself standing before the audience dressed only in my bra and black leather pants.

So many pairs of eyes, intent on my every word, every gesture. There were some real hotties out there. Playfully, I told them that if they showed me theirs, I'd show 'em mine.

Five or six tops flew off, and one girl even chucked her bra up on stage. I held it up: "C'mon! Is that all you got?"

This time quite a few more girls opened their bras and flashed me.

Even the guys were baring their chests. I signaled to Lars and we broke into our last big number—the one Mike had nicknamed "The Money Song" because he said it was going to land us a recording contract. All the way through, I kept teasing the audience, lifting a cup here, a cup there.

Finally, right before we went into the bridge, I ripped off my bra and threw it out into the crowd, baring my breasts under the stage lights, a burnt offering.

ENTRY FORTY-FIVE

Back in the land of the living where everything is lush and green: Sometimes I forget how beautiful Oregon is. LA's a dust-filled crypt, all the dead lawns with plants wilting in people's front yards. Cars lined up on the freeways. Pollution so strong it makes your eyes burn. And in the distance, the hills glittering, almost white.

Los Angeles can be wonderful, too. The nights are cool and breezy, that's one good thing. Stars winking through a quilt of city-wash that spreads out in all directions, almost as if it's trying to one-up the sun, to usurp daylight and give some of the glory to night. Going out after sunset is different in LA for this reason. More magical. There's a certain edginess Portland will never have. You can feel the power of the whole human race, of America, pulsing, burning, crying out for recognition: "Look at us! We made a huge oasis out here in the middle of the desert!"

And the day time, you ask? What about the days? They're a different animal completely. At first, it almost feels like you've died and gone to heaven: not a cloud in the sky, low humidity, temperatures pushing ninety.

But speaking strictly for myself, three days under that blue screen was more than enough. I started to miss my big Oregon fluffies. So I guess the old adage is true: LA is a nice place to visit, but I wouldn't want to live there.

Portland's more honest. Everyone here accepts the fact it's going to rain. A lot. Rain is a good thing. Farmers need it for their crops and it helps keep everything fresh and alive. The Pioneers built our biggest city where nature could best support it, and because of this foresight, Portlanders will never have to "steal" water from other states to preserve our way of life. We have more H_2O than we'll ever know what to do with.

Yet, despite our reconciliation with all things wet and soggy, no one else on earth knows how to appreciate a bright sunshiny day more than an Oregonian. After a few weeks of rain, it feels like a gift from God.

Deeksha's giving me the silent treatment today. Last night when I came in she frowned at my leather pants, calling them "vulgar." I don't know what her problem is. Everything gets amped up to eleven. It's like she's looking for a reason to get pissed.

No more dragging my feet: I'm moving out. Deeksha can drool on her next roommate, whoever she ends up luring back to the lair. Another young one. Who knows? Maybe she'll get a brunette this time, or a red head. I wonder how long until they figure out she's not really looking for something in the bathroom while they're in the shower, that she really just wants to sneak a peak at their "soul patch." She should do herself a favor and pick a lesbian exhibitionist who doesn't mind walking around naked in exchange for cheap rent.

Of course I'm really one to talk—flashing the audience the other night. Displaying my wares. That's all people were talking about after the show at the party.

The next day in the *LA Tattler*, there was a picture of me onstage lifting my shirt: "Shirt-Lifter Extraordinaire." It never occurred to me that they could take pictures. I didn't see any flashes in the audience. But there they were, my perky tits, right on the front page! Underneath, it said my name but there was no mention of our band, the show, nothing. Just some trashy blurb about how Jack Thorne's latest girlfriend was a stripper from Portland. A *stripper!* I should sue them for slander, the yellow-bellied sapsuckers!

Maybe Deeksha's so angry because she knows I'll be moving out soon. Probably overheard the call I took this morning from Jack's agent (now *my* agent). He woke me up out of a sound sleep to tell me that I'd already gotten, count 'em, THREE offers from two different labels. I'm not sure quite how that works. At AMI, I guess they have two separate divisions bidding against each other. Hart Drake (the agent) said that could definitely work in our favor.

I haven't told the rest of the band yet. We're having a powwow Thursday night at the Compound. I'll spring the news on them then. When I told Hart that I'd need to consult with the rest of the band before we went any further, he seemed surprised. "What's the point? Form your own band! With a deal like the one I'm sure to get, you can handpick some of the best musicians in LA. Or you could go the studio route and hire some big names to come in and lay down the tracks. And when it comes time to hit the road, you can hire whatever talent you need. That's the smartest way to approach it. Forget those Mammy Jammers. They'll hold you back from realizing your true potential."

Instead of going off on a tirade about loyalty, the ethics of being a team player, etc., I just asked Hart very politely to please never say anything like that again. The band always came first.

"OK, it's your call," he said. "Sooner or later, you'll come around."

You know, it's funny. I've been Jonesing for a record deal ever since I was a little kid singing along with videos on MTV. But now that it's really happening, I just feel numb.

One thing's for sure: I could never have done it without Jack's help; true to his word, he'd passed out the demos that I'd sent him, and he even told Hart to make a few calls. I found out after the show that four A&R guys had been in the audience. The one from AMI only caught our last song but he was so impressed that he gave us the thumbs-up; his boss called the next day to make an offer.

According to Hart, it's still too early to tell how much money we could get up front. A few other labels might catch the buzz and want a piece of the action. So everything's happening exactly as Jack predicted; he'd told me that if his pull didn't do it, then Tawny was my ace in the hole. She knew even more people in "the biz" than him.

I suppose this means that I owe her the favor she'd asked for. I'm supposed to get a Fed Ex today, some kind of a waiver to sign. She's making a documentary about the music industry, "behind the scenes." So far, she's interviewed twenty-five bands and about a million producers and managers and agents.

That night after my show at the Del Rey, Tawny had a video camera glued to her right hand; it went with her everywhere. At first, the documentary was kind of novel, amusing, but it got old fast. I couldn't relax with a camera pointed in my face. Later on, at Tawny's place in Bel Aire, the whole thing really started to get to me. She even got a close-up of Jack shooting heroin. And I think she filmed him shooting me up, as well.

Afterwards, when we all climbed into bed, Tawny giggled mischievously: Lucky for us she'd run out of film! Thinking back on it now, that moment stands out in my mind. In 20/20 hindsight, it's plain enough: I never should have gone over there. A lamb to the slaughter. Once the H hit my brain, I was bye-bye. Tawny could have stood me on my head and shoved the lens up my pussy for all I knew.

Speaking of which . . . the next morning, when I woke up, my pussy *was* really sore, stretched out, like I'd given birth or something. And if that wasn't enough, my period had just started. So whatever had happened the night before could have been potentially messy.

ENTRY FORTY-SIX

Actually, come to think of it, maybe I will hold off signing that waiver. Tawny acted like she needed it right away, but she's nowhere near being done with the project.

I should definitely get legal advice. When I have a lawyer look over my recording contract, I'll bring Tawny's "waiver" and see what they think. How embarrassing, though, telling them about what happened. I'll just say I was drunk and may have gotten myself into a compromising position. They'll get the idea.

Jack and Tawny did me a *huge* favor by turning on the record companies to Mammy Jammer. I know I'll probably never be able to repay them, but there's only so far you can go without losing all self-respect. This whole thing's spiraling out of control.

Besides, once the so-called "documentary" comes out, Jack might change his tune. Especially if Tawny decides to put in the footage of him shooting up. Even his reputation as the reigning bad boy of rock n' roll wouldn't be enough to save him. *MTV*, *Rolling Stone*, and *Spin* would gobble it up like candy.

No more "black & white" nights for this gal. Nothing good has ever come out of it, even if I did get the chance to party with Jack Thorne. Now I've got my own career to think about. Time for a little damage control.

I should give Jack a call, anyway, to thank him for everything. I wouldn't have to say much to get the wheels turning in the old dog's head. If he and Tawny ever got in a fight, she'd have a serious weapon at her disposal that could ruin him—especially with those scenes of us shooting up. Did he really want to take that chance?

ENTRY FORTY-SEVEN

Just got back from PHSU. Ruth took the day off work to come with. She's such a sweetheart. I couldn't have done it without her.

The hospital looked identical to the day I'd gone to see my dad for the last time. Part of it was the weather: Blue sky without a cloud anywhere in sight. Ruth assured me that today's been the first nice day we've had in Portland for a week. I must have brought the sun back with me from Los Angeles.

Strange as it may seem, a few clouds would have helped out. Anything to make today seem different.

Before we went inside, I had to get my courage up. Ruth sat in the car with me while I prayed that someone had painted the neurology wing a nice comforting shade of purple. With pink polka dots on the carpet. And the doctors all dressed up in Hawaiian shirts and Vans, riding their skateboards to surgery. I didn't care if the whole place burned down, just so long as I didn't bump into my father's ghost stumbling towards me in the hall with that stupid grin on his face, blank zombied-out eyes . . .

Before we'd left for the hospital, Ruth had made double-sure I ate a good breakfast. She came over with all these groceries: my favorite breakfast patties from Morningstar Farms, two grapefruits, hash browns. No coffee. She must have gotten her daily dose of caffeine already because she wasn't cranky or anything. If that girl doesn't get her double shot in the morning, look out!

Thank god the neurology program isn't in the exact same wing as where they put my father, along with all those ninety-year old basket cases with Alzheimer's. The woman at the front desk was very nice. She gave me this stack of forms to fill out. I didn't have all the information, but she said I could bring it with me when I came back for a follow-up visit.

Come back? I didn't like the sound of that—no, not at all. I couldn't stop picturing my father's room, how I'd end up like him with tubes sticking out of my arms, a catheter stuck up my gown.

Ruth was super-supportive, helping all she could. When the nurse practitioner arrived to escort me into the back room for the tests, Ruth even went so far as to ask if she could "accompany" me. The nurse sized up the frantic expression on my face and said OK.

They took practically every bodily fluid I could part with and some things I didn't even know I had to give. Then they ran these other tests on high-tech machines that looked like they'd been beamed down from the Starship *Enterprise*.

After all the tests were finished, the nurse led Ruth and me into an adjoining office and asked me all these questions about my symptoms. She wanted to know everything. I told her a lot, but when it came to the really juicy stuff, I held back because I was too embarrassed. I mean, shoot, demons in a bookstore? No way. She'd just write me off as being a mental patient. I tried to stay medical like a doctor would: sights and sounds being distorted, warped. My brain on the fritz.

The nurse smiled a patronizing smile when I said that last part, as if to say, well, now, let's just let us decide that, shall we? She told me to hold out my hands. Considering how nervous I was at the time, they weren't shaking. Not even a little. I'd been feeling much better lately. The symptoms must be temporarily in remission.

I asked the nurse about the possibility, and she said she wasn't surprised. The same thing happened to her the last time she'd taken her car in to a mechanic with engine trouble. A thorough diagnostic had been needed to locate the source of the trouble. Just because my body wasn't cooperating at the moment didn't mean I was imagining the whole thing. Some of the tests had indicated "irregularities."

And then I came right out and asked the nurse point blank: "So, do you think I have scrapie?"

She got this surprised expression on her face. "That, my dear, is *highly* unlikely." The way she said it with such a confident tone in her voice that bordered on arrogance almost made me relax and give up the whole thing, my nagging suspicions. I asked when they would be able to tell if I had it or not, and she said probably by the next visit.

But then she went on to say a few comments that have been bothering me ever since:

"Please bear in mind that our methods will be strictly trial and error. We'll be able to rule out 'scrapie' as soon as we make a positive match for something else or determine that the cause isn't physiological in nature."

I asked her what she meant and she said at the present time there was no way to test for Creutzfelt-Jakob Disease, the human form of scrapie or Mad Cow.

I got pretty freaked when I heard that. *No way to test for it!* Then how did they know it even existed at all?

The nurse set down her pencil and sighed this annoyed little sigh. "Ms. Fleischer, I was speaking in terms of the *living*. After a patient dies, a standard autopsy is more than adequate to make a diagnosis. Then it's merely a question of knowing what to look for."

I came really close to asking what they did to a corpse that they couldn't do to a *living* person, but then I thought better of it. That would make me paranoid for sure.

Ruth took me to lunch afterwards, but we didn't really talk about what the nurse had said. I couldn't eat a thing. Ruth said she wasn't leaving until I'd swallowed at least two pieces of sashimi.

She tried to keep the conversation on a positive note, begging me to tell her all about LA—especially Jack Thorne: The man, the legend. Had I slept with him again? Was he any good in bed? Alright, spit it out: Exactly how big *was* the package?

I bluffed my way through this friendly interrogation. What a drag. I wanted so desperately to tell Ruth about all the terrible shit that went down at Tawny's place, but I couldn't do it. She would definitely frown on me trying hard drugs, especially heroin. She doesn't even smoke pot.

Come to think of it, Ruth's never done *anything* except drink alcohol. Depending on the night, she can usually drink me under the table even though I'm way taller than her. And now, since I've lost all the weight, she definitely has the upper hand in that department. Oh yeah. Girlfriend can pound.

ENTRY FORTY-EIGHT

Finally got Jack on his cell this morning. He was in Toronto, so it was early afternoon on his end. He didn't sound very glad to hear my voice. I asked if it was a bad time and he said no. What did I want? I said that I'd just called to see how he was doing. There was an awkward silence. Then he spoke: Uh-huh. Right. Did I *really* want to know or was I just saying that? I told him I really wanted to know, he could tell me anything.

OK, fine, he said. You're asking for it: My bass player's sick with some parasite he caught from a restaurant in Boston. So now I gotta find another bassist by the sound check tonight who can fill in until Shamir feels better, and that's really busting my chops because nobody, I mean NOBODY can replace Shamir, even for a couple of shows. The guy's a complete motherfucker. He's been holding down the entire low end ever since we hit the road on tour; it's been cursed from the beginning. This new hot-shot drummer the label sent me, he ain't so hot. Keeps speeding up faster and faster and *faster!* like a goddamned carnival ride. Without my man, Shamir, I'm gonna end up singing like Michael Jackson on helium just to keep up with the tempo.

Oh man, I said, that's rough. But if anyone can do it, you can. When I told him that, Jack softened up a little. He said that he missed Tawny. She was all set to fly out and meet him in Toronto and then something came up at the last minute and she couldn't make it. So now he was stuck with NO LOVE except from the occasional "flounder" (his word for groupie).

In fact, Jack confessed, he had one in his room right now giving him a back rub, this cute little French Canadian *puta*. I told him that was a Spanish word, not French.

There was kissing, moaning in the background: The unmistakable sound of two naked bodies slapping together. *Oh. My. God. They were going at it! He was actually fucking her with me on the phone!*

I had to really work at staying calm. This was a side of Jack the world knew all too well, practically his trademark, but something I hadn't been exposed to—at least not personally. I should have hung up the phone right then and called him later, but instead I changed the subject, launching into the bidding wars, all the latest offers coming in from the record companies. It looked like AMI was going to give us the highest one, just over six hundred. Did he think that was high enough or should I hold out for more?

Jack growled into the receiver, how the hell should he know? Half a mil was plane fare as far as he was concerned. Hart handled the finances. Talk to Hart. I could trust him. He'd always been a real stand-up guy. Watch out though, when I signed the contract. Don't let him take more than fifteen percent off the top and try to get him to take it out of the sales profits, not your advance.

I got a little nervous, hearing that. If Hart was so trustworthy, then why would he ask for more than a fair commission? Right as I was getting ready to thank Jack again and say my goodbyes, he yelled at someone else in the room with him and the line went dead. Maybe his little *puta* had spilled the massage oil?

I hung up the phone, lay back on my bed, running my fingers through my hair, biting the split ends, an old habit from high school. Something had definitely changed between Jack and me. There wasn't the same magic, the warmth of when we'd first met, when he'd comforted me after my show at The Crystal. Why? Why had he been so cold on the phone? Was it because I couldn't give him my body right this second, because I was so far away, untouchable?

I took off my clothes and stood naked in front of mirror.

My ribs were really starting to show. No matter how much I ate, the pounds kept sliding off. Now I looked as skinny as Fiona Apple in her first video: "I've been a bad, bad girl . . ."

Screw Jack, the cold, heartless prick! The nerve of him, boning some flounder when I was trying to say thanks! Was he jealous of my newfound success?

No, that wasn't it. He was just having a bad day. Whatever. I needed a shower to help myself relax.

Once I'd turned on the water and I knew that Deeksha couldn't hear, I let myself start to cry, but nothing happened. No tears. I consulted my reflection in the mirror.

Faker. Don't make me laugh.

All of a sudden, I felt dried up, hollow inside: An actor who couldn't get into her lines. Even alone in my bathroom, I was on camera: Doing the right thing, what society expected of me.

You're nothing but a whore and whores can't cry.

In the shower, I kept the temperature all the way to the left, as hot as it would go. The scalding jets felt good on my skin: One variety of pain replacing another. I held my face under the water until I thought it was getting close to doing the kind of damage that might actually show up in a photograph.

ENTRY FORTY-NINE

Met at the Compound yesterday to go over our last show and tell the guys the good news. When I got there, Lars and Mike hadn't shown up yet. Niles and Ernesto were sitting out on the patio drinking beers. I popped the cap off a bottle and joined them. They were both in good spirits. Ernesto got up and gave me a hug. "*Los nenes de Julia son la sonrisa de su corazón!*" I asked him what he meant by that, and he said he was talking about our music, our babies. How each song had grown up and become full-fledged adults in LA. And I was their mother— especially of "Cowslip."

God, that was so nice to hear, such a poetic way of putting it. I kissed him on both cheeks and sat down. It was overcast out, a heavy cloud cover like it might rain, but it was warm enough to sit outside comfortably without a coat. I watched the sky, pondering the way the clouds in the southeast often took on a reddish hue after dark, reflecting the lights of the city. We sat drinking the rest of our beers and then Niles went to the store for another case. He still hadn't gotten back when Lars and Mike strolled in. By the way they were walking (staggering) it was obvious we weren't going to get any practicing done.

Lars came over and gave me a hug, but Mike stayed in the shadows unpacking his gear. He didn't say a word.

When Niles got back, we sat down with another beer and kind of zoned out, trying our best to relax. It was quiet and I could see there was tension between the synth boys and Lars and Mike. I knew instinctively that the band had already met without me. I broached the subject, making sure to keep out any hint of accusation. The synth boys squirmed a little in their chairs and Lars set down his beer. It was Mike who spoke first.

"That's right," he admitted. "We hashed out a few details. After we got back from the *long* drive home."

"Look," I said, "if you're trying to guilt me about flying, the ticket was a gift. From Tawny."

"Of course . . . a *gift*."

"Besides, I don't see what that has to do with you guys getting together and talking about me behind my back. At the very least, one of you should have called."

Mike said to hear him out. Despite being "colorful," my performance at the Del Rey had only reinforced concerns about several key issues: Most importantly, the lyrics. Not only had I changed over half the songs, but this time around, I hadn't improved on them. My rhymes had been downright childish in places. And I'd been drunk again, worse than at The Crystal.

I laughed. Man, this was so hilarious. Here was Mike, grilling me, and everyone else just sitting there watching him do it. I asked if he was done and he said no, he wasn't. The last thing he wanted to bring up was my attitude. On stage it was fine, a little over the top, but that was part of the act. I'd generated a lot of hype in LA. They'd all seen the front page of *The Tattler* and I'd even gotten a mention in the big industry tabloids. But he was talking about my attitude at practice *with the band*. Throwing hissy fits and trying to kill him with a bottle was totally unacceptable.

Mike sat back and took a pull off his beer, gazing out into the yard. The king in his castle. Now that he'd gotten that off his chest, I knew exactly where he stood. No one else said much of anything. We all just sat there and drank. I could feel the anger welling up inside me, a poisonous spring, but I was too upset to speak.

Ah, fuck it. I got up, went to the bathroom. A few minutes to catch my breath. I soaked my face in warm water and sat down on the toilet to think.

So this was it? The rest of the band was going to let Mike do their dirty work for them? I didn't exactly blame Niles and Ernesto; they were in kind of a ticklish position, having joined the band after Lars and Mike laid the foundation. It was Lars that I was most concerned about. If he backed Mike up, then I was through. I could rinse my hands of the entire matter and sign the recording contract with a clean conscience.

Back outside on the patio, the atmosphere had shifted. Mike was standing out in the yard apart from everyone else and Lars was joking with Ernesto. I sat down, took a hit off my beer. There was no point in delaying the inevitable. I asked Lars if he agreed with everything Mike had said.

He thought very carefully before speaking. That's one of the things I've liked about Lars from the beginning, even in the classroom. Basically, he's a thoughtful person. He said that Mike hadn't been speaking for the band. And what he'd said about the meeting had been misleading. It was just a spur-of-the-moment thing. They'd run into each other when they were unloading gear and one thing had led to another.

That's not to say that everything Mike had brought up was wrong. I'd forgotten a lot of the lyrics in LA, but oh well. It was only my second big show and I'd compensated for it in other ways. As far as the antics on stage went, he loved them.

Niles and Ernesto both nodded enthusiastically, mumbling in agreement. Lars went on to say that he'd seen a professional entertainer on stage. I'd been transformed into a different person and he'd been fascinated to see what I'd do next. And these days, that was the kind of presence that got noticed by the record companies.

Niles spoke up: Personally, he was blown away with my performance in LA. The crowd loved us. Afterwards, he'd been at the bar drinking and he'd heard people talking. They were saying that our show was the best they'd seen in a long time and we were going to blow Red Angel off the stage. Ernesto said he'd heard similar things and so what if I'd messed up a few lines? It was a lot to remember. I'd only been in the band for how long, a little over a month? "*ay! Dios mío!* He could never have memorized so many words in such a short amount of time. I was doing great. Just keep it up and everything would be cool.

Mike had come back from his little foray out into the yard. I could tell he was surprised by everything he'd heard. I looked him straight in the eye: did he have anything else to say to me? No comment. He just smiled this really cheesy smile.

"Alright then," I said. "I quit."

Everyone did a double take, even Mike. "That's right," I said. "I'm quitting Mammy Jammer and starting a new band. If any of you want to join that's up to you. All except Mike, he's on his own."

Ernesto and Niles started chattering like schoolgirls and Mike laughed as if the whole notion was ludicrous. But Lars . . . he wasn't doing either. A faint smile had formed on his lips. He kept one twinkling eye on me, waiting for what was to come. He knew. The bastard had already figured it out.

I held up my hand for everyone to please listen as I explained the situation: Hart, our new agent; the offers he'd orchestrated from what now amounted to four record companies. So far, no one had topped the offer from AMI, but who knows? It was open season. The bidding war still had another few days to go.

Mike was pacing back and forth in the yard. He threw his beer down on the ground and screamed this was bullshit! I couldn't do this! How dare I keep this from the band? "How long have you known? How long, goddamn it! You're a traitor, that's what you are! A fucking turncoat! I knew from Day One that you were only out for yourself!"

I stopped him right there: "You haven't had one nice thing to say to me since I joined the band! You were *never* on my side. Take tonight for instance: when I walked in, you didn't even go, 'Oh, hi Julia, nice to see you,' or some other half-assed attempt to be civil. No, you waited for the right moment, then you went straight for the kill—running through the list of petty grievances you prepared on the 'long' ride home from LA, as if I were some hired hand you could dismiss whenever you felt like it."

"You call getting drunk and forgetting half the songs 'petty?'"

"*Enough*! I have nothing more to say to you. Now or ever."

Mike looked at Lars and Lars just shrugged. That did it: Mike stormed into the Compound, grabbed his axe and slammed the front door behind him. We all listened to him start up his car, the squeal of tires as he roared off down the street.

Both Ernesto and Niles were giggling giggles of sheer joy. Ernesto got up and danced over to give me a joyous hug, and Niles shook my hand. Lars wasn't far behind. He was the only member of the band who was taller than me and he leaned over, wrapped those big strong arms around me: "OK, Julia. You're the boss. Congratulations."

I started crying then, happy tears, shaking my head—*no, no, no!* Forget all the possessive control-freak bullshit! It had never been *Lars'* band or *Mike's* band, and now it wasn't *my* band. It was *our* band. From now on, we'd vote on everything! ABSOLUTELY EVERYTHING! Speaking of which . . . did anyone have any ideas for a new name?

Silence. Lars and the boys weren't sure what to do. We were in virgin territory, so much had happened in the past five minutes.

"Well," I said. "I was thinking of something, but don't feel any pressure to agree."

"Tell us, " Ernesto said.

"How about 'Gringo Complex'?"

Ernesto couldn't help frowning.

"OK," I said, "scratch that one."

"'Bang To Rites,'" said Niles. "It's from *Trainspotting*. The book, not the movie."

"Bang To Rites?" Ernesto asked. "What does that mean?"

"I'm not sure," said Niles. "I just remember liking it when I read it."

"Not catchy enough," Ernesto said. "How about *Los Gatos*."

"The Cats?" I asked.

"Yeah."

"Sound too much like the musical," Niles said.

"I have a couple of ideas," Lars said. "I'll name them off and you stop me if you like one: Tom Paine . . . The Furies, Dispossessed, Man Ray . . . let's see, what else? Oh, The Skalds! I've always like that one."

I couldn't help cringing. "You mean like being 'scalded' by hot water?"

"No, no," Lars corrected. "Skald with a 'k'. It's a type of poetry in the Scandinavian sagas."

"Too bookish," Niles said.

Ernesto laughed. "You're really one to talk, *cabrón*. You got your name from a book."

"Yes, but it doesn't sound pretentious. You can accuse Irvine Welsh of many things, bookishness isn't among them."

I closed my eyes. Words and images floated through my mind. I must have conjured up dozens before one leapt out of my mouth: "The Compound!"

No one said anything right away. I knew that was probably a good sign, or it could mean that no one wanted to shoot down my second try.

"It has a nice ring to it," Niles finally said, breaking the silence. "Yeah," Ernesto piped in. "Not bad." We all waited on Lars. He was mulling it over. I could tell by the curious look on his face that he found it interesting, to say the least.

"Open-ended," he said, finally. "With several meanings."

"What meanings?" Ernesto asked. "It's the name of this building."

"Well," Lars said in his teaching voice, "the word is edgy: a 'compound fracture.' But it can also lean the other way: a salve, an ointment. Drug connotations."

I spoke up: "To me, it's cool because it holds a special meaning for us: our space, our home, the center of our universe."

"So obvious," Niles agreed. "Right under our noses . . . *The Compound.* It's a bit 'industrial,' isn't it? But not to the point of being obvious."

"I like it," Ernesto said.

"Me, too," said Lars. "The Compound has my vote."

"Let's give it a day or two and let it soak in," I said. "Next time we get together, we'll put it to a vote."

Everyone seemed happy with this arrangement. In the past few weeks, I'd learned my lesson the hard way, dreading each time I told a new one of my friends that I played guitar and sang for "Mammy Jammer." It was hard to get behind a band if you couldn't get behind the name. And once your music was labeled, it would ride you to the grave—that is, unless you quit and formed another band.

Even then, an old name could haunt you for years—especially if your previous band was better known. Lucky for us, Mammy Jammer had never really left the Portland scene. It would die a short and painless death. Nothing more than an unpleasant memory . . . along with a certain ghost by the name of Mike McKay.

ENTRY FIFTY

I've been surfing the web, trying to find out more info on CJD. It's easier than I thought. PCC has this database called EBSCO Host and I can access all sorts of things from my computer at home. Most of what I've found are articles from medical journals. There's so much information, almost too much to go through. I even found this one article on researchers in France who have already established a link between sheep and a certain type of CJD.

That guy from APHIS obviously hadn't known what he was talking about when he reassured my father. All he had to do was spend a couple of hours surfing the web and he would have seen that scrapie should be a huge concern among ranchers everywhere. God, I swear, the livestock industry is so messed. All those ignorant hicks that don't want to know the truth because it could mean they'd have to change their ways. Kind of like when you try to tell a person holding a hot dog why they shouldn't eat it. They'll pretend not to care, or even get angry. But once they find out what's really inside, they lose their appetite.

Initially, I chose not to eat red meat because I couldn't bear the thought of killing cows and sheep and pigs. They're just as smart as any dog or cat, and most people would cringe at the thought of eating pets. But the whole CJD thing is different. It's a health issue. A personal safety issue. I wonder how many people out there know that CJD isn't just a disease that's affecting the French and the British. Americans are coming down with it more and more. And since doctors can't test for it yet, there's no way to tell if you have it. They have to wait until you die, and then they cut open your skull and check out your brain to see if it's riddled with holes, the telltale sign of CJD.

Today, I've come to find out that lots of other animals are getting this sort of brain-wasting disease, not just cows and sheep. Deer all over the western United States are coming down with it. And fish. There's these farm-raised salmon in Michigan that caught it from run-off near a slaughterhouse.

Next time I visit PHSU, I'm going to bring a notepad full of questions with me. I'm going to ask them why they didn't give my father an autopsy. That would have proved what he'd been telling us all along, that his illness was a form of scrapie. The doctors all humored him, OK, Mr. Fleischer, we'll look into it.

But they didn't. They just wrote him off as an Alzheimer's patient and called it good. Not unlike police detectives who find the wrong killer who's guilty of other equally atrocious crimes, so they let it slide. Meanwhile, the real killer is still out there, and if he's killed once, chances are he'll do it again.

CJD is out there and people are eating burgers and catching it whether they know it or not. US ranchers are no different than UK ranchers. If a cow gets sick, they just call in the meat wagon to butcher it before it's too late. Three or four cows can make or break a small rancher. If he has to destroy them, he's out a lot of money. So he doesn't, instead he passes the buck to the meat packing industry and they pass it on to the people who eat hot dogs and hamburgers.

Americans need to know the risks. They need a "Mad Cowgirl" to tell them like it is. And, I'm just mad enough to do it. If I've got CJD, I'm not going to let myself get swept under the rug at some hospital, buried quietly in a cemetery. This journal is a living testament to what I'm going through. If I die, then they sure as hell better do an autopsy. It will be my dying wish: Cut me open or be damned!

My hands are starting to shake. I've got to quit typing and give it a rest. Ever since that showdown at the Compound, I've started to feel sick again. I think there is a fairly strong link between your emotions and your physical health, at least on a day-to-day level. Strong negative thoughts make it a lot worse. Got to try and keep a positive state of mind.

As soon as I feel up to it, I'm going to start work on that newspaper article. Lars told me to read whatever publication I want to get published in, to get a feel for the kind of writing they want. But I already know, I've been reading the local rags for years. It's between the *Willamette Week*, the *Mercury*, and the *Portland Sun*. One of them is bound to pick up my article. Lars will help me polish it and get it ready for publication.

The other day, he asked why the sudden interest in Mad Cow Disease? I corrected him: Not Mad Cow, *Creutzfeldt-Jakob*. Mad Cow is the bovine version of the same brain-wasting disease. I think Lars might suspect something now. He's really perceptive, much sharper than he looks. If you bumped into him backstage at a nightclub, you'd think he was a bouncer for sure. Then he'd say "excuse me" in Latin and you'd have to eat your words.

ENTRY FIFTY-ONE

Lars is being extra nice to me these days. I know why, and it's kind of sad. I'm in the driver's seat even though we always vote on everything as a band. Lars told me confidentially not to worry about that, every band needs a leader. I was the natural choice, especially considering it was my wheeling and dealing that got us signed. But we haven't reached the finish line yet. There's still an album to be recorded, a few hundred cities to tour. And then a second album and a second tour—maybe around the world, who knows? The point is, we haven't earned our keep yet. AMI showed us the money, now we have to show them the goods.

You know, hearing Lars say that really depressed me. Everything's about the almighty dollar. Bowing down to the golden calf. Whatever happened to art for art's sake? I'm an artist, not a businesswoman. Little strings are being pulled from directions I didn't expect. I'm starting to feel like a glorified marionette.

The other day at practice Lars dropped a hint, admitting that he works at PCC on a part-time basis. He also teaches online for Chemeketa Community College in Salem. That means he has a lot of "flex time" but no benefits. And his pay is about one-third less than full-timers even though he teaches five classes per term and they only teach four. I asked him what he taught and he said Writing 122.

Can you believe it? What a sneak! That's the next comp class I need to complete the writing track at PCC! I asked would the Chemeketa class transfer to PCC? He said yes, of course. All community colleges in Oregon were part of the same system. Go for it!

Thinking about it now, I'm not so sure I want to take any classes in the fall. I probably won't have much time, what with recording the new album and all. I've got more than enough material between my stuff and the old Mammy Jammer stuff that Mike didn't write. Lars seems to think we can get another guitarist and we'll be set to play live shows again.

I'm not so sure. If Mike wrote the guitar parts and came up with a lot of the music, we probably shouldn't use those songs. Definitely, we shouldn't record them. That would leave us wide open for a lawsuit.

Speaking of recording, I got a call from Hart yesterday and he's urging me to take the offer from AMI. He said he could probably squeeze another two hundred out of them because Pentagram Records has just upped the ante by a cool hundred. That brings the grand total up to $800,000 for two albums with an option for a third. I asked Hart if I could use some of it for living expenses and he said sure, but that was up to the band, wasn't it? I detected a little irony in his voice when he said that. He still wanted me to ditch them and move to LA. I laughed. "Alright, alright. Forget about it. I'll never move from Portland. We've already got an 'in' here, this place called 'The Cell.'"

Hart had never even heard of it. He brought up Seattle. Would I ever consider relocating further north? According to his sources, they've got some decent studios up there. The grunge movement pumped a lot of money and hype into Bell Town. And now that grunge was dead, a lot of the studios were hurting for business; a band like ours with connections could get a sweet rate, especially for a whole album.

I asked Hart what he thought of our new name and he said it had a certain ring to it. Kind of "underground." I guess that's a polite way of saying it's not the kind of name people will immediately warm up to. We'll have to win them over with our music first.

Hart said that we should keep playing live shows if we get a big enough venue to make it worth our while. Knowing me, I'd generate a buzz so that when our CD came out next year, the band would already have a grass-roots following. Just be careful not to get lumped in with the post-grunge scene in Seattle. That's the kiss of death. If I got a call from any trades, don't even say the word grunge. Instead, tell them all my techno influences. Stick to the newer stuff and drop a few compliments about musicians in my favorite bands. They would definitely hear about it, and if they warmed up to me, so much the better. At this point, it's all about networking.

I said I thought that was Hart's job and he laughed. Yeah, well, to a degree. On the business side. But I was on the *other* side, hanging out with musicians, the darlings, and that's where all the real action was. I must have sounded intimidated when I heard that because he told me there was no need to worry. Just go with my instincts. I was a natural. Musicians could spot a kiss-ass a mile away. But I was the opposite of that, thank God. I had integrity. Why, in less than a month, I'd hooked up with two of the most powerful people in the music industry without even trying!

I asked if he meant Tawny along with Jack and he said yes, of course. She was a prominent "broker" in the field. She even had a nickname, "The Baroness."

When I asked why the allusion to royalty, Hart seemed evasive. He told me about her line of work, how she sniffed out young talented musicians and groomed them for the major labels. She'd even gone so far as putting up a generous advance if necessary—all her own money— on the condition that she'd earn "points" once the album was released. Hart had been the middleman between her and industry executives for the past five years, and he'd done quite handsomely by her. It hadn't been hard. Once her name was mentioned, the office doors of presidents opened like magic. Among the industry elite, Tawny Davenport's nose for talent had reached legendary proportions.

Hart paused, as if deliberating whether or not to go on. "As a matter of fact," he said, lowering his voice with an affected hush, "she was all set to groom *you*. That is, until your show at the Del Rey triggered all the offers."

This bit of news caught me by surprise. So Jack had, in essence, sidestepped Tawny's interests by passing out copies of our demo to "friends." Once the offers started to roll in, she'd become the odd-woman out. There was a moment of silence, and then I had to ask: How much would Tawny have been willing to fork over for my advance, more than AMI's offer?

Hart's laugh boomed deep and full over the line: "Julia, Julia, Julia. There, you see! That's *precisely* what I'm talking about! You're a natural!"

When I hung up, I wasn't quite sure what to think. The rest of the guys would accept eight hundred from AMI in a heartbeat. They'd even let me take out a "comfortable" chunk for my living expenses while we recorded. You could see it in their eyes: I was their meal ticket, they had to keep me happy at all costs. From now on, I'd never really know what any of them thought of me. Not unless I kept my ear to the ground or put out spies. But that would be paranoid and wrong.

It's too late to pull the "sensitive artist" routine. I knew what would happen from the very first moment I stepped onto the stage at Crystal Ballroom. I just hadn't expected it to happen overnight. The wheels of industry are turning. Julia Fleischer's an investment, a commodity. A piece of property for companies to buy and sell.

And what, pray tell, is the harm in that? David Bowie incorporated himself into an actual corporation and then sold it on Wall Street for a killing. This kind of thing happens all the time. *Money, money, money.* It makes the world go round. And my songs are no exception.

Be that as it may, I've almost reached the breaking point. I just want to disconnect my phone, crawl under a rock and recharge my batteries. Reconnect with my old friends, real people who appreciate me for me.

Like Jeffrey. I'm supposed to meet him for drinks in a few hours. He seemed really excited when I called him up last night. I kept the conversation brief: Hey, what's up? *Yada, yada, yada.* Let's get together soon.

He mentioned tomorrow night and I hinted that I could stop by

Ringlers to pick him up when he got off his shift, but he'd said that probably wasn't such a good idea. We could meet someplace instead. Around nine. How about Old Town, I liked Old Town, right?

Yeah, yeah, I said, but I was kind of bummed. We still had unresolved issues and everything was coming back. An ickiness that made my heart feel muffled. Jeff tried to sound all peppy to make up for it: Hung Far Low. Nine o'clock.

Old Town is quite a ways from Ringlers, a "comfortable" distance as the crow flies, and that's no accident. Jeffrey anticipated what the "new Jules" was capable of. He probably heard all about me through the grapevine.

The music scene in Portland is worse than a high school cafeteria at lunchtime. And this week Julia Fleischer's the dish. All the local rags are blazing with news about Hart and his fancy wheeling and dealing, pushing up The Compound's advance with a bidding war.

Despite all his careful, passive-aggressive maneuvering, Jeff made one very large tactical error: The new Jules is not only reckless, she's crafty. If he didn't want me to meet at Ringlers, that could only mean one thing: *You-know-who* must be working.

What time is it? Seven-thirty. Perfect. Off I go, straight to Ringlers. I still need to have a word with Jeff's little "pole" vaulter.

ENTRY FIFTY-TWO

Jeff thinks I should get help. That's what he said last night. He wouldn't even have a drink with me because of the scene I made at Ringlers.

Nadja had been there just as I'd thought, serving the tables in front. I recognized her from the photo at Jeff's house immediately and went over to a table in her area. I think she recognized me as well, but she pretended not to. I ordered a beer and started into this article in the *Willamette Week* on organic food and how it's all a scam, how it costs more energy to grow one organic tomato than a whole bag of regular ones.

Nadja brought over my beer and I said, "Thanks . . . *Nadja*." She said no problem and walked off. I think she was starting to get worried. I kept staring at her, giving her the evil eye. Finally, she came over and asked if there was anything else she could get me. I said, "Yeah, how about a stick of butter."

"Butter?"

"Yeah, so I can grease up this pint and shove it up your ass, all the way into the red, you whore."

Just like that. Totally deadpan.

It took a second for the English to compute in Nadja's brain. I watched her expression change from puzzlement to shock to anger. I smiled sweetly, blinking my eyelashes to compound the effect. She snorted indignantly and stamped her foot, muttering some foreign curse. Off she went, shaking that fat ass behind her.

The manager came out sooner than I expected, his head bobbing up and down, a flurry of dreadlocks and hempware with a pencil tucked behind one ear. When he got to my table, he leaned over, informing me in hushed tones that it was time to go.

I reared my head back in surprise: *What! You're booting me?* He told me to drop the innocent act, I knew perfectly well. My behavior was unacceptable. I couldn't speak to the wait staff like that—not here, or anywhere else for that matter.

Evidently the next table had overheard the whole altercation. Some girl got up and went over to comfort Nadja, who was crying. That's when I noticed everyone over there was dressed in the same kind of cheesy sweats that I'd seen in the snapshots and they were speaking in some other language. I asked the manager if he was going to believe a bunch of Pollacks or a patriotic American like me.

At this point, some old grey haired dude at the table started berating me in what I assume was Polish. I stared him right in the eye and told him that if he had something to say to me, speak English or Spanish. This is America. If I ever visited Palookaville, then I'd be sure to speak whatever dialect of Pig Latin he was speaking. He threw his napkin down on the table, knocking over two glasses of beer. One of them rolled off and shattered on the floor.

This got the manager's attention. He told grey-haired Polish dude to leave right along with me. Well, this just totally enraged dude. He shouted in broken English that I'd just told his daughter to put a beer glass in a very disrespectable place. The manager went back to the bar, picked up the telephone, held it up. If we all weren't out in ONE MINUTE, he was calling the police.

So much for having a word with Nadja. She was on duty anyway. It would have been a one-sided conversation. Honestly, I don't understand what Jeffrey saw in her. She looked like she'd grown up on a diet of fat sandwiches and curdled milk. Zits all over her face, bags under her eyes. No wonder she let Jeff peel the onion. It probably smelled better than her moneymaker.

When Jeff finally caught up with me at Hung Far Low, he didn't look pleased. He sat down at the bar. "That was a really terrible thing you did," he said, lighting up a cigarette. "I almost got fired. And now, Nadja's father says he's going to teach me a lesson." "Well," I said, "he's probably not too happy about what you did to his daughter."

Jeff shook his head sadly. He said he'd hoped we could get past all that. He'd really been looking forward to seeing me, hearing about all the new and exciting things happening in my life. He took a package out of his backpack, set it down on the counter. I asked him what it was and he said a gift, he'd picked it out special for me. Then he said I had problems, seriously. I should consider getting help. Like from a professional.

After Jeff had gone, I ordered another drink and tore open the package. It was a big hardback book. When I turned it over and saw the front cover, I couldn't believe my eyes: *The Holy Bible.* Oh, man, that was too weird. Jeff had bought me an expensive copy of the King James Bible. He wasn't even religious, so far as I knew. I wondered if he'd decided on the gift before or after what happened in the bar. He could very easily have picked it up on his way to Old Town. Powell's was right across the street.

I hadn't so much as looked at a Bible in years. I flipped open the cover and started reading Genesis quietly to myself until I got to the part that went, "And God said, Let there be light: and there was light. And God saw the light, that it was good: and God divided the light from the darkness."

Two guys down the bar were staring. They seemed offended that I was reading the Bible. Maybe it was just a little ironic. This was the only bar in town with a huge statue of Buddha sitting cross-legged amidst bottles of liquor. I asked the guys what their problem was. One of them sneered, "You can always tell a leopard by its spots." What? I asked. Did you just say what I think you said? His buddy put up a hand wearily, apologized, they were both having a bad day.

But I wasn't satisfied. I told them if they didn't mind their own business, I'd sick Jesus on their asses. *Je-sus*! Then I pounded the rest of my G&T and went back to reading.

God was one busy dude on the first six days. The world went from being a lump of mud spinning around and around in the dark, to this place literally bursting with life: *Poof!*, you're a bird. *Poof!* you're a whale. Be fruitful and multiply!

At this point, God decided to create something beautiful in his image, after his likeness: *Poof!* you're a man! Be fruitful, overpopulate! And while you're at it, would you mind watching the store while I'm away?

That's how we became these wardens for God, naming everything and having dominion. Go figure.

ENTRY FIFTY-THREE
A lot of business-type stuff has happened over that last five days. First of all, I talked with the band and we decided to take AMI's offer. The contract came by Fed Ex yesterday. I took it to a famous entertainment lawyer downtown and had him look it over. He said it was very well written, one of the best he'd seen. I still had all the rights to my written music; that's where the money was, at least in the long run. He thought Hart's commission was a bit steep, even by LA standards, but it sounded as though he had done a lot of work facilitating the "bidding war" so it was more or less understandable. I asked whether it was reasonable to try to get him to take his commission out of the profits rather than the advance and the lawyer said that wasn't very likely.

After skimming through the whole contract, he circled a clause buried in the middle, a "brokerage fee" of $50,000. Did I know anything about that? I leaned back in my chair. So Tawny was still trying to get her teeth into me. That snake, Hart, hadn't even mentioned it.

Man, that really rubbed me the wrong way. If she would have asked me outright and made a case for herself things might have been different. But this was underhanded. Almost like "protection money" from the mob. I told my lawyer to cross it out and see what happened.

Despite his assurances that the contract was airtight, he still made over a dozen suggestions and then gave me a bill for his fee. He said that I could pay him after I got the commission as we'd agreed. Or he would cut his rate by 30% if I paid him today.

Yeah, right. Good one. As if I had that kind of money I could just throw around. Besides, he'd agreed to work on spec. That meant I didn't owe him a penny if the contract was never signed. And yet here he was acting like he was doing me this tremendous favor by offering a substantial discount.

Lawyers, agents, brokers: they were all blood suckers. How could this guy look me in the eye and smile like that? He knew full well the contract might not go through and he just wanted to make sure he got his money. Sneaky sneak! I felt like a wizard pitting one dragon against another. The secret was in achieving a balance so the evil forces were always on different sides, attacking each other. Because if they ever got together and ganged up on you . . . forget about it. You were history.

I sent back the contract to Hart by fax and he hammered it out, conceding about half of the points that my lawyer in Portland had suggested, then he Fed Exed me a new contract and I had my lawyer look at that; he agreed to half of what Hart had done, etc., etc. This went on for another two days until the contract was ready to be signed.

I called up the band and we met at the lawyer's office. It felt so good when everything was finished, like a huge weight had lifted off my shoulders. We went out and celebrated, drinking ourselves silly until two o'clock in the afternoon, even Lars. I don't even remember what happened after it got dark.

The next day, I woke up at the Compound. Ernesto and Niles were already up drinking coffee. We all had these monstrous hangovers but it was beautiful, the ache of victory. Niles said it was already about six in the evening, did I feel like heading over to Pub At The End Of The Universe? Hair of the dog. He smiled, baring his fangs. A Scottish werewolf in America.

The check came four days later. When Lars and I took it to the bank, the representative suggested we put the money in seven separate accounts to get everything FDIC insured. That was so weird seeing all that money. It finally sunk in: We were seven hundred thousand dollars richer (900K minus all the fees we owed).

The best part is, we can keep it all, barring an Act of God. So if we only use, say, $400,000 recording, the rest is ours. Everything will come out of the profits from our album once it gets released sometime early next year, so it's not exactly free.

AMI's been calling me non-stop, but I haven't returned any of their calls yet. They want me to fly down to LA and discuss my plans for the album. Hart says I don't have to, but it would be the professional thing to do, an act of "good faith," whatever that means. When Hart sensed I wasn't overly enthusiastic about the idea, he said that I might also be able to weasel more money out of them, maybe score a credit card for dinners with "business associates" of mine, which is a fancy way of saying other famous musicians that come through town looking to get sauced.

If I do end up flying down, I'm not staying at Tawny's house again, that's for sure. No more black & white nights for this girl.

ENTRY FIFTY-FOUR

For the past week or so, I've been pretty much living in the Compound. It turned out that Lars held the lease, not Mike, so Mike got all of his shit out. Lars said it was cool if I wanted to crash there, like, indefinitely.

I called up this real estate agent in Northwest about a loft. She said tons of things are open right now, especially in the Pearl District. Ruth and I are going to look at places this weekend. Since The Cell is located right in the heart of the Pearl District, it would make sense to find a place there.

When Hart called up the owner and discussed The Cell's technical specs, he seemed to feel it was fine, but he insisted we take the producer that Tawny had picked for us. I was kind of surprised to hear that. I thought she'd pretty much washed her hands of everything.

The producer's name is "Dig Low" and he's done all this work for practically every famous techno band on the planet. He's got a list of credentials as long as the Dead Sea Scrolls.

That's fine with me because obviously I'm not planning to work with Cynthia anymore, what with Mike being out of the band and all. I haven't heard what Dig Low is charging these days. If he wants points, he can put his lips together and blow. Every day, my piece of the pie keeps getting smaller and smaller. Now that Julia Fleischer has hit the big time, everybody wants a taste.

Today, I drove out to Fry's Electronics and bought myself a laptop. It's really sweet with a built-in mouse. A Sony with a zillion bytes. I'm typing this entry on it right now.

The midget keyboard will take a little getting used to. If I never warm up to it, the salesman said I could get another bigger, roomier keyboard and plug it into the laptop. I still have to get a printer, but I'm not in a hurry to do that. I haven't proofed anything yet. I'm kind of afraid to go back and look at all the stuff I've written. Some of it's a little on the harsh side.

As of this entry, the word count is: 64,137. Can you believe it? I just figured out I could check for a word count in the "tools" pull-down menu. My computer did it in about one second. Lars called right after that, and when I told him how many words I'd written, he just about passed out. He said that I'm every writing instructor's dream.

"*Wet* dream?" I asked. He wasn't so sure about that. But he said I'd inspired him to pull his old novel out of the closet and start writing again. *Furor scribendi.* My enthusiasm was contagious.

ENTRY FIFTY-FIVE

Holy cow crap, I didn't know we had to pay taxes! Hart said better safe than sorry, we should sock away forty percent, then wait and see what kind of magic his accountant could work for us. I told him that was cool, we'd get our own accountant, but thanks.

Hart seemed a little hurt that I didn't trust him. I almost changed my mind and waffled. Then I remembered what Jack had told me, how much money I'd already made for management, the exorbitant fee. *Boo-hoo-hoo.* Let poor Mr. Drake cry all the way to his estate planner's office.

Moving on to more important things: The band, recording. We're getting down to the wire. Only $460,000 left to produce two albums. $180,000 apiece. That's chicken feed compared to the nine hundred we started out with. I'm tempted to call up that entertainment lawyer downtown and run these numbers by him to see what he thinks.

Even though I'm grateful to Hart for all he's done, I still can't trust him. Not after that sneaky move he tried to pull with Tawny's "brokerage fee."

ENTRY FIFTY-SIX

Talked to Dig Low on the phone this afternoon. He's pretty smooth.

Maybe he sensed my sketchiness about all that's happened with our advance because he started out by saying that he'd seen our show at the Del Rey, Tawny had loaned him her videotape, and he was sold on us. We had the potential to become a household name if we wanted. And that's another thing: the name. But we could talk about that later.

Talk about what? I asked. He said "The Compound" was cool, but he had a few other suggestions, names that might go over a little better in Middle America. What a pisser! This guy had balls! I told him thanks but we were sticking with the name. It wasn't up for discussion. He laughed and said right, right, just an idea. And speaking of fresh ideas, since he was so impressed with my voice and moves, he'd be willing to do the first album on spec. I knew what was coming: *Points*, he wanted points. When he tried to sell me on it, I could feel this shiver of frustration go down the back of my scalp. What a drag. So many sets of teeth trying to get a bite.

Dig's deep, sexy voice kept working me, massaging the feminine side of my ego, messing with my head until I almost wanted to scream. He had this way of flattering you into complacency. A sprinkling of East LA gangster mixed with the polished delivery of a Harvard law professor. He knew all the right names, all the right words, all the right buttons, and he pushed them until you felt like you were the most important person in the universe. Every word calculated to make you feel good about yourself and good about him at the same time.

But whenever you questioned him about something, calling attention to a fine point, there was nothing to grab onto, he just kept talking, wearing you down, overwhelming you with facts, figures, charm.

To close the deal, "Mr. Low" mentioned that the last album he produced had already gone platinum. And he predicted it would go double platinum before it was done. "So, Jules, tell me, would you like to have a platinum record on your bedroom wall?" I laughed. Maybe the bathroom. He totally busted up over that one. A playful tone had crept into his voice, as if he sensed he'd finally won me over.

After that, Dig eased off, playing it cool. Before I knew what had happened, I'd just hung up the phone and agreed to pay him the points he asked for: Talk to Hart, get it down on paper.

I was ready to go to sleep and forget everything. Time for a marathon snooze.

ENTRY FIFTY-SEVEN

Oh, and there's more. This whole thing just keeps getting worse and worse. I found out yesterday. Now that we've got all this money and we're not working with Cynthia, The Cell is trying to ream us, charging these astronomical fees. Kobo Yoshikawa, the owner, said the additional costs are related to support staff, engineers, technicians . . . stuff like that. I told him we'd get back to him.

Meanwhile, Lars said we should snoop around and see what else is out there. But he emphasized that finding a place to record isn't our top priority right now. We've got to get all the songs down *cold* before we even set foot in a studio. That will save massive amounts of capital. So I guess even if I end up taking a loft downtown, I'll still practically be living at the Compound.

I was kind of hoping to buy a new car, but I'm going to hold off for now. Charging my rent and living expenses on the account is bad enough. I don't want the rest of the guys to start feeling resentful. So I'll keep on driving my beater. That's cool. I'm kind of attached to her anyway. But I'm definitely going to go ahead and replace her radiator now that summer's here. That should only cost about five or six hundred dollars.

All this shoptalk between Kobo and Hart and Dig is making my head spin. I gave Lars Hart's telephone number. He can hammer out all the final details with Dig, The Cell, etc.

Or maybe Dig can fly up and scope out the Portland scene for us. With all his experience, I'll bet he could see through Kobo's smokescreens instantly—that is, if Kobo really is jacking up prices because he knows we've got AMI funny money to throw around.

Let the vultures do what they may. I'm rinsing my hands of the whole thing. No more journal space wasted on corporate masturbation or the precious "bottom line." Screw all the lawyers and managers and agents and producers. Deep and hard. I don't care anymore. If this whole deal went up in smoke tomorrow, I'd almost be glad. It's draining me dry. I haven't picked up my guitar in a week.

There he is, resting in the corner. My boy, Martin. I'm going over there right now and take him out of his case!

Come to me, baby. Come to Jules. I'll let you touch mine if you let me touch yours. So smooth. *Mmmm.* I'm running my fingers down the back of your neck, lingering on your favorite fret, squeezing it, tugging at your heart strings until your voice fills the air, deep and true.

They don't care about us. They only care about themselves. But we love each other, you and me. We're still best friends, right? Martin?

ENTRY FIFTY-EIGHT

Ruth went with me yesterday to look at apartments. Man, it was such a breeze. All we did was walk into this real estate office—a really nice one downtown.

The agent showed me these pictures of spaces and where they were on a map of Portland. I made it clear right from the outset that I wanted to stay in the Pearl District. She said that was a great decision; it was so hopping these days with all the galleries and restaurants. The big century-old warehouses created a definite mood.

Ironically, because so many artists had moved there, attracted by the ample space and low rent, the area had gentrified practically overnight and now the rents were comparable with—even higher than—many neighborhoods downtown.

Those are the breaks, the agent said. It's certainly not bad for business! People aren't just renting apartments, they're *buying.* It's the difference between a liability and an asset. You should think about it, Ms. Fleischer. A loft on Everett or Flanders could conceivably double in value over the next five or six years.

"Yeah, and if I'm lucky, I could kill two birds with one stone."

"How do you mean?"

"Not only could I get a great living space for myself, I could also push out some starving artist and watch them freeze to death right in front of my building!"

The agent laughed nervously. Her eyes darted to Ruth for help. I had to fight a strong urge to get up and walk out. What a black hearted bitch. Most likely from California, center of the yuppie universe, judging by the way she talked so fast with that unmistakable San Fernando twang.

Her fee wasn't bad, though: One month's rent plus an application fee of $50, which was refundable if I took one of the apartments she was showing.

After being dragged through the first two places, I promptly fell in love with the third—this amazing loft above an art gallery on the corner of Flanders and 13th. The building's really old. It has curved brick archways with the biggest windows I've ever seen. And there's a big steel door hanging in the living room area that looks like it goes to a blast furnace or something. "Very outré," said the realtor. "The owner obviously has taste. He owns the gallery downstairs." When I asked if the door lead anywhere, she assured me it had been bricked off.

I didn't even know spaces this cool existed in Portland! Brand new wood floors . . . a spiral staircase leading up to the bedroom. It's all open, with a ceiling that's probably thirty feet high. I asked how much and the agent said an even two per month.

When I heard that I practically fell over. Two *thousand*? Maybe in LA or New York but in Portland? Lil ole P-town? That was about twice what I'd been planning on spending. But then I remembered what Hart had said about having guests over and entertaining. I could throw some killer parties to help offset the cost.

I asked the agent if there was a month-to-month lease and she said no, unfortunately, but she could probably talk the landlord down from a one year to a six-month.

"OK, fine," I said. "I'll take it."

Both Ruth's and the agent's eyes bugged out. I don't think either one knew I had that kind of cash to throw around.

Once the paperwork was signed, Ruth and I went out to lunch (on me) at Karumazushi. We started off by ordering this big expensive bottle of chilled sake. I'd never had sake over ice before but it was damn good. Much better than the hot stuff. I took one look at the sushi menu and said alright, one of everything.

Ruth ate most of the weird pieces when they came. I gave a couple of deep fried shrimp heads to these guys sitting next to us. They were very discreet, but macking hard on us, nonetheless. Ruth thought they were hotties. I wasn't so sure about that; they looked too formal in those suits. Ruth said they were expensive, probably Armani, right out of *GQ*. They asked us what we'd been doing today, and I said I'd just signed a lease on a loft.

The cuter of the two, a blond with a pretty boy mug, wanted to know what we did for a living and Ruth said she was working at Spree Athletic Wear as an assistant to the VP of Corporate Promotions. Instead of asking her what that was, the guy turned to me. I said I was unemployed at the moment.

Ruth laughed and said *hardly*, she's the lead singer for The Compound. We'd just got signed to AMI. I kicked her under the sushi bar for that and gave her the raised "shut up" eyebrow. But she seemed to feel these guys were harmless. They introduced themselves formally then and said they were having a party tonight, would we like to come? Ruth said sure without even asking me.

She had it bad for Peter, the dark haired one. Ken, the blond one, wrote a time and an address on the back of his business card. There was this street name I recognized and then a "slip" number. I asked what's a "slip"? He said the party was on his yacht down in the marina. Dress casual. Then he and Richard had to go. They shook hands with us and took off.

ENTRY FIFTY-NINE

I was late getting to the party because Jack called right as I was heading out the door. He sounded really depressed like he wanted to talk, so I went back in my room and shut the door.

He said the tour was falling apart. He'd already gone through two bass players and they both sucked and now it looked like Shamir might need some kind of operation. Must be some bad-ass bug, I joked, but Jack got really serious. He said the doctors had been wrong. It wasn't his stomach at all but something to do with his liver and he might die so shut up. Last time Jack saw him in the hospital his eyes had been bright yellow.

Oh my God, I said, I didn't realize. Jack said it's OK. But it was serious. The doctors think Shamir ate some kind of worm that burrowed up from his stomach and now was camping out in his liver. Antibiotics weren't good enough, they were going to have to open him up and pull it out.

When Jack said that, I really started to squirm. OK, fine. Time to change the subject. Had Tawny made it out there yet?

He said no, but they were hooking up in New York when he played the Symphony Space. I asked how big was it? He said a little bigger than the Del Rey, but classier, with reserved seating. Tickets had gone for $52 dollars a pop and it was already sold out. Damn, I said. That's sweet! Yeah, Jack agreed, but he'd better get the bassist problem smoothed out or there would be a riot. His last show had been a disaster. I asked if there was any talent in New York and he said, sure, that was the good thing about it. They already had this studio guy lined up to meet with them the afternoon before the show. He was good. A ringer. He'd sat in for two songs on Red Angel's sixth album.

We had a nice talk after that. It was the old Jack, the *real* Jack that I'd almost fallen in love with. He didn't apologize for the last phone call, but I could tell he felt bad. He said that he wanted me to warm up for the band at this two-hundred year old concert hall they were going to play next month in New Orleans and I said, OK, I'd think about it.

But there was no way it would happen, and we both knew it. Jack said he'd heard I'd gotten $900,000 for the first three albums and congratulations. I corrected him: the first *two* albums. There was an option for the third. Jack laughed; didn't I know that was the same thing? He asked if I had a cell phone number and I said no, but I was planning on getting a cell right away. Then he moved on to what I was wearing. *Panties and bra.* Are you in your room? he asked. *Yeah.* In your . . . bed? *Yeah.* Lying on your back? *Yeah.* Miss me? *Oh yeah.* How much? *This much.* Miss me more. *This much?* More! *Ahhhhhhhh.* More, more, more . . .

After we both finished, I lay back, caught my breath. It was almost better this way, over the phone. I didn't have to worry about getting attacked by a stray needle or a hundred things that go bump in the night.

Jack asked about that journal I'd been writing, was he in it? I said sure, in lots of places. He liked that. I asked how Tawny's project was coming and he said fine, he guessed. They never talked about it anymore.

Gradually, I worked toward what I'd been planning on telling him, about the heroin, etc., how it could potentially hurt both our careers.

Yeah, he agreed. He'd already thought about it, but there was nothing he could do. The tapes were on the west coast and he was on the east. But when he got back, first thing, he was going to find them and snag anything over the top. I told him that was a very good idea. And while he was at it, maybe he could grab the tapes of me having sex. He laughed nervously. How did I know about that? Well, I said, just a hunch. He lowered his voice. Sometimes Tawny could get a little rough. She was a Grade A sex fiend. A chip off the old block, just like her father. Trust those Brits: The most perverted race on earth—even before the Germans and the Japanese. Probably all that Druidic blood still coursing through their veins.

I felt better all of a sudden. *Tawny.* So it had been her, she'd been to blame. My curiosity got the best of me and I had to ask what she'd done. Any toys? No, Jack said, just her hands and a tube of K-Y. She was very good with her hands. Or very bad, depending on how you looked at it.

Jack wanted to change the subject, so I let him. It was easier talking to him now that I knew he hadn't been the one. We talked about a lot of things: money, politics, art. He wanted to know if I had any books to recommend. Novels, preferably. I told him to get *Jesus' Son* by Denis Johnson. It was right about his speed. Then I asked what he'd been reading lately. He said he'd gone back to poetry—Ginsberg and Blake, mainly—but he was ready for a switch to prose.

I sat up. *William* Blake? Jack laughed, who else? Oh my God, I screamed, he's my favorite poet of all time! Have you checked out the "Marriage of Heaven and Hell?" Sure, Jack said he'd read that. But his favorite was "America, A Prophecy." That's where he'd gotten the name for his band. He cleared his throat: "Fiery the Angels rose & as they rose deep thunder rolled around their shores, indignant, burning with the fires of Orc."

I clapped, jumping up and down on my bed. Wonderful! Jack asked how I'd gotten turned on to Blake and I said that I'd read about his poetry in *No One Here Gets Out Alive,* the biography of Jim Morrison.

Jack sneered, that piece of garbage? Lies, half truths. Nobody could ever write a book on Morrison and capture his true personality on paper. Val Kilmer had come much closer on film, so close at times it was almost eerie. Especially his voice, a certain presence behind the eyes. Still, on the whole, *The Doors: The Movie* had been Hollywood imitating Hollywood.

Jack had personally known dozens of people who'd hung out with Morrison and they'd all had something different to say about him: The guy had been a chameleon, a shape-shifter, always looking for a new angle. And he'd been evil. More evil than Jack, himself, and that was saying something.

I said, Hey!, be careful what you say about my friends! Jack Thorne's not evil. Slightly problematic as a human being, but not evil.

When he heard that, Jack totally cracked up. From the sounds coming out of my receiver, you would have thought he was a raving lunatic. He must have laughed for a whole minute. I pictured him wiping the tears out of his eyes. He said he loved me and wished to God I could fly out to New York and be with him. He'd rather hang out with me than Tawny any day of the week. I was different. He liked the way I made him feel, even days after he'd been with me. A little bit of something rubbed off on him and lingered, he couldn't say what exactly. But it was good. *Really* good. Better than smack.

Ruth and I were supposed to meet at Hung Far Low and then head over to the docks for the party. Unfortunately because of the call with Jack, I was over an hour late. She wasn't there, so I drove to the marina and ran down to the docks. This big yacht was chugging out into the river.

With my eyes, I followed the trail of bubbles from its big engine back to a slip along the far side of the marina. Sure enough, it had the same number that Ken had scribbled on the back of his business card.

Shoot! I'd just missed the boat!

As I was dragging my heels back up the stairs, totally bummed at myself for being a lousy friend, I happened to run into these catering guys who were loading boxes into a boat.

Here was my chance. I asked them if they were taking the stuff to a party out on the big yacht that had just left. They said, yes, they were, had I been invited? I said yes, but they didn't seem convinced. My appearance was less than stunning. I hadn't really had time to get ready, no make-up. Just this silk shirt and my leathers, which were starting to get a little on the "gamy" side.

I showed them Ken's business card and they said, OK, follow them. They took me with them and about a hundred bottles of champagne. The yacht was already out in the middle of the river, chugging full speed ahead, leaving a wake that stretched from shore to shore. When I saw the name spelled in big gold letters across the back, it made me want to puke: *Yuppie Scum.* How could anyone have the nerve to actually name their boat that? To me, it said all the wrong things: self-deprecating, but in a really smug way.

My initial bad impression was only reinforced by what I found on the boat. A big disgusting swirl of yuppie scum, all manner of it, dressed in the most obnoxious "casual wear."

No sign of Ruth. I walked around for at least twenty minutes without any luck. People looked at me like I was some kind of genetic mutation. I started wishing I'd never come.

And then, right as I was getting ready to give up and resign myself to a night alone at the bar, who should I run into, but Gretchen and Alex! They were talking with this group of the nerdiest looking geeks I had ever seen. Dressed in matching Intel baseball caps. They all took one look at me in my black motorcycle boots and leather pants and whatever homicidal look I happened to have on my face and kind of went, "Yeah, OK, right" . . . and went back to their conversation.

But I held my ground—crossing my arms, impatiently tapping the heel of my boot that boomed like a timpani on the hollow metal deck. Gretchen exchanged a quick glance with Alex; he nodded and she took me by the arm, escorting me off to one side to chat. Was I, by chance, looking for Ruth? She was talking to some guy out on the poop deck.

I kind of did a doubletake and asked Gretchen if she meant the bathroom. She tittered this annoying new laugh I'd never heard before and said, well, *nooooooo.* Just go right over there, up those stairs out onto that little balcony.

Without saying another word, Gretchen went back to her group of friends and picked up where she'd left off, as if I'd never even been there. I couldn't believe it. What a cow! I stalked off toward the poop deck and, sure enough, there was Ruth, trying to put the moves on Richard.

Alright, that did it. I'd seen enough. I marched straight toward the nearest bar and proceeded to get sauced, all the way up to the gills.

When Ruth finally caught up with me, I was shouting at some loser down the bar, telling him he could take his microprocessors and fuck off! They were probably the same size as the one in his shorts!

Needless to say, my "inappropriate behavior" didn't exactly help

Ruth's chances with any of the Ritchie Riches aboard. I guess I pretty much put a dent in her evening.

Sorry, honey! If you click your heels together three times and say "there's no place like home" you might even end up out in Beaver Town with Gretch, ignoring your old friends while you get ahead. "Let's play musical wives, shall we? Strap on those knee pads, ladies, open wide, and remember: *No teeth!*" All so hubby can get that big promotion he's been wanting.

And why not? Stranger things have been known to happen. Especially in the Silicon Forest, where, contrary to popular belief, money *does* grow on trees.

ENTRY SIXTY

Got this really harsh email from Tawny today. She didn't mention anything about my lawyer nixing the so-called brokerage fee, but it's pretty much inferred. I owe her three grand for all the clothes she bought me. That seems a little steep, but I'm not going to sweat it. I'll send off a check today, along with an extra three grand just to show my appreciation for all she's done for me and the band. Hopefully that will get her off my back.

In the email, Tawny mentioned that she really needed the release for her documentary. There's no way in hell I'm going to sign that thing. Not after what happened at her place. She totally took advantage of me and I never want to see her again. And there's something really sinister about the way she went about it. A sadistic inference hanging in the balance: "I own you."

I wish Jack could help. From what he said on the phone, it definitely sounds like Tawny's got some kinky video footage of me when I was butt-naked and strung out. Maybe I'll call Jack again. He was there when Tawny worked me over, but he was also strung out. He probably doesn't remember what happened either. In a way, he's a victim almost as much as I am.

If Tawny sends me another dark email like the one today, I'm going to call her up and just say, "Look, I'll give you another 44K if you just hand over the tapes." It would be worth it. But then there'd be no guarantee she hadn't made copies.

Oh, God, this is really starting to feel like blackmail. I should come clean with my lawyer. He'd understand. Nothing new under the sun. Those tapes could really come back and bite me once the first album is released and we go on tour. It would feed right into the "bad girl" persona I've been cultivating and then push the whole thing over the top. In a morally fickle country like America, you're flirting with disaster whenever you play that role. Public opinion can flip-flop overnight. I've seen it happen so many times with movie stars and pop singers.

No matter what, I've got to patch things up with "The Baroness." Now I understand why they call her that (even though she's more of a robber baron). I wish I'd never met her. Then none of this would have happened.

ENTRY SIXTY-ONE

Ruth helped me move in yesterday. Niles and Ernesto also pitched in with the heavy stuff. I told them it was their apartment, too; they could stop by any time. I'm getting one of those refrigerators with a beer tap on it for kegs. And a fully stocked wet bar. *Mi casa su casa.* Party central. Like Hart said, I want to do a little networking, and what better place to do it than here!

I've never had a place like this before. It's amazing. I met the gallery owner yesterday, who's also my landlord. His name is Mélange. I said, oh, that's a beautiful name and he said why, thank you. He'd changed it from Richard because he never felt like it fit his personality, which was a mixture of lots of different things. Besides, he couldn't possibly keep a name that shortened to "Dick."

Since I have all the money in the bank and our new accountant said to spend as much as I could before next fall in order to reduce my taxes, I paid the first six months up front. Mélange couldn't believe it; he said I was already the perfect tenant. I laughed when he said that, don't be too sure. I was totally forthcoming about the parties, etc., and he said they'd be no problem at all because there weren't any other tenants in the building. In fact, there aren't any other apartment buildings on the block. So who would complain? And since we were on the subject, he might as well warn me that it gets loud some days over at the construction site, this huge one-block gaping hole in the ground where they're building a high rise. I didn't think I'd be able to hear the construction from here, and Mélange said it's more like "white noise." I love these artistic types; they have the nicest way of putting things.

Downstairs in the gallery, there's this amazing art show going on right now. I'm on the third/fourth floor and it's on the first/second. Technically, Mélange isn't the landlord for the whole building, but the rest of it isn't being used for anything right now. His gallery downstairs has all these glass sculptures on display.

Upstairs, the exhibit is called "Lindow Revisited," done by an artist from Iceland. This little plaque explained how he got inspired by a two thousand year old man that had been pulled out of this bog in England. Archaeologists could tell his throat had been cut. All the sculptures have to do with Lindow man's body parts. They're super creepy—especially one that shows the inside of his stomach.

Because the primary medium is glass, the artist was able to illuminate some of the pieces inwardly. The biggest one, set up in the middle of the room, is life-size. There's this really ancient-looking boat with glass leaking out of it. And if you look closely, you can make out Lindow Man, floating in his watery coffin.

The whole thing glows and part of it even changes color. From the way the glass was blown, with bubbles and ripplets inside, you'd swear it was dark, peaty water rising up through the mist.

Ruth said she hates the entire exhibit; she wants nothing to do with it. Especially the creepy dead guy upstairs. Finding him was an evil omen. Digging his remains out of that bog was bad luck; but shipping glass replicas around the world takes it to a new level of depravity—no different than a snuff film or Michael Jackson collecting the Elephant Man's bones.

I guess I can see Ruth's point. But still, I can't help admiring the way it's so creative and well done. Mélange said the exhibition will be here for another two months, then it's off to Vancouver, BC.

The floor plan of the gallery is quite a bit like my loft. When I was sitting in Mélange's office, right before I signed the lease, he told me that originally the top floor was going to be part of the gallery. That's why they left that big rusty steel door on the wall and kept the space so authentic, with many of the original furnishings.

When I asked what the building had been used for originally, Mélange said he wasn't for sure, but he thought it might have been a slaughterhouse. When he said that, I must have turned grey because he immediately corrected himself: No, no, wait. How silly of him! That was the other place he owns on Flanders! This building had been a gristmill where they ground wheat and grains because there was this place on the other side of the ground floor with all these bolts and braces for a giant wheel of some kind.

I told him that's a real load off, because I could NEVER EVER live anywhere that had been a slaughterhouse. Not in a million gazillion years! I grew up on a cattle ranch and I have a very strong aversion to killing animals.

Mélange took my hand across the desk, squeezed it affectionately, and said we were going to get along just fine, him and me. He could tell I had a very big heart. Then he passed me this fancy antique fountain pen to sign the lease.

ENTRY SIXTY-TWO

Dig Low's up from LA for the rest of this week to square things at The Cell. Yesterday, he checked it out and said with a few minor changes, it would do fine. Still, he tried like gangbusters to get me to come back with him to LA. I could see he was going to get all lovey-dovey like he had on the phone, so I just cut him short and said nope. Uh-uh. I wouldn't even consider it. We're staying right here in the Rose City. End of conversation.

Dig told me and Lars not to sign any kind of contract that roped us into more than one week at a time. That would put more pressure on Kobo to keep our rates low. He snuck a peek at the client book and noticed that the big studio was open through the whole month of August and even part of September.

I was correct about Dig working Kobo. He managed to get the rates cut in half. Even a little less than half for some things. Dig said he had his own support staff, so that eliminated a lot of the cost. I'm not sure how many of his own people he's going to bring up from LA, though. I don't like the sound of it, especially if we're footing the bill. Still, the rates are so low now I can't really complain.

Dig said that if this project works out, he might move his base of operations up here to Portland because everything is so reasonable. He even commented on how nice the weather had been. I laughed. Fall, winter and spring were a different animal. But it's true, you can't beat

Portland in the summer: Everything so lush and green, sun almost every day. Even the nights were toasty warm. Dig said it was almost like a vacation, coming up here. His hotel is super-nice but dirt-cheap and all the restaurants are amazingly reasonable. I asked where he was staying and he said the Governor. I nearly choked. That's, like, the most expensive hotel in Portland. I felt him out to see if he was planning on staying there when he came up again in August to record and he said maybe. I had to bite my tongue. No way is he staying at the Governor for one or two months, unless he wants to pay the difference. The Doubletree, maybe, but not the Governor. I'd rather he just sublet a house in Southeast or something. Tons of really nice places open up when people go out of town on vacation.

Dig arranged with Kobo for us to record first thing in August, but Lars said that might be too soon. He didn't want to commit to a definite time yet. Dig said the record company won't like it if we drag our heels. Preferably, they'd like us to get started ASAP. That means we'll have our work cut out for us in July, getting all our material worked up and polished.

Lars asked Dig to stop by the Compound tomorrow and see what he thinks of a few songs. We still have to decide which ones we're going to put on the first album. Dig said he's thinking about going ahead and doing the first two albums back-to-back. I'm not sure that's a good idea because it means all our good stuff will probably go on the first one.

According to Dig, that won't matter. If the first one sells really well, the labels won't mind kicking in a few extra bucks if we need to spruce up the second one with a couple of ringers. I'm not so sure about that. I seem to remember Hart saying that AMI would get pretty upset if we tried to ask for more money, especially considering they've already shelled out close to a mill.

ENTRY SIXTY-THREE

You won't believe what happened today. My car was stolen! My bug that I've had since I first moved to Portland. Honey baby's gone! I filed a police report and they said there's a pretty good chance she'll be recovered.

When I walked into the precinct, I was so flustered that I said I wanted to file a missing person's report! The lady behind the desk asked me how long the person had been missing and I said a couple of hours. She laughed and said that wasn't exactly long enough. Then I realized what I'd said by accident and corrected myself.

What a serious bummer. Even though I'd been debating on getting a new car, it feels so wrong to have your baby stolen. Like I've been violated or something. I'd just gotten back from shopping for furniture and I was feeling guilty because I'd spent way too much money. I had this lamp and a few other things and I was trying to carry them all in one trip. When I got to the door of my building, I realized I'd left my keys in my car, but when I walked back around the block to get them my car was missing! Someone had seen the opportunity and driven off with it. I didn't even get a chance to see which way they'd gone.

So there I was, standing in the middle of the street holding this gigantic lamp. I lugged it over to the gallery. Thank God Mélange was there. He was so nice. He took me right up to my loft, gave me a spare key, and even dialed up the police while I got a drink of water. I really like him a lot.

ENTRY SIXTY-FOUR
Jeff called to say he wants to patch things up, let's go out to dinner. His treat! You know, those words sounded so nice to hear. These days, all my so-called "friends" are asking *me* for favors. I'm starting to hate going out with them because when the check comes they get up to go freshen up in the bathroom and I know what that means: Jules the millionaire, dinner's on her. Well, I've got news for them. I'm no fucking millionaire. I'm practically broke! It's just that I have money for high profile things that make me seem rich. I can't even afford to buy a used car! I've been taking the bus everywhere and it's driving me crazy. If this keeps up, I don't even see the point in renewing my driver's license next week.

I'm really looking forward to seeing Jeff. When he called, I asked him if he forgave me for my performance at Ringlers and he said sure. Where did I want to go for dinner? I said, where else, Karumazushi! He sounded kind of unenthusiastic so I asked what was wrong. He mumbled something about sushi being a little out of his price range.

God, I felt like such a jerk. Anywhere that served fish would be totally cool. He perked right up, you're eating fish now? Yeah, I admitted, he'd been right about the protein; now I was a regular "vegaquarian." He asked if the shaking and bad dreams had gone away, and I said not totally, but the symptoms had gotten a lot better—at least for the time being. Protein really helped and sashimi was the purest form of protein on earth.

Jeff suggested we meet at Shanghai Tunnel and decide over a drink where we wanted to eat. That was fine by me. It used to be our favorite place, back when it was still hopping. But it's nice these days, too, because you can relax without having people bump into you, crowding your space. Plus, it's not so hard to get a table, even on the weekend.

ENTRY SIXTY-FIVE
Jeff and I had the best time last night! We drank a couple of beers at the Shanghai, and he retold this story that a customer at work had told him the other day about all these tunnels that run under Portland. Usually, he gets sick of hearing drunks run off at the mouth when he's bartending, but this guy was a walking encyclopedia; if you asked him the right questions, he'd go off on these fascinating tangents.

He said that in Old Town there's still a whole network of tunnels underground, but the city has converted them into ducts for pipe and wires. A few of the bigger ones are rumored to stretch all the way up to the Pearl District. Last year, the construction crew working on the high rise next to Powell's uncovered a huge one; they had to halt work until the historical society checked everything out, photographing the inside of the tunnel, collecting artifacts, etc.

Back a hundred years ago, there was a whole industry built up around the tunnels—a smuggling trade that dealt in opium, stolen horses, even people.

When it came to "human" cargo, the streets of Old Town provided ample stock to chose from. Saloons would hire girls to pick up guys and spike their drinks with something to knock them out, then they'd take the wobbly victim into the back, where he would promptly pass out. Then a bouncer would push them down a chute into a tunnel that led down to the docks. It was really a form of slavery. Captains who were short on crew members would bid on the guys and imprison them in the holds of their ships.

By the time the poor drugged fellow woke up, he'd find himself out in the middle of the Pacific Ocean where the captain had absolute authority. Most men who were shanghaied like that never made it back to Oregon. Either they died on the high seas or ended up sailing all over the world and becoming hardcore sailors. The girls at the saloons tried to pick customers to shanghai who were fairly young and didn't come from money. There usually wasn't much fuss on the part of friends and relatives; in those days, it wasn't uncommon for men to set off in search of fame and fortune.

Instead of Japanese food, Jeff took me back to the same Chinese restaurant we always used to eat, just down the block from Magic Garden. I got an oyster platter that really hit the spot. Plenty of protein, but not quite as good as sushi. Not as clean of a burn. My head felt groggy; it was probably just nerves, hanging out with Jeff. He looks really good. I think he's lost some weight, himself. He didn't mention anything else about my weight or my health. We just had a good time.

After dinner, I was planning on taking him back to my place, but as we were passing the Magic Garden, my curiosity got the best of me and I took a peek inside. I've always wondered what it was like in there.

They had one big stage with fancy lights and this dancer weaving her body under them. It was exactly as I'd expected, really sleazy, but sexy at the same time. Jeff and I sat at the bar for a drink and shared a cigarette. The girl up there on stage caught my eye. I felt this little leap in my heart. She was a brunette, about medium height, with a body that reminded me of Ruth's.

Jeff gave me a couple of dollar bills and told me to go ahead. He seemed kind of amused by the whole thing. I went over to the stage. For some reason, I was extremely nervous, maybe because the place was packed with these gnarly old horn dogs who were crowding up around the dance floor. They probably thought I was a dancer, part of the act. I took the money up to the stage and the girl smiled this surprisingly genuine smile. It wasn't the same way she'd looked at the men. I knew she wanted me. I put the money on the rail. She turned around and bent over.

The guys started cheering, egging me on. By that point, they must have figured out that I couldn't have been a dancer. I was too freaked out. The girl just kind of eased her ass down on the rail and picked up one of the dollar bills between her cheeks.

Later, as Jeff and I were getting ready to leave, the girl came over to the bar and ordered a drink. She sat down next to me and introduced herself. We talked for a few minutes and she asked the bartender for a pen. "I'm not supposed to do this," she said. "Here's my number. Call any day before six. I've got a place on Burnside. It's not much, but there's a great view of the river from my fire escape. We can hang out, drink a few beers. That is, if your boyfriend doesn't mind."

Jeff was impressed by my loft. He said it was a lot bigger than he'd expected and asked about the gallery downstairs. I went over to the bar, poured him a glass of whisky.

"Single malt," he said, holding up the bottle. "Wow, this stuff's expensive." Yeah, I told him, it's part of my new job, entertaining. He seemed surprised. What the hell was I talking about, "entertaining." I regurgitated Hart's little spiel about networking and Jeff laughed this cynical laugh. He said that was the biggest load of crap he'd ever heard. I didn't have to do anything except play music and sing. Who was this guy, Hart, anyway? He sounded like a charlatan.

I told Jeff he was the one who got me a $900,000 record deal, that's who.

Jeff closed his eyes, then opened them and gazed directly into mine: "Look, I saw you at The Crystal. I was there, remember? Jules, you were amazing. That was the best concert I've ever seen. And I'm not just saying that because you used to be my girlfriend."

"Are you sure?"

"Why do you think Jack Thorne came up on stage at the end of your set?"

"I don't know."

"He could tell what you were going to become and he wanted to be seen with you, to make it look like he discovered you. That guy needs all the help he can get to jump-start his career. His last three albums were duds."

"I hear them play his stuff once in a while on KUFO."

"Since when do you ever listen to UFO?"

"At work, sometimes."

"Yeah, well, the station manager at UFO probably gets paid off. Nobody wants to hear Red Angel anymore. They suck. Ten years ago they could sell out the Coliseum, no problem. Now they can't even pack Crystal Ballroom. Believe me, Jack Thorne is nothing but a tired old junkie and he knows it."

"Hey! Don't talk that way about Jack! If anyone helped me score a record deal, he did."

"Jules, will you listen to me for one frigging second! Jack didn't get you signed. Hart didn't get you signed. You got *yourself* signed, and don't let anyone tell you any different. I know this new band and the record deal seems like it happened overnight, but your whole life has been leading up to this. Sure, you're talented, but you've also worked hard. Really hard. Practicing the guitar day and night, taking lessons from half a dozen teachers around town, playing your synth, writing songs, poetry . . ."

"That's not what got me signed, though. It was my presence, my persona on stage. Wasn't it?"

"Oh, sure. That didn't hurt. But in all honesty, I kind of missed seeing you rip on that Fender Mustang of yours. Pete Townsend style, remember? You're more than just a tall, skinny piece of ass. You're a musician, an *artist*."

When I heard Jeff say that, I wanted him so bad. He must have noticed because he raised an eyebrow. "Yeah, that's what I'm talking about. That look. How come you never gave me that look before?" I shrugged, dancing into the bathroom.

Jeff came to the door, pushed it open.

"Hey, don't you knock?" I was peeing. A real gusher from all the beer. He didn't exactly watch, but he didn't leave either. He just kept talking, asking what had happened to make me change so much?

"I could tell you. But then I'd have to kill you."

Jeff passed me the towel after I washed my hands. And then his lips were on mine and I could taste the whisky and he was right, it *did* taste good, so I pushed my tongue deeper into his mouth.

We retired to my futon mattress upstairs. As I was turning out the light, Jeff chuckled. "You've got the most expensive loft in Portland and you're sleeping on the floor. Jules, I swear. You crack me up."

I told him not to say another word. Just do me a favor and remove those dirty jeans. And the boxers. Before I shred them into ribbons with my bare teeth.

ENTRY SIXTY-SIX

I've been reading Jeff's Bible since the night he gave it to me. Now that I feel like I'm on the verge of getting really sick, it isn't a laughing matter. I need whatever help I can get. No more joking around. If I'm really dying, then I need to make sure my horse is saddled. Otherwise, I might slip off in the middle of the stream.

That's not to say I believe in heaven as a physical locale, but I know the principle *behind* heaven can apply to crossing over to a "higher" plane of existence. Hopefully someplace better than here.

The next morning, I finally remembered to ask Jeff what his motivation had been for giving me that King James Bible. He got this embarrassed look on his face and grudgingly admitted it was a re-gift. His grandmother had given it to him about a year before she died. She'd asked him either to read it or to be sure and give it to someone who needed it more than him.

I made Jeff a cup of coffee and myself a cup of herbal tea. He smiled as I went through the old morning rituals. Watching me get his coffee for him. Despite the fact that I hate being "domestic," it's bred into me from growing up on a ranch. So part of me kind of enjoyed going through the motions, being of service.

I asked Jeff if he believed in God and he said sure. Believing wasn't the hard part. Anyone could believe, but that was different from faith. Faith means that you think that God actually *wants* to help you, even if you're a total loser. Jeff wasn't so sure how he felt about that. What did I think?

I said I was definitely sure: God cares about everyone. Even the serial murderers and rapists of this world. I told Jeff that I'd gone to Powell's a few days ago and bought a concordance to help study the Bible. He asked what a concordance was, and I explained how it was a big index of all the words in the Bible.

Jeff wanted to know some of the words I'd looked up. I told him "light" and "love" and "truth." My favorite so far had been truth. Especially what Jesus says about it. He uses the word like a key to unlock the mysteries of the prophets. If we "know" the truth, it can work for us. And this understanding brings us into alignment with God, the Mother of Everything, All-Mother, so we can hear what She's telling us all the time. Her angels singing in our ears: *Ye shall know the truth and the truth shall make you free.*

"Man," Jeff said. "You sound like some kind of born-again. I can't believe you're talking this way after the things we did last night."

Ouch. Where had that come from? I felt the smile evaporate off my face, hardening from shock into resentment. How dare he say such an ugly thing? He had wanted me as much as I'd wanted him. Would All-Mother hold it against me that I needed a little comfort last night, someone in my bed next to me so I could fall asleep without the horrible dizzying sensation of being watched from all directions . . . eyes without faces, teeth without lips, dead souls thirsty for life?

Besides, it wasn't like I'd just committed adultery. Jeff was the expert in *that* department. He sipped the last of his coffee in silence. I got up and went to the window. Outside, this old homeless guy was carrying a big parcel up the street, trying to hold it in his arms. The way he carried it so carefully, you would have thought there was something really valuable inside, but from my elevation, I could see down into the bag. Nothing but useless garbage: a broken TV antennae, bent coat hangers, bundles of filthy rags. He was talking to himself, shuffling from one side of the sidewalk to the other. Drunk at ten o'clock in the morning.

Jeff gave me a kiss on the cheek, reached for his coat by the door. "I'm late for work. Lunch prep."

"I thought you were done working in the kitchen."

"I wish. They've only got me tending bar Monday through Wednesday."

"When it's *really* busy."

"Hey, you gotta start somewhere."

Jeff opened the front door to go. "When can I see you again?" he asked without turning.

"Beats me," I said. "Maybe never."

"What?" he asked, coming back inside.

"Oh, nothing," I said.

He came over, put his arms around me, trying the same Romeo routine from last night. Good one. "You have band practice today?" he asked. "When are you guys going in the studio?"

"Soon," I said.

"How many songs are you working up?"

Rolling over, I pushed my head into the couch so my face was cradled between two cushions. Jeff got the hint.

I listened to him going down the stairs until his footsteps faded into the purr of a jackhammer in the distance. No more heckles. At least not until I had a chance to recharge my spiritual batteries. It was daytime now, I could go back to sleep without worrying. The apartment was filled with light.

ENTRY SIXTY-SEVEN

Ruth called and woke me up. She was at work on lunch break. *Lunch?* I groaned. What time is it? She laughed, called me a bum. "But don't worry, it's OK for rock stars to sleep in. One of the perks of your job."

"Who's worrying?"

"*Oooo.* Attitude. You're really starting to fit the bill."

"Sorry. I'm dead to the world. Beddy-bye's calling."

"OK, I'll get to the point: Next Wednesday's your birthday, right?"

"Yeah."

"So what are you doing? Got any plans?"

I hadn't even thought about it. And then I read Ruth's mind. "Oh, no. Forget about it. I don't even have furniture . . . well, one couch. But that's not enough. How can I throw a party with only one couch to sit on? There'd be a riot."

Ruth said she'd get the ladies together and they could set up while we went out to dinner and celebrated at Karumazushi. It'd be awesome. Christen the new pad with champagne. Or at least a few drops of good Oregon stout.

Hmmm. I still wasn't convinced. It was hard to think about the next party when you still had a hang-over from the last one. Ruth told me to sleep on it, then give her a call tonight. Maybe we could go out and see a movie or something. She wanted to know if I'd seen *Crouching Tiger Hidden Dragon*, it was playing at the Baghdad. I told her that I wasn't so sure about that one. Jeff had called it "Crouching Bottom, Hidden Fart."

When I said that, Ruth couldn't help chuckling. Then, silence. I knew what was coming. "Hey, since when have you been hanging out with Jeff?" Since last night, I said. "Jules. Did you sleep with him?" None of your business. "Jules! You did!" So what if I did? Leave me alone.

"You're tired because you made wild and passionate love all night. With your estranged lover."

I'm hanging up now. Goodbye. Call when you get off work. I'll probably still be in bed.

ENTRY SIXTY-EIGHT

Every time I open up the Bible, it's like there's this big, invisible hand reaching out, trying to shut it. When I say cruel or nasty things and think cruel or nasty thoughts, the hand leaves me alone.

These days, I don't even recognize myself half the time. Another person takes over. Filthy words come gushing out of my mouth, but I can't seem to stop them. Like that guy in Ruth's short story out in the desert when all his friends heard him speaking in a strange tongue. If it wasn't for the CJD, I might actually be tempted to entertain the notion that I'm being possessed by some kind of demon.

It's obvious to modern sensibilities that people in the Bible simply didn't know the difference between, say, schizophrenia and "possession." They mixed the two up, personifying mental illness: *Wisdom that descendeth not from above, but is earthly, sensual, devilish.*

In my case, the prognosis isn't much better: Deadly prions rotting my brain from the inside out. And therein lies the crux of my dilemma: No matter what I tell myself logically, there's always a nagging primitive fear that the Israelites and the Babylonians may have been right after all.

Who knows, maybe livestock can serve as a "gateway" for evil forces to enter the world. Feeding cows and sheep their own kind is a sort of cosmic blasphemy, transgressing the natural order of things: *What goes around, comes around. You are what you eat.* That's how scrapie and Mad Cow got started: By using feed that was manufactured from cows and sheep, transforming peaceful herbivores into cannibals.

To Moses, this would certainly have been punishable by death, right along with blood transfusions and other commonplace medical practices we take for granted today. No matter how many gadgets and machines doctors come up with, they still can't explain the basic notion of a soul dwelling inside the body. To them, the difference between life and death is simply a matter of heart rate, brain waves.

Man, I swear, the thought of being possessed is utterly terrifying. Whenever I feel that telltale rage welling up inside, I've got to make an effort to fight it. That's not the real me. I am Julia Fleischer. I am good, not evil. Get thee behind me! I know you not!

Otherwise, if I let the changes take over, I'll end up like my Dad: Something else altogether—something inhuman, *raging in the wilds, where lions roam.*

Beautiful kind Ruth. She knows an awful lot about the Torah, which is the first five books of the Bible. I was a little surprised to discover that she knows many of the passages by heart; she can even read some of them in the original Hebrew.

The way she approaches scripture is totally different than the Lutherans who went to my church in Mt. Angel. They used to grasp on each word like a drowning man in the middle of a flood, clinging to anything nearby, just to keep from going under. But when Ruth reads, she approaches the words with *fondness*, like they're telling her about a dear old friend—the great grandmother she never knew but wishes she'd met.

Even though she says she doesn't know if God exists or not, I still think Ruth's approach is more comforting. There may be a lot of religious guilt associated with all the impossible Jewish customs she has problems observing in a land of Goyem, but there isn't *fear*. None of that Christian desperation. Instead, there's love, real love, the kind that I imagine Jesus felt for his people.

Despite the fact that Lutherans can be fairly close-minded, it was fun being one in Mt. Angel because most of the town was Catholic and you didn't have to do all the things they did, like smearing ash on your forehead and eating fish on Friday. You could always throw a Catholic off by quoting the Bible. None of them ever read much scripture, they just knew how to say Hail Mary's and stuff like that. So whenever they tried to flick me guff about being a heathen, I'd quote some passage from the New Testament that my Sunday school teacher had forced me to memorize.

Actually, I kind of enjoyed it when a Catholic bully tried to put me down because it gave me a chance to show off my book smarts. Now, I realize that I wasn't any better than them. Unless you *know* the truth, it can't help you; it's just empty words.

Lutherans are nothing more than glorified Catholics who read the Bible and drink too much coffee at bake sales. If a demon came for a

Catholic, the Catholic would hold out his cross. And if it came to take away a Lutheran, the Lutheran would say "get thee behind me." Either way, they'd both be screwed because their fear would give the demon power to blot out God's light and drag them kicking and screaming into darkness.

Judging from my encounters with the dark side, I'm pretty certain that demons are really just a manifestation of being afraid that there might not really be a God who can help us. That there might not be a God at all. But I know every time I feel a pure kind of love, separate from being turned on or wanting something from somebody, that's All-Mother's light shining through me. She is the source of all true love and if I try to live my life as an expression of that love, then I'm doing my best to move toward the light. This kind of unselfish love has no fear; it acts like an antibiotic to drive out fear—the possibility that I could be cut off from God's light.

Besides, fear is really just a form of guilt, remembering how I've been cruel to people instead of loving them as All-Mother's blessed children. If I can try to love whores like Nadja, then I'm being a real Christian. And I'll be safe from demons and the Shadow People.

ENTRY SIXTY-NINE
Ruth's been staying over, spending the night here at my place for the past week. I gave her a drawer in the bathroom and her own closet. *Mi casa, su casa.* That's what I told her. I don't know what she's thinking about me these days. She acts so sweet, but she must think I'm a complete nut-job: At least one nightmare a night, shaking like a leaf in a wind storm, throwing up.

But she's always there. The rock of my salvation. Coming with me to my next appointment at PHSU, the day after tomorrow.

There's not a lot of joy in my life right now. I took the bus to Motor Vehicles last week and they refused to renew my driver's license. The woman behind the desk took one look at me and referred my case to her supervisor, who promptly rescinded my license. She said it's only temporary, I've got to bring back proof from my doctor that I can operate a motor vehicle safely.

Man, I was so pissed. A little shaking and bloodshot eyes? Big deal! That doesn't mean I can't drive a car! I've never had even the smallest fender bender and my driving record is spotless. I reminded the supervisor of this fact and she looked at me funny, like she was trying to determine if I was a drug addict going cold turkey or fighting off the DTs.

There's something about my condition that makes people think I'm high. The woman said she couldn't understand quite what I was saying. Please speak up and try not to mumble.

I was going to say "I'm not fucking mumbling," but then I remembered how I was going to try and be as loving as possible to everyone, even to jerk-offs like her. So I just smiled and nodded and said, OK, if that's how it has to be, fine, thank you. I practically skipped out the double doors, trying my damnedest to be upbeat and positive. But part of me felt like I was skipping to my own funeral.

When I got outside, I broke down and cried in the parking lot. This Mexican guy came over and offered me his handkerchief.

God, I love Mexicans. Such a decent and kind people. You'd never see an American do what that guy did—not for a girl dressed in black leather and squinting through these little round pink sunglasses. Americans would label me as a freak and just assume I was some kind of drug addict Jonesing for my next fix. Not that Mexican guy. He goes, "*Qué te pasa, mi chivita?*" which means something like, "What's wrong, my dear?"

The cops still haven't found my car, so I guess there's no hurry to go back to the DMV. I hope the nurse practitioner at PHSU can give me a clean bill of health, at least clean enough to get my license back. I feel like a 'tard without one. Guess I'll have to go down and get an ID, or I'll get carded from every bar I walk into, even though people say I've aged five years in the past couple of months. That would put me up around 27, not nearly old enough. With OLCC cracking down like the Keystone Cops, pretty much any bar in Portland will card you if you look under forty.

Last Wednesday night at my birthday party, some of my old friends didn't even recognize me. They looked worried, asking if I was OK. I just kept my chin up and said, sure, what makes you think I'm not?

Despite the worried glances and cloistered interrogations from my older friends who hadn't seen me in a while, I ended up having a fairly good time at the party. Ruth must have spent a lot of time organizing things.

Everyone was there. And I mean *everyone*. All my old friends from PCC—even a few from John F. Kennedy High in Mt. Angel! Knowing Ruth, she probably set up chain letter-style invitations: if you come, bring three other friends of Julia's.

Well, I should probably sign off and get ready for band practice. These days, I have to leave over an hour ahead of time. I take the bus over the Hawthorne Bridge to 25th and Division, then I walk the rest of the way. Transferring buses takes longer than walking. That's one reason. The other is I need the exercise; it helps keep body and mind whole.

Lars noticed that I had the shakes at practice the other day and wanted to know what was wrong. I said, nuttin' honey. At least he didn't grill me like that lady at the DMV. Instead he asked if I'd been to see a doctor about it, and I said yeah, as a matter of fact, I had an appointment next Thursday. That seemed to satisfy him.

I've been working super hard to polish the songs for when we go in the studio next Tuesday. My voice isn't as strong as it was a few weeks ago, but it's still a hell of a lot stronger than Helena's ever was. Also, I'm learning all of Mike's guitar parts.

Dig Low said he's planning on bringing up a guitarist from LA, but I don't really think that's necessary. The parts Mike played are simple enough; it's knowing which effects go where that can get confusing.

Niles told me the effects pedals I'd be needing and I picked them up for dirt cheap at Rose City Music. Some of those pedals are pretty damn cool. I especially like this one called "The Experience." It's painted with swirly paint like a tie-dye, and it's manufactured locally, down in Eugene.

I also put new pick-ups on my Fender Mustang. It's always tended to go out of tune, so I might splurge and buy another guitar, probably a Stratocaster. There's one at Rose City that I've had my eye on. Steve promised he'd let it go for a good price. Because I quit work only two weeks ago, he said he would still give me the usual discounts through July, but would I mind wearing a Rose City Music T-shirt at my next show?

God, I swear, that guy is *always on*. Hearing him say that made me so glad I didn't work there anymore. I just smiled real sweet and said sure, I'd wear the frigging shirt, why not?

Speaking of shows, I think we might warm up for this band called Wasp Factory at The Orpheum next month. It should be a total breeze. I know the lyrics a lot better and it would be fun to get up on stage again. The whole town's buzzing with gossip about us, so I'm sure we could help sell tickets!

According to Lars, Wasp Factory was all set to play downstairs on the small stage, but if we get added to the bill, management's talking about moving everything upstairs to the big auditorium.

I've always wanted to play The Orpheum. I saw Peter Burnes there recently and he really packed the house. It was a great show, no hype, no pressure. He even played a couple of songs from the old days when he sang lead for Head Shots. And he really let his (grey) hair down, gabbing with the audience, laughing, cracking these lame-but-endearing jokes.

Oh, shoot. Look at the clock! I'm late for band practice! Maybe Ruth can drive me over. That's the third time this week. The guys are going to kill me!

ENTRY SEVENTY

Ruth and I were hanging out last night sipping G&Ts at this bar called Oba just up the street from my loft. It's really swank and pretentious, but Ruth likes it so we've been going there fairly often.

This one bartender, Brice, gives us our drinks for free half the time. Ruth thinks he's "soft" on me. I told her that he gives us so many for free because I'm the lead singer of a famous band, it's good for business. But Ruth said he was giving us drinks *before* he found out who I was.

Tonight, when Brice was mixing two double G&Ts, he goes: "So Jules, you're a big shot rock star. Tell me, how come you don't have any tattoos?"

Before I could answer, Ruth was already running her motor mouth. She said tattoos were cliché. Just because you're a rock musician doesn't mean you have to turn your body into a comic book.

I shut up because I knew Brice wasn't going to let that one slide. After he finished mixing our drinks, he nodded for us to follow him into the kitchen.

Once we were both inside, Brice shut the door and proceeded to strip out of his shirt and show us this whole menagerie of tats covering his back and chest. He said he had more in his pants, but he'd leave those to our imagination. Standing there, eyeing that gorgeous windsurfer's bod lit up under the lights, I nearly took a pound of flesh.

Back at the bar, I wrote out my phone number and told Brice to give me a call. He should stop over at my place for a drink after work one of these nights. It's close: a big loft on the corner of Everett or Flanders, right over The Black Pearl Art Gallery.

Brice laughed, pushing my number back across the bar. He said his girlfriend probably wouldn't approve.

"Since when has that ever stopped you?" I asked.

"What do you mean?"

"Just what I said."

"You don't know the first thing about me."

"Oh really. You've been giving us our drinks for free. Would your girlfriend approve of that?"

"Good question," Brice said. "Two Sapphire G&Ts doubles . . . that'll be twenty-two dollars."

After we finished our drinks, Ruth and I started back to my place. Halfway there, I said, "Who cares about the spike? I'm goin' for it!"

Ruth didn't know what I was talking about, so I asked her in plain English: "Do you feel like watching your best friend get inked?"

She laughed and screamed, the drunk *yenta* routine: "No way! Are you for real? *Getthefuckout!*" It took some convincing, but I eventually won her over and she agreed to come.

There's a tattoo parlor over on Burnside that stays open late. On the way there, we snuck in downstairs into Powell's and I got this big beautiful hardcover book with all these pictures of flowers. The security guard who threw me out last month wasn't there, but even if he had been standing at the door, I wouldn't have been too worried. Enough time had passed since "the incident."

Besides, I hadn't done anything so terrible. Wolfing down a roast beef sandwich in public isn't exactly a criminal offense.

The tattoo parlor was still open. They had all these daunting pictures of monsters and dragons on the wall. Ruth took one look and goes, "Alright, we're outa here," but I caught her by the waist—not so fast, girlfriend.

There was only one guy minding the store, so we had to wait. Ruth went out to get beers. She'd seen the other customer drinking and it had made her thirsty. I also think she just wanted to get out of there, hoping I'd follow, but I didn't.

After a long wait, the tattoo artist finished whatever he was drawing on a customer and came over. I held up my book and pointed to the illustration of a cowslip flower. Could he draw that on my arm?

He said no problem, but original artwork would cost extra. I pulled out four hundred twenty-seven dollars in cash (everything in my purse) and laid it down on the counter. Would that be enough? The guy smiled. "Uh, yeah." He pocketed the bills, led me into a back room.

First, he designed a pattern on regular sketching paper, then he traced it onto transfer paper. He asked if I was ready and I said sure. But when he turned on the motor and held up his needle, I started to get the shakes real bad. He turned off the motor and said, whoa, hey, are you alright? I told him yeah, it was just nerves. No worries.

The tattoo artist laughed and told me to wait right there, he had just the thing. He went to the closet, took out a vial of little blue pills. "Here, down one of these." Since I didn't have anything to chase it with, I chewed diligently. It tasted kind of like the way urine smells.

The artist held out a can of Coke. "No thanks," I said. By now, my mouth was full of a chalky saliva and I was able to swallow without gagging.

We waited for the pill to work. It did. Warm fuzzies. Next thing I knew, I was back in the chair and the artist was telling me to hold still, think beautiful thoughts. But try as I may, nothing "beautiful" came to mind. It's hard to get nostalgic with a needle biting into your arm.

I closed my eyes, gritted my teeth and fought off the memory of that horrible night at the guesthouse with Jack's weight pressing down on me—so heavy I couldn't breathe—and Tawny driving in the spike.

Ruth came back with a couple of beers soon after. She squealed when she saw me sitting in the old-fashioned barber's chair with the needle snarling angrily.

The artist was magnificent with that tool of his, a virtuoso. I watched in the mirror as the cowslip took shape on my arm. It was kind of scary because I knew it would be permanent—but it was exciting, too. I'd always wanted to get a tattoo, especially after hanging out with Jack, who was covered from head to toe—the Illustrated Man.

Ruth read to us from the flower book while she waited:

> . . . The word origins of Cowslip are somewhat dubious; it has been proposed that the name is actually a bastardization of "Cow's Leek," which had been taken from the Anglo-Saxon word, "leac," or plant. Cowslip flowers have a delightful bouquet. When pressed, they yield narcotic properties. Indeed, like the poppy, these bright yellow perennials have been applied to a variety of uses over the past millennium.
>
> In the Dark Ages, monks discovered they could use the plant to make "Cowslip Wine," a fermented liquor. Today, this drink is still enjoyed by rural folk across Europe, and in some parts of Northern England it has undergone a popular resurgence.
>
> Bars and dance clubs now offer their own variety of Cowslip Wine called "Yellow." But this beautiful and versatile primrose also has a serious side: Naturopathic physicians use the corolla as a sedative or antispasmodic. . . .

I asked the artist if he could fill in the petals of my tattoo with yellow ink, and he said, sure, but he'd recommend against it. The black outline was enough. Any more and it would look overdone. I liked the fact that he told me that; it meant he had integrity since the extra color would probably have earned him a few extra bucks.

Right before Ruth and I left, the tattoo artist stopped us at the door and said, "You know, I hope you don't take this the wrong way, Julia, but have we met someplace before? You look really familiar."

Ruth laughed. "You've probably seen her face plastered on every telephone pole and lamp post between here and the river. Or maybe in the newspaper. She sings lead for The Compound."

When the artist heard that, he snapped his fingers and said, aha!

That's it! His girlfriend had seen our show at The Crystal, but he hadn't been able to come. She'd been raving about us ever since. "But you guys were called something else. Mam Jam, right?"

"Close enough," I said. If nobody remembered our old name, that was fine with me.

ENTRY SEVENTY-ONE

Jack called this afternoon. He asked what was up, trying to make small talk. There was something in his voice, a humility that was highly suspect. He kept on jabbering.

Gradually, the conversation shifted away from us to Tawny. Jack started going into all these really personal details: Did I know the documentary had all been a joke? She'd never do anything like that. Can you imagine? In her line of work? *Ha!* That would totally fuck up her career—even more than she'd fucked it up already!

And the stupid title she went by: "The Baroness," it was just for show. Left over from a German relative she'd never met, a castle in Bavaria she'd never been to. It was true her family on the British side could trace their lineage back to Henry VIII, but then again, most of the aristocratic deadwood from the eighteenth century could pull a monarch or two out of their butts.

By and large, the Davenports were just a bunch of Geordie suck-ups. Take that hint Tawny had dropped about her family, the shipbuilding tycoons: completely misleading. She'd very conveniently left out the part where they lost everything during World War II because of an ill-timed partnership with some Nazi-owned steel company.

Oh, and her father, the illustrious director? In case I hadn't noticed, he wasn't listed in *Leonard Maltin's Movie Guide.*

Originally, he'd had started out filming commercials. But over the past decade, he'd moved in a different direction, where the real money was. Did I know that porn films in California grossed the same amount annually as Hollywood? Well, it's true. Davenport had taken the Hollywood porn machine and moved it over to Eastern Europe where some of the most beautiful women in the world had been living in abject poverty since The Wall came tumbling down and East Germany changed overnight from commies to capitalists.

That's where most of Tawny's bankroll came from. She'd never made any substantial money "brokering." Whatever she made one year, she ended up losing the next. And this time around, she'd finally hit bottom—*rock* bottom.

Dear Old Dad was not pleased since it was mostly his money she'd pissed away. And that's why she'd had started her documentary film project: As a ruse to get him off her back. She'd kept promising to get some juicy footage in the same vein as the Pamela Anderson/Tommy Lee exposé for the better part of a year, stringing him along when she needed another loan.

It didn't take a genius to figure out where the conversation was headed, so I asked point-blank why Jack had called. No more bullshit. Say what he had to say and get it over with.

"Got a pen?" he asked. "Write this down: *bluevault.com.* It's a website."

"A website!"

"It's not what you think. Your face isn't in any of the pictures. Only, well . . . other things."

"OTHER THINGS?"

"Look, Jules. Nobody will know it's you. There aren't any tattoos, birthmarks . . . nothing to give you away. And if people start to talk, just deny—"

I hung up the phone, ran downstairs, dialed into my server. C'mon, c'mon, hurry up . . . BlueVault.com . . . Oh, great. A pay site. They wanted a ton of information: credit card number, birth date, social security, everything under the sun. It took forever, cutting through all the "blue" tape.

As I sat there helplessly, waiting for my credit card to clear, I came so close to picking up my laptop and chucking it through the window.

Goddamn Tawny and Jack. Death to the perfect couple. Death!

Right as I was reaching over to log off, my card cleared and the site came up, BlueVault.com in big letters across the top of the screen: A black shadowy background and blood-red wallpaper with all manner of sadistic paraphernalia. And in the center of the screen, a grid of "thumbnails."

So many to choose from. Despite the fact they were practically microscopic, I knew instinctively which one to click first: Down near the bottom. *There.* That looked like Tawny's bedspread.

The picture downloaded very quickly. In a matter of seconds, my screen was filled with an image that my brain couldn't quite process. So much skin! And then I realized it was *my* skin, my legs and my . . . *Jesus, God, no.*

I made it into the bathroom just in time. My lunch came up along with what was left of breakfast. *How could Tawny do this to me? What had I ever done to her?*

I pulled myself up by my elbows, rolled over into the tub, turned on the shower. *I'm un-dead now, there's nothing left to take, can't go on, can't get up, can't move . . . what if she posts one with my face, everyone will see—all my fans, the guys in the band, Jeff, all my friends at PCC, my brother, the whole world.*

Boiling hot jets ate into my scalp, frying the skin off my ears, scalding my shoulders, my back . . . erasing what was left of the girl I used to be . . . not a shred of innocence left . . .

When I couldn't stand the pain anymore, I leapt out onto the floor, curling up in a ball, fetus-style. And that's how Ruth found me when she came home from work.

"Jules? You here?"

A clatter of keys on the front table. High heels clicking across the living room floor, over to the laptop. "*Ewe,* what's this?" Tawny's hand reaching deep inside me—deeper than was humanly possible—a vampire ripping my heart out, pulling it through the bloody hole between my legs.

ENTRY SEVENTY-TWO

The next morning when I checked my messages, I heard Jack's voice. My finger hovered above the delete button. But something kept me from pressing it. There was a desperate tone in his voice, so unlike the macho prick I'd come to know the hard way:

"Thank God you didn't answer. I hope your machine doesn't cut me off. This is the last time you'll ever hear my voice. The last time, Jules.

"I never told you, but, uh . . . from the first time I saw you, up there on stage, singing like an angel, I felt this amazing . . . *rush.* My throat went dry. I could feel my heart pounding, blood rushing to my head. You were like an angel.

"Later, when I comforted you backstage, that was the real me. Not

'Jack Thorne,' but John David Lardner from Madison, Wisconsin. The teenager with a cracking voice and wobbly knees. God, I wish that moment could have lasted forever—holding you tight in my arms.

"Life doesn't always work the way you want. Too many skeletons hanging around, waiting to sneak up from behind and tap you on the shoulder: 'May I have this dance?'

"That was Tawny's line. In the green room, she noticed my sweaty palms, watery eyes. *Love? Bah!* To her, it was a sign of weakness. That was the real reason she went ahead and sold those pictures—to get back at you for reminding her boyfriend how to be human, how to feel alive—really alive—how to love . . .

"But that's over. Finished. *It's better to burn out than to fade away.* Now my heart's finally black enough to match hers. We're supposed to have this romantic tryst, just Tawny and me, in New York: Dinner at Tavern On The Green. A carriage ride around Central Park. And then, a night to remember . . .

"Goodnight sweet princess. I should have been a poet instead of a rock star. Or both! A rare bird like Dylan, the Poet Laureate of rock n' roll!

"When I was a kid, I used to imitate everything about him: the walk, the talk, the chord changes. But something happened on the way to the record store. John shed his skin, and Jack was born. Got my first tattoo, a giant swastika across my chest. '*Yeahrightsowhatgetfucked!*' Already, it was too late.

"The poet inside me stayed underground, tapping out Morse code, even though he knew it would never reach the surface—at least not in time. How could a skinhead with a bigger chip on his shoulder than Johnny Rotten possibly admit his idol was a peacenik Jew who sings ballads?

"Ah, Jules. Jules, Jules, Jules. I keep seeing your face, a delicate flower among thorns. So young, so fresh. Petals rinsed by the morning dew. Your daddy was right: 'It don't matter what anyone else says.' If you stay true to yourself, those petals will never wilt, their golden brilliance will never fade.

"Alas, not so for the lost prince: *he fades from earth, scarce seen by souls of men, but tho' obscur'd, this is the form of the Angelic land. . . .*"

ENTRY SEVENTY-THREE

Went back to PHSU with Ruth. They ran more tests, lots more. Then a doctor called me into his office, a big corner office with all these windows. Dressed up in that suit of his, he looked more like a politician than a physician. He told me they'd reached a tentative diagnosis: I appeared to be suffering from Parkinson's disease. He was very sorry, but the hospital could no longer pay the cost of my treatment.

I asked him why not, and he said that originally, they thought my case might have some sort of connection to a study they were conducting that had to do with a new form of neuritis. But that obviously wasn't the case because I was in no visible pain. I laughed. What a joke. Every muscle and nerve in my body was crying out, shouting for someone to do something. Ruth asked the doctor if he could recommend any medication and he said he could but that it would be quite expensive.

Sitting there, I could feel my brain start to shut down. This place was making me feel more sick, not better. The quacks. Fluffing up their feathers to look important. I didn't have the letters M and D after my name, but I knew what to look for. All the warning signs were staring them right in the face. If I'd had even the slightest inclination, I could have run through the symptoms for CJD, how my case matched them precisely, how my father had died of the same thing despite the fact they'd misdiagnosed his condition as Alzheimer's. Basically, how they were all full of shit, how they only saw what they wanted to see, their minds already made up.

As Ruth and I were leaving, the nurse practitioner met us by the elevator. She gave me a few vials of pills and said these should help. Take them!

Before I could ask her what she meant, the elevator had come and she was hurrying off down the hall.

Of all people . . . for her to do that? Especially after our meeting when she'd been so patronizing. Something was rotten in the state of Oregon. The bastards weren't coming clean. Ruth asked what was wrong.

"Never you mind," I said. "Let's hit the library on our way home."

Go ahead and call me a laywoman and a hypochondriac, but after researching those little yellow pills, I know for a fact that the symptoms they treat have absolutely nothing to do with Parkinson's. So either that nurse was trying to give me a signal that I'm on the right track, or else she's got a sick sense of humor.

ENTRY SEVENTY-FIVE
Today was our first official day recording at The Cell. Dig Low got everything set up in the big room. It's great. Before, when we were doing the demo, Cynthia had used the same board, but she asked us to set up in a cramped little room off to one side.

This time, we're getting the royal treatment. Dig's posse was there, all six of them, setting up mics, tuning the drums, getting everything just right. Even the food. They asked me what I needed, and I said a large order of sashimi from Karumazushi and some Quaaludes.

About an hour later, they showed up with both the sash and the ludes. These guys don't mess around. They remind me a little of Malcolm X's soldiers: Very articulate but never speaking unless spoken to, short cropped hair, natural 'fros—none of those artificial white-boy straighteners for them. And you can tell they don't do drugs or party much. They're not what I expected at all. I thought the music biz was full of boozers and users.

Now I see how Dig gets so much done. Even *he* borders on being a teetotaler. I've seen him drink an occasional glass of cognac, but never on the job. Very professional.

Dig said he wanted to record all the instrumental parts first, preferably guitar. He introduced me to this guy, Marvin, who's from LA, a big shot studio musician down there. Marvin brought a phalanx of guitars along with three gym bags stuffed full of effects pedals and things.

Dig played the demo of the first song we planned to record and Marvin listened. After hearing it once, Marvin played Mike's part exact: Every note, identical. But there was something missing. It felt cold. Not enough fuzz, and the attacks were weak. I picked up my old Mustang and played the intro for him, to show him what I meant, how to tweak the ghost notes to give them an extra punch.

Dig came running in from the control room. "Whoa, whoa!" he shouted. "Since when have you played guitar like that!"

I laughed and said, like what? I was just showing Marvin, here, how to whip the horse's eyes.

"Do it again."

When I laid the chords down just like before, Dig started jumping up and down. "Yes, Yes, YES!" He ran back into the control booth, waving frantically at the engineer: "Roll it, quick!"

After that, Dig only used Marvin as backup. I played all the rhythm parts and most of the leads. Near the end of the day, Dig brought in a tray of glasses filled with champagne.

He held up his glass for a toast: "To Jules. She got the Midas Touch. 'Cept she ain't gonna turn this record to gold. Uh-uh. It's goin' platinum, baby! *Platinum!*"

Everyone took a sip. Dig noticed that I'd spilled some of my drink because my hands were shaking. He asked what was wrong, and I told him it was nothing to worry about, just a touch of Parkinson's. At least that's what the doctors at PHSU seemed to think.

When he heard that, the smile vanished off his lips. He clapped, "OK, folks, we're done! Same time tomorrow!"

Then he put his arm around me, led me outside, and hailed a cab.

At Front Street, Dig told the driver to let us out. It was overcast and kind of cold out. My man looked cute all bundled up in a sweater and a jacket; he'd also pulled down the beret he always wore so it covered the little black ears that were out of proportion to his big head.

We walked along the river, stopping at this deck with observation binoculars to sneak a peak at the boats sailing by. Down below, the water flowed dark and heavy, like a dream. I watched a log pass under the Steel Bridge.

Dig was the first to speak: "Now what's this you about Parkinson's?"

I filled him in about my two visits to PHSU, a basic thumbnail sketch of my symptoms, leaving out the juicy details. "Alright, now, girl," he said when I'd finished. "Listen up: I don't want you to speak about this to anyone. Not another living soul. Understand?"

I started to interrupted, but he put up a hand: "If AMI ever catches wind of it, they'll pull the plug so fast we'll both get whiplash."

"What about the advance?" I asked. "It's mine."

"At the moment, yes. But that can change faster than you realize. You see, there's a clause in the contract whereby they can . . . well, to put it simply, if Michael Reiser smells blood his first reaction will be to cut his losses. And that's when you kiss your beautiful contract goodbye. 'Cause once the bullets start flyin', we done."

"How? They can't—"

"Wanna bet? AMI's got a whole army of lawyers. One call from them and your bank will freeze all assets. Even your own personal account. Then it's a waiting game. One year, maybe two. Before you know it, your own lawyer will have sucked you dry."

"No."

"Yes, Julia. I've seen it happen before and it's not a pretty sight. Most people have no choice but to declare bankruptcy. You'd be lucky to keep the panties on that sweet ass of yours. Meanwhile AMI walks away with your advance—at least whatever's left."

I shut up. What more could I say? My lawyer hadn't mentioned anything about a clause having to do with sickness. Must be standard practice for all recording contracts, like "Acts of God" in home owner's insurance: Earthquakes, fires, floods . . . Creutzfeldt-Jakob Disease.

My hands were shaking again, so I popped another of those pills the nurse had given me, along with a lude. Dig watched nervously as I tried to swallow them dry. I could see him sizing me up, trying to decide whether or not to bail.

The way he was looking into my eyes, I could tell he was worried, too. For my sake. It wasn't all about money, self-preservation. He came right over to where I was standing by the rail.

Before I could back away, he'd wrapped his arms around me. Tight. At first I resisted, but he didn't loosen his hold.

Little by little, I felt myself relax, succumbing to the power of his embrace. So strong. We stayed like that for a long time. After the moment passed, Dig held me out at arm's length to get a look at my face. I was still crying, but I felt a lot better. I even attempted a smile; it must have looked pathetic because he touched my cheek fondly, wiping the tears away with his big hand.

"*Shhhhh,* c'mon, hey . . . you my shortie, right? Dig's here for you. Nothing bad's gonna happen, a'right? We gonna make it. No matter how the lightning flashes and the storm may rage: Together, we shall get to the Promised Land."

You know, the way he said it, so confident and firm, I almost believed him.

ENTRY SEVENTY-SIX

Last night, had a terrible nightmare. Ruth couldn't stay over because she had to get to work early for a presentation and the commute is worse from Northeast. So I was alone upstairs.

In the nightmare, I heard a faint rapping on the door, the big decorative one on the wall, the one that's bricked off. Someone on the other side trying to get in. I'd been having the same recurring dream for almost a month. But then I heard a creak as the latch turned and the door swung open.

"Who's there? Is somebody there?"

No answer. I tried to stay awake because I knew someone *was* there and they were waiting for me to fall asleep, which I did (in the nightmare).

But eventually, the gravity of sleep took over and I fell back into visions of other places, other times. Within seconds, I'd slipped far beyond the pale of humanity, into a future of glaring sunlight, water and sand . . . the ruins of ancient civilizations lying deep under a sea filled with tiny animals crawling around in their armored shells, but not like any crab or lobster I'd ever seen. And then, I was sliding backward through history—wars, disasters, great waves of human suffering washing over Asia and the Americas and Europe—and further still, past bygone empires I'd never read about in school, titanic buildings made of glass (except they were shaped differently, more like the pyramids of Egypt or Mexico). I tried to stop myself, but I couldn't keep from sliding, farther and farther back, until I was hovering above a great swampy ocean, watching dinosaurs feed on each other: Huge, brightly colored things—beasts of burden, beasts of prey. They moved a hell of a lot faster than I'd expected. Not like any bird or lizard. More like mammals, huge bears or lions. Some of them had fur and some had brightly colored plates that glittered with every color in the rainbow. And then I was speeding past them, into another place, much like the first, a great shallow ocean with trilobites and brachiopods, things I'd read about in biology class. I kept spinning, past all those cute little guys, until everything went dark. I could see magma lurking in the pits of volcanoes, glowing blasphemous red and orange, wanting to explode. The world was spinning on its axis, but I had stayed in one place. Each time it spun, a different scene rushed past. I was above it all, hovering with the angels.

I looked up and there they were! So beautiful, I gasped in wonder. I could actually *see* them: billions, trillions of cherubim flourishing over my head, the trains of their garments flowing through the cosmos, a holy procession, God's true handiwork, glistering with rays of love.

Back in my apartment, quiet and dark. Fingernails brushing over my skin, up the backs of my legs, along my spine, slowly working their way up towards my neck, where they hesitated; then opened and began to squeeze, ever so slightly.

I sat up, pulled the sheets around me. There, in the darkness, I could just barely make out the shape of a man standing beside my bed. He didn't seem exactly like a killer. More like a child who'd been caught stealing some incidental yet forbidden thing, a shrug of guilt on his face. He was trying to speak, to explain what he'd been doing, but he couldn't seem to get his mouth to work. As I stared at him, his shadowy features came more into focus: *Mr. Green,* Ruth's landlord!

When he saw that I recognized him, his bashful manner changed into desperation: "Holp! Halp, halp!" He dropped down on one knee, begging, imploring. I could smell the whisky on his breath, yet he didn't seem drunk. And there were other smells, vaguely nauseating.

In time, Mr. Green figured out that I couldn't help him, and this seemed to wash through his veins like a plague. He fell onto the floor, quivering, as if the weight of the earth was pressing down on his back.

Right when I thought he would be squashed between the floorboards, he turned his head and looked up at me. Somehow, my presence calmed him enough so that he stopped fighting whatever it was that had thrown him down so violently. A smile crept across his lips revealing a row of yellow teeth stained by a lifetime of smoking.

One elbow jerked up, then the other. He rose to his feet, moving awkwardly at first, and then faster and faster until I could barely keep my eyes on him. I watched in disbelief as he flitted about the room, frantic as a moth in a killing jar—banging into the walls, crashing against the ceiling, the floor.

"Stop!" I screamed. "Go away!"

In a final spasm of dread, Mr. Green knocked the lamp off the nightstand. The bulb shattered in a flash of brilliance.

And then I saw them all around me: greedy faces half-hid in darkness. They were pushing in around my bed, hundreds of them, within seconds of doing whatever they had come here to do!

I jumped to my feet, calling out the first thing that popped into my head: "Mother of lights! No variableness, neither shadow of turning!"

Instantly, my body lit up with some kind of illumination. I could feel it pouring out of my skin like sweat, heating up my pores from the inside.

Thank God, it was enough to dispel them. I saw them back away. But still, the room was filled with shadows.

ø

Woke up screaming. So vivid. The worst one yet. I reached for the light—jumped back in surprise.

The moon was shining in through a window. Not a full moon, but enough to help me make out the shape of my lamp where it lay knocked on its side on the floor, the shade partway off and bits of glass shimmering on the floor.

My first reaction was to run downstairs for my cell phone, but then I remembered the steel door, how it had opened. If it hadn't been a dream, then that meant the Shadow People might still be hiding somewhere in my apartment. And Mr. Green, he might be here, too. I drew the blanket up around my neck, shivering in spasms, my legs thumping mindlessly against the mattress.

Every muscle in my body was strung so tight that if I moved, even an inch, I felt as if my body would shatter into a thousand pieces.

Oh, God. I needed another one of those pills the nurse had given me to help ward off the headaches. My lips: parched. I could barely swallow my throat was so dry. If I didn't get something to eat and drink soon, the Shadow People would find me for sure.

Creeping down the stairs, every nerve in my body straining to sense any of the familiar clues: humming in my ears, whirring under my feet. I made it to the kitchen, drank some water from the tap, wolfed down a few pieces of sashimi.

There, that was better. I belched, so loud it echoed through the apartment. On my way to the toilet, I caught sight of myself in the bathroom mirror. Pale as a ghost, teeth chattering. Yet somehow, beloved, innocent.

My skin was still tingling from the dream; I could feel positive energy crackling all over my body, toasty warm, like rays from the sun. Everything was going to be alright. Even if I passed on to the next plane of existence. Death was an illusion perpetrated by fear of the unknown.

But I wasn't in the dark anymore. I'd seen the other side: Shades of doubt, from grey to black . . . and yet, beyond the Vale of Shadow there was All-Mother's power! Strong & eternal, glowing, radiant! She was absolutely real—the *only* reality. Everything else was either Her reflection or just smudges on life's window—so many distortions of the truth—and this knowledge was my secret weapon, a light to dispel the darkness.

As I sat down to tinkle, a nervous little fart squeaked through my cheeks, echoing in the toilet bowl. *Hmmmm. Could it be Saaaaaaatan trying to get the last word?*

The Church Lady's voice in my head. Well, that did it. Great peals of laughter rose up from deep inside. The face in the mirror laughed right along with me. I jumped off the pot and danced around the bathroom, turning on faucets, blinking the lights.

"Thank you, All-Mother! Thank you! THANK YOU!"

My head was clear for the first time in weeks. No more pain, it had vanished like the morning dew.

Despite my newfound peace of mind, I decided to give Ruth a call. Just to be on the safe side. She picked up on the third ring. How I loved hearing that sweet groggy voice!

"H-hello?"

"Hi baby doll."

"Oh Jules. What's going on? You OK?"

"Yeah, fine. Sorry to call so late."

"What time is it?"

"I don't know. Is Mr. Green there?"

"Who?"

"Mr. Green."

"Uh, yeah, I guess. He was when I got home from work."

"Alright, listen: I need you to go upstairs and check."

"What? *No!* I can't just barge in on him like that. He'd have a conniption."

"The upstairs door, it doesn't lock, right?"

"Huh?"

"The door upstairs. You can open it?"

"Yeah, but—"

"Are you on your cell?"

"Yeah."

"OK, I need you to go up there for me. Just listen at his door, see if you can hear him snoring."

"Why? What's this all about?"

"Ruth, please! I'm begging you!"

"God, Jules, I swear. The things you make me do. It's cold in here. Where's my friggin' robe. Oh, here it is. Alright, I'm going. Turning on the light. Walking through the hallway, the kitchen, living room. Now, I'm on the stairs. *Wait.* I hear something. Oh . . . never mind. It's only the TV. But that's weird. No channel, just static . . ."

When Ruth said that, my heart stopped. I knew exactly what she would find once she opened the door. Mr. Green hadn't fallen asleep in front of the television. Mr. Green was dead.

ENTRY SEVENTY-SEVEN

One of the local rags here in Portland somehow caught wind of the whole Internet fiasco. Their gossip columnist, Tom Unfried, published an exposé about "naughty Jules Fleischer" along with the website address to bluevault.com.

So now everyone's the wiser. I can't help suspecting that Mike had some kind of hand in all this. He knows Tawny and he's shrewd enough to call her up nosing around for some kind of lead now that he's out of our project.

When we were down in Los Angeles, Mike was the only one who said he actually could deal with living there. I could have guessed as much. His type thrives on tinsel, why not live in Tinseltown.

So where does this article leave me? In a tricky position, but nothing I can't handle. I'm beyond stressing out. Besides, if I show any sign of anxiety gossipmongers like Peeping Tom would smell it right away and go for the kill. They'd love to paint a big scarlet "PQ" on my chest. Jules Fleischer, *Porn Queen.*

Like Jack says, I'll just deny everything. There's no way anyone can prove it's me in those pictures. Just close-ups of a pussy with a hand in it. Unless you got down on your hands and knees and compared the real thing with that picture, you'd never know it was mine. And the only two people who could do that are Jack or Jeff.

Jack's ancient history, but I am kind of anxious about Jeff. What's he going to think if he sees those pictures? He was such a sweetheart the other day when I ran into him at Everyday Music, I've been fighting the urge to call him up.

ø

Went online today and checked out those pictures again. Still the same old thumbnails. I swear, if somebody put a gun in my hand and Tawny in my line of fire, I'd probably shoot. I really would, and it pains me to admit it.

Why? Because love is the only way to conquer your demons. Tawny's just another excuse for riling me up inside. Poor creature: she's had a pair of idle hands her whole life, and the Devil found work for them to do.

No one has said anything yet about the article except Lars. Of course, the paper just came out today (Wednesday). Lars kind of fished around to make sure the rumor wasn't true. I denied everything in the coolest and most collected way possible. He seemed relieved and even suggested I consider a lawsuit against Tom Unfried. Slander is a serious issue, especially when it's your career at stake. I said I'd think about it.

I'm so glad that Ruth's moving in. I told her she could stay here rent-free as long as she likes. Mr. Green's brother assured her that she was more than welcome to stay in the house; he's going to rent it out as a duplex (top/bottom). She said thanks but no thanks. She could never live there. Not after what happened.

Ruth didn't tell me so, but I think my prophetic dream really scared her. She's not sure what to think now. Even she had to admit there might be a "supernatural element" to my condition.

Well, I beg to differ. Supernatural is the wrong word entirely. I consider that dream *divinely natural*. My brain's been temporarily rewired, that's all. In my state of inbetweenness, I can't help noticing things most people miss. Like the shadows. They make me feel like that annoying little kid in *The Sixth Sense* who went around whispering "I can see dead people."

Maybe there is such a thing as a ghost, but I've never seen one. The closest I've ever come was the other night with Mr. Green. And even then, I wasn't convinced it was really him. If it was, I don't think he was quite like the Shadow People. He seemed more like a puppet on strings, the way he danced.

Shadow people can't even come close to that: Jumping into the air, coming down hard on the floor, huffing, puffing, sweating. No way. They've forgotten too much about this world.

Even when they pretend to walk away, it's just a pretense. They're gliding, legs aflutter, upside down wings. And their faces? Ha! Don't make me laugh! Sloppy patchwork, as if God threw up his hands in disgust. If you look closely, you can see they've been taken apart and reassembled: Blanks filled in with the next best thing . . . and believe me, that's way too much information.

Getting back to Ruth, she said her internship is going to turn into half days starting next week. Then she can devote more time to help with my research. I think she's actually starting to get interested in the project, especially after what happened at the hospital when that nurse gave me those pills. Ruth told me to surf on the web and try to find out more about the drugs in them. If her hunch is correct, they might be used to treat CJD.

So now it seems that Ruth is finally on my side. Or at least she's not such a skeptic, like she is about the "supernatural."

One of the things that interests me most about the whole thing is the spiritual side effects I'm experiencing. I want to find out if other patients with CJD experience anything similar or if I'm just a total freak or something. Religion has never really interested me before, but God always has.

When I was little, I tried to talk to God sometimes. I would say, "Hey, Big Guy, what's up with you? Hard day at work? Save any souls today?" And with the innocent expectation of a child, I half-expected to hear an answer.

My Sunday school teachers didn't like having me in their classes because they said I was a disruptive influence on the other children. I asked too many questions.

Well, I've got news for people like them: Now I have answers to a lot of those questions they hated because they couldn't answer them. I know things you can't read in the Bible.

After all, like Ruth says, "Bible" is just a word that means "library." It's not the whole truth. It has enough of the truth to enlighten you, but there are plenty of other sources out there, especially all the books that didn't make it into the Bible, like one in the Apocrypha that has a really wonderful story about Jesus when he was a little kid.

Mary, his mom, told him to go down to the river and fill this pot she had with water, but he broke it along the way. So instead of turning back, he just filled up his shirt with water and carried it home filled with more water than the pot could have held. His mom was astonished, but to him it was no big deal. It wasn't "supernatural." It was divinely natural. Everyone else was living out their lives as "subnaturals." They must have seemed like spiritual retards to Jesus.

And the same goes for Buddha. All those dorks trying to get him to be a king or whatever when all he wanted to do was find Nirvana. Now *that's* devotion.

ENTRY SEVENTY-EIGHT

Arrived at the studio this morning to find Dig wasn't there. We sat around for almost an hour waiting for His Highness. Eventually, one of his lackeys showed up. I knew what the guy was going to say before he even open his mouth. Dig was real sorry, but he got called to LA on business. One of his previous clients had an emergency and Dig had to bail him out. Something to do with changing the lyrics in one of the songs at the last minute because of legal concerns.

Yeah, right. Give me a little credit. I could see through the smoke and mirrors. Dig's assistant was polite, it was clear he didn't know the details. Why shoot the messenger?

Lars and the rest of the guys didn't seem to get it, and I wasn't going to spell it out for them. Dig was finished with us, off the project. I went to this coffee shop near my house and ordered my usual steamed soymilk with almond. Then I called up Dig's cell.

To my surprise, he actually answered. The guilt in his voice was palpable. It went from "yo!" to "oh, hey, Jules, waz'up?" Evidently, he'd been expecting someone else. I asked him how he was doing, had he gotten to the Promised Land yet? Because if he had, he'd left me behind. He laughed this embarrassed laugh, which only confirmed my suspicions.

"You know, Dig, I thought you were different than all that LA trash down there. But you've just proved me wrong."

"Now, baby, don't get the wrong idea. Didn't my boy, Yakara, fill you in? I'll be back up there in another couple of days. One week tops."

"No you won't. You're bailing. Just admit it."

"What? Now, look, you're new to the business, you don't know the routine. These things happen."

"Yeah, so who is this other client that's more important than us?"

"I'd love to tell you, but I can't. It's a legal thing. I'm being sued, right along with my client. Anything I say could foul up the case."

"Don't give me that jive. I may be new to the business, but I know a rat when I smell one. Especially if he's jumping off a sinking ship."

"Who you callin' a rat?"

"Oh, I'm sorry. Did I offend you? Let me rephrase that: You, Digger, *baby*, are a jive-talkin', two-faced black devil!"

I hung up. What a phony. Anyone who puts five platinum records on his bedroom wall is a loser, no matter how much money he's got in the bank.

And Digger's heart? That was made of platinum, too. Even his name was fake. I wondered what his real name was, Jerome Washington? Or was it Lincoln? Some president before the Civil War.

As I thought all these hateful things and sipped my drink, I couldn't help admitting to myself that the real reason I felt betrayed was because I'd liked Digger. A lot. I could still feel that marathon hug he gave me in the park. Big strong arms holding me tight and that yummy cologne with a musky tang underneath. What a disappointment. We could have been good friends, business associates, and who knows what else?

Not more than two hours have gone by, and already I'm starting to feel bad about what I said to Digger on the phone. A part of me is disappointed because, frankly, I'd wanted him in my bed. Not for his great body or his black charm, but because I'd liked him. The *real* him, the nice guy underneath it all who had let some corporate lawyer talk him into ditching us.

Ah, well. Time to move on. No use dwelling on what could have been. Mr. Low's definitely in the past tense. Any bridge that might have been left is on fire now. And that means one thing: it's only a matter of time before AMI wants their money back. So I don't have long to spend it.

What goes around comes around. The whole thing was bad karma from the start. Hooking up with a charmer like Tawny and Hart Drake, her pet cobra. Forget about it. He'll find a way to keep his commission, but our advance is history. The president of AMI should be covering his losses right about now. By the end of the month, at least. What a shame. Before we've had a chance to finish our first song.

But still, even if the bridge is burning, it hasn't caught the shithouse on fire. I still have some time to get my kicks before the whole thing goes up in flames.

Tomorrow, I could go into the studio by myself and tell the secretary to hire the first producer she came to in her Rolodex. Tell her I'm doing a few songs on my own.

Hey, now that's an idea! I could read some of my favorite poems over a guitar track, kind of a Jim Morrison *American Prayer* type thing. I could even read a passage from this journal. Who knows? Maybe after I'm gone, the band will go back in the studio and lay down some tracks over top. I can hear it now, the synth boys ameliorating my raw guitar chords with a few nice, soothing washes up and down the ivories, my words coming through at just the right moment:

> "This is probably the one and only chance I'll ever get to write my own personal liner notes . . ."

ENTRY SEVENTY-NINE

When I told Lars about the Dig Low's advice, he seemed to think I was overreacting about the label. Even if I was sick with "Parkinson's" why would they drop me? I told him that I was already too sick right now to go on a long tour and labels depend on tours to help promote their albums. Lars brought up The Beatles and Squeeze and The Smiths and a bunch of other bands that didn't do much touring but were hugely successful. That was really nice of him to say. I could have mentioned that the Beatles didn't need to tour after their first few albums because they were already so famous, but what was the point in contradicting him. He was on my side. If he and the other guys still want to think that I'm going to be around long enough to record another two albums, who am I to burst their bubble? They've got eyes, they can see what I'm going through.

So if they chose to overlook the symptoms, I should be grateful for the support. They don't need to hear all the gory details and I've decided that I'm not going to belabor them in this journal either.

Suffice it to say my body's falling apart and I know it. It's not your imagination when your period is next to nothing and your head aches all the time and you can barely hold your food and all these swirly colors keep flashing in front of your eyes like some kind of acid flashback.

But the point of this journal is to glorify life not bum people out about death. I'm keeping at this thing, writing to make a difference like William Blake or the prophets. I know that I'm not in their league, but in my own way, I'm heading in the same direction. Jim Morrison always wanted to "break on through to the other side." I have already and I'm still here to talk about it. I've seen the other side, and if you ask me, the rest of humanity's not missing much.

Nobody (except maybe Jesus) has crossed that great grey divide that separates our world from the other worlds and come back unscathed. I say "worlds" plural because I don't think Jeffrey Dahmer ended up in the same place as Mahatma Gandhi. But there's not some big bearded jolly Santa Claus-style God up in heaven deciding who's been naughty and who's been nice.

Divine logic is inscrutable; it operates in much the same way as nature, which reflects its sense of order, if in a slightly distorted fashion like a carnival funhouse mirror. In the natural realm, life-forms are divided into phyla and species and so on. Human beings are evolving right here on earth, our spiritual selves developing into a form that can embrace the infinite.

Most animals have two eyes for a reason, two ears, two nostrils, they have fur, all of the physical amenities that nature has bestowed upon them. Indirectly, God has provided for them, but she didn't give them hairy butts so they can sit on the snow and not get cold. Their evolution mimics the divine sense of order. Sunlight falls upon everything in the world, it doesn't withhold its rays from some and give extra ones to others. Animals and plants take advantage of this bounty. The same holds true in spiritual terms. Those people who take advantage of All-Mother's love here, will benefit from it hereafter. And that's the only thing they'll take with them.

I felt Her love in my dream when I told the shadows in no uncertain terms who my maker was. That I come from one grand unification of Love, not the flesh. I'm evolving towards a higher level of experience, and I will naturally gravitate in the same direction after the death of my earthly body.

But my death won't be what finally propels me there, toward the Grand Unification; it will be my attraction to goodness, to the light. Feeling grateful, giving thanks. This glowing state of mind draws me to the best place for me to go when my body is ruined.

ENTRY EIGHTY

Ruth's been digging up all this amazing information about CJD. A blood hound on a cyber-trail. I know she's doing it for me and I love her for it. But it's starting to get me down thinking about all the symptoms involved, the "nuts and bolts" of my disease. I'm going to die, that's inevitable, but dwelling on the negative things happening to me only seems to make me feel worse.

Take for instance that time in the kitchen after my nightmare, when I laughed out loud; that made me feel so much better. It was like laughing in the face of adversity with a genuine optimism that stems from happiness. I've got to quit wallowing in the mud and look up into the light.

These days I've been really noticing the sky and how it works. The way clouds move. I think the really high ones, cirrus clouds go fastest, except because they're so high up, they look like they're moving slower than, say, a low-hanging cumulus or alto-stratus. Another thing I've noticed are the exhaust trails left by jets. I guess most of it is condensed water, like in a cloud, but whatever's in them, they seem a lot bigger and fluffier than they were when I was a kid. Yesterday, I saw one that seemed to grow and grow until it engulfed half the sky.

This got me to wondering about it, and when I mentioned it to Jeff yesterday at dinner, he said I should listen to the Art Bell Show on KEX, AM 1190. He turns it on at work sometimes when he's in the kitchen. It comes on after ten o'clock and Art even had a show about weird exhaust patterns one time. He called them "contrails." All these pseudo-experts came on and gave their paranoid theories about how aliens are spiking jet fuel with extraterrestrial additives to change the climate or how the government is putting aluminum dust in it to combat global warning.

When Jeff started ripping on all those conspiracy theories, I realized that he'd never buy one word of my new insights about life and death. He'd think I was completely off my rocker. It's kind of ironic, too, because he's the one who gave me that King James Bible and it got me thinking along these lines. I've read most of it now, except for the boring books with family trees that go on for pages and pages, not to mention all those cleansing rituals of the Israelites.

Anything with a decent storyline grabs me. Especially the healings and prophecies. I've also started reading William Blake again, especially *The Marriage of Heaven and Hell* and *America: A Prophecy*. I told Jeff about what Jack had said about William Blake being the inspiration for his band, and Jeff totally cracked up. He said Jack was pulling my leg. Everyone knew he'd copped the band's name from an old song by The Clash called "Red Angel Dragnet," and The Clash had copped some of their lyrics from the movie, *Taxi Driver*. Everyone was always copping everyone else's material. That's what makes the art world go round. Even William Blake lifted most of his stuff right out of the Bible, isn't that right?

I said I really didn't like where this conversation was headed, it was turning ugly. Every great artist got their inspiration from God, whether they knew it or not, and that wasn't "copping," it was reflecting.

Jeff got this look on his face like, oh boy, here she goes again. That really ticked me off, so I told him I wasn't feeling so hot. Maybe the Chinese food wasn't agreeing with me. It was greasy compared to Japanese.

Jeff laughed and called me a racist. Ever since he started working at Ringlers, hanging out with 21st century hippies, they've slowly been brainwashing him into a PC mindset. It's pitiful. Second guessing yourself anytime you mention another culture or race.

And believe me, there's no one more confused than a hippie in the new millennium. Flower power went corporate years ago with Jane Fonda and a million other yuppies who preach hippy drivel but live in multi-million dollar homes from the way they've exploited the system.

Fuck Jeff. If he's going to judge me because I don't buy into the corporate machine that's slowly sucking him in and changing him, then so be it. He can sleep alone. I don't need any hypocrites in my bed, thank you very much.

As William Blake says, "I must create my own system or be enslav'd by another man's." I dare Jeff to find out where Blake "copped" that one.

ENTRY EIGHTY-ONE
Today I went to Safeway on Burnside and bought every yummy thing I could lay hands on. At the checkout counter, I had the clerk call over the manager. Could I possibly borrow a shopping cart for about an hour? He asked why and I said that I needed to get the food down to the Mission for the homeless. He said I couldn't borrow the cart, but since I'd bought so many groceries, he would have them delivered for me.

I sent everything anonymously. It would have been satisfying to see the looks on all those people's faces, but I like the idea of giving unconditionally. It cost me almost four hundred dollars, but that's nothing when you think about it. Almost the same price as the tattoo on my arm.

After I got home, I told Ruth. She said that was a nice gesture but it wasn't really my money to be giving away. It belonged to the band. Part of me understood why she said it, but part of me kind of bristled because she'd never complained before when I'd bought her sushi dinners on the band's money. I guess nobody's immune to hypocrisy.

Even me. I'm a hypocrite, I admit it. A sell-out, peddling my wares just like all those hippy bastards working Ringlers, even that dick of a manager. Even Nadja, who came to America from the land of communist thugs so she could sleep her way to the top of the food chain. By now she's probably let the manager peel her onion once or twice.

ENTRY EIGHTY-TWO
I've almost finished recording all the personal stuff I want to record. So far, I've had three producers come in, but I finally settled on Cynthia for "Cowslip." She says she's not together with Mike anymore, he's the biggest prick on the planet. I think she wants to work on The Compound's project and she's confused as to why I'm doing this little side project, but she didn't complain. She said she promised to keep it totally confidential.

That got me to thinking, I probably shouldn't be doing this "pet" project on the side with the band's money. Even if AMI is going send their corporate sharks up here any day now to find out what's going on. They keep calling and leaving messages. I haven't returned any of their calls. It's only a matter of time before they call Lars. They've got his number, so let them. He can do the talking. I'm a mess right now.

Despite the fact that I'm recording these songs, it's not costing very much. I moved into the cheapest studio, a board with only twenty-four tracks. For what I'm doing, that's more than enough.

If Lars wants to add tracks later, he can do whatever he wants with the ones I've put down. I'll be sure to leave the masters with him, in his safe keeping.

As a matter of fact, I think I'll even sign over the rights to the band. If they ever want to do anything with it, that's their prerogative. I hope they do. That would make me feel so good to know people were hearing it, even if another singer was singing it.

But still, I like to flatter myself that my vocals are pretty strong. I still have a killer set of pipes. So maybe a song or two will end up like that one by Suzanne Vega that got turned into a big hit when some British DJ laid down a dance beat under it. Stranger things have been known to happen.

ENTRY EIGHTY-THREE
Lars called and said he'd just gotten off the phone with the president of AMI. Michael Reiser had screamed at the top of his lungs: "What the hell's going on? How many songs have you recorded? Overnight everything! I want a copy on my desk tomorrow morning!"

Lars told Reiser that Dig Low had quit, we were shopping around for another producer. When Reiser heard that, he blew a head gasket. "Goddamn you Oregon hillbillies! Why didn't one of you call! How long ago did this happen?"

Lars said a little over a week. Reiser told him even a day was too long. He'd put his ass on the line for us and if we didn't keep his stockholders happy, it could mean his job. Lars managed to calm the man down and said that from now on he would personally call Reiser with a weekly update. Or he could call as often Reiser liked. Every day if he preferred.

Reiser's temper peaked again. He was the president of the second largest record company in the world, did Lars think he had time to hold Lars' dick every time he decided to take a leak?

Eventually, Reiser's tone changed. He gave Lars the name and number of some VP to call. This guy had the time to baby-sit. "Call him every day until you've got something to send me! And tell your sex-pot singer, 'Jules,' to give me a call at her earliest convenience."

I think Lars was surprised that I didn't get upset by the news. I might have even sounded a little relieved.

Actually, I was elated. Reiser's call meant two things: 1) Dig Low hadn't blabbed about my so-called "Parkinson's," and 2) AMI would give us a lot more breathing room than I'd expected.

Lars listened to my thoughts carefully. He was a great listener. Then he went on to say that he'd had an "epiphany." We had to get our shit together—and fast. Because the next time Reiser called, frightening as it may sound, he wouldn't be so nice. In the phone call, he'd also thrown out the names of some really respectable producers who would be willing to fly up to Portland immediately. Did I feel up to going back in the studio next week, say Tuesday?

I told him I'd consider it. Silence. Lars was thinking long and hard, trying to phrase what he was going to say next in the best possible words.

"No offense, Jules, but do you think you'll ever get better? Because if not, then shouldn't you be making the most of each day?"

He went on to say that he'd seen the Barbara Walters interview with Michael J. Fox a couple of years back and he remembered Fox saying that Parkinson's was "a slow decline" or something like that. It didn't just get you right away; it snuck up, little by little, day by day. So if I really wanted to do this, there was no time like the present.

Hearing those fateful words shook me awake. Even if I wasn't really sick from Parkinson's, Lars' observations were just as valid. I remembered how hard I'd worked to get where I was. These past few weeks, I'd resigned myself to "dying with dignity" instead of working to make something truly exceptional.

I told Lars about the side project I'd done in the little studio and he said yeah, that's cool. But it was small potatoes compared to what we could do as a band.

Part of me was offended and part knew he was right. *American Prayer* would have passed into obscurity if it hadn't been for all the Doors other albums.

"Alright," I said. "Count me in. I'm definitely down with recording on Tuesday."

Lars was thrilled. "Excellent!" he said. "Oh, before I forget, there's just one other thing: Are you still interested in playing The Orpheum with that band from Detroit, Wasp Factory?"

"Oh yeah. I forgot about that."

"Lou Gamble, the promoter, called this morning. He needs to know today if we can warm up. He even said there's even a chance we could headline this particular show because we're so popular in Portland right now."

"How do you mean? We've only played one show."

"KPDX, the college station, has been playing two songs from our demo on heavy rotation."

"Get out! PDX is playing our songs? Which ones?"

"'Burn' and 'So Close'."

"Really, they're playing 'Burn'? But we never even finished back-ups."

"Go figure."

"That's hilarious. Obviously this guy, Lou Gamble, has never been to Portland. Or else he'd know that nobody listens to PDX. It's a college station with, like, ten watts. I could barely get it when I lived in Southeast."

"Well, actually, there are additional factors."

"Oh? Like what?"

"You know, the latest rumor. That you've got AIDS."

"Who's been saying that?"

"Your favorite gossip columnist at the *Sun*.'"

"Tom Unfried? The Peeper?"

"He never came right out and said it, he just raised the possibility. Either that or anorexia."

"God, I hate that little man. The things I could do to him with a cattle prod and a jar of Vaseline."

"So let's do the next best thing. Make him eat his words! August 2nd we play The Orpheum and blow the doors off the place!"

"Well . . . I don't know."

"C'mon Jules. You've got all the songs down cold. It'd be a breeze."

"Yeah?"

"Yeah, and it would also send a good signal to AMI if they hear we've played a monster show. Even more publicity for when the album comes out."

"Are you kidding? No one would remember the show in a year."

"Don't be too sure. They're still talking about The Crystal like it happened yesterday."

"What makes you say that?"

"Jules, *hello*! Where have you been for the past month? That's all people are talking about. Like it or not, you're on your way to becoming an urban legend."

"Those aren't real."

"This one is."

"Not all of it."

"Only the good parts."

"OK, you win. I'll play the damned gig. Just to shut you up."

"Are you sure?"

"See you at The Cell. Shall we say high noon?"

"I hope you don't mean 'high' in the way I'm thinking."

"Alright, smart ass, make it one."

"One o'clock it is. Oh, and Jules: do yourself a favor. Get some rest."

"Lars, do yourself a favor: go fuck yourself."

"Now you're talkin! That's the urban legend we all know and love!"

ENTRY EIGHTY-FOUR

My brother Hans called early this morning and woke me up. I've been getting most of my sleep in the mornings these days. At night, I'm just too freaked out. The changes start up once my head hits the pillow. I can hear the Shadow People outside, on the street, whispering.

Sometimes their voices mingle with cars swooshing past outside, but I know why that is: They're trying to make me second guess myself. When they imitate the sounds of cars or trucks or construction they do it to confuse me. They even try to blend in with the sound of the toilet flushing when Ruth is downstairs. I don't think they know the difference between night and day, it's all the same to them; but *my* attitude changes at night, I get more fearful, and they always try to use that to their advantage. Fear is their butter and hatred their bread. They feast on the sorrows and blight of the world. It falls like crumbs from a rich man's table and they nibble each morsel with a sickening delight. I hate them, but I have to control my inner loathing. It's exactly what they want.

Hans was all worried about me. He said one of his friends mentioned that I was sick, it had been in the papers. Was it true I had AIDS? I laughed. Oh, Hans, what do you think? He said he didn't know, but my picture in the *Portland Sun* didn't look so hot. I was very thin and he could see the bones in my face, like a skeleton.

"Gee, thanks," I said. "I haven't heard from you since I invited you to my show at The Crystal, and now you're calling me Skeletor." Hans laughed and said he was sorry, but was I OK? I told him no, but I wasn't HIV positive.

"Well what is it, then?" he asked.

"You remember what got dad? Now it's working on me."

I could hear his brain processing the information. He wanted to say something, couldn't. And then I heard a sniffle and I knew he was fighting back the tears. "H-how. But how do you know? Have you been to the hospital?"

"Several times."

"But how could you get Alzheimer's? You're only twenty-two."

I felt my lips harden into a knowing smile. "Hans, you of all people. Christ. Dad didn't have *Alzheimer's*. You know that. Before he went to PHSU, you're the one who said he was acting just like the sheep, like he'd come down with scrapie."

"Yeah, but . . . did the hospital say you had scrapies?"

"People can't get scrapie. The human version is called CJD:

Creutzfeldt-Jakob Disease. It affects the brain with these deadly things known as 'prions.' They get in your stomach when you eat infected meat, and then they get drawn into your blood. Once they hit your lymph nodes, they get sucked up into your brain, where they have some kind of reaction and start eating away tissue. Until eventually your brain ends full of tiny holes like a sponge. The scientific name for all prion-related diseases, from Mad Cow to scrapie, is called 'spongipathy' because of the way it turns your brain into a sponge."

"Now, Julia. C'mon. That's messed up. Are you sure this isn't just another one of your *X-Files* theories?"

"Surf the net and find out for yourself.."

"The doctors said you've got the sponge disease?"

"No, they falsely diagnosed my case as Parkinson's. I still have to call this nurse back. She gave me some pills that are used to treat the symptoms associated with CJD, not Parkinson's. So there's something fishy going on over there. I think it has something to do with prions. They aren't like other diseases, organic. You can't kill them by sterilization. Instead, you have to remove them; but doctors don't know how to do that yet. So all the instruments they used to test dad and other patients with CJD are contaminated now, especially the surgical instruments. It could cost hundreds of millions to replace everything."

"Gosh, Julia. You're so smart. Since when did you get so smart?"

"Since I left Mt. Angel."

"Don't say that. It's beautiful here. The most beautiful place on earth."

"Yeah, like Marilyn Monroe in the casket. Not a hair out of place, but dead. That town is about as dead as they come."

"I like it here. You did too. Once. No matter what you say it will always be your home town."

"How's mom doing?"

"OK, I guess. She thinks you're mad at her, but she says all she wants is to see her daughter. She loves you, Julia. Can't you come visit?"

"No, I can't."

"No? Well, can we come visit you? Mom knows all about your new singing career. She's been clipping articles out of the paper. All her friends and customers at work ask her about you, and she kind of has to pretend that she knows how you're doing. I think it makes her real sad because she misses you."

"She said that?"

"No, but she does. You know how she is."

"Why didn't you come to my show?"

"Well, I tried. But I couldn't get no one to take me. If you'd a sent me a *pair* of tickets instead of one, I could've bribed a buddy to drive. Even if they don't much care for that style of music. Heavy metal, I mean."

"Hans, we don't play heavy metal. That went out in the 80s. Our band plays a style of rock that's more like Depeche Mode. You remember them?"

"No."

"I played them all the time at home."

"You played a lot of stuff. Mostly, I hated it. You used to be such a good country singer. I'll bet if you sang country again, you could sing all them gals off the stage, like the Dixie Chicks and Shania Twain. You ever listen to them?"

"Can't say as I do."

"What about Sheryl Crow? She's kind of rockish."

"No, I don't listen to her, either."

"*The Globe Sessions.* Check it out. All her videos are on the TV. We've got cable. I seen her play all kind of songs. She's real pretty. Tall, like you. 'Cept her hair ain't as nice as yours. It's mouse brown."

"Hans, how are you paying for your hospital bills?"

"Huh?"

"Your medical treatment. Is mom paying for it?"

"We got the Healthnet card. Pays for pret'near everything."

"Where'd you get it?"

"Daddy, 'fore he died. You got one too, don't ya?"

"No. No, I don't. Can you put mom on?"

"You want to talk to mom? She's right here!"

"I love you Hans."

"I love you, too. Here's mom! *Sssssssh. C'mere! Yeah, she wants to talk to you. No, I didn't. Mom, take the golldarn phone!*"

"H-hello?"

"Hi."

"Julia! It's so good to hear your voice."

"It's good to hear you, too."

"Oh, isn't this just the cat's meow! How are you, sweet heart?"

"I'm fine, fine."

"The newspapers say you're sick. Are you sure you're fine?"

"Which papers?"

"I don't know. The bad ones, I suppose. I only read *The Oregonian* and they haven't had much to say about you, just the concert dates when your band is playing. There was an article about your next concert. At The Morpheum, right?"

"The Orpheum, yeah. Who's been saying I'm sick? What have they been saying?"

"People talk . . . honey, now . . . you can tell me, I'm you mother. Have you got the AIDS?"

"No! I don't. Is that what they've been saying?"

"Just Mildred. She's got a mean streak a mile wide. I wore a red dress to the Biergarten last Saturday night and she told me I looked like a whore. The nerve of that woman!"

"Mom, listen to me: I don't have AIDS, but I am sick. The doctors say I have Parkinson's disease."

"Parkinson's! You mean like that nice boy from Family Ties? What was his name, Alex?"

"Yes, mom. That's part of the reason I called. Do I have any health insurance? Hans says he's got a Healthnet card."

"Oh yes. You're fully covered. When daddy died, he took out an expensive policy that pret'near broke the bank. Those creditors got so angry. But they can't touch the policy. Your daddy made sure of that. Hans got an extension, and you're fully covered until your twenty-fifth birthday."

"Oh, thank God. What a relief! Did it cover dad's bills at PHSU?"

"Yes, yes. Everything. The deductible was a few thousand. Less than three, I think. Let me see, I can check if you'd like."

"No, that's OK. I need you to send me my card and all the paper work. Can you mail it to me?"

"Well, I don't know. Why don't you come out and pick it up? I can make supper, your favorite: vegetarian lasagna!"

"To tell you the truth, mom, I don't really feel up to the drive. I'm pretty sick."

"How bad is it? Can you get around on foot?"

"And there's something else I want to tell you: I don't really have Parkinson's."

"I knew it! Oh, honey, why didn't you say so! You can tell me anything! I'm your mommy! I'm not here to judge you, all the bad things you've done. The Good Lord will forgive. All your sins, washed away with the blood of the lamb."

"Sssssssssh. I don't have AIDS, I already told you. It's something else. What dad died from. Creutzfeldt-Jakob Disease."

"Now why on earth would you say such a thing? You know Buck died from Alzheimer's. That's what the death certificate says."

"Yeah, I know. But I've found out some things out since then. Important facts. I'm pretty sure the hospital knew the truth by the time dad died, but they didn't want us to know."

"Why . . . that's crazy! Oh, dear. I thought you'd grown out of those crazy theories of yours. Everyone out to get you."

"Mom, would you listen to me for one second? It's not a *theory*. The head nurse insinuated that I had CJD. She gave me some medication, snuck it to me, these pills used to treat CJD, not Parkinson's or Alzheimer's. That's how I know for sure. My symptoms are identical to dad's."

"Portland, that wicked city has corrupted you! Come home to us. There's an extra bedroom. When I picked out the house, I chose one with three on purpose. It's a guestroom right now, but you can have it. It's your room. I can put all your things in there, your stuffed pink dinosaur. What's his name?"

"Deano."

"Julia, honey. We all love you so much, the whole town. Pastor John would certainly welcome you back into the flock. He asks after you almost every Sunday. Everyone in Mt. Angel, even the Catholics, will forgive the sins you've committed if you come home to us!"

"Mom, I'm not asking for anyone's forgiveness. I just need you to send me my Healthnet card. Can you do that?"

"No, I don't trust the post. Things get lost. I'll drive there myself. What's your address?"

"Well . . . I'm not sure that's such a hot idea."

"It's not open for debate."

"OK, if you promise not to mention any of that stuff about coming home."

"Yes, yes. I promise. We'll just talk about happy things. Like the way we all used to ride horses down to the stream. Do you remember Misty?"

"Of course!"

"She loved you very much—thought of you as her colt. Very protective. You remember the time that hateful ram, Buddy, when he broke down Mr. Conner's fence and charged. We were down by the stream and your father rode as fast as he could, but it would have been too late if it hadn't been for Misty. She saw what was happening, where you were picking wild flowers, and she came over and stood right in front of you, she wouldn't let Buddy touch you. That Misty; she was the smartest horse ever."

"She wasn't a horse, mom. She was a pony."

"Do you ever think about Misty?"

"All the time. I still miss her. But it makes me sad because I'll never see her again."

"Oh, poo! Why not? You think God keeps ponies out of heaven? I'm sure there's a place for Misty up there. If any animal deserved to walk through the pearly gates, it was your Misty."

"OK . . . well, I've gotta go."

"Wait! We haven't set up a date and time. When should I bring the packet?"

"Soon. How about the day after tomorrow? At, say, three o'clock."

"I suppose I could come then. But I am scheduled to work Fridays until six . . ."

We hammered out the details of the visit. It took a while, but eventually we both hit upon an agreeable time: Seven o'clock, Friday.

When I hung up the phone, it was like this fifty-pound saddle had been strapped on my back. Hearing mom's voice reminded me of all the bad times. She was still carrying them around with her even though she tried to keep a cheery outlook and never said a negative word. The pain and suffering had changed her, made her seem brighter on the outside, when really she was the most unhappy person on earth.

Even when times had been good, before Hans' accident, she'd still had a dark, gloomy disposition. And then at other times she'd be bouncing off the walls—so much so, it frightened Hans and me. Looking back on it now, I'm fairly certain that mom was, and still is, bi-polar. Her mood swings, oh my God. They were enough to knock a little kid off her feet.

Hans and I used to play this game we invented called, "Watch Out For Mommy." One of us would come giggling to the other and say, "Watch out for Mommy! She's saying mean things again." Then we both knew it wasn't really her, it was the wicked witch of the west pretending to be her. Our real mommy was locked up in a dungeon under the house. If we listened through the floor, we could hear her calling for help, warning us about dangerous things the wicked witch might do. I'd put my ear to the floor under the dining room table and say, "Hans, *shhh*! Be quiet. Mom said not to eat the cookies. They're poison!"

Kids have an amazing way of coping with almost anything. In some ways, they're a lot more resilient than adults. I'm twice as old now, and the thought of seeing mom is enough to drive me to drink, even though it's only one o'clock in the afternoon. I just hope it's not the wicked witch of the west who pulls up in front of my house. Because if it is, I don't think I can face her—with or without that Healthnet card.

ENTRY EIGHTY-FIVE

The conversation with mom got me to thinking. How many other people think I have AIDS? The Peeper is ruining my life. All he cares about is his own stupid column, making his weekly quota of lies. God, how I resent being put in this position. Even if I did have AIDS, it would be no one's business but my own.

Peeping Tom Unfried. It's worth spilling the beans just to spite him! But how can I tell the world? There's no way unless I throw myself at the mercy of AMI. Once the word's out that I have CJD, either they'll drop us from the label or work with us.

Judging from what Reiser said to Lars on the phone, it sounds like they're still behind us. He definitely unbuttoned his collar on this deal, and to be perfectly honest, if I'd been in his position, I wouldn't have done it. Not from a business perspective. He'd allowed himself to get caught up in the hype, the bidding war. Hart had sucked him in.

Of course, if it wasn't for the CJD, he would have gotten his money's worth and more. But now, I'm not so sure how much longer I can hold out. The shadows are following me everywhere like buzzards circling a cowgirl in the desert who's lost her horse. They're waiting for the end, hedging their bets, keeping me off balance so I'll become one of them like Mr. Green.

When I saw him in my dream, he hadn't lost his earthly energy yet, I could tell. He wasn't himself, but that's because something else was manipulating him, telling him lies, trying to trick him. Soaking up what little light he had left, what little love he could still feel from God. And now the demon, whatever it was, discarded the love part like the rind of an orange; but it kept the juicy power, converting it for its own evil ends.

Well, alright then. So be it. I've made up my mind. I'm throwing a party next Thursday night. It'll be perfect, the first Thursday of August when everyone comes to visit the art galleries.

My first instinct is to make it kind of small, inviting only my best friends, but I don't think I should be uptight about that. Whatever happens happens. Since my loft is so big, I think I'll have Lars and the guys bring over some gear, maybe even the PA from the Compound and we can play a few numbers. Two or three songs. Then I make the announcement: I've got Creutzfeldt-Jakob Disease. But it's not contagious, so don't worry about sitting on the toilet seat! Just don't use my toothbrush! There might be a couple of prions hiding in the bristles.

Ruth will help organize everything. She's a wizard when it comes to planning. I'm going all out this time, nothing's too good for my friends. Just like Henry Chinaski in *Barfly* when he gets that check from his publisher. "HEY, BARKEEP: ANOTHER ROUND FOR MY FRIENDS!"

Speaking of which, I should also hire a caterer. Oh, and a bartender for behind the bar. Except instead of some stale beer in an old man bar, it will be champagne and caviar! FOR MY FRIEEEEEENDS! Maybe Jeff will work for free. Naw, that would be cruel. I'll ask him to bring one of his bros from Ringlers—but no hippy-dippies.

Just thinking about it, I'm really starting to get excited! This is going to be a blast! Maybe the Dandy Warhols will show. I hear they're in town. Or the leader of Pink Martini: that cute piano player, Thomas.

ENTRY EIGHTY-SIX

My mom came about an hour ago. It was great to see her. At first. She seemed genuinely glad to see me. But as soon as she stepped into my apartment and goes, "Oh my, what an odd place," I wanted her out. Immediately. She went over to the decorative steel door and rapped on it with her knuckles. "Where does this lead? The meat locker?" I guess it reminded her of someplace in Mt. Angel where they process livestock.

She couldn't have said a worse thing if she'd tried. Now I'm thinking about what Mélange told me before I signed the lease.

No—I'm not even going there. I love this place and nothing can make me move. Not unless I find blood between the cracks in the floor. Mélange asked if he could bring a few friends from out of town to my party, big time dealers from Europe he's trying to impress. It was so adorable, the way he came right out and admitted that. Most people try to hide it when they want to make a good impression. Not Mélange. I told him sure, by all means bring them. Please keep it under ten, though, if you don't mind. He said no problem.

Getting back to mom, she walked around and wanted to see every nook and cranny. I felt like she was appraising my abilities as a housekeeper, running her finger along window ledges to look for dust, annoying things like that. Well, I'm sure she found plenty. I haven't dusted since the first week I moved in.

Mom's always been a little on the anal side. It's in her blood. Germans are the most anal people on earth, except for maybe the Japanese. Kobo's absolutely *psychotic* about messes. One time he came by the studio and saw all the beer cans and wrappers on the floor and started picking them up, himself, with this surly expression on his mug.

Mom asked about the furniture, was I planning on getting more than the mattress upstairs on the floor and this one couch? I said maybe, but I liked the open space, that's part of the reason I chose this place. I wanted to explain how the ranch house had been so cluttered when I was growing up that it had made me claustrophobic for life, but I thought better of it. That would hurt mom's feelings.

I made her a cup of coffee. She said it was the best she'd ever drunk. What was that gizmo I'd made it with? I told her it was a French press and a grinder to grind the beans. Then I washed it off and gave her the press and the grinder as a gift, along with this big two-pound bag of Ruth's most expensive beans.

Mom tried to refuse, but I said, oh please, it's nothing. Take! Enjoy! I can't drink coffee anymore. Don't ask why. I could tell she wanted to, but she was afraid to go there. Didn't want to get me started. It was obvious that she hadn't believed a word I'd told her on the phone about CJD. I don't think Hans had either. They're both convinced I'm crazy as a loon. I can hear my mom now, gossiping with Hans as she makes dinner: "All those drugs she takes: Marijuana and who knows what else. It's no wonder she's on edge." The two of them jabbering away. Enough to make you stand up and yell "SILENCE!" at the top of your lungs.

If only they'd seen Tawny drive a spike into my arm, then they'd really think I was nuts. And in a way, I suppose they'd be right: I *am* nuts, at least by most people's standards. But I'm glad because most people would have said the same exact thing about Blake and that Swedish mystic, Emanuel Swedenborg.

These days, I'm touching the fringes of eternity and if that makes me loony, then so be it: I'm a loon.

Sorry if I'm rambling. It's hard for me to concentrate. The changes are tugging at my sleeve, pulling me towards . . . well, I don't want to talk about that now.

Let's get back to mom, her visit. She didn't stay long. I think my shaking made her nervous. Maybe she thought I was strung out, I don't know. She probably still thinks I have AIDS. The way she looked at me with a combination of pity, disappointment and loathing. The worst combination of motherly qualities you can imagine. I'd rather she just slapped me in the face and told me I was no daughter of hers: A whore and a sinner. That would have been easier to take.

I asked why Hans hadn't come, and she made some lame excuse. I think he's afraid of me now. I intimidate him. All of the promise he once had—the brightness, the down to earth smarts—it's like it's all been drained away. Living his whole life in Mt. Angel, he's turned into a full-fledged hick. Whenever I see him or talk to him on the phone, I've got this mother hen urge to rip off the blinders; his fear of learning about the outside world.

Everyone in Mt. Angel justifies that same fear with quotes from the

Bible. "Remove thy foot from evil," stuff like that. But what they fail to realize is that Jesus said not to judge anyone. Evil is only a mask that covers people's True Selves, like a disfiguring disease. The real person, the good person, is always under there. Portland is not evil. There's plenty of good if you look for it.

Hiding out in the sticks and burying your head in the dirt is certainly not the fastest way to heaven. It doesn't get you brownie points with God.

Now, if you help the so-called "sinners," people everywhere who, for whatever reason, are blind to the goodness within themselves, that *will* bring you closer to God because you're reflecting Her loving kindness, reflecting Her light into other people's lives. Completing the cycle that ultimately returns back to the source.

That's what the Scriptures mean when they talk about glorifying Her name!

I wish Hans was brave enough to move here and hang out with me. I'd introduce him to all my friends and be the sister I never had the chance to be. Whatever he wanted to do. You name it, I'd support him. I love him so much.

I love you, Hans, my big *strong* brother. I'm so sorry about what I did. It was an accident, but it was still my fault and it's been eating away my insides knowing that I'm the cause of your misery. You could have been so much more: All-state high school champion, star quarterback of OSU, the U of O, whatever. You could have done it, I know you could! Anything you'd set your mind to, and you still can! Maybe not on the grid iron, but football doesn't last forever, even in the NFL. Your legs might be shot, but you've still got a good head on your shoulders and the biggest heart around.

Oh Hans! You have so much to give to the world! Get out of that prison, get away from mom! She's poisoning your mind, draining away your ambition, transforming you into a companion for rainy days . . . and there are so many rain-filled days in Oregon.

I can't write anymore. My keyboard is wet with tears.

ENTRY EIGHTY-SEVEN
Found out both *Willamette Week* and the *Mercury* take electronic

submissions, so I emailed them my article on the Mad Cow/Scrapie/CJD connection. Yesterday, Lars emailed me back suggestions about ways to improve it. He caught all these typos and grammar bugs that Ruth and I totally spaced on. Plus, he showed me how to spice up my text with these things called "headers" to make it read easier. In journalism, you have to lead your reader by the hand. They don't have the patience of someone sitting down to read a novel (or a journal, *wink, wink*).

I guess I'll hear soon enough what those guys think at the weeklies. Ruth thought I should also mail it to the *Sun*, but I said forget that, they print Unfried's column. Any paper that publishes that flaming cow dung isn't worth my consideration. Besides, wouldn't it be kind of bizarre if I was published right after "Peeping Tom?"

Ruth said that's exactly what they'd do. And it would open the door for me to write a comeback editorial about Unfried: Battle of the Pens. I have to admit, she almost had me convinced. Maybe if the *Willy Week* and *Mercury* pass, I'll consider the *Sun*. I could use that cattle prod pen, after all. Get Unfried where it would hurt him the most.

ENTRY EIGHTY-EIGHT

Finally, I got through to that nurse practitioner at PHSU. She called me back after I'd left about a dozen messages on her answering machine. In the last two, I mentioned that I was FULLY INSURED WITH OREGON HEALTHNET. I knew that would get her attention. She's just like all the rest, a money-sucking vampire.

But I have to admit she was rather nice on the phone. It sure beats her bedside manner. She has one of those faces with sharp features that are painful to watch, especially when she's telling you about life and death. She said that she'd been meaning to give me a call about the test results but things had gotten hectic around the hospital lately. I asked her what she meant about the tests and she sounded almost a little apologetic. She said that there was some indication that my suspicions had been correct.

Part of me got really excited when she said that, and part of me sunk even deeper into despair. I started throwing out some words that I'd learned in my research and she seemed impressed, responding on a more advanced level, almost as if I were a physician. It was flattering, but I have to admit she lost me.

Now that I had Healthnet coverage, she was all fired up to have me come in for more tests. Tapping my spinal column for fluid, gnarly stuff like that. I said thanks but no thanks. Just the medication, please. Could she write me out a prescription for more pills? Anything to stop the headaches. They were getting unbearable.

The nurse was very sympathetic and said, yes, of course, I had a few options there, she'd consult with a doctor and get a second opinion.

I asked if she meant the guy I'd met with and she said no, he wasn't affiliated with the hospital anymore. She wasn't at liberty to discuss the matter, but it had a direct bearing on my situation. That's when I knew they'd fired his ass. Did it anything to do with all the equipment over there that might have come in contact with prions, per se? She didn't laugh. I think it might have pissed her off, actually. So I backed off and changed the subject to the new doctor who'd be taking my case. The nurse was even willing to give his name, Dr. Eastman.

Doctor *Lawrence* Eastman? I said. The nurse seemed a little surprised that I'd heard of him. I almost told her about that article I'd just finished writing, how I'd come across Eastman's name in several different places, and then I thought better of it. Instead, I made up a lie, that I'd heard of him when my father was being treated at the hospital. The nurse didn't seem at all surprised. Her response made me wonder if Eastman had somehow been involved in treating my dad or studying his case.

So today, I'm making a quick trip up to the hospital for another prescription. The nurse said she'd have it ready by three o'clock. That's a relief because I don't think I could last much longer without some kind of help aside from the alcohol and pills. That giant baggie of ludes that Digger's people scored is almost out. One day without those and I'd probably go insane from the pounding in my temples.

Every time my heart beats, I can feel this rush of voices flooding through my consciousness. It's the Shadow People, calling out in unison, like they're being guided by something else, trained to key in to my frequency, the resonation of my imperfect self commonly described as a "soul." I don't believe in souls, not like most Christians think of them. It's a cop out, an overly simplistic way of explaining what happens when we leave our bodies and most people get it all wrong. They think of our bodies as these vessels and our souls as our True Selves, but that's not really correct. We aren't in our bodies right now, we're with the All-Mother but we just don't know it.

The whole idea of being good so our souls will join a patriarchal God in heaven is a shortcut to thinking. It leads to darkness, not light. Demons get off on that kind of thing, manipulating us into believing we're all doomed unless we live perfect lives.

Well, I know differently. We're not shits out of luck—that's like calling God the creator of all shit, a title I reserve for the demons and whatever force seems to be guiding them. The Shadow People answer to them and they probably answer to other higher-ups. And at the top of this unholy pyramid, a single red eye.

ENTRY EIGHTY-NINE

The party is nigh upon us. It's Wednesday afternoon here at "the meat locker." Ruth's taking the day off work tomorrow to help me get ready. So far no one famous is coming, but that's just as well. I know things tend to pick up at the last minute, especially in the heart of the Pearl District on First Thursday.

The *Willy Week* and *Mercury* both turned down my article. Polite rejection emails, standard form letters. Maybe they didn't realize who I was. I could have mentioned the band in my cover letter, but somehow that felt cheesy, relying on my pull as a celebrity. Or maybe they thought I was just some idiot using a controversial rock star's name.

Getting those form letters was a sobering experience. I couldn't help but wonder if my writing was professional enough. Lars seemed to think so. He even added a few minor touches of his own to help shore up "potentially dangerous prose landslides" as he put it, the show off. I'll give him a landslide falling on that fat head of his if he doesn't watch out. But seriously, I'm going to tell Lars tomorrow night about my sob story and see if he has any advice on how to get published.

This morning over breakfast Ruth finally convinced me to send my little masterpiece to the *Sun*. I emailed it at about two o'clock this afternoon and I haven't heard back. They'll probably freak when they figure out who wrote it. Everyone in their offices must be familiar with my name by now, considering I've been a target for the past four or five issues. I wouldn't be surprised if Unfried's tacked my face on a dartboard in his office.

If he hasn't yet, he will after I get through with him. I'm going to make him eat every vile word he's said about me. Forget the sword or the pistol, uncap your pen! It's a showdown at the OK Corral!

Peeping Tom better come prepared to do battle because I'm not only bringing my favorite ballpoint to the table, but also my laptop and printer, which is basically the equivalent of a .38 special with hollow-tipped slugs for maximum impact.

Last night Jeff called and said we're all set bartender-wise. Some kid from Ringlers Annex. I've hung out a few times at the Annex; it's in this really cool triangular building wedged between Stark and Burnside. I haven't been there lately because I've pretty much banned all things "McMinnimal" since that episode with Nadja, but even I have to admit the place has a certain quality you can't find elsewhere.

I'm really excited about the food at our party. Ruth hired this caterer who owns a fancy-schmancy restaurant in Sellwood and hosts a cooking show on television. Everything's going to be either seafood or veggie. I thought about sushi, but that could get sketchy unless it was properly chilled, and tons of ice would be a mess. So nix on the sush. We'll have plenty of other delectables.

On the phone, Jeff mentioned that maybe I should also think about hiring a Big Punisher to stand in front of my building just in case there's trouble. He said to keep in mind that I'm living in a fairly rough part of town. Not like Southeast where you can almost leave your doors unlocked at night. Jeff asked if I was willing to go up to a hundred bucks. If so, he could get a professional from Crystal Ballroom. Two of the guys might even do it for free if I let them trade off at the door and mingle the rest of the time.

I think Ruth hid my leathers. Can't find them anywhere. The other day, she complained they stunk. At the time, I'd just taken them off to go to bed, so I picked them up and smelled them to see what she was talking about. They didn't seem so bad to me, minus a stain here and a stain there.

The crotch was a little gamy, but, hey, that goes with the territory, right? Leathers are leather. They're supposed to be like a seventh layer of skin. And what's wrong if I spread my scent around? Furry pheromones.

It might have been a tad noticeable, but it didn't smell disgusting. Just the hint of a clean well-oiled *purrrrrrr* beneath my perfume.

Besides, how do you wash leathers? They're too stiff for the washing machine. I guess when they "resurface" after the party I should take them to the cleaners.

I'll go shopping tomorrow morning for something equally dashing. Maybe a leather mini to show off my long legs that look even longer now that I'm a beanpole. You know what they say about beanpoles: Every Jack in town wants to climb them.

Ouch. Sorry for the cheesy pun. That's what I get for hanging out with an English prof. But seriously, I must not look half bad because I still get more than my share of whistles in the street and heads turning when I walk into a bar or nightclub.

So for those of you who think the "waif look" is out, I'm here to tell you it's alive and well. And horny. I've been getting really horny lately. It's hard being a good girl. Keeping a "pure" thought so God's light will shine through the holes multiplying in my brain. Even though I can barely stand up because of the headaches, I still occasionally want to get down and do the nasty.

Well, OK: more than just *occasionally.* Strange as it may seem, being sick makes you horny. Mother Nature knows she might not get another crack at reproduction, so she gives it all she's got. In the great scheme of things, you still can come out a winner, even if you pop out only one kid. Because if that kid's *exceptional*, it could pass on your genes to any number of potential mates. Hence, your DNA legacy.

Come to think of it, Kurt Cobain was right: Nature *is* a whore. So even if I get drunk tonight or tomorrow night or whenever, it's really not such a big deal. Maybe that could be my new come-on line: "Hey there, you hunka burnin' love, you: *Touch me I'm sick.*" With my luck, the first guy I say it to would be Mark Arm. I wonder how many fans have used that line on him? Mr. Mud Honey, himself.

But seriously, it's not like I can *give* anyone CJD. It's not communicable. Even if I wanted to infect another person, it would be virtually impossible—at least according to all the information I've gathered from the web. Short of drinking my blood or eating a pound of flesh, any potential suitor is safe.

Well, maybe I should qualify that: he's safe from catching a *disease* but considering half of Portland is convinced I've got AIDS, his reputation might suffer considerably in the "safe sex" department. Kind of ironic. The only contagious disease I've ever caught was the clap from Jeff and that's been history ever since I took those antibiotics.

I've just had an epiphany. Scratch everything I just said about getting laid. There's one notable exception to the rule and her name is R-U-T-H. It wouldn't matter if every guy on the planet wanted me, I'd pass them all up for one night of passion with girlfriend. I'm convinced beyond a doubt that she's the most beautiful person on earth. Jeff's a hopeless clod by comparison.

Even the slickest, meanest, baddest hipster can't compare to my baby doll. I know why that is: I'm in love with her. Not a crush, not lust. I truly *love* her and I want to show her how I feel. To express my love, give it shape, form. Motion.

Ruth's known how I feel about her for a long time, even if I've never said it in so many words. To tell the truth, I was kind of surprised when she took up my offer and moved in with me. That must mean I don't make her uncomfortable like Deeksha the Dragon made me feel living in her midst.

On the day I moved out of her lair, The Great White Worm had been shocked. Especially when I gave her the rest of June's rent plus the first week of July's. She said I didn't have to do that. Could we just sit down and talk so there aren't any hard feelings?

Right off, she apologized for coming onto me in the garden; it was totally unforgivable. She'd given in to her weak side, violating all the principles she held sacred. Osho would never have approved of such opportunism. Could I ever forgive her? I said I could, no hard feelings. We hugged then, and I felt a lot better.

However, I can't say as though I've missed her. Not even a little. It's such a relief to be away from that heaviness, the way she lumbered around the apartment like an overweight panther in a zoo, ever-watchful—stalking, almost by force of habit, trying to find a way to get at me through the bars.

If I ever came across that way to Ruth, I think I'd shoot myself rather than face the fact that I was being a "Deeksha." Be this as it may, I still find myself doing some of the same things that Deeksha did to me, like watching Ruth out of the corner of my eye, the way she moves around the apartment, the way she regards me . . . just generally being aware of her sexually.

Girlfriend waltzes into the bathroom without a second thought when I'm in the shower or peeing; it doesn't seem to bother her, so I've been doing the same. I think on a subconscious level she's attracted to me, but that doesn't mean she's full-out "bi."

All women have that nature-nurture instinct, it's part of who we are as physical beings here on earth, our role as custodians at the gate. But my passion for Ruth goes beyond that. I've had dreams about her, holding her, tasting her lips, *all* of her, reveling in her love. Part of it is obviously the fact that we sleep together in the same bed like children. In the middle of the night, I'll feel her leg resting across mine, and it makes me start to tingle all over.

Try going to sleep with that kind of frustration! You just want to slink downstairs and pleasure yourself, but even that might be overheard. Especially with the acoustics: wood floors, open balcony, bare walls.

Sometimes I almost get the feeling that Ruth wouldn't push me away if I touched her, especially in bed. I know it sounds stupid, like *duh!* But it isn't so simple. I have to make sure I'm not overstepping my bounds. The signals are there. Ruth hasn't said anything yet about getting another bed for herself. I keep waiting for the subject to come up, but it never does.

So, in a way, maybe I'm just being paranoid about being rejected. Maybe she's waiting for me to make the first move.

I'll never forget the look Ruth gave me in the mirror that night before I went on stage at The Crystal. If it wasn't sexual then I don't know what is. I think part of it was her attraction to me as a rock star on that particular night. I wasn't ordinary Jules anymore. I was *other,* a stranger insofar as the situation was concerned.

My power as a celebrity—it's intoxicating, but sad at the same time. Before that night, Ruth had seen me entirely naked many times, but never reacted quite the same. In all fairness, I think part of it had to do with my outfit, the leathers and open shirt; I looked different, so thin, my hair longer than ever before. It made me feel superhuman: "I'm the Lizard King! I can do anything!"

Part of that energy came across as sexual. And part of my success that night was due to my encounter with Ruth in the dressing room. While I was singing, she was in the back of my mind the whole time. I knew she was watching me, so I projected my love to her via the audience; they amplified the signal and she got it loud and clear.

Later on, after the performance, Ruth had seemed flushed, literally bursting with excitement. It wasn't merely, my success, it was *ours*. I'd shared my moment in the sun, intoxicating her with the raw power of celebrity (as well as the complimentary G&Ts).

Throwing this party with Ruth is almost giving me the same kind of vibe that I got helping Jeff throw one of his keggers. I feel almost like we're a couple and I'm fairly sure that Mélange thinks we're an item, if only casually. He's seen Ruth and me take guys up to the apartment separately, so he probably thinks we're in an open "bi" relationship.

Mélange is almost like a girlfriend or a mother, the way he notices things like that. Every time I go out, he waves. And if Ruth and I happen to stumble home drunk and he's in the gallery, I've seen him step over to the window and scan the street nervously to make sure we get inside safely.

He said the Icelandic artist who designed the glass sculptures might be coming tomorrow night; she's very interested in meeting me. I was surprised when Mélange said "she" because I just assumed the artist was a man. With a name like "Hafdis Sollilja," it was anyone's guess. Mélange hadn't put a picture of her on the wall. He laughed when I confessed my surprise. "Yes, well perhaps it was also her subject matter," he joked. "A two-thousand year old corpse set in a block of ice isn't exactly what one thinks of as 'chick' art." I smacked him on the arm for that one, the sexist bastard.

In Portland, they have a tradition called "First Thursday." On the first Thursday of every month, the galleries in the Pearl District stay open late and welcome visitors. Some of them even serve snacks and drinks to get people in the door.

Lately, I'd been to so many galleries that the thought of going out and mingling tomorrow night on Broadway or somewhere just isn't appealing. But I don't have to, the gallery-goers are coming to me!

All of the displays start to feel the same after you've been to enough of them. Especially in Portland. In my nightly sojourns over the past few weeks, I've noticed several things—not least of which is that often the best artists preferred to remain anonymous, even to their patrons. Hence, no picture of Hafdis in the gallery. Let the art speak for itself! How refreshing that must be. Unlike the music biz: all glitter & glam, where substance is forced into the back seat.

Yeah, the more I think about it, the more anxious I am to meet the face behind those intriguing displays—especially the ones upstairs. Hafdis Sollilja: Her name's a mouthful, but she's definitely on my wave length. I wonder if she knows Björk or anyone from Gus-gus?

ENTRY NINETY
Last night was probably one of the most horrible and wonderful nights of my life. I'm so happy, I could sing. In fact, I think I will!

"LAAAAAAAAAAAAAAAAAAAAAAAA!"

I suppose I could go ahead and cut to the chase, tell you what happened after the party, why I'm so elated to the very core of my being. But I'm not going to. I'm going to be a good girl for once. You gotta eat your mock-meat and potatoes before dessert!

Typing this journal has taught me a thing or two about suspense. Better to keep the reader guessing .

Let me start out by saying that the party was by far the most successful I've ever thrown. No snags or glitches whatsoever. I guess the old saying is true: you get what you pay for.

This one set me back almost five thousand dollars. I can't believe I spent that kind of scratch. But it was worth every penny and the rest of the band had the times of their lives. Not one of them complained, they all seemed to acknowledge we needed a break to blow off steam and since we had the cash, why not spend it.

I told Lars what Hart had said about spending as much as possible in a hurry to avoid taxes on the full amount. He seemed skeptical, but said we could talk about it some other time. Tonight was all good! No shoptalk.

A few hours later, he proceeded to break his word, after I'd made the announcement about the CJD. He came over and said he'd noticed how much I was shaking and how my voice sounded different. Maybe you should take a rest until after The Orpheum and hit the studio then. I said I was so relieved to hear him say that. I could really use the rest. Singing only three songs had exhausted me and my throat was sore. He said that our top priority now would be The Orpheum. He'd mentioned it to the VP at AMI and the guy had thought it was a good idea considering how we'd gotten "derailed" with Dig taking off. He said AMI had blacklisted Dig for breach of contract.

Hearing that surprised me because I'd thought his contract was with us, not AMI. We hadn't even thought to bust him for breaking his word because he'd been working on spec. Maybe that's why he hadn't badmouthed me despite what I said on the phone.

So Dig would be out quite a bit of capital for his act of desertion. Those suits in LA don't mess around. I'm kind of nervous. They're going to hear about the CJD for sure now that the word's out. I've got to be brave and put it out of mind.

Ruth and I invited our buds from PCC to come over and help set up for the party. They're not really gallery-goers anyway, unless it's to hook up with a guy. Not exactly the "artsy" types like us. Well, like me. I guess Ruth's not exactly the artsy type either, but she does her best. She's the only person I know who could put up with my eccentricities for any length of time. Regardless of my "artistic" temperament that only seems to keep getting worse as my art gets better.

When the caterer finally made it, she was really impressed with the space: much larger than she'd expected, one of the largest lofts she'd ever seen in Portland. More of a warehouse.

I told her it *was* a warehouse. And this was one whole side of it, about a third of the entire floor space on this floor. The rest was vacant for now and so were the floors above us. The owner was in the process of converting the entire building into lofts but his bank loan hadn't gone through yet. She was quite impressed and said, "OK, let's get started. We don't have much time."

I pointed her over to the tables we'd rented and had some guys set up for us earlier in the afternoon. Then Lars and the guys came with the drum risers and the PA, which they set up in the corner by the "meatlocker." Niles and Ernesto said we should hold band practice here. It was way bigger than the Compound.

Lars seemed just a tad irritated when they said that and asked what the rent was. I told him and I could tell he was trying not to get pissed. He went over and started unpacking his drums from the cases, biting his lip to keep from saying something he'd regret. Ernesto, bless his Latino heart, came over and gave me this great big boyish hug and asked how I was doing. I could tell by the look on his face and Nile's face that Lars had told them everything.

That kind of rubbed me the wrong way because I'd told Lars in confidence, but it was the band, after all, we were like family, so I decided it wasn't too far out of line. Ernesto took me aside and said he'd brought a gift for me.

What a sweetie! I took him into the kitchen and got him a beer from the fridge (the kegs weren't set up yet). He took a big gulp and a drop of beer snuck out that cute little mouth of his. I wiped the drop and then I couldn't resist, I gave him a little peck on the lips. He jumped back and nearly dropped his beer. He was laughing, this high-pitched nervous laugh, saying if he'd known that giving me a present would have gotten him kisses like that, he would already have spent all his money!

What a darling! I opened the wrapping paper carefully because it was very interesting, with all these cool Spanish words on it and these bright shapes of party favors that I'd never seen before, not like we have here in America: Seashells and little horns and things like that.

When I commented on how much I liked the paper, he said, oh, it's not "party" paper. It's ceremonial. Part of the gift, a tradition in Santeria, kind of like Christmas. I said, oh, that's very cool using religious paper. And then I opened it up. How beautiful! A little statue, very strange but charming. He said it was the first step towards building a shrine. If I wanted him to, he'd help me. I could build one right here in my home for protection against evil spirits.

I marveled at the statue. Ernesto called it *"oshé Changó"* and said it was very *very* powerful. It was about one and a half feet tall and made of bronze or some kind of gold colored metal (obviously not gold). An African woman holding her pointed breasts. Erenesto explained the thing balanced on her head was actually a special double-edged axe called *"edun ara."*

Everyone came over to see. Ernesto jumped in between when Mae-Ling reached out to touch it. He said he was very sorry, but no one else must come near for the first three days it was in my apartment. After that, I'd be free to show anyone, but they still were not to touch it. Such precautions ensured that I could welcome Changó into my heart.

I got a little nervous the way Ernesto spoke with such reverence and just a hint of fear, like the statue was alive or something. He must have noticed because he said it was perfectly alright if I didn't want the protection. But he would have to take the statue back immediately; it was a sacred object blessed by his Babalawo and it could anger the gods if I rejected it.

At this point, I didn't actually consider whether I wanted something like that in my home. It went directly against my religious beliefs, but it was so beautiful and I didn't really believe all that mumbo jumbo. So I said, OK, I'd go put it away in my closet for the rest of the party.

Ernesto seemed relieved. He went up into the bedroom with me and asked if there was any other way I wanted to repay him. He sat down on the bed, raised an eyebrow. I almost got angry and then I saw that he was only joking. *Mierditas!* The little shit!

By the time people started arriving we had the bar set up complete with a keg on tap (Newcastle brown) and a fully stocked bar. Jeff had told us everything to get the day before: We should put all the really good stuff away because that was too expensive. So we had well drinks, one bottle of good tequila and one bottle of good whisky. But when those went, there would only be the well drinks.

At the liquor store, Ruth and I had bought this giant bottle of Sapphire, our private reserve, to mix with our tonics. Hey, it was out party, right? We could do whatever the hell we wanted! And now all the good stuff was up in my closet with Changó's statue. I hoped his priestess didn't mind being up there in the dark with all that booze. She was certainly free to help herself!

After the first hour, I could tell that we wouldn't be hurting for guests. Already, the place was filling up: People talking in little clusters everywhere. Ruth and I walked around, playing the cordial hosts, asking if everything was OK and trying to stop by each cluster to welcome the newcomers. Everyone seemed really impressed with the whole thing. I didn't know at least half of them. Assumedly, the percentage would get higher and higher as the evening wore on. Most of the galleries were closed by now, but I knew that the true late-nighters hadn't even left their homes yet.

At exactly midnight, The Compound did a mini sound check. A crowd gathered around the stage that Lars had set up. He'd worked really hard on it and I felt kind of guilty that no one else had offered to help. It was amazing how my loft had been transformed into a club-like atmosphere with the help of a few decorations and a few black lights tacked up here and there.

Lars had even brought this light for the stage: a big portable lamp with a lens on it that the band used back in their old days when they'd played at various coffee shops around town. The light was red, which I didn't really care for. I asked Lars if he could change it and he said, sorry, no, he'd forgotten to bring the other colors, but he could dim it if I wanted. I said, yes, please. It was shining up into my eyes.

We started out with "Close," what evidently was turning out to be our biggest hit (that is, if you went by what they played the most on KPDX, that college station downtown that had been giving us a generous amount of air time). I felt really good with plenty of protein in my gut and a few G&Ts under my belt.

By the time we got to "Burn," I'd started to loosen up. Instead of being my typical "sex-pot" self, I just stood there at the mic and sang. But I knew I looked good in the leather mini that I'd bought and the shirt that was made out of this shimmery fabric to reflect the light. Also, I was wearing a new pair of lace-up boots with long heels.

After we finished the song, I began talking to the crowd, thanking them for coming. Over the past couple of days, I'd been rehearsing my little speech, but now that everyone was staring up at me with these friendly and slightly confused smiles on their faces, I almost froze. I asked if perchance there was a Tom Unfried in the audience? Some people laughed but most of them booed. A few called out obscenities that made me laugh.

Then I began my brief little explanation of Creutzfeldt-Jakob, the disease I was suffering from, how I'd been examined by neurologists at PHSU. They'd wanted to give me all these painful tests and experimental treatments but I wasn't interested. And then I warned them about the serious danger prions posed to Americans everywhere, even in Portland and the Willamette Valley: So watch out for those hamburgers and hot dogs!

The room was filled with hushed whispers. I bent over to get a drink of water and when I picked it up my hand was shaking so badly, I couldn't drink. Niles came over, held it for me. I noticed several of my friends in the audience were crying, especially Tina and Lilly and Mae-Ling, who were standing near the front of the stage. I told them not to be sad. This was my going away party and going away parties were supposed to be happy occasions!

I signaled to Lars and we launched into our third and final song for the evening, the one we used to call our "money maker" because we thought it would be the most popular. Strange how KPDX didn't seem to agree. It was a very powerful song with a well-developed chorus and bridge. And the lyrics were some of my favorites. I even sang the ones I remembered from the ad-libbing on stage at The Crystal.

Everyone in the room was grooving and trying to be extra supportive. They almost were overdoing it, to make me feel better. It was a little embarrassing and I was glad to get off stage.

After singing those songs, I was seriously dying for a drink and I don't mean water. As I reached the stairs, Mélange caught me by the arm and pulled me over to his cluster. They were all gathered by the front door, in a little nook that served as the foyer to my loft. It was a nice spot to smoke, because the window over there opened, and since it was so hot in the room it felt really good with a slight cool breeze coming in. I shook hands all around and said thank you to everyone who complimented me. Mélange introduced everyone and finished with Hafdis.

My mouth nearly dropped open. She was drop-dead gorgeous, at least six feet tall with long whitish-blonde hair. In America, you just don't see hair like that unless it comes out of a bottle. She called my songs "enchanting." I recognized the accent from hearing Björk onstage in concert and also in that Lars Von Trier movie, *Dancer in the Dark*. Except Björk had a higher, raspier voice. Hafdis's was deep yet melodic. She reminded me of one of Tolkien's elves—the queen, Galadriel.

Well, that was enough for me. I wanted her instantly and from the flicker in her eyes, she sensed this. She was definitely gay, or at least bi.

And then I came to myself and noticed the rest of the little clique had been watching the two of us with interest. How long had I been standing there gaping, I wondered. Had I momentarily slipped out of time?

I asked if anyone had a cigarette. Mélange said he didn't know I smoked. I said I didn't but sometimes when I was drinking I'd have one just for the taste. I never inhaled. Kind of like a cigar. I told him the only thing I inhaled was *de Rasta wizdom, jah.* Everyone laughed. Then Mélange said wasn't it remarkable? So striking. Another man, dressed immaculately, with a strong European accent I couldn't place said yes . . . it *was* remarkable, the resemblance.

I didn't follow what they were talking about and said so. Hafdis laughed a deep, beautiful laugh and said they all thought we looked like sisters aside from the fact that I was a bit shorter and thinner.

I was flattered by this, deeply flattered. Hafdis could easily have been a runway model. She put her arm around me, turning us toward the big mirror by the coat rack. My hair was in my eyes, so she brushed it back and let me see for myself.

My God, it was true. And not just sisters; we could have passed for twins!"I think we shall be great friends," Hafdis said. She looked at my glass, curious what I was drinking. I told her it was just tonic and a twist of lime, but follow me upstairs.

"What have you got for me?" she said. Blushing, I opened the bedroom closet and took out the bottle of Sapphire. I poured a stiff G&T, took a sip, poured in a little more Sapphire. Then I passed the plastic cup to her.

Instead of taking a little sip like most girls I knew, she drank precisely half, never taking her eyes off me. When I took the glass, to my surprise, I noticed I wasn't shaking. Somehow, her presence, intimidating as it was, put me at ease. I was thinking of immortals, of those few people in the world who seemed outside of time.

Hafdis was one of these, but not in the same way as Jack and Tawny. No, hers was a magic of *light*, of natural goodness, but still otherworldly and almost frightening. I imitated her, drinking down the rest of the gin, but it was so strong, I began to choke.

Concerned, Hafdis came over, patted me on the back. I put up my hand to signal that I'd be alright, it had just gone down the wrong pipe. But when I didn't stop coughing, Hafdis ran out of the room and came back with a glass of water, which I took gratefully.

"There," she said. "All better, *já*?"

"*Já,*" I said.

She picked up my empty glass. "More please. It's very good."

I laughed and she laughed and then everything was cool again and we were drinking straight Sapphire right out of the bottle like a couple of winos. *Blah!* It was too strong for me, but Hafdis took a good, healthy pull.

"Hope I'm not interrupting."

Ruth standing in the doorway: She was smiling, but somehow not amused. I felt a tinge of guilt. The bottle of Sapphire was so big. More than we could ever hope to drink in one night. Still, the inference was there and I could tell what she was thinking. She asked if I was going to introduce her to "my new friend" and I said, oh, how barbaric of me. Hafdis held out her hand.

Ruth shook it limply. "They're taking pictures down there," she said. "A professional photographer. I think he's from the *Willy Week* or something."

I followed her down the stairs. Hafdis stayed put. Clever girl. Now that she'd found our hiding place, she would be helping herself to another drink of the good stuff. Good for you! Drink one for me, elven queen!

The rest of the party was unpleasantly surreal with people wanting to ask more about the CJD yet reluctant to broach the subject.

The bolder ones did ask, with a dramatic show of sympathy that came across as a little less than sincere. At least to my paranoid state of mind. I was already starting to regret "coming out of the closet."

Everyone now thought of me as a dying woman and that somehow made me feel sicker, much sicker, like the air in the room had been polluted with negative thoughts, labeling me, pigeon-holing me into yet another slot. And yet, it was also a relief to know that all the weekly rags, even the *Sun*, would probably sniff out the story and print that I didn't have AIDS. True, they'd obsess on the CJD thing, but that was OK because it would raise public awareness of the problem and cause people to think twice before they went to a fast food restaurant and ordered that Big Mac or Whopper.

Later on, Hafdis rejoined me, strolling around the room at my side. Everyone was enchanted and joked that we made the perfect couple. I noticed Hafdis didn't laugh or even smile when they said this but accepted it graciously, as if it was an established fact. Part of me was flattered, but part of me found it a little irritating and presumptuous. Here was a woman who had been drop-dead gorgeous her whole life, who was extremely talented and basically had it all; whereas my good fortune had been the product of a lot of really hard work.

Mélange thanked me for everything and said goodnight. His guests had to be going. Most likely to another, swankier party somewhere up in the West Hills. Maybe even Mr. Davenport's estate. Good riddance. Mélange asked Hafdis if she would be joining them. She shook her head with a stoic smile of thanks. He said fine, she had his cell number if she decided to catch up. She could always cab it, don't forget about the Portland cabs. They were a hell of a lot cheaper than London.

Once the rest of the group had gone, I asked Hafdis if she'd been living in London and she said yes, she'd been there for the past two years. And then I asked her about Iceland, where she'd been born. She laughed, Reykjavík, where else? The rest of the country was little farm towns sprinkled in amongst the volcanoes and moss. I told her that I had been born here in Portland, that I'd grown up in the country on a ranch about thirty miles east of here. She seemed interested and asked a lot of questions but when she noticed that I tired of the subject quickly she changed the conversation back to herself.

She had spent her teenage years in Reykjavík because the schools were better there, but she'd grown up on a farm tending sheep. It was near a little town called Hveragerði, about the same distance south of Reykjavík as Mt. Angel was from Portland. Wasn't that a coincidence?

I totally wigged out when Hafdis mentioned the sheep. I told her about my childhood and she couldn't believe it. *Sheep?* Yes, I said, and cattle. My father usually kept the balance of livestock at about fifty-fifty. If prices for beef were low, the prices for wool or lamb were usually high. So it worked out well. Hafdis asked about my disease, had I caught if from the sheep then?

When she said that, I nearly dropped my glass in surprise. As a matter of fact, yes, I was fairly certain that's where I had caught it. She said that scrapie had been a serious concern in Iceland when she was a girl: several cases of premature senility had occurred in farms nearby, down in another town called Grindavik. All the papers covered the story extensively. It was commonly believed that ranchers had been exposed to some kind of scrapie-like disease while feeding their sheep.

Later on, around three in the morning, after everyone was either tipsy or asleep in various nondescript corners of the apartment, I crept upstairs for another dash of Sapphire to replenish my drink.

When I got near the top of the stairs, I could hear arguing. Two of my dearest friends duking it out. I couldn't believe my ears:

Jeff: She hasn't returned my calls for a week! I wonder why?

Ruth: Umm, maybe because the last time you guys went out you made a total ass out of yourself?

Jeff: What do you mean?

Ruth: You offended practically everything she holds dear: William Blake, Jack Thorne, even the Bible.

Jeff: She told you that?

Ruth: It really bothered her. She was depressed the whole next day.

Jeff: Because I told her that Jack had gotten the name of his band from The Clash instead of William Blake?

Ruth: God, I swear. Sometimes you can be such a deadhead.

Jeff: Don't get all uppity on me! You think I meant to hurt her feelings! I love her!

Ruth: Yeah? Well you have a really fucked up way of showing it.

Jeff: You're one to talk. Turning her into a dike!

Ruth: Nice try, you did that all on your own.

Jeff: Fuck you! I know you're sleeping with her!

Ruth: And if I was, it would be none of your business.

Jeff: If it wasn't for you, she'd be back with me right now.

Ruth: God, you are such a *guy*. Always thinking with your little head. Don't you even realize how bad you hurt her? She's only now just recovering.

Jeff: No shit. She came by Ringlers and almost got me fired.

Ruth: Serves you right! Two-timer!

Jeff: Look, don't think I'm totally in the dark. I know all about bluevault.com. You dikes are all the same! Trying to one up the guys, our "little heads." Christ, you hurt her so bad she was bleeding!

Ruth: I don't know what you're talking about.

Jeff: The *pictures*! I saw them! Half of Portland's seen them!

Ruth: Those aren't of Jules. Or me.

Jeff: Bullshit. I know her cunt when I see it. Even if it is stretched out by your fist.

Ruth: That does it! Get out! Get the fuck out! Get out of my house!

Jeff: This isn't your house. It's Jules'. And you're living here rent free, you suck-up! If I wasn't raised to be a gentleman, I'd give you a taste of *my* fist!

I ran back down the stairs just in time, before Jeff crashed through the door and rushed out of the apartment without even saying goodbye. I could see tears welling up in his eyes. Poor baby. He didn't want me to see him like that.

Hafdis came over and asked what all that was about. I must have been on the verge of tears myself because she opened her arms to give me a hug. I could feel the muscles flexing under her sleeves—by far the strongest woman I'd ever touched. Probably could have beat up Jeff; she might actually have tried if she'd heard what I'd just heard. How could he have said those terrible hurtful things to Ruth?

Part of me was dying to go up there and calm her, but I just didn't have the strength. Everything was unraveling in my life, even my relationship with her. I realized for the first time since I was a little child that I had absolutely no idea what to do next. So I pressed my wet face into Hafdis's chest and she held me, stroking my hair, murmuring words of comfort in a strange and wondrous tongue that made me feel the universal nature of my plight, the way people had cried and been comforted like this for thousands upon thousands of years.

The Changes. They were here, the hum of machinery under my feet, vibrating up through the floor, through my bones. But Hafdis was steady as a great rocky fjord. The vibrations couldn't touch her. She had a deep, deep pool of energy to draw from, the pure strength of her ancestors, the Vikings she'd told me about, how her language hadn't changed all that much from when Leif Erickson had sailed across the Atlantic and struck ground on what was now Canada. I imagined what she had told me, how if she were somehow transported back in time, if she were standing on the beach when Erikson landed, she could have welcomed him as a fellow Icelander and he would have understood nearly every word.

When I was finished crying, I looked around the room. Even though a dozen or so stragglers were left, no one seemed to have noticed. They were all in their own worlds, drug-addled realities tempered only by their need for sleep. I wiped the tears out of my eyes. No more giants rumbling in the earth. Hafdis had held me, kept them from taking me. Together, we'd waited it out. I felt this surge of gratitude.

She must have noticed because she laughed that deep full-bodied laugh of hers that made me want to lay my head against her chest again so I could hear it reverberating like a huge sub-woofer. I wanted her to take me inside that place, the center and circumference of her being, to where the strength lay.

Maybe I still possessed a little of the same strength, I was no weakling. Before the CJD had hit, I would have seemed more like her, offering my strength to others. My friends always called me the steady one that nothing could shake.

Not any more. In the past three months, I'd cried more than the whole rest of my life put together. Death has a way of making you feel your own vulnerability, but also a new kind of strength. In my own way, I was a thousand times stronger than before. If Hafdis and I had been standing in No Man's Land, our astral bodies teetering on the brink, I could have done the same thing for her that she had just done for me, and more.

Even if it was Jeffrey, I'd reach out and guide him towards the light, even now, after he'd said all those cruel things upstairs to the one I loved.

Ruth. I should go to her, tell her I love her, how I feel. She was as strong as Hafdis in her own way. She'd been my rock over the past few months. On her, I could always depend. But now wasn't a good time. Her hot Jewish blood was still boiling from the argument. She'd joked about her temper with me in the past, saying that Mediterraneans had a lower boiling point because the Dead Sea was the lowest point on earth. God, how I loved her, that sharp double-edged sense of humor. I had to be careful what I said after a joke like that. Part of her Jewish side was always on the lookout for hidden signs of racism. If I'd agreed too heartily, it would have put her on the defensive. And now the poor thing was upstairs in a funk and I couldn't help her. She had to work it out herself.

Ruth, dearest Ruth: How I love you! Sticking up for me like that. Sticking up for me like a girlfriend would, a *real* girlfriend. Tonight is the night. After everyone's gone, I'll take you into my bed and tell you my greatest secret, confessing the full extent of my love, how I've been aching to touch you for so, so long.

Hafdis came back from the bar with an affectionate swagger. Tonight, she'd consumed more alcohol than any man I'd ever met and yet she didn't show the faintest sign of intoxication. She held up a set of keys, jingling them. Would I care to join her downstairs for a nightcap? She could personally show me her work. And she had a bottle of something that might interest me down in her suitcase. I looked upstairs. The light in the bedroom had gone off. It looked as though Ruth was turning in for the night.

But Niles, good ole Niles—he was still here, spinning records, ever the faithful DJ. I went over and asked if he'd mind keeping an eye on things. "Deal," he said. "Would you m-mind [hiccup] if I stayed over? I'm just a wee bit [hiccup] knackered." I said no problem, the couch was his. I'd kick off the people who'd crashed on it when I got back. He smiled and gave me the "OK" sign with his thumb and finger. Then he slumped back against the wall. Poor Niles. He was a complete runt compared to Hafdis. Despite the fact he was so drunk, he probably hadn't consumed even half of what she had.

Downstairs in the gallery, Hafdis went straight to her suitcase. "Brennevín," she said, holding up a bottle. "In Iceland we call it 'The Black Death.'"

"Sounds appetizing."

She laughed. "It's good. Here, try some."

I took a sip. *Whew!* It was stronger than I'd expected. Hard liquor. Kind of a cross between German Schnapps and Listerine mouthwash. The worst thing I'd ever tasted.

"Have more," Hafdis urged. "It's good for you, keeps the blood pumping through your veins."

I took another drink, handed it back to her. In one gulp, she'd downed three times what I had and wiped her mouth on the back of her hand, a few strands of hair caught between her wet lips. Holy mama. She took my hand, led me upstairs to the largest of the displays.

The room was totally dark, except for an eerie greenish-yellow illumination coming up through the glass around her statue of Lindow Man.

"You see," she explained, "I made the outer circumference to resemble the shape of a boat. What most archaeology texts leave out, is the boat they found near the victim when they pulled him from the bog. I believe when the priests sacrificed him, they probably pushed him out in that little boat. He was not drowned. Nay, his throat was cut so deep, he could not have drowned."

"Foul play?"

"No, I think not. He was a sacrifice to their gods. A blood sacrifice for the harvest, something like that. The wood from his little boat was stained with blood. Enough to fill the entire bottom."

I shuddered at the thought. Hafdis smiled, apparently charmed by my skittishness. "Fascinating, *já*?" This time, as she said "já" a curious inhaling sound accompanied it, almost as if she'd been caught by surprise. How adorable. Right away, I wanted to hear her do it again.

She took my hand once more, leading me around the gallery, giving me the grand tour, showing countless pieces, commenting on their design, the inspiration behind them. Eventually, I tired of the whole thing and we sat down together on the sofa with that horrible bottle of *Brennevín* wedged between us. I couldn't stomach another drop, no matter how eagerly she offered.

And then, before I knew it, she'd leaned into me, tasting my mouth, giving the faintest hint of tobacco and smoke on her tongue . . . along with the Black Death. When presented this way, it tasted delicious. I fought back the urge, but couldn't stop myself from throwing my arms around her and pushing my tongue deep into her mouth. Very soon, we were both stripped down to the waist, running our hands over each other's breasts, lapping up the sight of them in the eerie glow of Lindow Man's tomb.

Hafdis was like an animal—a big man—getting all worked up. Her breathing, heavy and labored. Clearly she wanted me even more than I'd realized.

Somehow, this eagerness put a damper on my lust and I remembered Ruth upstairs. When Hafdis slid her long fingers up my skirt, brushing them lightly against my pussy lips, now drenched with excitement, I moved away. In her disappointment, she made that adorable gasping sound. The look on her face said it all: *But why?* Perhaps this was the only time in her life that another human being had pulled away. She seemed confused, out of sorts. I put on my bra, scooted back over next to her. We sat together in silence under the hot track lights, as if on display.

I was the first to speak: "It's not that I don't want to. It's just . . ."

"I understand," she said, nodding at my apartment above us. "You already have a lover."

The frankness of the world "lover" caught me off guard. I hesitated before nodding. "Well then," Hafdis said. "I admire your loyalty. It's a quality we Icelanders sometimes take for granted . . . at least in the bedroom."

I smiled, grateful she understood. Yet still, despite what she'd just told me, she left her shirt off. The sight of that perfect body was almost more than I could take. A second longer, and I'd lose my resolve. I stood up, took both her hands, squeezed them together warmly.

And that's where I left her, Hafdis Sollilja, in that strange room with her sculptures, half-naked, swallowing the Black Death in gulps of defeat. She was a beauty. If it hadn't been for Ruth, I would have eaten her alive. And I'm quite sure that she would have returned the favor.

Back up in the apartment, everything was quiet. The couple on the couch had left and Niles had taken off his shoes and laid down to sleep. I went around nudging the last few stragglers: "You don't have to go home, but you can't stay here." Then I went into the bathroom to brush my teeth. I almost took a shower to get the smell of Hafdis off me, then I figured that would be dishonest. I had nothing to hide. Ruth was probably asleep anyway.

When I came out of the bathroom, the stragglers had left. I turned off the light and crept up the stairs to bed: Ruth's steady breathing in the dark. I slid under the blanket next to her and shut my eyes.

"Jules?"

"Yeah."

"Where have you been?"

"I went down to the gallery."

"But why? Mélange said he was going to another party somewhere in Southeast. That singer from Pavement's house, I think."

"You're kidding! Malkmus was throwing a party tonight?"

"I don't know. Maybe."

"That figures. No wonder no one famous came to mine."

"I thought you didn't care."

"Well, I don't. But still. I invited Pink Martini and the Dandys. You'd have thought *someone* would have showed up between the two of them."

"Jules."

"Yeah?"

"Did you go downstairs with that artist from Iceland? What's her name?"

"Hafdis."

"Yeah. Did you?"

"She wanted to show me her work."

"Oh. Was it fun?"

"For a while. Then it got boring."

"What's that smell on your breath?"

"She had this awful schnapps from Iceland. Called the 'Black Death.'"

"You drank alone with her?"

"Only a sip. It was so bad I almost threw up."

"Jules."

"Yeah."

"Do you like her?"

"Well, sure. She's . . . nice."

"You know what I mean."

"Am I *attracted* to her?"

"Mélange said she was really excited to meet you. They had a nickname for you. The other guy, the European in the fancy suit, he kept calling you that and Hafdis told him to shut up."

"What did he call me?"

"Faustine."

"*Faustine*?"

"Yeah."

"That's not so bad."

"Jules, I thought you knew German."

"I do."

"So do I. It sounds an awful lot like 'Faust.'"

"Yeah, so? He's one of the most famous characters in German literature: Herr Doktor Faustus, the man who dared make a pact with Satan!"

"Maybe, but it also's their word for 'fist.'"

"Are you sure?"

"Pretty sure."

"The bastard."

"Yeah, and Mélange was saying it too. They were all gay, even Hafdis, but I'm sure you found out for yourself."

"Hey, what's *that* supposed to mean?"

"I can smell her perfume all over you. It's very distinctive, like that musk hunters use to trick deer and elk when they want to sneak up on them."

"Ruth. You're jealous."

"Am not."

"Yes, you are!"

"*Well?*"

"Ruth?"

"Yeah?"

"Do you love me?"

"Yes, I love you."

"Feed my sheep."

"Huh?"

"Sorry, it's just a joke. A really bad one. God, I must be drunk."

"Feed your sheep?"

"Never mind."

"Jules. Does that mean what I think it means?"

"Indirectly, by way of a really blasphemous allusion that I wish I could take back."

"So you don't want me to 'feed your sheep'?"

"No, well *yes!*"

"C'mere. I've got something to show you. Put your hand right here."

"Between your legs?"

"Between my legs. I got something the other day and you're the first person to feel it."

"Is that what I think it is?"

"Yep, a puss ring."

"I can't believe you did that! Usually you're so . . ."

"Straight?"

"And conservative. You know what this means don't you?"

"What?"

"I'm going to have to get one to match, and you're coming with."

"OK! That'll be fun! When I was waiting to get it, I found myself wishing that I'd had the nerve to invite you along. And then, later, when I was lying back on the table, and the girl was putting it in, I couldn't help daydreaming about this moment. How I'd broach the subject. Whether I'd tell you . . . or *show* you."

"I'm glad you showed me. And now, I'm going to show *you* what can be done with such a unique setting."

ENTRY NINETY-ONE

These last six days have been a little slice of heaven. Ruth quit her internship so we could hang out 24/7. I haven't called Jeff or Lars or any of my other friends. The only thing on my horizon is our gig at The Orpheum.

Ruth wants to take a trip somewhere glamorous, Rome or Paris. And why not? We have the money and the time. I told her yeah, but let's wait until after The Orpheum. I think she's against me playing the show and I know why she wants to go somewhere exotic. It's because I'm dying. When we're in bed at night, I get the shakes so bad it feels like one of those vibrating mattresses at a cheap motel. Ruth says that after I fall asleep, I barely shake at all unless I'm having a bad dream.

Sometimes when we're out eating in a restaurant or walking across the Hawthorne bridge, through Forest Park, wherever, she just starts crying. At moments like these, we switch sides and it's me saying, "Shhhhh, shhhhh, it's OK, everything's going to be fine, you'll see." But that technique doesn't really work on Ruth. She's a pragmatist, so it only makes her cry harder.

Bless her heart. I love her so much. I've never loved anyone more. The way I feel about her makes my relationship with Jeff pale by comparison. I've told her so and this seems to make her feel really good, validating her choice to be with me and put the rest of her life on hold temporarily.

Ruth's already hooked up with gay friends who only hang out with other gays. We've gone to a couple of places where they congregate. But really, I don't like that whole scene. Watching older women dancing together makes me think of Deeksha. Especially when they come over and ask me to join them, like it's supposed to be fun shaking your booty with someone twice your age just because you're in a gay bar.

Ruth could just as easily have been a man and I wouldn't care in the slightest. I'm in love with *her* not her sex.

The other day, Ruth and I were in Powell's, hanging out in the coffee shop as we often do, and she said, "Jules, are we lesbians?" I laughed and said I could only speak for myself, but no, I didn't consider myself one. I'm a free agent, a *free radical*. Ruth laughed because she got the double meaning from biology.

After the joke, she seemed to feel a lot more comfortable with her alleged "new sexuality," her choice to love my body as well as my spirit. In the past couple of days, she hasn't pushed for us to going dancing at The Egyptian. I'm glad because I know what that means. She knows we're really no different than before. We're still the same two people we've always been.

I couldn't sleep tonight, so I got up to type this entry because I didn't want Ruth to feel obligated to keep me company. She's bushed, little meow-meow. We made love tonight and it was so good. Really simple, nothing tricky, not trying to break any new ground or have multiples together. In fact, I didn't come at all. Ruth did, and that was enough for me. I watched her face the whole time. Her eyes went wide as she looked up at me, her pussy shuddering around my fingers like a hummingbird drawing nectar from a flower.

Afterwards, she smiled and brushed her fingers across my tattoo. "Cowslip, my Cowslip." I must have frowned when she said that because she immediately looked up and apologized.

But I wasn't mad or anything. It just caught me off guard. I told her it was OK, but maybe she shouldn't say it again. I guess a part of me was afraid my dad might be listening and it would hurt his feelings.

Speaking of "feelings" I've been getting this strange one like he's nearby these last few days. Last Wednesday, Ruth and I were shopping at Nordstrom's and I noticed this man walk by. He looked right at me, and for a split second, he looked exactly like my dad. I almost called out to him. But then I saw he wasn't my father, just another cowboy. He tipped his hat, kept walking. That's one thing I miss about cowboys, their simple manners. I didn't take offense at the fact he tipped his hat "for a lady," trying to mack on me or something. He was just being friendly.

I'm starting to understand that when a man holds a door open for me, it isn't because I'm a member of the "weaker" sex or because he wants to jump my bones. It's just a way of being polite, of acknowledging me as a person who happens to be female. If I were male, he'd say, "howdy" and it would mean the same thing.

Life can be so simple if you just let it. I only wish I'd come to understand this fact when I'd had more living left to do.

ENTRY NINETY-TWO
Ruth says we're going to the coast and that's that. It's not open for discussion. She called Lars herself and told him what happened (my latest collapse) and he agreed. Under the circumstances, they'd call off practice. I could listen to the demos on the way to the coast to make double sure I had all the lyrics secure in my memory banks and the others, we could sort those out after the sound check, which ones I felt most comfortable with.

Obviously, "Cowslip" was a dead ringer. A few more after that and we'd have enough for the show. There's no rule how long you have to perform, and besides, for a lot of it we could just jam on our instruments and I could free-style my lyrics. That's my favorite thing to do anyway. I can make up a song in my head on the spur of the moment almost better than I can remember the words to one that already exists.

This fact puzzled Lars and the boys for a while, but they understand now. It's because of the CJD. My creative mind is still intact; it's my memory banks that are somewhat in question.

A year ago, I could have memorized all the songs with no problem. If I could memorize the whole periodic table of elements the night before the exam, then I sure as hell could remember a few measly lyrics.

Ruth's not here right now. She's out shopping for the trip. I hope Lars isn't too bummed out that I can't make practice. You can never tell with him. He's always got up this front that's impenetrable, a shield. When I talked with him on the phone, he said that the coast would be just what I needed, a break from the daily grind. Get away from the old haunts. Whenever he felt down and out, he always went to the beach.

After he said that, I knew that he'd inadvertently given Ruth the idea. She's never really mentioned it before. I think she just wanted to get me out of the city, take me someplace fresh, and the coast is the perfect choice.

Talk about fresh air! Those ocean breezes coming in off the water, they taste so fresh in your lungs, wonderful! I haven't been to the coast in ages. The idea sounds better and better as I type this entry. Nothing's more beautiful than the Oregon coast: rocky beaches with the crashing waves, huge crags of volcanic impatience rising up from the deep water like huge titans wading ashore . . . and the lush avalanche of the Pacific rainforest rushing down to meet the water with its own green tide!

Alright, now I'm getting psyched. Hurry up, Rooty! Let's go! She's taking the brand new Volvo (nicknamed "Volva") that her father bought her last year for Hanukah. Maybe if I'm good she'll let me drive. At least on the beach.

Driving Miss Volva! Straight into the Pacific! Time's wingéd chariot gliding out over the waves, revving to one million RPM's . . . next stop Albion!

Well, it's almost dark and Ruth hasn't come back yet. She's taking forever. I suppose I should say a word or two about the dream, what happened the day before last, the whole reason Ruth called Lars in the first place.

After that fiasco with Mr. Green, she tends to take my dreams pretty seriously, and there was the one part of it, the part that even freaked *her* out because of the coincidence. She said there was a perfectly rational explanation, but she's wrong.

The whole thing started at exactly three in the morning. I know because I looked at the clock. I'd just been woken out of a sound sleep. There came a tapping down below, a tiny set of knuckles gently rapping, rapping at the steel door. I hid under the covers, coward that I was, but then I noticed that Ruth wasn't in the bed. I called to her, and when I did, the rapping became more frantic, louder and a voice called out.

"Julia! Julia! Are you there? It's me! Jack! Open up!"

A part of me relaxed when I heard Jack's voice, no matter how absurd. I knew there couldn't be anyone on the other side of the door; it was bricked off as Mélange had said, but then again, he'd lied about other things, why not about the door? If he'd confessed there was *another side*, then nobody in their right mind would have moved in.

"Julia! Please answer!"

I crept downstairs into the living room. The bathroom was dark. No sign of Ruth, but her coat was still there on the rack by the door.

"Julia!"

"OK, sheez. How do I know it's really you?"

"Open up!"

"Jack? How'd you get back there?"

"I . . . I was on a historical tour of the city. I got separated from the group."

"What tour?"

"Portland Underground. It starts in the Shanghai Tunnel and ends in a pizza parlor on Front Street."

"Really?"

"Would I lie?"

"If you're really Jack, prove it."

"Prove it?"

"Tell me something only Jack could know."

There was a moment of silence. I could have sworn I heard whispering, the sound of a woman's voice. It, too, vaguely familiar. And then the clearing of a throat.

"'Fiery the Angels rose & as they rose deep thunder roll'd around their shores, indignant, burning with the fires of Orc!'" I went to the door, pulled on the latch. To my surprise, it actually shook loose from its foundation. There was a great pounding on the other side. A few of the blows were so powerful, they made the whole building shake on its foundations.

I stepped back as the door swung open. And there it was: The grinning face of Jack Thorne covered in white dust. I expected him to come out into the room and hug me but instead he beckoned for me to join him.

Part of me knew better, but the warm smile on his face was so happy, so joyful to see me after we'd had that horrible falling out on the phone and then that creepy last message on my phone mail.

Ah, what the hell. I passed over the threshold and Jack's strong arms embraced me. I could feel the shudder of his chest as he cried tears of happiness. "Oh, Julia. I've missed you so much. If only you knew."

He took my hand. "C'mere. I've got something to show you." I tried to hold my ground, but he tugged playfully, Cracker Jack up to his old tricks.

"Shouldn't we go out my front door? I mean, it's cold down here . . ."

"Don't be such a wimp!"

"But Jack . . ."

"Shhhhhhhh. No more if's and's or but's. Especially *but's!*"

"Why no 'butts?' I thought you were rather attracted to mine." Jack laughed, his voice reverberating through the tunnel. It was dark, but a faint light through the chinks lit our way. And then I saw the other end up ahead. The light was grey and bleached, obviously from the moon.

Another few minutes and we'd made it. But instead of being outside in the moonlight, we were standing in the middle of a huge deserted lobby. All of the furniture was old and rotten, the floors covered with such a heavy layer of dust that it felt like dirt underfoot.

Jack led me through an archway. There was a set of stairs, but they didn't look very trustworthy. Some of them were slanting inwards, as if they'd crumbled from beneath. Jack had this amazing knack of avoiding the weak stairs. His hand buoyed me up, almost as if he was floating on air.

Or was it the other way around? Was I the one who kept Jack from sinking down? For some strange reason, I couldn't tell who was lifting whom. It didn't matter. He squeezed my hand tight. I wanted to ask where we were going, but for some reason the words got stuck in my throat.

After a dizzying array of flights, we emerged onto a floor. I was huffing and puffing, but Jack had barely broken a sweat. He led me down a hall that was in a similar state of disrepair. The carpet made these disgusting squishy-sucking sounds with every step. I held my breath and tried my best to ignore the swampy stench.

The door of a room was ajar and Jack pushed it open. "Darling!" he bellowed. "I found her! She's here!"

Tawny came waltzing out of the bathroom completely naked. She looked awful. There were track marks all over her body. Huge, swollen boils that looked like if you so much as touched them they would burst.

She reached out her arms for a hug. I tried to back out into the hall, but Jack was right behind me. He shut the door. By now, Tawny had put her arms down. She picked up a big, rusty needle on the night table by the bed. "Jules, honey. You're shaking all over. How about a little something to help you relax?"

"No!" I screamed. "Get that away from me!"

"Oh, Jules . . . you always were a light weight. C'mere. Black tar straight from Mexico. It doesn't get any better."

I tried to get away, but it was no good: Jack grabbed me around the waist; he lifted me up, tossed me on the bed. Tawny cinched a belt around my neck, slapping my forehead to get a pulse.

In the distance, a horrible bellowing laugh: It didn't sound human at all—more like the way a bull sounds. I thought of cattle, the ranch, the meat wagon, that horrible slaughterhouse on wheels.

"Close your eyes," Tawny purred. There was a grinding crunch as the spike pushed through my skull into my brain. Everything went all swimmy. And then, darkness.

When I woke up, Jack and Tawny were gone. I reached up, felt for the hole between my eyes where the needle had gone in.

Nothing. It hadn't left a mark. I was no longer shaking; whatever they'd shot into my veins had worked. I felt completely calm inside. Pretty vacant. I got up, walked to the window.

No, it couldn't be. Impossible. I rubbed my eyes, but there was no mistaking all the familiar sights of Times Square. I could see the television screen where they flash people's faces on the David Letterman Show, all the familiar buildings, and on the other side, that big hotel or whatever it was where the ball always dropped down every year, glowing with a million lights, Dick Clark shouting, "Happy new year!"

And then it hit me: *A dream, this is only a dream. You can wake up any time you want.*

I closed my eyes and tried my hardest to conjure up the sight of my bedroom: Ruth sleeping peacefully at my side, her long black hair spread out like a mane across her pillow, the tick of the clock, the droning rush of traffic outside. But try as I may, I couldn't force it into being. Everything was dim, grey matter—little more than shadow.

Oh, man. Don't tell me. Those bastards were going to make me walk all the way home through that god forsaken tunnel? Three thousand miles. That would take forever, or at least until the sun came up.

"Fuck you!" I yelled through the floor. "Fuck all of you! Creeps."

Back at the big steel door, it was such a relief to see another shade of light other than the dismal grey. Instead everything was bright yellow—glowing, shimmering, wonderfully animated! I burst through the door like a pearl diver coming up from the dark, watery depths for air.

As soon as I'd passed over the threshold, I felt this terrible weight descend on my body, pressing in from all sides, compacting every inch, every corpuscle of my being, as if I'd been thrown into a decompression chamber.

Ruth's voice screaming, frantic: "Jules! Don't do this to me! Jules! Goddamn you! Wake up! Don't die! Wake up!"

I opened my eyes. There she was, pounding on my chest like a mad woman, blowing into my mouth as if I were some kind of air mattress. When Ruth saw my eyes come into focus, she cried out for joy and fell on my neck, kissing me, hugging me, pressing her face tight against mine, until I felt that I would be smothered under the weight of her gratitude—a hot, wet face drowning me in a shower of tears.

The next morning, in my room at PHSU, I could tell Ruth was terribly agitated. She'd been going over that night in her mind, trying to figure out why she'd woken up, because if she hadn't, if she'd stayed asleep and not noticed the way I was breathing differently, in these little gasps, then . . . well, she didn't want to think about that. It was a miracle she'd noticed. We were on the same wavelength. She'd known instinctively like a wife who knew when her husband was in danger.

But still . . . there was something else. Something she wasn't telling me. I looked over to where she was standing by the window, gazing out over the Willamette River down below.

"What? What is it?"

Ruth shrugged, feigning ignorance.

"Something's happened," I said.

"*Duh!*" she laughed. "You bozo. You almost croaked on me."

"No, not that," I persisted.

"Oh, Jules, honey, please. Not now. Later, when they let me take you back home."

"When?"

"Soon. They just have to run some tests."

"Forget it. I don't want any tests. I've already had more than my share, thank you very much."

"But Jules! They can help! They can . . ."

"What? Stretch my life out a month, two months, a year?"

"Yes! And that's one more year that we can spend together!"

I felt my cheeks burning with frustration. It wouldn't be like that. I'd end up like my father, a vegetable. I wouldn't be myself anymore, I wouldn't be her girlfriend.

She put her hand on my forehead, brushed away a long lock of hair. "Oh, Jules. I love you so much."

I smiled weakly. "You've got a funny way of showing it . . . pounding on my chest in the middle of the night."

She giggled for a second, the woman I loved, and then I could see the tears coming and I rolled over and just stared at nothing in particular, at the tube sticking out of my arm.

As soon as we got home early the next morning, I asked Ruth to please tell me whatever it was she'd been keeping from me at the hospital. "Check the voicemail," she said. "it's all there."

Hart's voice: The usually pleasantries, and then a nervous pause. Dead air. I stepped back. Was this possible? Hart Drake at a loss for words? He almost sounded upset, which was clearly impossible. How could a man be upset if he had a cold stone in his chest that was incapable of beating?

Hart said there was no point in trying to sugarcoat the facts, out with it: Jack and Tawny had been found dead, the day before last, overdosed, in a hotel room. The Marriott on Times Square. Please call him ASAP.

When I heard that, I went straight for the bottle of Sapphire next to Changó's priestess.

Ruth was right behind me. "No!" She yelled. "Julia! Goddamn it! You're killing yourself! I won't stand by and watch you do it! If you keep this up, I'm leaving! Do you hear me, Jules! I'll leave you!"

I didn't say anything. What could I say to that? Calmly, quietly, I tilted up the bottle and took a long, satisfying hit. In my mind's eye, I saw Hafdis gripping the neck at the same angle, gulping the same heroic gulps: A Valkyrie standing in the middle of the Road of Excess, taking a short break on her way to the Palace of Wisdom. My throat burned and my eyes watered but still I drank.

Ahhhhhhhh. If she could do it, I could do it. After all, we were almost twins. Everyone had said so at the party. She was "William" and I was "Wilson." Just like the story by Edgar Alan Poe.

ENTRY NINETY-THREE

Sorry I haven't been writing in the journal. I don't think I can keep it up much longer. Maybe just until we start recording again and then I can dictate to Ruth. She's taken quite an interest in this "little" writing project of mine. I've only let her read bits and pieces, but when she saw how many pages I've written, she was astonished.

We're on our way back from the coast. I might sound calm, but that's only because I don't have the energy to be scared anymore. I've got about an hour to write the rest of this entry and I'll need all of it.

The way Ruth is driving, it's a wonder I can type anything at all. She's a speed demon, but that's just as well. If she doesn't break the speed limit, I'll miss the entire show at The Orpheum. Good thing they ended up booking us as headliners instead of the warm-up band. It's already six-thirty, so I'll definitely miss the sound check.

But that's cool, I guess. As cool as it could be, considering. I called up Lars and told him what happened, how I got "disoriented" on the beach and couldn't find my way back home, how Ruth had ended up calling the police and how nice they'd been to send out a car to look for me.

The trip started out fantastically. We found a nice little motel room with a kitchenette in Lincoln City overlooking the beach. I convinced Ruth to bring a bottle of champagne. We carried a blanket down on the beach to watch the sun sink behind a watery horizon: The vanishing point for water & fire & air. It was one of those moments in life that just couldn't get any better: The warm sea breeze, gulls crying out over the waves—crashing foam, soft sand.

I lay my head down on Ruth's lap and she stroked my hair, pouring the occasional sip of champagne into my mouth. And beneath us, the rumbling of machinery under the sand, churning and turning, the wheel of a great combine. It was coming up through the earth for me. Ruth couldn't feel the giants in the earth because she was whole. I shut my eyes and took a deep breath, resting my head between her legs.

The next day, around noon, when Ruth was making breakfast in our room, I went out for a walk on the beach. It was nice weather, some big clouds in the distance. Warm sand between my toes, not yet painfully hot from the sun, just warm. I watched this guy out in breakwater. He'd just finished clamming for the day and from the way he was lugging his bucket, it looked to be a good one. I waved and he came over to where I was sitting next to this big log.

As he got closer, I almost screamed. It was my dad, his face, the same easy smile and the big white teeth with a crack in the one where that bronco threw him off during the rodeo at St. Paul when he was eighteen years old. He seemed worried, like maybe he was scaring me, so he said, "Hey, are you alright there, missy?"

And then I saw that it wasn't dad at all, but this grey-haired local with a kind smile. I asked him how many he'd caught and he said he didn't know but enough to eat for supper. He showed me his bucket brimming with steamer clams.

"Here," he said, holding out a handful. I thanked him but said that I didn't know the first thing about how to cook them. He was about ready to give me instructions when he saw that I didn't really want them, I was just being polite and he took them back, not offended but sad that he couldn't share his catch with this nice young woman, especially after he'd spooked her.

The man waved goodbye and left me to contemplate the beautiful day. One thing I can never quite get used to about the coast is that wide open place where the curve of the earth reaches up and touches the sky. So magical, like nowhere else. The way the sky reflects in the sea, it almost looks as if the two were actually meeting, commingling in a celestial embrace.

As if by way of a response to so much beauty, my stomach growled, so I started back to the motel. Usually, I eat first thing when I get up, but today Ruth had wanted to make eggs benedict and have mimosas out on the deck. She was trying to learn how to cook, it was a new challenge for her. I'd been cooking since I was a little kid, helping my mom every step of the way, but Ruth had never been responsible for anything in the kitchen.

The changes were coming and that was a very bad sign. If I slipped out of time, who knows what would happen out there on the beach?

I started running back to the motel. When I got a fair distance, I realized that I was lost. Nothing looked familiar. Instead of retracing my steps, I kind of lost my head and panicked.

I'm not sure how long I went on like that, running, the sand pushing between my toes. Before I knew it, I'd reached the base of a cliff. Waves were breaking really hard against it and I could feel the draft of a big cave.

For some reason, it was terrifying. There in the shade, I couldn't feel any heat from the sun. All I was wearing was this T-shirt and a big pair of boxers. My hair whipped back and forth in the wind and sand blew against my cheeks, chiding me for being so careless.

I turned around and looked back toward the motel, but it was nowhere in sight. No buildings at all—just these big trees that I didn't remember being there, hundreds of feet tall, virgin timber. I thought of the stand at Opal Creek, a nature preserve on the upper fork of the Santiam River with acres upon acres of virgin Doug firs and hemlocks. These trees were just like them and they came right down to the edge of the beach. Waves hissed against the rocks. I could almost hear words in them, but it sounded like a language I didn't know, not like the usual Shadow People I'd encountered in Portland. The voices seemed proud and brave and fearless.

That kind of freaked me out because I knew I was hearing a different kind of shadow person, much older and not afraid like the ones in Portland. They called gently from the sea and from amidst the ferns and mossy glens of the rainforest.

Whoever was calling didn't come out, though. They didn't crowd my space. None of the usual desperation, the ravenous hunger. I knew for sure that I was lost, I'd slipped out of time, but it almost seemed enjoyable in this beautiful place, like the way a drowning person, once her lungs fill with water; she quits fighting and opens herself up to the welcoming embrace of the sea, letting it carry her down to the bottom . . . a gentle rocking, the rise and fall of time swirling around the ears, a tide of space and time.

I went a little way over and sat in the sun. It felt good, nice and warm. The changes were still upon me, but they weren't scary like before. They were peaceful and reassuring. No need to face the strangers. I couldn't even hear their voices in the sunlight. They seemed to prefer the shadows over along the whispering cove. I looked up and saw movement in the mouth of the cave.

A girl was standing there looking down at me. She was very beautiful, dressed in a deerskin, and she was waving. I turned and looked over my shoulder. Nobody there. She laughed and gestured at me. When I pointed at myself, she laughed even harder.

A plume of smoke rose into the sky. They had a fire going in there. I smelled something delicious, salmon cooking over the flames. My stomach lurched, driving me to my feet. But I knew if I went inside the cave, I'd never come out again.

The girl was dancing now, swirling her hips. She was very young, no more than fourteen or fifteen with sweet buttercups for breasts, the nipples dark brown against her chest.

I turned away and walked into the sun. It felt good on my face. Another ten, twenty paces. Who was I kidding? I could never make it back to the hotel. Aside from the fact that it had vanished, my legs were shaking so bad there was no point in going on. I sat down cross-legged in the warm sand, locking my knees in the Lotus position.

And then I saw them, three of the same figures I'd encountered before when I'd slipped out of time in my bedroom, their garments flowing over my head, shimmering in the light. I called out to them. "Hello! What's your name? Have you come to take me away?" Their faces were covered in a flourishing train, obscured by the celestial fabric of their robes.

I remembered that quote from the Bible: "No one shall look upon my face and live."

Oh, but they were so beautiful, the way they swam through the air, moving effortlessly, balancing on the pinions of space & time. One grand unification. I wanted them to come down and scoop me up in their arms.

Yet, even as I pondered those celestial visitants, I felt a pang of guilt in my heart. All the disgusting things I'd done in my life: sinking needles into my flesh, consorting with vampires, letting them reach inside, desecrating the sanctity of my womb.

What right do you have to look up and contemplate God's divine plan? None at all. I was abomination. Slime of the pit. As such, I had no right to ask for their help. This realization shot through my brain like a diamond bullet, leaving behind an empty hole of regret.

I looked down at my knees knocking together in the sand, my arms shaking out of control. Nothing but flesh and blood. Silly, stupid meat. Julia Annika Fleischer, the girl with CJD. Rock star, sinner . . . demon bait.

Oh, how I wanted to look up and see if the angels were still there. Maybe they loved me enough to forgive me. Maybe I could love myself enough to strip off the husk of death and reach for the hem of eternity.

But instead of angels, I saw a hearse driving up the beach. *And at my back I always hear, time's wingéd chariot drawing near.* Blue and red lights, the familiar growl of a police radio as it pulled up: "Excuse me, miss. Is your name Julia? Julia Fleischer?"

I tried to tell the officer that I only needed some protein and then I'd be fine. Right as rain. Did he by chance have a Power Bar? His answer was measured and even: Everything had been prearranged. He'd already called it in. We were going straight to the hospital. My friend, a Ruth Cohaine, was already there, waiting. Just sit back, miss. Don't try and talk. I'll have you there in about ten minutes.

Ruth met me at the door of the emergency room. Poor thing, she didn't have any tears left to cry. No expression on her beautifully stoic face, none at all. These precious little tragedies of mine were becoming routine. At least I hadn't pulled up in an ambulance this time.

The rest of the afternoon was spent trying to explain Creutzfeldt-Jakob Disease to a bunch of country doctors who were convinced that I'd taken some kind of drug, most likely a newfangled type of speed or perhaps ecstasy. Would I mind giving them a urine and blood sample before I left?

Ø

Ruth. Sweet, darling Ruth. So loyal. She's speeding down the Vanduser Corridor in her red Volva, trying her best to get me to the show on time. We're going to make it, I can tell. The crowd might have to wait an extra half-hour, but that's show biz. I've been in their place more time that I can count.

And The Orpheum, well, they won't really care if we go on a little late, so long as we rock the house. More of an opportunity for them to sell beer. Extra manna in the coffers while people wait around and get drunk, complaining to each other, "What time is it? Man, this better be good!"

Some of the best shows I'd ever seen were a combination of a late band and teenage angst rebuffed: *Who cares if we made you wait five extra minutes or an hour? Cover your eardrums, kiddies. We're blowing the doors off this place!*

I'm watching Ruth now, her eyes straining, so intent upon the road, anticipating every curve. The sun has already dropped down below the tree line. You know you're in a real forest when it sets behind the trees, illuminating their crowns, halos of light. This moment will never be lost, my appreciation of Ruth: her love, the love of one divine being towards another.

Next time the angels come, I won't let myself look away. Next time, I'll open my arms and my heart: "Friends! I know you have always been here and I have always been with you! One grand unification of lights!"

Thank you! Thank you, Mommy for sending your kids to pick me up! I love you so much! Eternal Love, the source of being. I exist to reflect that smile of contentment on your face: And behold, it is very good. For everything that lives is holy.

Afterword

Julia's physical decline was swift and dramatic after that horrible night at The Orpheum. A part of her passed away on stage and never returned. After the medics finally were able to revive her in the ambulance, Julia wasn't the same person who had sat in my car only a few hours earlier faithfully typing what was to be the last entry of her journal. She seemed completely at a loss when I tried to comfort her, almost as if a complete stranger was holding her hand. As we pulled up to the emergency room entrance, she looked out the window and said, "There went up a mist from the earth and watered the whole face of the ground." I'd been so upset at the time, it hadn't even occur to me she was quoting scripture.

The next day, I remembered a previous discussion we'd had on that very passage in Genesis. Julia believed it was the point at which a different narrator took over and mankind went from being the image and likeness of God to mortal, finite beings created from "the dust of the ground."

Several weeks later, while planning her funeral ceremony, I mentioned the incident to her pastor in Mt. Angel. He seemed deeply touched and asked for my permission to use it in future sermons. He even quoted the passage at her funeral, saying it breathed new life into the phrase "ashes to ashes, dust to dust," because it meant Julia was, in essence, confessing her sins and making her peace with the world.

In retrospect, I think she was doing the exact opposite. The look on her face hadn't been one of submission, but more of a stubborn resolve—almost as if she were confronting a life-long adversary, the herald of death, who'd been sent to take her away.

Before I go much further, I should say a few words more about Julia's last performance. It is only fitting, especially considering how frank and open her journal treats such matters.

We arrived at The Orpheum about five hours after Julia was supposed to be there for the sound check. She went straight on stage without a chance to catch her breath.

The audience was especially rowdy. They'd been waiting for over an hour since Wasp Factory had left the stage (after playing a third encore). Julia didn't apologize when she went out, which was wise considering. The band broke into "So Close," one of their songs that had gotten airplay on KPDX. Quite a few people in the audience knew the lyrics, especially the chorus: "Far away, so close / take my hand, feel the pulse / inside my veins, wash out the pain / far away, so close."

I noticed several guys in the front row were holding up their fists. It wasn't until after the song that I heard what they were chanting: "Sit on this, sit on this!" Julia didn't seem to notice until she'd made it through the next song. The guys kept it up, raising their fists obnoxiously in the air, laughing, whistling. A few of them called for Julia to "show us your tits."

By then, more of the audience had gotten involved. A fight broke out near the front. Half the crowd was falling-over drunk and this reflected badly on the management for allowing the bartenders to serve drinks to so many people who were obviously intoxicated.

Julia went to the edge of the stage. She leaned over and asked one of the guys to speak up. If he had something to say, say it to everyone. She held out the microphone and he yelled for her to "fuck this!" (his fist).

Instead of reacting, Julia looked him straight in the eye. "What's your name?"

"Dick," he said. "Dick Gozinya."

"Tell me, Dick, why are you so filled with hate?" The kid just laughed. "Is this what you want?" she asked, tugging at her shirt. The whole front row erupted in applause. "Well," she said, "then I guess you're out of luck. I'm an artist, not a stripper. And that goes for all the rest of you: Anyone who came here to see my breasts might as well leave."

At this point, I was praying that Julia wouldn't do anything controversial. She didn't have the strength. Not tonight, not after what happened on the beach. "C'mon, honey," I whispered under my breath. "The next song, start the next song."

Lars clicked his sticks, but Julia cut him off. She shielded her eyes in an effort to see out into the audience: "I want y'all to know that I forgive Dick & Company . . . for they know not what they do. They're from the Devil. Everything they say comes from him. And he's nothing but a lie, himself. The father of lies. . . ."

An eerie stillness passed through the crowd like a shiver. Nobody knew quite what to expect. The band skipped a few songs on their play list and went straight to "Burn," another popular one from their bootlegged demo.

I could see right then that Julia wasn't going to make it; her hands were shaking so badly that she had to put the microphone back on the stand. She peered up into the stage lights, rubbing her eyes.

But Julia's fans weren't about to let the show end. They came to her rescue, singing for her. It was amazing how many of them knew the lyrics.

The effect on Julia was instantaneous. She yanked the microphone off the stand, held it out. More and more people sang, encouraged by the sound of their voices booming through the PA.

Julia went over to the edge of the stage and closed her eyes, letting the music wash over her like a healing balm. Yes, she was back in her element. Not even the changes could stop her now.

And then it happened: One of the frat boys threw a bottle, hitting Julia in the side of the head.

Fortunately, it glanced off without much of an impact. But the shock distracted her just enough so she toppled over. The crowd gasped. A bouncer jumped up on stage. The second he realized she was unconscious, he shouted for someone to call 911. Then he started giving her CPR.

A tall, grey-haired man that I'd never seen before stepped through the curtain. He took the microphone, told everyone to go home; the show was over.

The blow to Julia's head didn't turn out to be serious. Only a minor concussion. A few stitches and she should have been fine. But she wasn't. The whole experience had overwhelmed her, being onstage while those boys raised their fists so lewdly, knowing they'd seen the most compromising moment of her life on the World Wide Web.

In her room at PHSU, Julia passed in and out of consciousness for several days and by the end of it, she no longer knew my name. Despite this, she did recall that she loved me, always brightening up when I came into the room. It wouldn't have been so bad if it weren't for the hallucinations. Sometimes I would be sitting there beside her bed, reading or sleeping and she would break into the most terrifying scream, pointing at the door, shouting at "them" to get away. "You'll never take me! The glowers won't let you!"

It took me several days to catch on. She was addressing the Shadow People, whom she believed were sneaking into her room for some unholy purpose, to rob her of her mind, I suppose. They were the most obvious outward manifestation of her illness: deadly prions eating away her brain. Instead of relating to them in abstract terms, her imagination clothed them in human form.

Julia's psychosis had taken over to the point that she became convinced she was in contact with the souls of people who had died in the hospital. Apparently, some of them were dim shadows. Yet others, the friendly benevolent ones, gave off a glow, some kind of illumination. She seemed to feel a kinship with these "glowers," whom she invited into the room on a regular basis for comfort. When one or more bright souls were close by, she could relax enough to sleep. In a way, they served as her guardian angels.

But when there didn't happen to be any glowers in the room, Julia was absolutely terrified of sleeping. She confessed to me that she was more vulnerable in a dream state. The Shadow People could find her much more easily; they would gather around her bed, pressing in upon her, trying to feed off her energy. This, in turn, drained her resources, nudging her closer to death. She seemed to think they couldn't help themselves. It was their nature to "feed" in this way. For whatever reason, they had squandered their share of the light while still alive and now they couldn't find their way into the next dimension. They needed some of Julia's illumination to fortify themselves for the journey. But this robbed her of the strength she needed to make it across No Man's Land after she died. So if the Shadow People drained her dry, she ran the risk of ultimately becoming one of them—cut off from the light, slowly filling up with dark energy. And then it would be too late: her identity would cloud over and perish. Never again would she reflect the divine effulgence of God.

For this reason, Julia was absolutely terrified of the nurse who came in every day to give her a shot to help her sleep. During the first couple of weeks, an orderly accompanied the nurse to strap Julia down so she couldn't resist.

It didn't matter which nurse happened to be on duty, Julia always called her "Tawny." At the time, I chalked this up to her condition—dementia, memory loss—but after reading the journal it's no wonder. A needle had been Tawny's weapon of choice; and so, by extension, the nurses had become yet another beast of prey out for the kill.

Near the end of August, Julia had some sort of seizure that robbed her of the ability to speak (except near the very end, which I will get to shortly).

Immediately prior to the seizure, she had a confrontation with a being she called "Urizen." Evidently, he was supposed to be some kind of emissary or messenger from Hell. I'm not really sure. I gathered from her conversation with him that he had two demons with him, held at bay like dogs on a leash; when he wanted to frighten Julia, he would threaten to set them loose.

Urizen's "visit" lasted about an hour. During this time Julia seemed to feel herself on trial. For someone with only a small portion of her brain left, she quoted an exhausting array of verses from the Bible and William Blake's writings (most notably "The Marriage of Heaven & Hell"). She told the dark being that she was not afraid of him because her love had been "perfected by truth, fortified through revelation." All-Mother was here with her and nothing he could do or say would make her believe otherwise. She was a "thought in the One Mind" and her physical existence had been a dream since birth.

Urizen must have attacked her on this point because she kept stating over and over that he, himself, was nothing more than illusion, a belief that All-Mother's thoughts could be circumscribed or limited and that She was less than omnipotent.

I find it extremely unlikely that CJD affects most patients in this way, robbing them of the ability to recognize their best friend and lover, yet bestowing them with an almost supernatural ability to summon long passages of scripture at will—especially verses which they'd read only recently.

Sitting there witnessing the spectacle of Julia fighting that imaginary demon was far and away the most terrifying experience of my life. Following her eyes as they locked onto Urizen's somehow gave him a sense of legitimacy and I found myself wondering, "What if she's right and I'm the blind one?" The idea that a real demon might actually be there in the room made me feel like screaming.

At no time during this so-called trial did Julia loose her cool. She indicated that many other "bright souls" were in the room supporting her, watching as spectators. Despite the fact they never stepped in on her behalf, their presence was no doubt comforting and helped assure Julia that Urizen wouldn't dare set his hell hounds loose on her, as he had several months before in Powell's.

After about an hour or so, Urizen left the room, apparently defeated by Julia's "Divine Logic." Thoroughly exhausted, she fell into a deep sleep and didn't wake up again for almost twenty-four hours.

When Julia finally awoke, she no longer possessed the ability to speak English. Her words had lapsed into the syllables of a nonsensical foreign tongue that seemed to hold an otherworldly grammatical structure of its own. She resembled an infant who had just returned from a separate dimension and was confusing our language with another, more frightful mode of communication. The rasping, lowing utterances were a strain on the ear. Ashamed as I am to admit it, several times I had to cover my ears while she was attempting to convey her thoughts to me. It was just too much seeing *and* hearing her like that.

And now, I've come at last to the final point in this afterword—namely the circumstances attending Julia's ultimate passing. It was a little after three o'clock in the afternoon on a rather unusually sunny day that came after three or four days of rain. I was getting ready to attend a service at temple with my parents, it being Rosh Hashanah, the first day of the new year on the Jewish calendar.

For some reason, I called them and cancelled at the last minute. They were quite disappointed but they understood: Julia was near the end; she could go at any minute and I wanted so much to be with her and support her when the time came for her body to die. (I say her "body" because, at the time, I believed her soul had already passed over.)

I was sitting next to Julia's bed reading from the Torah. I heard a whisper, very faint. To my astonishment, when I looked over she was smiling at me, a familiar sort of smile that I hadn't seen since our drive back from the coast.

When she opened her mouth, despite a heavy slur, I could understand the words perfectly: "Ruth, my love. He's come." I leapt to her bedside and took her hand. "Jules, is it really you?" She nodded, squeezing my hand three times to let me know that indeed it was. (In the course of our romance, we'd developed a code where three squeezes meant "I love you," one squeeze for each syllable.)

This was too much. I burst into tears and now it was Jules who did the comforting.

She said that everything was all set, he'd come to make sure she got through No Man's Land. "Who?" I asked. "Who has come?" She blinked at me. "Who do you think, silly? *Daddy*! He's standing right next to you." I looked up, almost as if I expected to shake Mr. Fleischer's hand.

Jules' breathing grew labored. The machine beside her bed started to beep. I didn't call the nurse. Instead, I reached over, unplugged it. "Thank you," she said. "I've wanted to do that ever since they put me here."

I couldn't help sobbing because she was really going and I knew that I'd never see her again, at least not in this world. She said it then: "*Goooooooooodbye.*" As the word passed through her lips, a rattle came from deep inside her chest; the familiar spark went out of her eyes and I knew she was gone.

In accordance with Julia's wishes, an autopsy was performed the next day; it revealed, beyond a shadow of a doubt, that she'd died from Creutzfeldt-Jakob Disease.

ø

Jules, this part's for you: I love you so much. For the past two years, I've gone over your journal time and time again in the hopes that it would bring me closer to you, and it has. Every time I open it up, I can hear your voice rising off the page "like milk-washed lips." I'll keep it by my bed forever. That way, you'll never be far from me.

There aren't very many people out there brave enough to bare their souls for all the world to see. I know I couldn't even come close. But you have proved that revealing our faults right along with the strengths is part of the healing process that brings us closer to Yahweh, the God of peace and love,

All-Mother. It is for that reason that I take the good with the bad and treasure them both as signposts in your soul's journey through this world as it struggled towards the light. I have read the Christian New Testament for this reason and, much to my surprise, found it deeply moving.

This is not to say that I'm convinced Yeshua really was the Christ; but he certainly cleared the way for divine love to come into this world and touch the hearts of people everywhere. It's been over two thousand years since Yeshua's days on earth and I find myself wondering if there ever will be a Christ. Maybe he will be a *she*? Who can really say. I think there's a little bit of Christ's love in all of us.

If I were an angel, the reverence you showed for God would certainly have drawn me closer to you. That moment on the beach could just as easily have been your ultimate victory if only you hadn't lost faith in yourself, your worthiness to be with God. Maybe those angels really were there for you. Who am I to poke holes in your theory about CJD—how it removed the natural barrier between this world and the next?

Jules, I want to believe. So much. To embrace your belief that you touched the fringes of eternity. Because if you did, then there's hope for me as well; there's hope for all of us.

Ruth Cohaine
New York City

Appendix

Despite vigorous protests from the publisher, I have insisted that this so-called "novel" include an appendix of Julia's article on the Mad Cow/Scrapie/CJD connection as it was published in the *Portland Sun* on July 11, 2001.

Many of you may find it a bit on the dry side, but Julia's light sense of humor comes through in places. Bear in mind that she wrote it while suffering from the effects of Creutzfeldt-Jakob. Imagine the burden that must have posed, knowing that with every keystroke she typed, a new hole was appearing in her brain!

Time was of the essence, as you well know from reading her journal. This having been said, it should be obvious that Julia's primary incentive for writing this article was certainly not the paltry two hundred and thirty-three dollars she earned from the *Portland Sun*, but rather to enlighten the world on the dangers of eating prion-tainted meat.

In this way, Julia picked up the torch that was originally lit by Upton Sinclair in *The Jungle*, his best-selling novel about the horrors of the meat packing industry in turn-of-the-century America. It is my fondest wish that *Cowslip* should spark the public's interest and concern in much the same way—prodding congress to appoint a special commission to investigate the practices of the USDA and any possible collusion from corporate interest groups.

At the very least, stricter guidelines should be imposed by the FDA to require the labeling of all food products which contain meat additives imported from England and other suspect countries.

All the basic facts you need to know are right here. Very little has changed since this article was written. Consider it a wakeup call.

—RC

It's a Mad Mad Mad Mad World![□]

by Julia Fleischer, special to *Portland Sun Times*

Portland, Ore. — In the past year new outbreaks of Mad Cow Disease have been reported in over a dozen countries, including the U.S. In addition, Scrapie, a closely related disease that kills sheep, is a problem in almost every state, including Oregon.

WHAT EXACTLY IS A "MAD" COW?
No, it isn't pissed off and ready to trample some poor, unsuspecting ranch-hand like a monster from Stephen King's imagination. The popular nickname "mad" comes from a decidedly British use of the word that means "crazy."

Mad Cow is one form of *spongiform encephalopathy*, a disease that pokes millions of microscopic holes in the brain, thus effectively turning it into a sponge.

In the United Kingdom, Mad Cow Disease was spread to cattle through feed tainted with a protein made from butchered "downer cows," too sick to sell on the open market. This common cannibalistic practice was not limited to the United Kingdom. France and other European countries used the same type of feed and suffered the same disastrous consequences as a result.

To prevent Mad Cow Disease from spreading to America, the FDA prohibited the feeding of mammal-based protein to cows, sheep, and goats in 1997. Since that time, manufacturers and distributors have been required to label feed that might contain suspect proteins along with a warning.

INFECTED SHEEP
Scrapie is a dangerous threat to the welfare of both livestock and people living in the Willamette Valley. Since it's a form of spongiform encephalopathy that occurs in sheep and goats, the general public should take no false comfort from the fact that Mad Cow has yet to show up here: Unbeknownst to most of us, the US Department of Agriculture has been fighting "Mad Sheep" for over half a century.

The first case of scrapie in the US was diagnosed in 1947 in a Michigan flock. The sheep, which had been imported from England, were consequently destroyed, but it was too late; the disease had already gained a foothold. Since that time, scrapie has been diagnosed in more than 950 flocks across the country, including Oregon.

Historically, it's been thought

---

that scrapie could not be transmitted to people; however, this assumption may not last much longer. A team of scientists in France recently announced they've found a causal connection between scrapie and a human form of the disease. They claim to have proof that several patients were infected and later died from a protein with the same "calling card."

DEER AND ELK SPREAD THE DISEASE

Wild game, such as deer and elk, has been shown to carry their own form of spongiform encephalopathy called "Chronic Wasting Disease." This means that hunters are a high-risk group, particularly if they aren't aware of the dangers associated with eating meat contaminated by the brain and spinal cord of animals they kill.

Since the problem is widely recognized among hunters in Colorado, Division of Wildlife officials came up with a plan to help. They offered to autopsy the heads of elk and deer free of charge if hunters brought them in. So far, just over five percent have been diagnosed with Chronic Wasting Disease. But none of the hunters who submitted heads have been notified, despite the fact that officials maintain a database with contact information.

Only one deer from Oregon has ever been diagnosed with Chronic Wasting Disease, and its case was rather unique. The animal had been relocated at the Foothills Research Station, just outside of Fort Collins

in Colorado. It developed the disease after living there for some time.

According to David Guthrie, a retired professor who runs a website out of Corvallis, Oregon (madcow-disease.org) the Foothills Research Station was a biological time bomb waiting to explode. "There is a very good chance that it's responsible for the spread of 'madness' to wild game in several neighboring states."

Professor Guthrie learned that in 1967 a visiting scientist diagnosed scrapie-like symptoms in some of the deer, but management declined to test them. Twelve years later, after eighty-five percent of the game had died from a "mysterious" disease, the first autopsy was finally conducted. As it turned out, the animal's brain was riddled with the telltale holes of spongiform encephalopathy.

"During those intervening years, the potential for contamination was definitely there," Guthrie says. "They were shipping out animals to zoos and wild game parks all over the place."

In Oregon, the Animal and Plant Health Inspection Service (APHIS) has yet to test a single deer or elk. Lack of finances can't be the reason, since a test kit costs around $17. It's more likely that officials in Oregon's Department of Fish and Wildlife share a certain lack of motivation with authorities at the Foothills Research Station. Game tag sales would plummet if studies found "mad" deer and elk roaming the woods. And this could hurt the state in two ways: a loss of important revenue, and a reduction in the number of hunters to help control the potentially explosive deer population.

Aside from animals that came from Foothills Research Station, Guthrie also believes that contaminated sheep could be responsible for the outbreak of "madness" among wild game around the country.

Another possible, albeit sinister, explanation seems to have been totally ignored by APHIS: Deer and elk could have wandered down out of the woods at night and eaten contaminated feed that was intended for cattle.

If this turns out to be true, then the US already has Mad Cow Disease on its hands. It has not ballooned into the size of the European epidemic, because American cows are being slaughtered and packaged for sale before their symptoms turn chronic. And that could mean vast amounts of people in the US have been eating contaminated beef without ever knowing it, leaving themselves open to the possibility of infection.

IN YOUR OWN BACKYARD

The human variation of Mad Cow, called *Creutzfeldt-Jakob Disease* (CJD), was discovered in the 1920s by two German neurologists from whom the disease takes its name. Since that time, it lurked virtually undetected until the mid-90s when the first outbreak happened in England, focusing worldwide attention on the disease.

Unfortunately, several Oregonians have died from CJD in recent months, and this means the potential for contaminated meat is a very real one, even here in the Willamette Valley. CJD is coming up more and more in the obituary section of Oregon and Washington newspapers.

Professor Guthrie believes the officially recognized cases may only be the tip of the scalpel. "Three to four may get reported every year, but this figure can be misleading because people are reluctant to list the cause of death as CJD. Family members don't want the memory of their loved ones stigmatized by public misconceptions about Mad Cow Disease, whereas many hospitals don't want the headache of tracing organ donations from infected patients. And there's also the problem of tracking down and destroying expensive medical instruments and equipment which may have been contaminated."

Josephine Melton, 47, Vancouver, Wash., who was suffering from the disease, died last month.

When Melton was first admitted to Midland Washington Medical Center, doctors were clueless about the cause of her symptoms, which included severe panic attacks, hallucinations, memory loss, and loss of consciousness. By the time Melton died, she had been moved from hospital to hospital in a desperate attempt to treat her "mysterious condition."

Doctors at Portland Health Sciences University finally made a correct diagnosis, but Melton never learned the name of the nightmarish disease; she had already slipped into a coma—the final stage of CJD.

THE HUMAN VERSION
Creutzfeldt-Jakob Disease is contagious, but certainly not in the same way as Chicken Pox. According to most reports, it can't be passed from one person to another through daily, or even intimate, contact.

In order to get the disease, scientists believe you must ingest a small amount of tissue that has been contaminated by a brain or spinal cord from an animal with spongiform encephalopathy. They aren't sure how much it takes, but a piece the size of a peppercorn has been shown to infect cows.

Blood transfusions are also suspect if the blood comes from someone who is infected. Canada already curbs blood donors who are at high risk for CJD. The policies are not unlike US precautions recently put in place to safeguard against an outbreak of foot and mouth disease in cattle—specifically targeting people traveling to America from the United Kingdom. Dr. Renee Danforth, VP of clinical manage-ment for the Canadian Blood Foundation, estimates the risk of contracting CJD in the UK is twenty to fifty times greater than the rest of Europe.

In the US, there's been a growing concern about beef, as well as secondary byproducts made from cows. Last month, New York City health officials investigated the sales of Samba fruit bites candy, which contains a beef-based gelatin. Flamingo USA, the company that manufactures Samba, announced it doesn't plan to change the ingredients in any of its products, despite the ongoing investigation.

Current research indicates that blood products, milk products, and gelatin are unlikely to carry Transmissible Spongiform Encephalopathies (TSEs), because they're pretty much free of protein or tissue, which carry the highest risk for transmission. TSEs have never been found in pork, poultry, and fish.

Part of the problem associated with beef protein comes from the unique physical make-up of Mad Cow Disease. It doesn't work like a virus or pathogen, so it's virtually impossible to kill.

Last year, Dr. Kristoph Von Werner, a central nervous system specialist at the National Bureau of Health, tried to do just that: He took some infected brain tissue from a cow, put it in a sterilizer, and heated it up to 1,112 degrees. The tissue itself quickly became toast, but the infectious proteins (call "prions") were not destroyed.

Von Werner's experiment demonstrates quite dramatically that you can't kill Mad Cow or scrapie simply by cooking meat or other derivative products. In other related experiments, it's been proved that irradiation, and even electrocution, is equally ineffective.

REDUCING THE RISK

Shopping at the supermarket can be frustrating these days, especially if you're health-conscious but still can't resist buying items with a long list of ingredients. Many of these names are either too long to pronounce or make some vague reference to "meat."

Livestock feed is clearly labeled, but you're out of luck if you want to know whether or not a beef-based ingredient has been imported from a country with Mad Cow Disease. And herein lies the irony: When it comes to deadly TSEs, the Food and Drug Administration seems more concerned about protecting cows than people.

Of course, there's a flip side to the coin: Overhauling the food industry to require country-of-origin labeling for all meat-based ingredients would be extremely costly. And the expense would be passed on directly to consumers.

At this point, most experts agree it is highly unlikely that very many people in Oregon or Washington will contract CJD. Dr. Lawrence Eastman, the neurologist who treated Josephine Melton, says "the risk of getting this disease even after exposure to infected beef is extremely remote."

Still, there are precautions you can take to reduce your risk even further:

- Avoid all beef and sheep products from the UK or France.

- Avoid food and health products with vague meat-based ingredients.

- Avoid hamburger, hot dogs, or sausages; if you must buy ground beef, look for particular cuts (i.e. ground sirloin).

- Avoid brains, tongue, or any other cut of meat that comes from the head of an animal.

- Buy beef that comes from cows raised and butchered in Oregon or Washington; to be extra safe, buy from stores that guarantee their beef comes from cows that have never been fed animal byproducts.

- If you are a hunter, take extra care when butchering your kill, especially if it is deer or elk; leave the head intact and avoid contaminating the meat with fluids from the spinal cord.

SINGING THE RED MEAT BLUES

Beef is the most obvious culprit, but as any died-in-the-wool vegan will tell you, it's nearly impossible to cut all beef and dairy products out of your life completely. You really have to work at it, especially when all those little things like candy and gel caps are brought into the picture.

Such restraint would certainly be overkill—that is, if you believe what most scientists and doctors are telling us. Yet, despite all their reassurances, one nagging question still remains: If the human form of Mad Cow Disease can incubate for up to thirty years without showing any of the obvious warning signs, how can doctors know whether or not an epidemic is lurking right now in the general populace? Answer: They can't. There's no way to test for the disease until after a patient dies, and even then, most deaths caused by CJD are probably being written off as pneumonia, Parkinson's, or Alzheimer's dis-ease—especially if the patient is over fifty. So right now, it's a waiting game.

"This is one of those illnesses where it's very difficult for the public to get beyond the mystical," Dr. Eastman says. "Most scientists don't understand it."

Thankfully, the British and French are way ahead of us. If the incidence of CJD becomes alarming here at home, we can look to them for direction and guidance.

Special thanks

Praise be to S.T. Joshi and T.C. Boyle for their help and support over the years. I would also like to thank my parents, Ed and Lyn, and my sister, Karin, for all the encouragement they provided as I unwound this yarn into the tangled monstrosity that is both diary & gothic tale. Tati: Your eagle-eyes are every writer's dream. Di, Burning Woman: Always let your love light shine and the world will be brighter for it! Nate: your advice on the text, the cover art, and book design was invaluable. Zank ja, Maria, for the headshot you clicked off in the 24-hour shopping center (bright light at night!) as we fled from an overzealous manager into the refuge of frozen foods. Muchas gracias, Trip, for your thoughtful suggestions on the text—especially in the passages with Spanish. Kurt and Jen, you certainly deserve a huge pat on the back for everything: "Jeezum Crow, it delivers the goods!" And most importantly, thank you, Dear Reader, for buying my book! Go to the TerminusBooks.com website and drop me a line . . .

Siggi
Portland, Oregon